From th
launchers v
riddled the west bank. Trees flew in the air, elephant grass ignited, and the Tigris churned as if on a high boil. Ray was down to the last of his ammunition and was now firing tracer rounds from his hell belt. He could see them zip across the waterway, joining the immense firepower that shone brighter than the sinking sun.

The Circle of Willis

by

H. G. Hedger

This is a work of fiction. Names, characters, places, and incidents are either the product of the author's imagination or are used fictitiously, and any resemblance to actual persons living or dead, business establishments, events, or locales, is entirely coincidental.

The Circle of Willis

COPYRIGHT © 2023 by H. G. Hedger

All rights reserved. No part of this book may be used or reproduced in any manner whatsoever without written permission of the author or The Wild Rose Press, Inc. except in the case of brief quotations embodied in critical articles or reviews.
Contact Information: info@thewildrosepress.com

Cover Art by *Rae Monet, Inc.*

The Write Advice
A sister company of The Wild Rose Press, Inc.
PO Box 708
Adams Basin, NY 14410-0708
Visit us at www.thewildrosepress.com

Publishing History
First Edition, 2023
Trade Paperback ISBN 978-1-5092-5345-6
Digital ISBN 978-1-5092-5346-3

Published in the United States of America

Dedication

To My Family
(My Everything)

Tract One:

Summer 2005 and Before
A Constellation of Glass

"Ray, are you there?"

The crackle of Ray's ambulance transmitter startled him from a deep doze. His rig was parked under a flourishing elm glowing green where the city streetlight suffused the foliage. But the interior was dark. Shadows shrouded Ray.

The familiar female voice continued, "Sheriff just got a call to the abandoned factory on Highway 51. He's dealing with a drunk driver, and wants you to check out the situation."

Ray straightened up and rubbed his eyes with the heel of his hand before buckling up and turning on the ambulance's lights.

"What am I walking into?" The radio static increased in volume and then quieted. Ray took a swig of coffee and grimaced. The joy of cold gas station java at 3:30 in the morning.

"It was an anonymous call. Some kids were out partying. Sounds more like a welfare check."

Ray turned off the flashing lights. No need to spook anyone. He eased the unit onto the empty street. Some things don't change. A few years ago, he was in high school and occasionally showed up for a party with his pals at the old factory. Now he was twenty-one, working as a paramedic, waiting for his military training in Fort Benning to start. His partner had called in sick for the twenty-four-hour shift, and there was no backup. But life in a small town is like that. You don't have the reserves big cities do. He didn't mind working alone, though—solitude gave him time to think.

Earlier, between the routine calls, transporting a dialysis patient back to the nursing home and patching up an elderly man who had fallen, all he could think about was the surprise he was planning for May, his girlfriend of two years. A few nights before deployment, he would bring her a big bouquet, take her to her favorite Italian restaurant, and then, getting down on one knee, he would propose. Grand gestures weren't his style, but he knew how much May loved the spotlight. He imagined her excitement as he opened the velvet ring box, displaying what the jewelry store saleswoman had assured him was all the rage, and what two months of his salary could afford.

Six months ago, May had shown him an advertisement for a ring in one of her fashion magazines. She had talked about how perfect the arrangement was, mentioning her finger size several times. Ray recalled the details with clarity. He felt confident in his choice and had made the last payment, getting the ring out of layaway just that morning. But now, he had to still the anticipatory excitement. He had to compartmentalize and focus on the task at hand. Someone might need his help.

Tahlequah, a small town nestled in the foothills of the Ozarks, was ringed by an outer circle, a road that cocooned its interior. Warm Oklahoma air washed over him through the open window. The ninety-eight-degree heat of the day had cooled. The dash temperature now read eighty-five, but the T-shirt underneath his technician scrub top was still damp.

He positioned the unit as close as possible to the crumbling building's entrance, took another swill of jitter juice, and swung the first aid trauma bag over his shoulder.

Broken glass, illuminated by the full moon's light, glinted a sparkling constellation along a decaying walkway. The interior was a quagmire of fallen plaster, old mattresses, broken bottles, and accumulated debris over collapsing decades. Navigating was difficult. Ray swept the beam of his flashlight in a trained, methodical fashion and moved deeper into the factory. He reached the innermost room, rumored to be where the factory supervisors once hung out to spy on their workers and pull them from the line if they were too slow, inept, or appeared drunk. Ray was ready to turn around when he saw movement in a darkened corner and heard a whimper. There, curled around a silent form, was a dog.

"Oh man," he whispered and moved toward the creature. He knew this dog, which meant he knew who she was protecting. They were inseparable. Leo went nowhere without her faithful companion, Sandy. Only weighing in around twenty pounds, she had the spirit of a much larger canine and, over the years, had been known, on occasion, to be a ball of protective fury. But now he could see how time had tempered her.

"Hey, Sandy." The aged dog, white circling her muzzle, looked at him with tired brown eyes and thumped her tail slowly on the filthy, sheetless mattress. Ray held his hand out for Sandy to sniff, and gently stroked the top of her head. Then he spoke to the crumpled figure. "Leo, it's me, Ray. I'm going to check you out and make sure everything's okay."

He eased back a torn hoodie that partially covered her and quickly assessed the fifteen-year-old girl. Her breath was shallow but regular–ten respirations per minute. Her pulse was thready but steady, with no audible arrhythmias, fifty-six per minute. Dried emesis clung to long, dark hair. Thank goodness she hadn't inhaled the vomit, he thought as he auscultated her lungs, listening carefully for wheezing or crackles. Aspiration pneumonia could be deadly.

What kind of person would leave her here like this, alone, discarded, unprotected? He called her name. She opened her eyes and then closed them with a soft moan. Scattered around her were beer cans, empty liquor bottles, and a prescription container with her father's name on it—Joseph Lightfoot: OxyContin 40mg prolonged-release. Take one every six hours, as needed, for pain. Coach Lightfoot. Ray's high school track coach and biology teacher. He emptied the remaining pills into a plastic baggie, then shoved the bag and prescription bottle into his pocket and helped the waif-like girl to her feet.

"Come on, Leo," he encouraged. She took one step and then buckled. Ray slid an arm under her, his training kicking in without thought. He gently slung her across his shoulder. The fireman's carry was easier this time than in training with his 200-pound partner. "Leo, I'm sorry." Ray wasn't sure why he was talking aloud. He was positive, even if she could hear, nothing was registering, but he continued, "I was hoping to take you home to your dad, but I can't now. You're not out of the woods. You might need naloxone, a reversal, and for sure, you need hydration. Let's get you to the hospital, where they can monitor you for any complications." As he started to leave, Sandy, whose watchful gaze had never left Ray, cautiously got to her feet and followed them over the rubble, out of the door, into the moonlit night.

****

"Coach!" Ray jumped from the bench. He'd been waiting by the hospital's entrance. "She's going to be okay."

Coach Lightfoot's face was a contortion of fear and anguish. Ray stepped in front of him. "I found these at the scene." He thrust the empty bottle forward.

Coach suddenly seemed to recognize him. "Ray?" He took the bottle, and his face slackened as if someone had opened a plug and drained all emotion away. "My pain pills. That's what happened? Oh, my God, this is my fault!"

"Alcohol was also there." Ray's voice was measured. "Leo wasn't alone when the party started. Someone brought the booze." He knew his words weren't doing much good, but he had to try. This man helped turn his life around and believed in him when he didn't even believe in himself. "She's stable now, Coach, and she's in good hands."

"They need to know what she took, along with the alcohol." Coach palmed the bottle and started toward the door.

"They know," Ray said. "The two pills I found, I put in a bag and gave to the emergency room doctor. He knows what she took, just not how much. Well, nobody knows. That's why they're going to watch her for a while."

Coach bent slightly as if in acknowledgment and then seemed to notice Sandy, who had been at Ray's feet during the entire exchange.

"She was lying beside Leo, guarding her," Ray explained. "I can drop her off at your house, if you want me to?"

Coach nodded. "If you could do that now, I'd appreciate it. That way I won't have to worry about her too. Put Sandy in the backyard. There's a doggie door," he spoke softly, sorting everything out. "Food and water are in the house. She should be good."

As Ray drove away, hanging out of the ambulance's passenger window, was a serious mutt, laser-focused on the receding hospital.

Thief of the Night

On the periphery of consciousness, Leo dreamed. She must be in some altered state, for the sounds and smells were foreign. When her heavy eyelids started to flutter to allow in fractionated light, nothing seemed familiar.

Then there was a voice reaching through the obscure—her father's.

He sounded worried, like she had never heard him before. "Nurse, she's not moving! She's cold, and her skin has no color." Leo felt his large, warm hand grab hers. She tried to squeeze back, but her fingers didn't respond. "Are you sure she's okay?"

"She's going to be fine. Take a breath." The husky voice wasn't familiar. "Look here, Mr. Lightfoot. These moving lines show variations in Leo's blood oxygen level, heart, and respiratory rate. Don't worry. Your daughter's vitals are within normal limits. She's on a central monitoring system. Alarms go off whenever anything happens outside the expected parameters. And someone is watching them twenty-four-seven. Your only job is to be here, by her side. Having family support makes all the difference."

Through a gauzy haze, Leo saw her father's head fall to his chest. She wanted to reach him, touch his face, and tell him she was okay. But her limbs and voice were rendered mute with torpidity. The last thing she remembered was driving with Jake to a party. Shoot, what had she told her dad? That she was studying with a classmate? He didn't know they were dating, even after eleven months.

Images flickered, vivid moments spent growing up in the Lightfoot household with her dad, Uncle Paul, and Sandy. She held them, immersed herself in them, and then let go. Another memory inserted itself. She was stepping into Jake's dad's house, the curtains were drawn, making visualization difficult. Jake came from behind.

"Don't worry. My old man's working the second shift. He won't be home till midnight." His breath was warm and smelled of smoke. Then he slipped a heavy chain with an attached solitary dark eye around her neck. "This was my momma's. She gave the pendant to me to protect me when I came to live with my dad. Now, I'm giving it to you. So, you know I'm always watching." He stood before her in his Beyond Fear T-shirt and crotch-hugging jeans, looking at her with the eagerness and attention she had grown to expect since her first week of high school when he relentlessly started pursuing her. "But you can't tell your dad or anyone who gave you the eye. It's our secret." He flashed his smile, the one that got to her every time.

Leo felt singled out and valued. A nineteen-year-old senior had fallen for her, telling her how mature she was for her age and how she deserved the best. Jake pushed his blonde hair off his shoulder and moved closer. "Come on, Leo, show your appreciation for the gift. Give me a hug. That necklace, that eye means I'm gonna protect you. It's my promise to you. Come on in." His arms tightened around her.

"What did that machine do to you?" Uncle Paul's voice interrupted Leo's detached reverie. "What are you looking for? Has there been any change?"

"The doctor tells me she'll wake up any time now, but I'm afraid to leave. I might miss something. I wasn't paying close enough attention at home and look what happened." There was a long pause, and then her father said, "I've been given something many parents never get, a second chance, and I don't want to mess this up. Only three years left until she graduates." Her father gently squeezed her hand. "I promise you, Leo, nothing like this will happen again."

Uncle Paul's voice moved closer. "What can I do?"

"There's only one other time everything seemed so out of control. The first, was the night she was born."

Uncle Paul returned. "Your life was incredibly complicated then."

The familiar voices kept her grounded even as memories of childhood and Jake spun around her. Her father and uncle were by her side, chatting as they had done her entire life. But this must be a hallucination. They never talked about the night she was born. She had a mother, Emily. But she died. How? When? Leo didn't have the details. All she had were a few pictures. She desired more than anything to have her mother's story. Filling in the holes, the empty pockets of longing Leo carried all the time, was impossible without information. Please keep talking, even if this is just a dream.

As if hearing her thoughts, her father's voice resumed. "Remember how we waited until visiting hours were over, long after Emily's parents left the hospital."

"You were terrified they'd return and find you. I had to peek into the room to make sure everything was clear."

"I felt like a thief of the night bearing gifts. The nurse told me not to be scared, and that fathers were welcome anytime."

She had been waiting her entire life to hear this narrative. Leo willed herself to focus on the words and not drift off.

Her father's soft-spoken voice pulled her along. "The room's only illumination came from a night light. When my eyes adjusted, I could see Emily had fallen asleep while feeding our little one. The bottle rolled onto the bedding. Emily's hair fell across an infinitely small body, and there, pushing tiny fingers through the baby blanket toward me, was the most beautiful baby I'd ever seen. As I took Leo from Emily's arms, her little face intently scrutinized me. And when her tiny fist gripped my finger, holding on for dear life, all the blood in my body rushed toward my heart. Thank goodness for the reclining chair. I knew then I would do anything, stop the earth's gravitational pull, or work a hundred jobs for my newly formed family. But I messed up, Paul. I lost Emily and almost lost Leo."

Hearing the pain in his voice, she somehow had to reach him. Through oppressive dullness, she willed herself to move. And finally, her fingertips responded, tapping lightly against the cotton sheet. As the brain fog dissipated, acidic smells of disinfectant, a scent so strong she could taste it, assaulted her–and a new reality sunk in. She was in the hospital. Something terrible must have happened. She could see fuzzy gray socks put on askew. The white tread on the bottom bunched around bony ankles. Were those her legs? They belonged to someone who lived in a nursing home, not those of a teenager. She was awake now. Leo looked toward the voices of the men who raised her.

Uncle Paul had a hand on her father's shoulder. "I can't reschedule my business trip. Before I leave, I'm going to grab us a couple of coffees." He walked out the door.

Leo tried to smile, but her lips felt cracked, dry, and swollen. "Daddy?"

Her father moved quickly to her side. The smell of dried vomit wafted as he pushed back her hair and planted a firm kiss on her forehead.

"Leotie, my prairie flower."

His eyes reached hers, and Leo could tell he was seeing her fully. Everything. The times she lied about where she was going–*to the library to work on a project*, wearing casual, baggy exit outfits, which covered tight tank tops and form-fitting leggings, when she was heading to Jake's house. Back then, when she was sneaking out to meet him, she felt like the adventurous Wonder Woman's alter ego, a modern-day Diana Prince. But now she could see, etched in the fine lines creasing her father's forehead, settling in his eyes lidded with sadness, what a betrayal of faith these acts have been. Will he ever be able to believe her again?

Hunger for Relief

Not even forty-eight hours had passed since Leo's hospital discharge, and the threads of her life continued to unravel. How could she not have seen this coming? She heard the rumors her father lost his coaching job because of the prescription pills she took and handed out like candy. The firing made sense. How could anyone trust a high school science teacher and track coach who couldn't keep his daughter out of his medications? Of course, no one at the hospital believed her when she told them this was the first time she mixed alcohol and pills. And all because Jake had told her everything would be okay. "Nothing bad ever happens."

But none of that mattered now. Her dad didn't deserve to be terminated because of her. Leo was familiar with the pervasive feeling of failure. She wore a mantle of anxiousness, one she could never quite shake. If her dad losing his coaching job wasn't enough, there was still the issue of Jake.

Maybe now he was her ex-boyfriend. He hadn't visited once while she was in the hospital. He hadn't called or returned her messages. The signal was clear. He never let her forget he could have any girl he wanted. He probably already moved on. After all, who would want a loser who didn't know the first thing about being a girlfriend, and who passed out in a pile of puke the first time she went to a real party?

But the most terrible consequence, what crippled her, above all, was the loss of Sandy.

Leo was so overwhelmed with the ramifications of her actions, her hospitalization, and the complicated discharge process that, at first, she didn't register Sandy wasn't at the door greeting her with tail-spinning abandon. Her dad had not left Leo's side since the hospital admission and was equally off-balance.

"Oh, no," he muttered as he peered into his daughter's room. Leo looked at her faithful companion's lifeless body and burst into tears. Sandy's last day on earth wasn't supposed to have been alone, devotedly waiting, lying on a pile of Leo's dirty clothes while she slept off a bender in the hospital.

At Leo's shattered insistence, her dad drove her and a blanket-wrapped Sandy to the vet to figure out what happened. He examined her and told them a ruptured splenic tumor was the cause. The veterinarian tried to reason with the disconsolate teenager that there was nothing she could have done. He explained because the lump was so deeply seated in the dog's compact body, often there were no external signs of this type of cancer. Only x-ray vision or ultrasound could have seen the buried lesion. But Leo knew better. If she had been present, if she had been clear-headed and not so focused on the turmoil of Jake, then she would have noticed. Something, an increasing lethargy, a dulled look in Sandy's eyes, would've told her. After all, she understood her pup better than anyone. Sandy, in turn, unconditionally accepted and loved the whole mess of her.

In a few moments, they were going to bury her

beast friend, as she used to call Sandy. Who needed a best friend when you had a beast friend? At least, that's what Leo told herself. She tried not to be envious of the close bonds she saw form among her peers. Not that she didn't want to braid someone else's hair and talk all night, sharing kept secrets and hidden desires. But friendships were never easy. Navigating those complexities required learned behavior, and having grown up without a mother, they simply were beyond her purview.

Over the years, Leo wished she had a mother. One in which she could confide and ask questions. A girl without a mother watches closely. She observes other children being tended to, in the neighborhood, at school, on television, and while shopping. She sees mothers wiping ice cream off their chins, cooing into their ears, kissing scraped knees, dropping off cookies for a bake sale, and organizing themed birthday parties. If her mother lived, Leo's life would be different.

Leo was on her hands and knees, frantically searching for something to put in the pinewood box with Sandy so she wouldn't be alone. Her dad and uncle were out back digging the hole. The problem was, everywhere she looked, Leo saw Sandy.

It seemed her memories, at least the ones that were reliable and true, started the day she got Sandy. I remember the day I got my dog, but I don't carry a single image of my mother, not even a memory shimmer.

What she does remember is seeing the scruffy-year-old pup, scorched around her ears from a house fire, come flying into her arms the moment the chain-linked door of the pound opened. She could still feel the heft of Sandy's warm body and soft, tickling licks on her face. But most of all, she remembered holding her tightly as the pup squirmed in her arms and stating with as much force as her three-year-old voice could muster, "I want *this* puppy."

Her dad had taken in the missing patches of fur, the scorch marks, and a jagged raised scar along the young dog's torso. "Are you sure, Leo?" he had asked softly. "There are still a lot of dogs to look at, including some newborn puppies."

"No, Dad," her voice had quivered, terrified that something so quickly gained could be lost. "No! This is the dog I want. This is the dog of my dreams." From then on, they were a team. The only time they were apart was during school, and even then, Sandy would accompany her dad or uncle and walk the three blocks with her. And afterward, the moment Leo walked in the door, Sandy greeted her with uncontrollable abandon.

Leo grabbed her favorite nightshirt, the one Sandy slept on when she was at school and a pair of socks that Leo had tied together to form a pull toy. She could still hear Sandy's low, fierce rumble as she tried to tug the sock from Leo's grip. That growl scared many people; such anger in a little dog. But Leo understood the snarl protecting the heart. She saw the playful glint in Sandy's eyes that seemed to say, "Isn't this the best thing in the world, playing tug of war with knotted socks?" Then that was it, wasn't it? Every moment Sandy spent with Leo was enough for the little creature. With her father, Leo often felt she was interrupting him in his woodshop or when he was grading his students' papers. And with Jake, when she said something stupid or when his friends showed up, he would walk away from her as if embarrassed.

On her dresser were a series of pictures. Leo peered at each one. A timeline of her life. Her Uncle Paul had been taking photographs since he joined the yearbook photography team his junior year of high school, a good long time. After all, he was a decade older than her father. Uncle Paul's 35mm camera was always slung around his neck or in an easily accessible cushioned duffel bag with various filters and lenses. Every few weeks, a new snapshot would appear on their refrigerator until replaced by the latest installment. Exceptional photos would be enlarged. Her father made and stained the frames. Then they would hang them on the walls of their home. But not with deliberation. The displayed photos were more a function of space than being in any chronological order. Once there, however, they remained, taking permanent residence, memories of memories.

"Come on, Leo. A storm is moving in. We need to get this show on the road," her dad called from the back porch. The screen door slammed. She grabbed a picture of herself sleeping on the couch with Sandy. She had been six. Leo raced through the small house into the backyard after him. Heavy, rain-laden clouds, twenty shades of jumbled gray, crowded the sky. Leo tucked the sock toy and snapshot between Sandy's front paws and wrapped the nightshirt over her body.

"Ready?" Her father looked at her, and she solemnly nodded. With a few whacks, he nailed the lid to the crate and carefully placed the pine box in the ground.

"I remember the day you brought Sandy home." Her dad was slowly shoveling dirt into the opening, trying to minimize the sound of soil thudding against the box. "I thought she was the mangiest, ugliest, sorriest excuse of a dog I had ever seen." He paused and smiled tiredly, "But you, my three-year-old daughter—"

"Thought she was the most spectacular puppy I had ever seen." Leo finished his sentence and took a fistful of the earth to release.

"I remember kayaking, about five, six years back," her uncle, a shorter, stockier, older version of her dad, broke in. "Do you remember?"

Remember? How could Leo forget? On one of those flawless Oklahoma days with a turquoise sky that rendered the Illinois River a deep jade, they paddled. The estuary rushed over creek stone and felled trees, then, in stretches, became still. They had spent all day on the water, occasionally stopping on rocky juts to snack and swim. Her dad sat in the back of the two-person kayak. Leo was in front with Sandy standing, paws resting on the bow, a scout for her pack. And when they saw a bald eagle flying along the bank, Sandy could not control herself. Leaping and barking at the raptor, twenty pounds of frenzied fury ultimately hurled herself overboard. In the process, she caused the entire boat to capsize.

"What a sight you three were." Her uncle chuckled. "The two of you looking shocked, soaked to the bone, with the little one paddling as fast as she could after that damn bird. We're lucky the predator didn't turn around and fish her out for dinner."

"And after kayaking, we went to the Crow's Nest for grilled cheese sandwiches." Leo picked up the story as a sudden flash of lightning streaked across the sky.

She looked at her uncle and dad, and from their expressions, she could see they didn't recall the most memorable part of the day. She wanted to stop now, keep this memory to herself, but their expressions were expectant.

"Remember, in the middle of the dance floor? They were having a birthday party for a dog. He was thirteen." Her dad slowly nodded, and she continued. "There were balloons and a cake, and everybody sang Happy Birthday. We all got to have a piece of cake, including Sandy." Leo stopped the story there, unsure if they remembered the rest, the most crucial part.

She had asked Pete, the owner, if she could have a birthday party for Sandy. He had looked at her and promised, "When she turns thirteen, the place will be all hers." Tears welled. Sandy's party would have been this year. Leo swiped her eyes with her hand, feeling the grit of earth smudge against her cheek.

Leo started shaking, and her dad quickly finished burying her childhood dog. The wind, laced with a fine mist, gathered force, and the clouds churned as he started saying a few more positive words about what a great pet she was, a futile attempt to shift the atmosphere. Leo stopped listening. She was doing all she could to hold everything together. After all, that is what you did in a household of men. She had done that her entire life: hang tough, be strong, and push through. When her uncle dovetailed in with another story meant to make her feel better, she knew the tears were unstoppable. She turned and ran.

From her core came choked keening. She needed something to stop the intense guilt and emptiness. Day after day, she would hug Sandy and confide in her. She pulled open the screen door and raced down the hall. In the bathroom, she yanked open the cabinet and reached for the bottle.

"It's gone." Her dad was standing behind her, his tall, solid form filling the frame. "I flushed every last one down the toilet."

Leo turned to face him.

"I'm done with them. I can handle back pain. But what I cannot handle, what I could not manage, is life without you." He opened his arms. She moved into them. Enfolded there in the warm, complex admixture of nutmeg, cinnamon, and orange, she was able to cry, to grieve the ever-present loss of her mother and the fresh loss of her best friend, her boyfriend, and her father's trust.

"I'm so sorry, Leo." He stroked her hair gently. "I let you down because I wasn't paying attention. But that is over."

Leo wanted her father to continue, to reassure her as he always had when she was young. She wanted so badly to hear him say, it's going to be okay, my daughter. Everything's going to be all right. But no more words were forthcoming.

As the intensity of rain pelting against the small bathroom window increased, a sudden gust of wind rose, rattling the glass in its splintered, wooden frame.

Throw that Gauntlet Down

Sept 11, 2001

"Ray, I mean it. I'm leaving without you if you're not down in thirty seconds! We're going to be late." Seventeen-year-old Hope Shipworth, Ray's twin sister, impatiently shouted up the thickly carpeted stairs, her backpack slung over her shoulder, car keys dangling from her right hand.

Ray scrambled, throwing his gym shorts and tennis shoes in a bag, and yelled, "Come on, give me a minute." He couldn't find his cross-country shirt. In the dirty clothes? Shoot. Today was an away meet, and he couldn't run without it. He had to start being more organized.

Taking the steps two at a time, he raced down and rounded the corner into the laundry room, where he ran into his mom, holding out his soiled shirt.

"For goodness' sake, keep the noise down. Your dad's working on his sermon. Your voices could raise the dead," she said with a slight grin and thrust the orange jersey into his hands. "You're responsible for washing your clothes now, remember?"

"Yeah, I know. I just keep forgetting." He grabbed the polyester pullover by the mesh lining and sniffed. The smell was like balled-up dirty socks. Maybe he'd have time to rinse the shirt in the school's bathroom sink and let it dry in his locker during classes, or maybe the coach wouldn't notice the odor, the grime around the neckline, or the sweat stains under the armpits. The recent talk about representing your school by how you dressed and behaved came back to him. This day wasn't getting off to a good start. He gave his mother a quick peck on the cheek and ran out the front door, trying to catch Hope before she pulled out of the driveway.

The morning was crystal-clear, the kind that often goes underappreciated by youth. The Sooner State's prolonged warmness, a reluctance to let go of summer, continued to nourish its trees' food factories, rendering the leaves a spectrum of lush, varied greens. Autumn's cooling process, which would ignite the foliage with golden yellows, crimson reds, and burnt oranges, was over eight weeks away.

Per her usual pattern, his twin sister quickly cycled through the favorite pre-programmed stations on their shared 1991 eggplant-colored Pontiac Grand AM.

"Hey, stop there!" Ray said. Hope did this every morning on the way to school—the driver got to choose the station, and the first one ready to leave in the morning got to drive. No matter how hard he tried, Ray was always a minute or two behind her. This channel surfing drove him crazy, and she knew it. Again, another reason to get his act together. "Stop, Hope! Go back one station—something about a plane hitting a building in New York."

"Come on. Is this news? In a city as big as that, this was bound to happen. One of those sightseeing helicopters, probably." Even as she protested, her sturdy finger punched the previous button.

Information flowed in and expanded. What was

thought to be a small plane hitting an insignificant structure, turned into a large, 159-foot-long, wide-body (with a seven-a-breast cross-section) airliner, slamming into one of New York's tallest, most recognized buildings—The North Twin Tower. What was considered an isolated, accidental event turned into something organized and horrific.

Ray pointed out an empty parking spot near the back of the lot, grateful there was one left this close to the start of class. Hope accelerated into the space and slammed the brakes.

Within moments, they huddled around Ray's homeroom teacher's television on wheels. In one of those jarring flashes seared into memory like a livestock brand, Ray saw the South Tower sliced in half by another 767 as the digital school clock flashed a bright red 8:03. With this, he had two simultaneous thoughts: class starts in two minutes, and our country is under attack.

There is the shared experience of witnessing a typical day unravel, seeing airliners dissect erect buildings, firefighters rushing up smoke-clogged stairwells, even as dazed masses stream down, out into a world so thick with clouds of dust that all move as ghosts. Then there is the personal immersion, where what you perceive sets in motion a series of internal responses. In this private, complex space, Ray made a decision.

****

Pastor Shipworth finished saying grace, and the nuclear family of four had their utensils poised for meatloaf action when he began expounding on what this day had wrought. Ray raised a singular eyebrow at his twin sister, who lifted both eyebrows (try as she might, she had never mastered the single eyebrow lift) in return. They knew their father would not be able to resist interjecting his views on the day's events. Family dinners were often a testing ground for observations and invectives that later became Sunday sermons. The twins were not disappointed. Today proved to be no exception. Their eyebrow exchange, or lack thereof, was a silent form of communication.

Bertrand Shipworth was a stalwart man, a five foot ten inch indomitable force, almost as wide as he was tall. He ran his household, church, and the personal lives of his family and congregation with exacting discipline. He would vigorously cheer you on if you adhered to his structured expectations. And nothing was better than having his support and approval. You felt on top of the world when he was on your side. Ray and Hope, his only children, spent their childhood vying to be in this spotlight and worthy of his praise. Yet the moment you veered off course, even a fraction, he became a bulldog. With ferocious and unyielding tenacity, he would not relent. Once you returned to the straight and narrow, he graciously yielded. He saw this as his God-given mission. While the Shipworth twins admired, respected, and sometimes feared him, as they edged toward adulthood and their worldview expanded beyond the confines of the church and home, they began to see their father in a shifting light.

"Evil is real." A smear of mashed potatoes clung to the edge of his mouth. "Today's events just underscore that the apocalypse is imminent." He wiped his face. "Archangel Michael will soon spread his wings in the lofty clouds and wearing God's armor will defeat the devil as predicted in Revelations. We must put our house in order and be prepared."

Ray saw the scene vividly in his mind, replicating a relief done by Christoph Daniel Schenck he'd seen in Art History. The Archangel Michael held a flaming sword over his head as he straddled the cowering devil. To Ray, he looked like an unconquerable, mythic hero. The devil exuded terror with his tongue hanging out of his open mouth and startled, lurching eyes. As evil descended into open flames, his clawed hand frantically reached out. Whether to hang on, or perhaps in a final attempt to pull Michael down, Ray couldn't tell.

"The true test is now." Pastor Shipworth reached for a second serving of potatoes and meatloaf. "We must remain faithful, despite this world filled with violence, despite our future suffering. God, the creator, the redeemer, will be victorious. He will reign."

Good and evil, these concrete concepts were immutable. Ray was raised believing this. How to differentiate between the two was found in the Bible, God's Law. The delineations were clear-cut and non-negotiable.

Ray drew on the inner strength he felt when running unencumbered through the woods of Eastern Oklahoma. He recognized a deep sense of patriotism, an emerging warrior spirit. Despite the opposition he would undoubtedly face, he knew what to do. When he was sure his father had finished, out of respect, you never interrupt your elders, he took a drink of water and said, "As soon as I graduate, I am enlisting."

Hope audibly gasped, her eyes widening in shock.

Ray's father put down his fork with measured fortitude and stared at his son. "The hell you are." Then he hurriedly looked away, as though the sight of Ray was something he could no longer endure.

"This is my calling, Dad." Ray knew he had to speak now, or he would never find the strength to stand up to him. "You raised us always to do the right thing, even if it's uncomfortable or unpopular. That's what I'm doing. Look at what happened today. Our country needs men who are willing to sacrifice everything. I can't just sit back and do nothing. I'll volunteer, do my duty, then return. After today, it's the least I can do."

"You are so damn naïve. Ray, this is a knee-jerk reaction. Your life will change forever."

"What do you know about being a soldier? You lecture us behind a safe pulpit. You said you'd be proud if we lived a life of service. Well, that's what I want to do."

The gauntlet was thrown. Ray wasn't surprised by his father's response for he held a fundamental belief. The religious conviction had been curated over generations, and was honed in his father's lifetime—violence was incompatible with his Christian faith.

Adhering to the commandment "Thou shalt not kill," Pastor Shipworth had counseled countless young men in his congregation to avoid the military, instructing them that there were other ways to serve one's nation. And Ray knew his father would try to change his mind. He would convince him that joining the armed services could be done in a non-combative way. A mechanic, medic, or communication expert were examples. Ray wasn't opposed to this, but he wasn't giving his father the satisfaction, at least not on this day when their country had been attacked.

"Maria and Hope, please excuse my foul

language," he said, dismissing Ray with a slight flick of his fork. Ray could tell his father, though displeased, was confident in his ability to manipulate his son, confident that by the time Ray turned eighteen, he would forget this enlistment nonsense. His father knew how to work his son; he had worked him his entire life.

Pastor Shipworth continued heartily ingesting his meal, acting as if the conversation and the day's events held little significance, as if nothing of consequence had transpired.

Ray stared at the congealing meatloaf, mashed potatoes, and peas turning cold on his dinner plate. Something had irrevocably shifted.

Even in its infancy, an immense longing for service to others and his country burned inside him. Though merely a flicker, it seared, leaving him eager and unafraid.

The Round-a-bout of Life

February 2005

"Thanks for picking me up." Ray threw his bookbag in the back seat and slid into the passenger side of his father's gold Buick Century. Heavy, dark charcoal clouds swiftly moved across the sky, furiously colliding with each other, a herd of terrified elephants escaping gunshots. "My car will be fixed by tomorrow. I won't have to bother you again."

Ray hated having to call and ask his father for a favor. Relations were strained since he moved out of his childhood home and started living with May, his girlfriend, but today there had been no other option. His coursework was finished, and all that remained was studying and taking the National Paramedic Certification Exam.

"No problem, son. I was heading this way to visit Mrs. Deedle. You remember her, don't you?"

It was a dig. Of course, Ray remembered her. He knew every one of his father's parishioners. Pastor Shipworth pulled into the senior living complex on the outskirts of town. "Why don't you come in with me and pay her a visit?" He focused his intent gaze on his son. "She would love to see you. Everyone in the congregation is always asking about you. Maybe you could see your way through to join us this Sunday."

The request was more like a demand, but distance gave Ray perspective and courage.

"No, thanks. Tell her I said hello. I'm going to study. The qualifying exam is next week. I've put in so much work. I can't fail now."

His father nodded, his jowls jiggled slightly, his jaw set, his expression stern. Ray knew this look meant a lecture, a private sermon, would happen on the tortuous drive home. He sighed. As Ray grabbed his backpack and pulled out his notes to study, fat drops of rain began slapping the windshield.

****

Ray hadn't seen this as giving in. Learning from his mother's advice, "Choose your battles wisely," he merely allowed his father's post 9-11 campaign to wash over him. The offensive started on the pulpit, the Sunday afterward, on the same podium his mother carefully polished with Murphy's lemon oil every week, giving the wood a burnished shine.

"Matthew 26:52—People who live by the sword, die by the sword." His father's booming voice reached the rafters. No falling asleep with this sermon. And the crusade continued, "Matthew 5:39, Don't fight against the one who is working evil against you...I tell you this, love your enemies." Another supporting bible verse, another Sunday, another missive, "Blessed are the peacemakers; they will be called the children of God."

Month after month, Pastor Shipworth's operation continued through Ray's seventeenth and eighteenth years. By the time he graduated, his father's careful grooming had dovetailed with an acceptance into the nearby paramedic program. The urgency to enlist

The Circle of Willis

abated when Ray met May. Ray wasn't going to join the military just out of spite. Life offered alternatives. He didn't mind that his father considered Ray another one of his successful interventions, a notch in his pulpit. His father was confident he had covered the bases. If his son's yearning to join the military reemerged, Ray would have a skill that would put him in a non-combatant role, a practice that was theologically in keeping with Pastor Bertrand Shipworth's belief system.

What he hadn't counted on was his son's free will. After high school, Ray attended his father's church services less frequently. "You want me to pass the licensing exam? I must go to the study sessions." He had been truthful. A handful of his classmates met religiously every week to review notes and study. What could he say? Sunday mornings happened to work best for the group. Sometimes, they would gather at a coffee shop or, if the weather was agreeable, outside on campus or in a park. Often, they would toss around a football while they quizzed each other on course material.

Immersing in his studies was easy. Ray found the human body fascinating, especially how an injury could throw everything off balance and how internal mechanisms quickly jumped into action, fighting to re-establish an equilibrium. He saw his role as a paramedic as an extension of this process–merely another tool offered to the body in a struggle to survive. Ray had learned a lot in school by job shadowing seasoned paramedics. He was realistic now and understood that the lights of his unit, often, would witness the mundane: stomach bloat from indulging in too many barbecued ribs or a pounding headache resulting from a night of drinking. Sometimes the calls were outrageously hilarious: a woman frantically called because she found her son sitting in a box full of foam packaging nuts. He was deathly allergic to peanuts, and she argued that he would have an anaphylactic reaction.

But, on rare occasions, the flashing lights represented an intricate intersection between life and death. Ray clearly remembered a lecture that took place over six months ago. His professor had stood before the class, her dry-cleaned pants pleated perfectly, and a white starched dress shirt unbuttoned at the neck, and she had talked about the Circle of Willis.

"One of the body's most amazing protective mechanisms is the Circle of Willis." She had taken her long wooden stick and pointed to a sizeable map-like chart showing a group of blood vessels in the brain that connected, forming a continuous structure that resembled a circle. "These oxygen-rich arteries supply blood to a large portion of the brain. As you have learned…" The instructor took a moment to survey her class and ensure everyone was carefully listening, "…every artery and vein in the human body has a preordained, one-directional blood flow, except for this incredibly adaptive round-a-bout of cerebral blood."

The room was quiet. Ray's professor nodded in appreciation and continued. "Remember, when a blockage or narrowing occurs in the body's blood vessels ischemia, damage, or even death to the affected area can happen. Think back to our discussion of the heart and how a major blockage in the left anterior descending artery can cause sudden cardiac arrest, often leading to death. That is why this event is called the

Widow Maker." She had taken a drink of water. "But in the brain, this circular system cleverly serves as a safety mechanism. If a clog or narrowing slows or prevents the blood from flowing in one direction, the change in pressure will cause the blood to reverse course to flow backward to compensate. The natural shape of the circle, and the way pressure acts, allow for a bi-directional blood flow, thus sustaining oxygenation to the brain. Nowhere else in the human body does this occur."

Ray was floored by this concept, by the brilliantly adaptive way the body fought to protect brain life. He thought of people's capacity to pull together, form shielding circles, preserve function and vitality, and how suddenly everything could be disrupted. If a tear or rupture occurred in one of the body's major arteries, no number of compensatory mechanisms would work. A person could bleed out in a matter of minutes.

****

Ray carefully put his study material away when he saw his father leave the long-term care facility and step into the rain. He braced himself for what was coming.

For the first few minutes of the remaining drive into town, Pastor Shipworth's hands clutched the steering wheel so tightly his knuckles turned white. "You move in with a woman, out of wedlock, no less. You are not even engaged. You stop coming to church. Why do you insist on driving a knife through your parents' hearts?"

It wasn't the delivery Ray expected. Of course, his father couldn't see Ray's choices as anything but directed at him personally, purposely meant to humiliate and embarrass him. When all Ray had been doing was trying to live his life to the best of his ability. Involuntarily, a smile tugged at the corner of Ray's mouth, and under his breath, he muttered, "Don't be so dramatic."

His father jerked the Buick onto the shoulder of the gravel road and slammed on the brakes, causing both to lurch forward. "What did you say?" His voice was quiet, but full of rage.

"You heard me," Ray returned. He kept his voice even, willing himself not to look away. Then, in a slightly louder voice, he continued, "I said, do not be so dramatic."

In a lumbering motion surprisingly swift for a man of such heft and girth, Pastor Shipworth was out of the driver's door. He grabbed Ray by his shoulders and pulled him outside into the pelting rain. "You know something?" The spittle flew from his bulging face. "You have always been a disappointment!"

"I'm a disappointment because you only want a son who is exactly like you." Ray fought to maintain control. He wasn't going to give his father the satisfaction of seeing him dissolve—something strong men didn't do. "The truth is you have no tolerance for diversity. For anyone taking one step off your ordained path. How is that Christlike?"

His father grabbed his son's backpack, stuffed with over two years' worth of class study notes, muttering aloud, "Dramatic?" Fistful after fistful, he clutched and tore into the papers, held them in his beefy palms, and released them into the stiff, rain-laden wind. "You want to see something dramatic?" With a flourish, his face red, he dumped the remainder of the papers and binders into the murky waters of a muddy, shallow drainage ditch and, as an afterthought, threw the backpack in. He stomped on the partially submerged canvas. "How's that for dramatic?"

Ray stood at the base of the ankle-deep canal as his father's taillights receded into the driving rain. Sticking out of his bag, flapping in the harsh wind, was a page, torn and mud-soaked, but Ray could still read his handwritten heading—The Circle of Willis.

****

Once Ray reached the main section of town, instead of turning toward the warm comfort of the apartment he shared with May, he moved in the opposite direction. Drenched but with a determination and surety that he had not felt since 9-11, he sat before the Army recruiting officer and committed himself.

When the officer asked if he had any special skills, Ray shook his head and said, "No, sir. Please sign me up for the front line–Army Infantry." And so, it came to pass.

Tract Two:

Fall 2005
An Unasked-for Gift

What he noticed, before his brain had time to register what this meant, was the door to their apartment shut tightly. Usually, on warm autumn afternoons in mid-September, the period between the necessity of air-conditioning and the need for furnaces, all the Redman Studio apartment doors were flung wide open, a living organism revealing its underbelly, the inner rooms pulsating cells. May always thrilled in these brief displays. "Look at the filth in 223. Come on, pick up your beer cans, and use the sweeper occasionally. How do they live that way?"

He remembered the first time they stood side by side, examining the lives of others under a microscope. "Oh, I always knew she would have ultra-frilly decorations, all those fake plants and flowers. And come on, don't you know the pillows are supposed to compliment the sofa, not be made with the exact same fabric? That's why they're called accent pillows!" May laughed, her voice high, "a chipmunk," his friend Miguel teased. Ray slung his arm around her curvy waist and inhaled her freshly shampooed hair, a smell that he now associated with her, an overwhelming concoction of perfumed fragrances not found anywhere in nature but one he nonetheless found intoxicating. She continued, "Our place is the best, don't you think?" May turned to examine their unit, a precise compartment, orderly, color-coordinated, mimicking the pages of one of her magazines.

When they first started living together, the run-down 300-square-foot studio apartment was the most economical place they could find, one they could barely afford. Yet, May, who had a knack for finding hidden bargains and high-quality cast-offs in second-hand stores, made their home look like a million bucks. Now that Ray was earning a more stable income, and she had finally found full-time employment, she had moved on to higher-class shopping and mastered the art of stretching their credit card limits to the maximum.

"Our home's the best because of you." Ray kissed her soft neck, and she squirmed out from under his arm, eager to continue her comparisons.

When he first met May, he felt like he'd discovered an exotic new breed, a vibrant, colorful adaptation of a previously known species. For May not to be part of this exhibition meant something was up. Maybe I should have told her I got the night off from work and was planning on taking her out to dinner. He found himself second-guessing his surprise. But then he rationalized she must be out shopping while reaching in his pocket for his keys, fingers grazing the velvet ring box. May found a new look for the apartment and was getting slipcovers, accessories, and accent pieces–notions he had never contemplated before she came into his life. How different she was from his steady, non-materialistic Mother and no-nonsense sister. The joy May exacted from a successful shopping trip, from a bargain find, never ceased to amaze him. As he fumbled with the chain, he noticed her parked car in its usual position, not out shopping. The keys fell to the cement landing. He bent to retrieve them.

Maybe she's napping. He turned the lock. Ray wasn't due to be home until much later. But he had picked up an extra shift last week to get this time off. He wanted the entire night to be one surprise after another, flowers, a candlelit dinner, and a proposal. He was leaving for boot camp in five days. There wasn't much time left. Ray turned the handle and entered.

Boxes were everywhere. May's heart-shaped face popped around the corner of their bedroom; her round eyes flashed quickly from surprise to irritable defiance.

"Well, at least you saved me the trouble of having to write a note." She forcefully threw an armful of her "fall" clothes into an empty carton, an open act of rebellion, for she loved her outfits. He had never met someone who had four separate wardrobes, one for each time of year. He could see that spring and summer were packed. The seasons of their time together, he evaluated, his mind taking over what his heart did not want to recognize. Winter was when they met and moved in together. Those clothes must still be hanging in her closet. Maybe this was an extreme act of reorganization.

"What's going on, May?" Ray tentatively placed the pink rose arrangement on top of a box of jewelry, makeup, and assorted toiletries, his six-foot, two-inch frame filling the doorway. His voice was measured. He had learned how important remaining calm was when faced with a disaster. His instructors had emphasized this fact repeatedly. "Don't forget your training.

Remain cool when arriving at a chaotic scene, take everything in, assess, then triage." Later in boot camp, when everyone had a nickname, this ability would earn him the moniker "Iceman."

"I'm leaving. Not that anything matters to you. You're outta here, anyway. I'm moving in with Marty, starting a new life." She laid the truth at his feet, an unwanted gift.

Marty? Her boss? Ray's chest felt tight and constricted, as though his lungs were collapsing, yet he remained motionless. Processing. She stopped packing for a moment, aware of her words' impact. "Look, you were always harping about the truth, so there you are." Winter came out of the bedroom closet.

She was right. The truth was always more manageable. Ray grew up believing this. He remembers his first lesson, courtesy of his father. Bored twins, Ray and Hope, finding a partially used gallon of fire engine red paint, wanted to surprise their mother and had covered half of the garage door up to the height their seven-year-old arms would reach. When their father returned home and saw their handiwork, he was furious. Out of fear, they lied, blaming the neighbor's teenage son. The repercussions were terrible. Worse than seeing his father's face knotted in rage and feeling the "board of education" on his bottom was how Hope shrieked before her "turn to learn." "Wait! Wait!" Ray had cried. Even then, an instinct, an unrecognized need to protect, kicked in. "It's not her fault. Painting the garage was my idea!" He stretched tall, his skinny rib cage puffed out, trying to appear larger, more believable. "Oh, and now another lie?" His father gave Ray a second round of education before turning to Hope.

There was simplicity in truth. Spinning elaborate narratives around a falsehood was exhausting and always seemed to trip the spinner up. Time and time again, Ray had seen this born out. Stepping into and owning his mistakes was easier than looking for excuses and laying blame at the feet of others. And he knew now, the exacting expectations of his mother and father allowed him to do so. Lying was not tolerated. The truth, no matter how difficult, was honored. And that is why he trusted her. When May called to say her boss was making her work late, night after night, he believed her. She would slip in at two or three in the morning, her scent strong, her body hard-wired. He would reach for her and pull her close. "You must be tired. I'm sorry you have to work so much overtime." Mostly she remained taut, but sometimes she fell into him. Now, this all made sense. He understood.

The pink rose petals of the bouquet were brushed brown at the edges. May remained confrontational, her arms on shapely hips, her orange top rising above the soft swell of flesh he used to lay his head upon after they made love.

"He says he cannot live without me!" Her eyes were resolute, unyielding.

But I cannot live without you. Externally, he remained stoic, for the price of forgoing truth-telling is silence. While honesty was valued and a sign of strength, a display of raw emotion was pathetic, a sign of weakness, leaving one vulnerable. And though Ray experienced profoundly and had a rich interior life, he knew little about expressing his thoughts and feelings. Why couldn't she see that all the small things put together over the past two years meant he loved her and truly cared? Every considered act had been a display of what he felt: the raised flower bed he had built for her in the community garden, the thoughtfully planned secret Saturday excursions, and the wildflowers he collected throughout the warm seasons (the ones he so carefully tried to color coordinate with her current decorating trend).

Her defiance continued, "I want to be with someone who loves me so much he says he would die without me." Okay, a bit theatrical, but he understood. He nodded, his eyes searching for the slightest crack or waver in her expression. There was none. With a prolonged pause he took in the whole of her, from the top of her head, where he could drop a kiss in her bleached blond hair, so light, she hardly noticed, to her carefully polished fingers and toes matching, of course, her outfit. He breathed in deeply, inhaling. But she was too far away, her scent already a remembrance.

It was better this way, his military buddies would say later, at boot camp and then in war; better that she did this before your deployment, before she raided your bank account and left you penniless and broken-hearted. But the truth was, he would have given anything to have her remain loyal and faithful, to have her value him the way he treasured her.

When he returned the next day, May had folded her belongings and two years' worth of memories into a Ford Fusion. They were all gone. As he walked out of the apartment for the final time, locking the door behind him, he could feel the infinitesimal weight of the diamond nestled in a velvet ring box, a tiny broken 0.5-carat embolism of hope, now coursing through his bloodstream, heading straight for his heart.

The Substance of Ordinary Days

On the last day of Leo Lightfoot's intensive month-long outpatient program, her father met her on the bench by the cluster of western redbud trees as he had for the past four weeks. He could usually gauge how the day had gone by her gait and posture. This late afternoon toward the end of September, she was fairly skipping. In her right hand was a sheath of paper.

"My certificate of completion." She grinned in a self-deprecating way. "You can hang that right up there with my kindergarten graduation diploma. Something you can really be proud of, your druggie fifteen-year-old finished a mandatory rehab course."

Joseph looped an easy arm around her shoulder and gave her a quick hug before releasing her. He knew public displays of parental devotion did not go far among high schoolers. "You make light of this, but this is huge, Leo. I'm proud of you."

She scanned his face and looked into his eyes as if reading his truth. For a moment, she grabbed his hand, as she had done so many times when she was young, and then let go.

Joseph let out a sigh of relief as they walked the downtown sidewalk on their way home. The past thirty days had not been easy. There were plenty of tears, and numerous times he had to walk Leo to the door of the Center to ensure attendance. But today, she seemed lighter. Initially, the admitting doctor wanted Leo discharged from the hospital directly into an inpatient rehabilitation program. Leo had burst into tears and clung to her father, saying the situation would be worse if she were elsewhere. She had never spent a night away from him in her entire life, and she wasn't ready. She begged, promising that if she could do the outpatient program, she would try her hardest and not let him down. Convincing the doctor that this would work was difficult, and Joseph worried he was making a mistake. But he petitioned for his daughter, stating that her home was now safe. All the pain pills were gone. The doctor reluctantly agreed. Today, Joseph was sure he had made the right decision.

"Dad?" Her voice pulled him back to the present. "This means a celebration is in order, right? Afternoon Delights' Ice Cream Parlor?" Her eyes were eager, alight.

"Me, turn down an invitation for ice cream? Never." Joseph sent gratitude into the universe as he opened the door to the parlor of goodness.

"Thanks, Dad." Leo took the cinnamon toast crunch ice cream roll from her father and beamed. Significant moments in the Lightfoot household were celebrated with delicious treats. Later, years into therapy, Leo would realize how unique her experience of growing up in a permissive, free-flowing family had been. If her mother had lived, would everything have been different? As it was, never was there an issue of spoiling your appetite with dessert before dinner. There had been countless times when snacks were meals and potato chips counted as vegetables. By age eight, she had memorized every aisle in the hardware store and often went years between visits to the dreaded dentist. Leo would eventually see that while searching for the missing pieces, memories of her mother, the parts that were there, the substance of ordinary days, were like diaphanous fibrin sheaths, steadily filling in wounds.

Autumnal dusk, still holding summer close to its breast, softly settled around father and daughter as they amiably walked home, enjoying their delicacies.

Leo needed to say something to her father while they were alone. Part of her recovery depended on her admission, and still, she stalled. "We have to finish our treats before we get home." Leo took a bite of her celebratory ice cream, slowed her pace, and glanced at her dad. "Uncle Paul would never forgive us for not getting him any."

Her father wiped the remains of his cherry jubilee from his mouth and grinned. "What he doesn't know won't hurt him." He threw his empty sundae cup into a nearby receptacle.

"The story of our family." Contained in her words was an implicit axiom. Leo was not smiling as she looked at her father.

She took a deep breath. "Dad?" As she started to speak, she was stopped short by the expression on her father's face. He was intently focused, looking straight ahead. She followed his gaze—the high school cross country team, out for a training run, sliced through the expanding twilight. A wave of motion, a sea of bare arms and legs, swelled in asynchronous unity. They moved effortlessly, swiftly, running with the lightness of youth and promise. When the lead runner saw his former coach standing on the corner, the senior raised his right hand in a sharp salute, a gesture of honor and respect. He led; the group followed. Each successive runner followed suit, a string of appreciation, a tribute of unassailable recognition. Leo's father knew each one of the young men. He understood their stories and their motivations. He had been coaching for as long as she could remember, and seeing them in training, brought back layered memory. After the last runner rounded the corner, in their wake, settled a palpable sense of recognition for coach Lightfoot's service to the program, their school, and their lives.

"Dad, I'm so sorry. I cannot tell you how horrible I feel you lost your coaching job because of me." She struggled to keep going, her voice wavered. "You're their coach. This isn't right. I made a mistake, not you." Her shoulders bent in a sob.

"Is that what you think, Leotie? I lost my job because of you?" He moved closer, folded his daughter into his arms, hugged her, and then held her at arm's length so he could look directly into her eyes. "Listen, my little one. Leaving was my choice, my decision. No one made me stop coaching." He paused before continuing. "I still have my job, don't I? I'm still teaching. They didn't fire me." He kissed the top of her head.

It was his decision. Leo struggled to put this in perspective, for she had always been the coach's daughter. The seasons of cross country and track had been part of their father-daughter narrative for her entire life. "Can you go back to coaching, will you, please?" The weight of his sacrifice was almost too much for her to bear.

"That's something I'll evaluate when you graduate. My resignation is indefinite, and I have no desire to return. You're my priority."

Apologizing, then making amends, was what she learned, what she must do. Leo held this mantra close to her. "I am going to show you how sorry I am. I will not let you down again, Dad."

****

The black walnuts crunched underfoot as they walked up the pathway that led to their home. Leo looked over her shoulder as she opened the weathered door and spoke to him, "Now I have to apologize and make amends to Mom."

She gave him a fragile smile. He noted tears glinting on her dark lashes and his stomach tightly twisted. He loved his daughter, her resilient strength, and her innocent determination. But he also knew all too well how challenges that lie behind rocks can spring, like a rattlesnake unbidden, and poison life's best intentions.

She pulled a letter out of her book bag and gave an exaggerated shrug. "Well, I can't make amends. Mom's dead, but I can say I'm sorry."

Joseph touched her arm. "Leo, there's some—"

"It's okay, Dad."

He felt unnerved. "What do you have to apologize for?"

"That's between my mom and me." She kissed him, a light graze across the stubble of his cheek. She exited the back door. "Don't worry, Dad. I've got this, I really do."

On the crest of their backyard slope overlooking the Tahlequah River, there were two stones now, one for Sandy and one for Emily.

From the kitchen window, Joseph watched his

adolescent daughter sitting cross-legged on the rose quartz memorial stone, her head bent down, reading a message, the content of which he would never know. Over the years, he saw her retreat to this special place when she was overwhelmed by life or just needed a quiet space. Joseph wanted her to have a spot to be able to connect and feel close to her mother, and Leo found solace there in moments of joy, frustration, and sorrow. The top of the stone was carved into a bench, an unyielding altar, where Leo had placed countless stuffed animals, wildflower sprigs, art projects, report cards, and even peanut butter and jelly sandwiches. Offerings made by an aching daughter. Beneath the bench, on the curved part of the stone that rounded like a just noticeable pregnancy, was a block etching: Emily 7/7/72.

****

Leo was seated at the kitchen table with her father, who was grading biology worksheets. Uncle Paul stood at the stove, flipping grilled sandwiches. The smell of butter and crisping cheese permeated the small kitchen. Leo could see her uncle's blue, soft-shelled suitcase packed and waiting by the front door from her position at the sturdy, circular, well-worn oak table. His camera case rested by its side.

"Leaving on a business trip tomorrow, Uncle Paul?" For as long as Leo could remember, her uncle left on these business trips, as they called them, several times a month. Often, he would just be gone overnight. Sometimes his work kept him away for a week or more.

Uncle Paul held a spatula in his right hand. He pushed back a shock of peppered gray hair with his wrist, looked at Leo, and smiled. "Yes, I think I'll be gone for three days this time."

"Before you go…" Leo reached into her rehabilitation folder and pulled out a list of names. "You guys have to help me choose my outpatient therapist." The next phase of Leo's recovery centered around continued counseling. "I must make my first appointment within a week. They just gave me a list of names that accept our insurance. How am I supposed to choose?"

Uncle Paul put a platter of stacked sandwiches on the table and grabbed the list. "Here, let me help." He scanned the paper. "They don't give you much to go on. They list their names and where they went to school, but not much else. Okay, listen and choose." In a dramatic voice, he switched to what he thought was a passable English accent and started to read, "Dr. M. Wertheimer, Dr. W. Glasser, Dr. J. Baker, Dr. E. Lopez." He gave the information back to Leo and captured a crispy square.

After a few minutes of companionable silence punctuated by the sounds of a well-appreciated meal, Leo put down her sandwich. She looked at her father and uncle, stating, "Dr. Baker is the one." She responded to their quizzical expressions with a quick laugh. "Because we could surely use a Baker in this family."

Uncle Paul guffawed, and Joseph chuckled as he raised his coffee mug. "That's as good a reason as any. Let's toast to Dr. J. Baker, whomever they may be, wherever they may be!"

Leo raised her water and Uncle Paul his can of diet soda; and met in the middle of the table, clanking. "To Dr. Baker!"

After Leo replaced her plastic water bottle on the table, her dad's arm, en route for another sandwich, clipped the edge, sending the container skittering across the floor, rolling until stopped by the refrigerator. She went to retrieve her beverage and saw the edge of a card, knocked off weeks ago, sticking out, dust covered. She retrieved the invitation and blew off the grit.

"Dad, tonight's Ray's farewell cookout. The send-off started at four."

Joseph looked at his watch and the stack of papers waiting to be graded. "Do you still want to go? It's getting late."

"It's only seven, and there's no end time listed. Sure, we might have missed the barbecue part, but we have to go, Dad. It's Ray."

Leo saw her dad trying to gauge how much this meant to her. He nodded as if resigned. "Yes, it's for Ray. We should go and wish him well."

Leo ran to change her shirt and met her dad in the driveway. After she jumped into the passenger seat, she buckled her seat belt, and as they pulled out, she smiled. "I bet he doesn't even recognize me. The last time he saw me was his senior year, when I was twelve. I've changed a lot since then."

She doesn't remember. Joseph started to say something, then stopped. The day had been long and emotionally charged. Leo was in a good place, and there wasn't a concrete reason to alter her narrative. Withholding information from his daughter was something with which he'd never been comfortable. But always, any omission was done with the sole intent of protecting Leo, to shield her from hurtful truths. He reached over and turned on the radio. Music spiraled around them and then fled out the open windows.

Here's to you, Mrs. Robertson

Ray stayed in the shower longer than usual. Fantasies of finding a way not to attend his "Farewell Cookout" ran through his mind. As he'd been staying with his sister since May walked out, pretending he was sick was impossible. He had just finished a six-mile run, and she'd be wounded if he suddenly bailed. Besides, this party was more for her, an act of being able to regulate something over which she had no control. The warm water was a rivulet. He rinsed his hair and watched the suds circle down the drain but stopped when someone knocked on the door.

"Hey, brother? Are you alive in there?" He turned off the water. There was a protracted pause. "You're hogging the bathroom, and I need to put on my party face." As he grabbed a thin, coarse, sun-dried towel and began to wipe himself down, her footsteps diminished.

The party looked like a high school reunion, no, more like a lifetime reunion. Hope invited everyone who had been part of his life since they were young. Sunday school teachers, little league coaches, teammates, family, and friends mingled, vibrant in the autumnal light, with a backdrop of 80s music piped in from loaned speakers. The grills Hope borrowed were full of barbecue magic, chicken thighs, sizzling beef, black bean, and turkey burgers. The feast his sister and her long-time friend, now housemate Gabrielle, had prepared was impressive, spread over three tables of varying heights decorated with red, white, and blue plastic coverings from Dollar General. As Ray stood in the doorway, his hair still wet from the shower, his dark navy T-shirt slightly damp from the heat his body was still generating from his run, he felt a deep sensation of abeyance.

He was standing between two lifetimes. His collective past was on a patch of green before him. His uncharted future was around the corner. Not a part of him would presume to be above another's experience. But here, in this still moment, the dividing line in his life was clear. After May walked out on him, there had been no reason to keep the apartment. The possessions he truly cared about were packed into a few boxes and stacked in the closet of Hope's rented 800-square-foot home. If his sister moved, she promised she would take them with her.

"Hey, Ray-Ban, get the hell out here!" Miguel, Ray's best friend from high school, spotted the reluctant guest of honor and made a beeline for him. Ray stepped outside and into a hug that lifted him an inch off the ground. Hope called him beefy. What could Ray say? Miguel loved the weights and carb-loading with beer. Already a little unsteady, Miguel slung an arm around Ray's shoulder. "Trying to get out of your own party?" He steered him into the gathering.

"There he is the man of the hour who also happens to have a voice like an angel."

Ray turned around. "Mrs. Robertson." He flashed one of his easy, broad smiles at the tiny choir director. She stood before him with a curved spine and tightly rolled silver hair that framed a face with more wrinkles than a catcher's mitt.

"We sure have missed your voice and your perfect pitch. The choir hasn't been the same since you left." Her compliment was sincere. In her hands was a paper plate piled high with food, and on top perched a piece of garlic bread.

When he was ten, he remembered asking his mother at the weekly potluck held after church services, "If Mrs. Robertson eats so much at breakfast, lunch, and dinner, why isn't she fat?" His voice had not been quiet.

"Shh, Ray." His mother pulled him into the prep kitchen and stooped to look him in the eyes. "That's probably her only food for the day. That's why these lunches are so important. Many people in our congregation live alone. They have limited resources and no one to share a meal with, so they just don't eat." Acts of service were concepts he grew up with and appreciated. Perhaps the most authentic part of his father's ministry was this. Though he stopped attending church on Sundays, Ray showed up when possible for community work events: food or clothing giveaways or when a parishioner needed help fixing a leaking roof or repairing a rotting foundation.

"Your teeth are white enough for a toothpaste commercial. With your thick dark hair and electric blue eyes, you look more like a movie star than a soldier. Are you sure you're heading in the right direction?"

"Ah, the million-dollar question." He paused and took a swig of Sprite. "No turning back now. Uncle Sam has my social security number and address." His smile was strained, out of politeness and respect for his elder. He understood the undercurrent of this exchange.

Like many adults of his parents' congregation, Mrs. Robertson believed war resulted from man's fundamental evil, an inability to live up to God's exacting standards.

She placed a weathered hand on his arm and gave him a gentle squeeze. "We'll be praying for you." The paper plate in her remaining hand wobbled, and her garlic bread toppled to the ground.

"Thank you, I need all the help I can get." He knew Mrs. Robertson had accomplished her mission. In her sweet, fundamental way, she performed a duty to tell him that although his actions went against the teachings of the church he was raised in, and he was considered lost, he was still worthy of prayer.

****

"It's your party. Get something to eat." Hope brushed past him on her way to the table with a new bowl of potato salad. "The crowds went through Gabrielle's batch like lightning. Time to bring out the reserves—my latest creative endeavor in the kitchen."

Ray looked at her askance. Hope's futile attempts to create culinary delights were legendary. Friends and family continued to find ingenious ways to avoid consumption. He was foraging for an excuse when she gently pushed him toward the food table.

"Come on, Ray, no FHB tonight."

His chortle was spontaneous. The acronym for Family Hold Back was whispered when unexpected guests appeared at their home for a meal or when the attendance of worshipers exceeded the amount of nourishment prepared. His mother would murmur FHB smiling, a mutual conspiracy; his father would say the words with seriousness, a strict mandate. Once the

Shipworth family had served everyone else, they ate. As adults, when Hope and Ray went to a mutual friend's home for dinner, they always found themselves waiting, being the last to put food on their plates. This concept was so ingrained they usually did not notice, but occasionally, they would catch each other's eye and nod, an understanding of a shared upbringing. Hope gave her brother another playful nudge.

"Will we ever be able to go in for food right away and not hold back?" Ray asked as he picked up an empty paper plate.

"Probably not." She took a large spoonful of the chunky medley. "But tonight, eat for me." She dropped the potato salad on his plate. "I don't want to have to worry about the mayo spoiling my delicacy."

****

"We almost didn't come." Straightforward speaking, there was only one person he knew who always cut to the chase. He looked up from his plate of food. She stood in front of him, and his breath caught. She looked so much like a young woman, with rangy jean-clad legs, a white T-shirt hugging narrow hips, long black hair swept back into a high ponytail that accentuated her wide-set eyes, perfectly centered aquiline nose, rose petal lips. She was not the same twelve-year-old child last seen during his senior year of track; this was not the same lifeless girl he found, a discarded afterthought, five weeks ago.

"Nice to see you too, Squirt." He stood, put his untouched food down, and shoved his hands in his pockets.

"Squirt?" She tried to act annoyed, but her smile gave her away. "Time to ditch that nickname. I'm almost as tall as you now." She pulled herself higher and, for a moment, stood on her toes, her eyes dark cinnamon, alive, flecked with gold, seeking his. "The last time you saw me, I was just a kid."

Ray laughed loudly. "I still have six inches on you, but you're right. You've done some growing." As Leo talked, it became apparent she didn't know he had found her in the factory. Bringing up something which held possible embarrassment and pain was pointless now. After all, he rationalized, chances are, after tonight, I will never see her again.

"The invitation fell off our refrigerator, and if I hadn't dropped my water bottle, we wouldn't be here."

"I'll have to thank gravity for that one." Ray noticed the blue horseshoes in her hands and gleefully rubbed his hands together. "A glutton for punishment, are you? Don't tell me you want to lose to me one last time."

Her laugh was soft and floated with the air. "Fat chance! You're on." They headed to the horseshoe pit, side by side, their steps light, unencumbered.

The first time Ray met Leo, she was eight years old. After Coach Lightfoot recruited him for the cross-country team, he was extra early for the first practice. Leo had marched up to him, wearing bright red shorts and an oversized Tiger shirt. "What's your name?" she demanded. He told her. Band-Aids were on both knees. "Coach is my dad," she continued. Her hair looked like a discarded bird's nest because, he found out, she had just rolled down a hill.

"I bet I can beat you in a race." Fist-clenched hands were hanging by her side, and her young eyes sparkled.

Ray did everything to keep from laughing out loud

because he could tell this was serious business. He looked around. No one else was there; Coach was talking to his assistant a football field away. "Sure. See that tree near the base of the hill? Let's go."

And she was off, skinny legs pumping as fast as they could, her Sandy sidekick flying by her side. With four strides, Ray was next to her, huffing and puffing. He pretended he was exerting himself as much as possible. She looked over at him as he kept pace with her and laughed. When they reached the elm tree, he slowed. Leo's small hand slapped the laced bark, and a triumphant voice yelled, "I won!"

"Good job, Squirt." He high-fived her, and she beamed.

"I know you let me win." Her honesty had surprised him: "You better not do that again. One day I'll beat you for real." Ray's teammates were starting to gather and do stretches. As he jogged off to join them, he called, "I don't doubt that, Squirt, not one bit."

When Coach Lightfoot held cross country practices in the fall, and track and field in the spring, she was always there, on the edges, doing cartwheels, making clover chain crowns, climbing trees, lying flat on her back, looking at cloud animals in the sky or making grass angels, sitting in the stands chatting with a runner's girlfriend or their parents. Leo lived in her own biosphere, enfolded by a larger world, constantly with her dog.

Before the freshman season ended, Leo gave him a nickname. "You call me Squirt, and I'm calling you Blink." When he asked why, she simply said, "Because a Ray of sunshine is so bright, it makes you Blink."

****

Sometime during the prolonged festivities, after the food was consumed, and the corn hole games died down, the bonfire was lit. People with young children headed home, and those without reached for another drink as they pulled chairs around the flame and placed blankets on their knees. Ray caught his sister's eye. She was unusually quiet. Hope came over, her arms full of plastic cups and disposable plates. Ray offered her the trash can.

"I am so mad at them. I sent an invitation, you know." Her voice trembled. "I can't believe they didn't show. Dad, I guess I understand. He sees your enlistment as a personal attack on him, a hostile affront to everything he stands for. But Mom? What's she thinking? You're her baby."

"Only by ten minutes."

"You're her only son." Hope's eyes filled, and Ray gave her an all-encompassing hug.

"Come on, Hope. You know the situation. She's supposed to be a supportive, obedient wife and follow the head of the household. Nothing has changed since we were little. Why expect a reversal now."

"I don't know, maybe because her son is going to boot camp and then to war." Hope continued to make the rounds, picking up and shoving trash into the receptacle Ray carried behind her. "You would think that maternal instinct we learned about in school would kick in, and nothing could keep her from saying goodbye."

Her anger was fierce. Though Ray understood, he didn't feel animosity toward his parents. Hope was grieving their separation. He felt the same. They'd always been close. The longest they'd gone without seeing each other, even as young adults, was a few days. Growing up, people said, "There's no special connection between you, except that you share the same birthday, the same parents, oh, and the same cake." But they were wrong. Unlike most siblings, the only time they sparred was over who got to drive. And, even then, that was short-lived, for they quickly devised a system: first one ready for school drives, and work takes precedence over pleasure. Though never spoken, they appreciated that their singularly unique childhood would not have been the same experience without the other. They did not feel physical pain when the other suffered, like identical twins often reported, but on an emotional level, they understood. They could read each other with a glance.

****

"Hey, it's all cleaned up inside. I think I'm heading to bed." Gabrielle stood behind the siblings seated around the fire and put a hand on each of their shoulders.

Hope leaned back and smiled gratefully. "Thanks for all your help tonight. Don't wait up."

Gabrielle bent to graze Hope's forehead. She then squeezed Ray's upper arm. "Take care of yourself, please. I don't want her to fall apart."

As Gabrielle walked away, Ray raised a single eyebrow.

Hope gave a quick, self-conscious laugh and shrugged. "I'm trying to figure this stuff out. As adolescents we didn't have the chance to explore our inner yearnings, let alone to test relationships and see what feels right. I like her."

Ray sized up his sister and replied, "Then that's all

that matters."

They stayed up long after the last guest left. Sitting by the dying fire, they talked, reflected, and laughed, siblings that had shared a reluctant womb and drawn their first breaths within minutes of each other. They intuitively knew this time would come—a point of separation, of diverging experience. As the horizon began to lighten and the last embers cooled, Ray and Hope looked at each other, eyes tired but gratified. There was nothing left to say except a single word they uttered simultaneously, "Coffee!"

Hours later, Ray would be far removed from this moment, his sister, and life as he knew it, on a plane hurdling through the sky.

Tract Three:

Fall 2005-Spring 2006
The Preacher's Kid

Outside the airplane window, dark clouds churned. In thirty minutes, they would begin their descent. Ray carried with him memories of last night's farewell cookout. So many people had shown up to wish him well.

Leo and Coach Lightfoot's attendance touched him. Without question, Joseph Lightfoot had altered the course of Ray's life. Coach probably didn't even realize this, but then he was like that, unassuming but present, always doing the right thing, trying to help the students he taught.

The aircraft suddenly dropped. Ray's stomach lurched as the middle-aged woman beside him white-knuckled her armrest. Tinny strands of Led Zeppelin's "Stairway to Heaven" emanated from her headphones.

As the rain slashed across his window and the visibility closed in, the aircraft's wings struggled to stay level against strong headwinds. Across the aisle, a man in a crisp business suit threw back a jack and coke.

Ray closed his eyes and reached back to a time in his past when he questioned what he was doing. He remembered tearing across a parking lot, and thinking how did I get myself into this situation? Under his T-shirt, tucked into the waistband of his jeans, was a pack of cigarettes. And he didn't even smoke. High School had not gotten off to a good start.

It began the first morning on the first day of his freshman year.

"Preacher's Kid." A pair of bushy hands sporting black leather wrist cuffs shoved him into his open metal locker. "Are you a softie, or do you have the guts to be a man?"

The voice belonged to a senior they called Bear, pumped up and burly with more facial hair than a grizzly. His reputation preceded him.

Ray wanted to turn and walk away, to let Bear toy with him and be done, but something inside of him couldn't let go. "Just because my dad's a pastor doesn't mean that I'm weak."

Bear grinned as if this was precisely the reaction he wanted. His yellow nicotine-stained teeth, crammed into a mouth too small for his body, leaned into each other like overcrowded tombstones. "We'll see about that. But you're gonna have to prove yourself." He gave Ray another poke in the chest. "We meet behind the school when the fifth-period bell goes off." Ray started to point out that school wasn't over then but was stopped short by the look in Bear's eyes of malevolent amusement.

The gang smoked and tore each other apart with words. They slapped one another forcefully on the shoulders and shoved tight fists into unsuspecting abdomens. They told raunchy jokes at the expense of others. Ray struggled not to let his disquietude show. Expectations escalated quickly. Bear pulled Ray before him.

The Circle of Willis

"It's your turn, Babyface." Smoke-filled, fetid breath slammed into Ray. He reflexively stepped back, flinching. Bear laughed. "This's the easy one. They ain't gonna do nothing but git harder. Then we'll see if you're a little boy or a man."

All new initiates were required to steal a pack of cigarettes and give them to Bear. For the first time in his young life, Ray fully understood his father's preaching about the hazards of straying from a virtuous path.

Already Ray could see the perils of this direction. A single pack of cigarettes would lead to activities other members bragged about, like breaking into and robbing stores and unoccupied homes at night. This wasn't what he understood being a man to be. He struggled to find a way out.

On the day Bear lured him in, Ray witnessed what would happen if he refused to participate. Another freshman, a boy Ray didn't know, balked at the initiation task.

"I'm not going to steal." The short, solid-framed adolescent's voice wavered, but he stood resolute. Within seconds, four of Bear's accomplices surrounded him and hauled him over the hill. When Miguel returned with a swollen right eye, split lip, and blood on his face, he compliantly completed his assignment. He threw the stolen pack at Bear's feet and was rewarded with a sharp shove. Ray's turn was up. Trapped against a wall, an ultimatum faced him: prove yourself or else.

Ray knew the manager of the Hit-N-Run convenience store. Mr. Ruggles was an usher at his dad's church and implicitly trusted him. When he crossed the threshold, and the store bell rang, Mr.

Ruggles looked up and beamed. "Hey, Ray, just give me a moment. I have to finish stocking these shelves."

Ray attempted to smile back. With the blood in his neck pulsating at the same rapid rate as his heart, he casually stepped behind the register, grabbed a pack of cigarettes, and put them under his shirt before putting the can of Sprite on the counter. He waited to pay for the drink.

When he left the store, Ray tossed the soda atop the overflowing trash and started running as fast as his legs would take him, as if he could untie the earthly bonds of his body and escape reality through this desperate act of all-out flight.

Ray raced across the road without looking. The black Civic screeched to a stop, barely missing him. The driver jumped out and put a steady hand on his shoulder. "Ray, what's going on?"

It took an instant for him to recognize his biology teacher. Hearing the kindness in his voice and seeing the concern in his eyes, Ray lost his bearing. Coach Lightfoot caught him as he collapsed, helped him into the air-conditioned vehicle, and let him sob.

Ray couldn't remember the last time he cried. He was taught that letting your emotions show was a sign of weakness and that vulnerability could be used against you. The words came slowly at first, then in a torrent. This time, Ray did not hold back. He told the truth of the situation. He expressed his fears and the sense of complete helplessness.

In the silence that followed came a tentative lifeline.

"There's a way out." Ray's desperation quieted. Coach Lightfoot continued, "If you decide to do the right thing, I have a solution." Ray listened intently. "Of course, the store manager must agree. It's ultimately his decision to prosecute or not. Your life is before you, Ray. Your choices become your history."

Though shocked at Ray's revelation, the store manager and long-time tithe usher recognized true contrition. He was a member who lived each day trying to embody what he learned from the pews situated far below pastor Shipworth's pulpit. The store would not press charges if Ray lived up to the agreed-upon terms. Coach Lightfoot stood by Ray's side as he confessed and asked for forgiveness. He was given a chance to course-correct; not every adolescent had this opportunity.

As they left the store, with the returned pack of crumpled cigarettes in the trash, a receipt of sale, and the cost of the purchase in the till, Mr. Ruggles pulled Ray aside.

"If you follow through, there's no reason for your father to know any of this happened."

Ray nodded. He was exceedingly grateful. Almost weighing as heavily upon him as the gang membership was the wrath and resultant punishments he would incur when his father found out.

The following day, when the fifth-period bell rang, Ray, his stomach in twists, not entirely understanding how this would go down, ducked out as he had for the past four afternoons to meet up with Bear and his accomplices. Coach Lightfoot and a Tahlequah police officer walked out of the red brick building. There wasn't time to disperse. Besides, Bear vociferously argued, other than skipping class, they weren't doing anything wrong.

The officer spoke first. "Ray Shipworth was busted shoplifting a pack of cigarettes yesterday afternoon. He went into the store with the intent to steal. That's a crime."

Coach continued, "The store owner isn't going to press charges provided Ray shows up every day after school for cross-country training in the fall, conditioning in the winter, then track and field in the spring."

The Officer looked Bear in the eye. "Do you understand what this means?" Bear let out a grunt, a begrudging acknowledgment. "Now, for the rest of you," the officer continued, "this is a one-time offer. If you've done anything like Mr. Shipworth here, swiped a pack of smokes, and you want to commit to Coach Lightfoot, I'll personally petition for you not to be prosecuted." He was bluffing, of course. The high schoolers could not get into trouble if the police hadn't caught them, but he was sure none of them knew this. "Any takers?"

Miguel stepped out of the pack, still sporting a swollen eye from his 'group lesson' given days ago.

"Good choice." The officer motioned him to stand next to Ray. "Any other volunteers?" No one else moved.

As Ray and Miguel walked away, flanked by Coach Lightfoot and the officer, Ray heard Bear's voice rise into the afternoon sky, "Worthless pieces of crap, anyway. Feels good to dump that load of shit."

Ray had never felt so relieved in all his life.

****

Bright forked lightning sparked and snapped through the coal-black clouds. The bottom had dropped out of life as Ray knew it. May had left him before he could propose, and his father disowned him. What was left for him back home? He could not fix what was broken, but he could make an impact on the world as an infantryman. There was nothing left but to commit wholeheartedly to the military. Ray resolved to be the best soldier possible. This would be his obsession; he had nothing left.

"Passengers and flight attendants, please prepare for landing." The pilot's voice broke through his reverie. Ray brought his seat to an upright position and braced for what was next.

The Duffle Bag Drill

Fort Benning Military Base, Columbus Georgia
"You wanna try me, bro?" A scrappy man with a voice that oozed southern vernacular, the way Spanish-moss saturated trees, stood before a towering form they called the Yank.

"Back off, hick! You're too close. I can smell your rotten breath. You got to stop eating all the roadkill. You're not leaving any for the vultures." The Yank shoved him in the chest and sent the bloke flying.

And it was on. Again.

Ray sighed. He stepped back and gave them space. This in-processing phase was taking forever. Ray and his fellow recruits had spent the week waiting for all sorts of calculated misery. There were physicals (all that poking and prodding), not to mention an endless series of immunizations. As he dropped his camouflage pants for another round of shots, he thought, what about the guys with minimal real estate back there? Additionally, there were haircuts, gear issuance, drug testing, x-rays, and all that mind-numbing paperwork which did little to subdue the restless servicemen. Instead, the required monotonous motions seemed to fuel nicotine-deprived, testosterone-laden infernos.

Fights, embers of spontaneous combustion, broke out everywhere. They happened in the lines waiting for chow, in the barracks while waiting for your turn to

The Circle of Willis

stand in line, or just when milling around, and over the most minuscule of things: Yo momma is so fat when she sat on Walmart, she lowered the prices. You're so inbred. They named a sandwich after you. I ain't as stupid as you look.

Ray watched the Yank swagger away, wiping a bloody nose with his sleeve, leaving his battered opponent looking even worse. How in the world will this volatile, cantankerous mass of seething privates ever get through boot camp without killing each other? We'll never make it, let alone become fully functioning soldiers.

Unbeknownst to the recruits, the transformation started the moment they arrived.

The fledglings were already shedding parts of their civilian identities, like molting insects discarding their exoskeletons. Everyone entered with their own stories and swag that rendered them unique. But by the time they boarded the buses from reception, all had been uniformly shorn, shaved, re-clothed, and in most cases, re-named. Those who still needed a handle would shortly earn one.

While Ray and his fellow initiates were driven downrange, the tenor began to shift from agitated indifference to charged unease. As different as they had been on that first day, one overarching element united them now. They were entering the unknown together. When they stepped off the bus, everything would change. They would be divided into platoons (Ray would be assigned to the third one) and then squads. But first, there was the duffel bag drill.

Drill Sergeant Sledge, heavily muscled and intimidating with his chiseled face and gruff megaphone loud voice, took control the moment their boots hit the ground downrange. "You are mine now!" he barked, and the rookies involuntarily stepped backward. "Don't go looking for your momma; she ain't here. She don't want you no more. Do you hear me? You don't talk, eat, or even fart without my permission. Total control, ladies, every breath you take, every move you make, I'll be watching you!" He paused to let his words sink in and took pleasure in the looks of terror on some of their faces. "Now, let's see what you got."

Two hundred identical army-issued top-load duffle bags with two hundred identical-looking locks were dumped into a mountainous pile. Sledge screamed, a thunderous gravelly voice Ray would hear intermittently in his dreams for the rest of his life. "You have one hour to find your bag, or else you'll be left behind."

It was madness, this scramble, this sea of panicked trainees trying desperately to find their belongings. Sacks were flying in every direction, being randomly tossed and discarded after the private's fingers stumbled, attempting the combination to no avail.

What is to keep the same person from trying the same lock on the same bag he found launched in another location repeatedly? Just like Sisyphus, doomed for eternity, pushing a colossal boulder up a hill, only to have the rock roll down every time he neared the top.

Ray saw a solution, a single conceivable way to get through this impossible exercise of futility. Not thinking of being singled out and punished for his brazenness (that would come later), he scrambled up the pile of olive-green canvas, a silhouette, backlit by the intense Georgia sun, atop an unlikely bluff. He waved his arms and whistled his Coach Lightfoot I-mean-business whistle.

Ray shouted, "There's only one way we can get through this mess." He took a quick breath. Most of the recruits were staring hard at him, listening; a few continued their frantic combination dialing. "We have to form a huge circle. Everyone grabs one rucksack and tries the lock. If the combo doesn't work, pass the bag to your left. When you find your pack, fall out." Or stay in the circle and help the private next to you, he thought, as he stumbled down. When his feet hit the ground, a rudimentary process was forming. The ring expanded as the nascent soldiers realized the benefit of working in coordination. The duffle bags moved, passing from one set of hands to the next. And then, as each private claimed their belongings and stepped back, the circle constricted.

When they finished, Drill Sergeant Sledge looked at his stopwatch. "Ladies, you set a record. Congratulations. But don't let this go to your pretty little heads." Beady eyes honed on Ray. "No matter how cute you think you are, everyone's shit stinks. Now let the fun begin."

****

He ran across an open, rock-strewn expanse at an all-out pace. Sweat dripped down his back and stung his eyes. His lungs could not take in enough of the condensed Georgia air to expand. Really, Ray, what were you thinking? You willingly volunteered for this insanity. Fifty pounds of infantry gear weighed him down in a "full battle rattle." His weapon, flak vest, Kevlar helmet, pistol belt, ammunition, canteen, and loaded, go-to-war rucksack slammed against him as he sprinted. Like many other boot camp experiences, this intense training pushed Ray to uncharted limits.

The psychological demands were as exacting as the physical. And Ray found himself in a constant state of flux, trying to establish some sense of equilibrium. In this moment of total exertion, Ray reached into memory. He was at the State Cross Country Meet, his senior year, and had just rounded the trail's final bend leading into the open concluding stretch. The crowd let out a roar as the top runners turned the corner and galloped by. Screams of encouragement came from the sidelines as they ran. At the end, he could see Coach Lightfoot furiously waving him in, jumping up and down, more animated than he had ever seen him. Ray heard the vibrant throng, rising in its swell, ascending from a silent Georgian wood— his energized Coach, in the guise of his Drill Sergeant. And he flew across the finish line as though not weighed down by the full combat gear worn by a soldier in a war.

"Iceman? Are you okay?" The private they called Yoda tugged nervously on one of his overly large tea-cupped-shaped ears, which made him look more like Dumbo (but that nickname had been taken) and handed Ray his canteen of water. "Drill sergeant says we have to hydrate."

Ray shook himself to the present. The two-mile run, in full battle gear, was over. He wasn't sure what time he had gotten or where he had placed. But he understood that hadn't been the point. The goal was to strengthen and prepare them should they ever find themselves in a situation like that in war, when all they had to save themselves was the allowance of weighted flight. As if we will ever have to run for miles with all our gear. In modern warfare, Ray thought, this will never happen.

Ray leaned wearily against the longitudinally furrowed trunk of a southern live oak and pulled off his helmet, his cropped dark hair matted with sweat. He took Yoda's offering and drank deeply. He couldn't account for how memory slipped in at the strangest times. Everything was different here, at Fort Benning. The way experiences and sensations of the present seemed to trigger the neurons responsible for thoughts and memories of the past was inexplicable. Somehow, they were forging new connections, rewiring his circuitry.

Drill Sergeant Sledge stood large before his recovering men and took a drink from his canteen, demonstrating by example the importance of fluid intake after an all-out effort. He surveyed the soldiers, some still breathing heavily, and calmly stated, "Chuck Norris doesn't breathe. He holds air hostage."

In the House of Pain

Time bent in on itself at the United States Army Infantry Training epicenter. During the Red phase, the period of total control, there was an all-out assault on the senses. Each detail of every assignment mattered. Starting at 0430 in the morning, every movement, how you made your bed, your hygiene, how you exercised, walked, marched, spoke to your superiors, even ate, was scrutinized and, if found lacking, was immediately corrected by the drill sergeant. There were no exceptions to the strict regime. Adherence was non-negotiable. When one recruit messed up, the whole team paid the unrelenting piper.

"Caught one of you slacking." Sledge held a private by his collar so everyone could see. They were cleaning their barracks. "This guy thought he'd let you do all the work. I found him sitting on the toilet, chewing tobacco. So, after you finish tidying up, there will be a contraband hunt."

Everyone groaned. They knew what this meant. During the search for anything that wasn't army-issued (a piece of gum, a can of dip, a candy bar, the butt of a cigarette with three puffs left), their superiors would toss everything asunder. "But first..." Sledge took the steel bucket and splashed tepid mop water all over the bay. "Everyone on your hands and knees and wipe up the damn floor."

Group corrective actions included extreme physical exertion taking the soldier to the brink of exhaustion. Ray and his fellow initiates quickly learned that these drills were called smoke sessions, a term originating in military recruit training. Two-hour hard-core smoke sessions held outside or in the barracks were typical. The components included endless cycles of unsupported sit-ups, side straddle hops, flutter kicks, supine bicycling, and pushups. *Chuck Norris doesn't do push-ups. He pushes the earth down.*

Maintaining the front leaning rest position for prolonged periods (while chanting *We like it, we love it, we want more of it, make it hurt, Drill Sergeant, make it hurt*), followed by running up and down steep hills with green duffle bags held overhead were also incorporated. Group repercussions also included menial subservient tasks: making your bed ten times in a row, scrubbing rows of toilets with a toothbrush, cutting blades of grass with scissors until the entire area was "beautified" (pruned so that every fragment of green was equal height), filling the 1,025-gallon water buffalo, with an eight-ounce canteen cup. And these consequences, even for perceivably minor infractions, say looking around during a drill or talking while in chow formation, during the first few weeks caused the platoon to turn on the inciting individual. *The quickest way to a man's heart is with Chuck Norris' fist, so damn it, Hollywood, do not screw up again, or else we'll unleash him on you!*

****

It was Ray's squad's first-time doing nighttime land navigation. Around them spun a black, moonless night.

"Shit, Iceman, we're lost and totally screwed." Perry, so named because, like the detective Perry Mason, he sniffed around in other people's business, was the team's point man. He threw his hands in the air and turned in a 360-degree circle. "Hell, if I know the way out."

Despite their careful plotting and dead reckoning with three compasses, they missed their first point. They were hopelessly lost, so far off course they could see the lights of Columbus, Georgia, shimmering in the distance over the rapidly moving Chattahoochee River.

"All right then." Iceman, the squad's leader, remained calm. No use getting upset now. He could see his team's navigator tense. "Look, ultimately, the repercussions will fall on me, and that's okay. We might have made an error in plotting our grid coordinates. Let's sit for a moment and re-group." The fatigue-clad soldiers climbed upon a fallen tree on the steep bank and drank water from their canteens. Ray assessed each of his team members quickly and then regarded the night.

Perry broke the silence. "We'll pay for this. Navigating is much easier during the day." He looked dejected.

Ray nodded. "Bet we aren't the only ones who messed up."

"I know how we can get out of it," Hollywood said. "We follow this river downstream as far as she takes us. We'll have a head start, and it's harder to track scents in the water." He was not serious, his teammates knew this, but he gave them pause—how easy walking away and returning to a life that was becoming increasingly difficult to remember would be.

They lost count of how many recruits had bailed, gone AWOL, absent without leave, which warranted a dishonorable military discharge, and followed you for life. And many others had fallen by the wayside for different reasons—a broken foot, a fight that resulted in injury, or a mental breakdown. One guy was chaptered out and went to jail for making and throwing an MRE (Meals, Ready to Eat) bomb (tabasco sauce in the heater, put the steaming sauce in a beverage bag, and voila). They sat solemnly in absorbed introspection.

"You know prisoners have more freedom than we do," Mud Cat broke the silence. "They can listen to music, read books, draw, and watch TV. They get to have their own stuff and get visitors, conjugal ones even." Ray leaned back against the heavily gnarled wood and looked upward. Dense clouds moved in. The coverage was so thick nothing was visible, not even the moving pinpoint glow of a plane. We have each other, our rifles, and rucksacks. And right now, I don't need anything more.

****

The entire company, close to two hundred men, were together, and they were being led ten at a time into the "gas chamber," a mandatory requirement for all burgeoning soldiers. Ray was in the first group of ten and listened intently to the instructions on donning and clearing his mask. He understood what was required of him once tapped on the shoulder. Some of the men in his platoon, he observed, were so nervous, they hadn't absorbed the information.

Ray gave one of his squad mates, who was shaking uncontrollably, a quick pat on the back. "Come on, Mud Cat," His voice was low. "You're going to be fine.

Think of all the soldiers before you who got through without the world ending." Mud Cat nodded, but his facial expression indicated Ray's words had not mitigated his fears, not one iota. Ray sighed.

He would always recall the night Mud Cat earned his moniker. During the first week of total control, two hours before Cat's scheduled fireguard, Ray saw him rise stealthily from his bed. He stated in a low, monotone voice to anyone who wasn't asleep and cared to listen, "Don't think I can do this anymore." He then walked out the door smack into one of those sudden Georgia storms, all anger and rain-drenched madness. He wanted to escape, though this would mean a dishonorable discharge. The need for release overrode all. An hour later, he returned, tripping over gear as he crept back into the barracks, creating quite a stir. Lights turned on, and soldiers sat up, rubbing their eyes and groaning, *Time to rise*?

When they saw him soaked and covered head to toe in mud, Perry cackled, "Look what the Cat drug in!" Mud Cat was born.

Ray never found out what transpired that night, if Cat had a change of heart, thinking of his eighteen-month-old daughter at home, if he had a come to Jesus moment under the pouring sky, or if he simply couldn't navigate his way out of the massive 280-mile installment. The following morning, Ray saw a change. Cat seemed resolute, determined to finish the course he had chosen, committing to the process with body and mind.

In the barracks, their bottom racks were next to each other, and in those impossible moments where sleep is elusive and minds race despite overly exhausted bodies, they whispered. Ray helped him through the Combat Life Saving course. And Cat kept working with Ray repeatedly to ensure that Ray, who had never touched a gun, felt comfortable loading, zeroing, firing, and cleaning his weapon. They both were agile learners, quick to help each other and those around them.

It looked like one of Coach Lightfoot's Bunsen burners in biology class. Ray quickly followed the memorized directions as the gas began to vaporize, filling the air of the enclosed space. He closed his eyes, held his breath, and unzipped the flap. Within seconds, he tightly secured the apparatus and cleared it, creating a firm seal. He inhaled; the gasmask was tight, the filters working, and each breath was easy. Next to him, Mud Cat struggled. Without thinking, Ray reached over and tightened the mask's straps. He cupped his hand over the vent and told Cat to blow air out, then put his hands over the filters and told him to breathe in. Cat calmed once he saw his equipment was working. Iceman and Cat breathed side by side, the chamber now so full of smoke, seeing was impossible.

Ray waited. Once he felt the tap on his shoulder, he removed the mask, put on his Kevlar helmet, held his rifle in his right hand and, as ordered, recited his name, rank, and social security number. He tried not to inhale, but even with his breath held, the gas attacked. His body's reaction was swift. Immediately, he began to choke, cough, and gag. Tears and mucus streamed uncontrollably from his eyes, nose, and throat. Panic and pain caused disorientation, where was the door? Some of his fellow soldiers appeared utterly incapacitated. Ray found the wall and followed the contours with his hand until he stumbled outside, where he promptly vomited the undigested remains of lunch. Mud Cat was close behind him.

As Ray's group took in gulps of chilled air in an endeavor to mitigate the gas effects, the other initiates, the ones who had not yet gone through the experience, looked on with fascinated horror. Some could not help themselves and laughed. They pointed and snickered at their compatriots' anguish, even though they knew the same fate awaited them. Ray imagined some rookies thought they would be immune to the gases' effects, that they were somehow more robust, and the gas would not impact them in any way. But they were wrong.

Ray looked at his teammates, the ones he had gone through the chamber with and the ones now pouring out of the enclosure, saturated with vomit and bodily fluids. They were all bathed in a harsh, unforgiving light, saturated with chemicals, retching and fighting for air exchange. Yet, despite their pain, they tried to help each other by rinsing out one another's eyes and pouring water over their fellow soldier's hands. Ray saw with clarity how important this band of brothers was becoming to him, the sense of camaraderie, the willingness to endure together and, when necessary, come selflessly to the other's aid.

When the organizers led the second to last group into the cell, just as Ray felt his body achieve a sense of normalcy, Drill Sergeant Sledge called him. Then he yelled at Cat to join Ray and stand before him at parade rest, never, *ever*, a good thing. "Iceman, you ain't always going to be around to help a brother out. Do you know what the insurgents are doing now? Do you!" he barked.

"No, Drill Sergeant Sledge, no."

"I didn't think so. Well, let me tell you, Private. In October last year, in Al Anbar province, they started using chlorine gas along with conventional vehicle-borne explosive devices. Every man here, Cat included, must know how to put on his mask. You two got it?"

"Yes, Drill Sergeant Sledge!" they responded in unison.

"Okay then." Sledge sized them up and then continued. "For your antics, Iceman and Cat, you get to join this group of virgins. You two ladies earned yourself another round of fun in the House of Pain." He pushed them in with the second to last group and closed the door.

This time, unprompted, Cat stepped up to the plate. Ray could see the fear of the unknown in the assemblage's eyes. Cat looked quickly to Ray for support, then spoke, "You will not die. It's a bit rough, but you can do it." Ray remained composed and nodded in agreement as the burner in the middle of the room swiftly released the volatile vapors. Ray and Cat led by example, going through the motions clearly and steadily. And when Cat saw a fellow private struggling, he reached over and did what had been done for him.

****

Who can tell the inner workings of a man of stone, uncompromising, unshakable, a seer of all, one who is tasked with the herculean undertaking of transforming mere boys by crushing their civilian identities, then building them piece by piece into unflinching warriors, soldiers who will unquestionably follow orders, risking even death for the protection of their country, a higher cause? Who can tell exactly what he thinks as he commands Iceman and Mud Cat before him again, then calls the novice, helped by Mud Cat, to join them? As he sends the three of them, still retching and reeling from their last go-round, into the House of Pain one more time with the final group, he knows that if faced with letting a fellow trainee fail, Ray and Cat will step up again and again despite the repercussions, despite their personal agony.

Though Drill Sergeant Sledge unflinchingly understands his duty and how hard he must push to get his men there, he also recognizes that the drill is over. Lessons have been learned, but even more importantly, true character has been revealed.

Chuck Norris Doesn't Wear a Watch

"You wanna die?" Sledge screeched at the top of his lungs so close to Ray's face that he could see nasal hair in his beaked nose and droplets of spittle fly from his mouth. His visage was purple with rage.

Ray still did not feel entirely comfortable handling his weapon. That would eventually come months and months into training, but Sledge saw all. He noticed the slight tremor, and with lightning speed, ripped Ray's rifle from his hands and shoved him back, pushing the gun barrel into the middle of Ray's forehead. "Girlies, see how a moment's hesitation can turn out, see how indecision could kill you? If you don't want your momma to cry at your funeral, then you gotta kill first!"

****

"Chuck Norris doesn't wear a watch. He decides what time it is! And he's telling me it's time for a midnight SMOKE!" Sledge's penetrating words reached Ray's ears before his eyes registered the harsh fluorescent lights turning on and off overhead.

"Who screwed us this time?" Perry's southern accent, thick with denied sleep, drawled. They were being ripped out of slumber one hour after lights out for an intense smoke session courtesy of Dumbo falling asleep during his watch. In their ears, as they threw on their gear and ran into the dark, star-splashed Georgian night, rang the words of their drill sergeant.

"If Dumbo were in a war zone, on the nighttime watch out in the field, and had fallen asleep, ALL of you would be dead!"

As the indoctrination process progressed, as men were broken down, then rebuilt with paracord strands of army core values, they began to recognize the seriousness of obligation. No matter what task was required of them, no matter how insignificant the action seemed, their duty was to fulfill that commitment honorably.

****

"Look here!" Sledge hauled two privates before the platoon, scattered across a brittle, desiccated field, recuperating. They just finished the marksmanship training course and were exhausted. Sledge had the soldiers stand at attention before their squad mates. Everyone held their breath, knowing this would not be good. Sledge instructed them to throw their heads back and expose their necks. Across the soft flesh, from ear to ear, were slices of jagged red lines drawn with the red sharpie Sledge kept in his pocket. "I caught these two nodding off when they should have been on alert. They didn't feel me approach them from behind; they didn't see me slice open their throats. Do you think this is a game, Privates? I see some of you smirking. This ain't a joke. Combat ain't no laughing matter, and neither is a dereliction of duty."

Hours and days flowed together. The Red Phase bled into the White, a period where essential warrior skills were honed and ingrained, a time when any youthful arrogance that remained was drained, like an oil exchange, and was replaced with a steady abiding sense of humility and expanding maturity. Loyalty, duty, respect, honor, integrity, personal courage, and selfless service. During this juncture, Dumbo finally proved himself and became simply Bo.

If the developing soldiers had a moment to analyze their metamorphosis, they would realize the smoke sessions had decreased while technical instructions escalated. The White phase seeped into the Blue, where everything was fused and sharpened to razor precision. Specialized live fire training and extended field exercises pushed self-discipline, along with tactical and leadership skills, to new realms.

Unaware of these stages, Ray and his platoon mates followed the tightly controlled system, seeped with a core of army values. Evident to Ray was that his father's phrase "there goes one, there goes all, in this case, had the reverse connotation. He began to see that his loyalty to the mission and dedication to his band of brothers mattered more. If one failed in combat, they might all fall. Conformity and performance took precedence over personal needs. He and his men were no longer individuals, and their autonomy did not matter. They were serving a higher purpose. He was learning a new code, a new way of life. Drill Sergeant Sledge, he mused, was in some ways like his father, commanding, exacting, transforming. Only he had more of a sense of humor. "You are the reason condoms have an expiration date. Private, you make me believe in reincarnation because no one could become that stupid in one lifetime."

****

Over and over again, Sledge demonstrated how, rapidly, a lapse could lead to personal death, the slaughter of one of your brothers, or, even worse, your entire squad. Ray's platoon was about to start bayonet training, a practice that the Army's basic combat training would remove in five years. It had been an integral part of a warriors' arsenal from the 17th to the early 20th century.

"This is the situation." Sledge's voice was eerily calm. His men were in a straight line. One hundred meters down range hung a series of tires on recycled playground equipment, moving gently with a cooling wind and a cloudless blue-sky backdrop. "You are at war. Your unit must make the ultimate sacrifice in a last-ditch effort to stop the insurgents. There is no way out. Your ammo is all gone. All you have left is hand-to-hand combat and your bayonet."

"FIX BAYONETS," he commanded. Within seconds, the soldiers uniformly attached the spears to the muzzle of their rifles and stood shoulder to shoulder, stock still.

"Many of you will die, but there is no other option—annihilate or be killed. Remember your training, maintain your footing, and tap into that fearless inner warrior. He is in charge now. The boys that came groveling into boot camp are gone. They are history. You are hard-core fighters now. Do not think, just act. Thrust your bayonet into the enemy and send them to their maker."

Sledge paused, and the men, their weapons pointed straight ahead, waited until he lifted his hand, then quickly brought his arm down as he yelled, "CHARGE." The exercise became real. The ferocity of the head-on charge into death, fueled by the purpose of getting the enemy before they got you, spurred the burgeoning warriors into frenzied action. Sledge knew his soldiers had repeated these killing techniques so often, and in so many varied ways, they had become ingrained. They could now repeat them unconsciously, leap from a deep sleep even, and respond instinctively. As Drill Sergeant Sledge witnessed the fury of his men, the brutal way the tires were slashed and obliterated, he folded his arms across his chest and smiled.

Turning Blue

Iceman's Third Platoon marched down a wintry dark path laden with crystalizing mist and surrounded by a forbidding forest. As they moved, parachute flares lit up the woodlands, throwing eerie shadows everywhere. The blinding light mixed with darkness would be enough to disorient an everyday man, but this highly trained team was focused, their sense of direction keen, ready for another competition among platoons. In the prior contest, they had come in second place. They were determined to show Drill Sergeant Sledge that he could be proud of them and prove they were becoming the soldiers he expected them to be. As the Third Platoon stepped out of the dense foliage into a clearing under a midnight sky half-filled with white clouds, half-clear, they saw a World War I-style trench leading to a wooden wall.

They silently lined up in the gully. A green light came on.

"Move out!" Sledge commanded. He ordered them over the wall and reminded them the challenge was a timed event. All was quiet for a moment as they advanced, crawling through the thick, frosty, sand-mud mixture. The silence was shattered as M240B machine guns spread live fire over the platoons' heads. Four feet over their crouching bodies also flew burning orange tracer rounds, temporary flashes of brilliant light streaking across the night sky, visual meteors. Explosions were going off on the sides. The soldiers high crawled as swiftly as possible, spurred on by the cracking sounds of bullets whizzing overhead. They flipped on their backs to go under barbed wire through sludgy mud water, their flak jackets weighing them down immensely. When the white parachute flare went off, which signaled the platoon was halfway through, a unified guttural cry rose from their throats and reverberated down the line, intertwining with the night's gun-fueled cacophony. All reached into depths they did not know existed before and pushed themselves and each other balls to the wall.

The Third Platoon stood in rigid formation before him.

"Before I read the finishing times, you've got some work to do." Sledge was stern, resolute. He stood unyielding as he smoked them, and they endured. Not one soldier fell out or slowed down. When they were back in precise formation, mud-caked, exhausted, and dejected with sweat evaporating and freezing almost simultaneously, he read the finishing times: "Second Platoon, 16:20, Fourth Platoon 14:08, First Platoon 13:13 and finishing in First Place," did the corners of Sledge's mouth turn a notch upwards? "Third Platoon, 11:36. Over a full minute better than second place. Good job, men. Nick at Night was a success."

The elated Platoon exploded in celebration, like a team that had just won the world series.

****

Drill Sergeant Sledge: You had a good job when you LEFT

Platoon: You're RIGHT

Drill Sergeant Sledge: Jodie was home when you LEFT

Platoon: You're RIGHT

The fifty-plus pound pack on Ray's back felt insubstantial now. He remembered how encumbered he felt on his first weighted march, over four months ago, with only thirty-five pounds. He could not see the physical changes in muscle tone, but he felt the strength in his body. His mental acumen was knife-edged, his spirit fortified. Iceman was hard-wired and ready for the next chapter in his life. He looked forward to these treks, appreciating the heft of his rucksack, the cadence of his platoon's footfalls, and the way the landscape would shift and change, infused with shadow and light.

Ray and his brothers had marched with the dawn, following the sun's steady rise. On an eight-mile ruck in the cold soaking rain, they had climbed the "Stairway to Heaven," their boots heavily saturated, each weighted step burning, as blisters formed, then opened. Still, they persevered. And as they neared the summit, the front moved on, a curtain across the sky, leaving smears of dark crimson across a distant horizon.

There is history here. Ray contemplated as he marched. Every step he took was in another soldier's footsteps. The storied past of service members who had trained and gone into battle from here heightened his focus. This twelve-mile ruck back to the garrison marked his company's last one together. They had just completed a week of physically and mentally intense field training exercises, the last component of his combined Basic Combat and Advanced Infantry Training. The drill was as close to war-like conditions as the Army could make it, representing the final step in becoming a full-fledged Infantryman. Tomorrow he would Turn Blue.

No family or friends would make the Turning Blue or the graduation ceremony. His sister, Hope, recently moved into a supervisory role at the food manufacturing plant and said she couldn't break away. And his mother, in her last letter to him, had written that if he were closer, if she could sneak away for a few hours, then she would come. As the drive from Oklahoma to Fort Benning was twelve hours one-way, attending was not tenable. She was apologetic.

Ray's father didn't know his mother was writing to him. She would mail the secretly crafted letters directly from the post office, and Ray sent all return correspondences to his sister's address. Ray thought back to the morning after his farewell party, the dawn he left for boot camp. As Hope was pulling out of her long driveway, she jammed on the brakes, coming to an abrupt stop. Standing by the mailbox was his mother; their family car pulled off the road. Ray climbed out of the passenger side. Maria had a thermos of a grain beverage in one hand and the other, a still-warm foil container of his favorite cinnamon doughnut muffins. She handed them through the car window to Hope and stood before him.

"I couldn't let you go without saying goodbye." She held him at arm's length for a moment, taking in the countenance of her son. "I told your father I was delivering these to our congregants in the nursing home. Don't worry. There's more for them in the car." In her eyes, he could see an ache, a sadness. She looked at him intently as if desperately memorizing every detail. Then she folded him to her and hugged him like there was no tomorrow, but she did not cry.

As for his father, Ray thought with detachment, he probably doesn't even know or care that I'm graduating. That complicated interconnection was something Ray could not afford to tease apart now. As hard as he tried, he could not help but remember how wounded he was after hearing the last meaningful words Pastor Shipworth had said to him. "You've always been a disappointment." With reinforced conviction and steadfast inner drive, Ray pushed the thoughts of his father and their strained relationship aside.

As far as he could see in front of him moved a cohesive unit, where individuals were indistinguishable, where in a few short months, their country would call them to the battlefield to risk life and limb. Why couldn't his father see that Ray's driving force was not dissimilar from his, a spiritual hunger for righteous service?

As he marched with the end in sight, Ray could visualize himself at the morrow's commemoration, waiting to receive the Infantry Cord. He would be in his dress uniform, in a sea of identically clad men, surrounded by fellow soldiers, yet isolated. Authorized to be worn only by the United States Infantry-qualified soldiers, the prestigious military adornment (a looped circle formed by a series of alternating left and right half knots) was awarded during the ceremony. Usually, someone significant to the soldier, say a wife, father, or mother, would place the light blue cord on their right shoulder.

Ray envisioned himself at the service, standing alone, putting the cord on his own shoulder, absorbing what the moment meant, trying not to focus on the words of congratulation around him, trying hard not to wish that someone had been there to witness his accomplishments, his transformation.

But what Ray cannot see is what will happen tomorrow at the ceremony. How, when the time comes, out of his peripheral vision, will step a form, a recognizable entity, who will stand before him to honor the journey that had led to this moment, the making of an Infantryman. He cannot see how, when the infantry blue cord is placed on his shoulder, this individual will level his gaze and look directly into Ray's eyes. Only then will Ray see reflected in Drill Sergeant Sledge's countenance, realized approval, and earned respect.

Tract Four:

Winter 2007-Winter 2008
The Road to Sparrowhawk Mountain

"Leo, come on. Let's get the show on the road," Joseph Lightfoot turned on the overhead light in his daughter's room and stood in the door frame, a thermos of coffee in his hand. "Your driver's test is on Saturday, and you need two more hours of nighttime driving to meet the requirements."

Her alarm clock read five a.m. "Really, Dad? On a school morning?" Even as she protested, she tugged on a pair of jeans over her sleep shorts and a sweatshirt over her cotton tee. "Won't we be cutting it close? After a couple of hours of driving, I still have to shower and make lunch. And in case you don't know, your daughter has a perfect attendance record. I don't want to be counted as absent or tardy."

"We're not going to be late. Besides, I have parent-teacher conferences tonight and tomorrow. It's now or never."

"And you can't see your way into signing off that I completed my ten hours of driving in the dark? Everyone says their parents fudged the time sheet. I have my daytime hours. It's no big deal."

"It is to me, Leotie." He turned and walked down the hall, the wooden floorboards creaking under his feet.

Leo sighed as she followed him. Delaying learning to drive was her decision, after all, and her father hadn't questioned why. He hadn't pushed. Late summer, before her senior year of high school started, she announced at a family dinner of macaroni and jalapeno cheese that she was ready. Uncle Paul stepped up to the plate first, and when Leo could handle his automatic vehicle with undaunted assurance, Joseph took the reins in late fall. He was adamant that Leo learn how to drive a manual. If you know how to drive a stick, you can drive any vehicle in any circumstance. This had seemed critically important to him, so she had not argued.

For two successive weekends, he took his daughter to the empty school parking lot and patiently taught her how to drive his 1999 five-speed Honda Civic. Leo learned the gears, how to engage the clutch, shift, and accelerate without stalling. Once she seemed confident with her newly acquired skills, he let her drive around the neighborhood, then to and from school on days they didn't walk.

Out of this frosty, pre-dawn morning, light snow, an unusual but not unforeseen occurrence in early December, was starting to take form, white brush strokes on a black canvas. Leo took a swig of hot coffee, performed her safety checks, adjusted her rearview mirror, pulled the driver's seat forward, and turned on her windshield wipers with the heater on full blast. She looked at her dad. "I'm ready."

She followed his directions, driving without question and shifting easily. When he told her to stop, they were on a steeply inclined road, flanked by bare-branched stands of oak-hickory interspersed with shortleaf pine, leading to the top of Sparrowhawk Mountain. Headlights perforated the darkness, giving the illusion the road was a tightly enclosed tunnel reaching into the sky. Leo looked at her father and waited. His usually steady eyes seemed hard-edged. She tensed. What was going on?

"Shifting gears and accelerating on an empty, flat parking lot or driving to school is one thing. But you need to know how to navigate balancing the clutch and gas so that you don't stall out on a steep hill in San Francisco or anywhere else, with cars bumper to bumper behind you. You need to be able to get out of tough positions." He took a deep breath, his face serious with intent. "I need to know you can figure this stuff out in any situation you might find yourself in. I need to know you're going to be okay."

Were there tears in his eyes? Leo knew instinctively this went beyond what was happening now. She nodded and swallowed. "It's okay, Dad. I'm going to be all right. I've got this, I really do."

She started, stopped, and stalled but hit the brakes when the car slid backward. Over and over, she tried. The initial panic she felt when slipping downhill was quickly replaced with inner grit. Determination and concentration fueled the need to show her father she could rise to the occasion and meet his expectations. She was resolute, above all, that she would do what was possible to assuage her father's fears.

On their way back home with thirty minutes to spare before the first bell rang, with hot showers and a cinnamon toast breakfast planned, her father pulled out Leo's driving log from the glove compartment and signed off that she had met the required fifty hours behind the wheel, including the mandate that ten of them be in the dark. As dawn's pale, icy fingers attempted to insert themselves, to nudge a reluctant night into retirement, out of the dense brush stepped a solitary doe. Standing stock-still in the middle of the glazed strip of road, she calmly lifted her head, looking directly through the windshield and into Leo's eyes. Leo slammed on the brakes, then rapidly turned the steering wheel, sending the little black hatchback into a full-on, out-of-control spin.

Two hours later, after the tow truck hauled the car out of the ditch and before proceeding to the repair shop, the driver dropped them off at the high school.

"No showers, no breakfast, what a start to our day." Leo's father shook his head, looking at his daughter, relief in his eyes. "Me and my bright ideas. Sorry about breaking your perfect attendance streak."

"Records are meant to be broken, right?" She smiled. "Who needs a certificate of achievement in that silly category? Sorry about your car." She shrugged apologetically.

"Vehicles are replaceable, but…."

"I know, Dad." Leo stood on her toes and quickly kissed her father's cheek. "See you after school."

****

"Today in class, we'll compose a letter to a soldier serving overseas." Leo's substitute English teacher taped a long list of names and their APO addresses on the chalkboard. She sighed; this day already seemed endless. A bruise was forming where the seat belt dug into her body. Her chest was tender to the touch. She was finally in the last class of the day, freedom only fifty minutes away. These filler exercises made up by the endless stream of replacement instructors were lame. She wished her regular teacher, Ms. Barkley, was back. How many months off did a person really need after having a baby?

Her classmates bunched around the posting, jostling and laughing. Judy Langard, a girl the entire school knew, seemed to be on center stage. Judy had been the lead in last year's musical production of "Beauty and the Beast." Leo had helped work on the set after being encouraged by Dr. Baker to get more involved and to make connections.

Unlike Leo, Judy appeared comfortable in every situation. How different her life would be if she had that kind of confidence. While Leo felt at ease in her skin, content living her life, she also felt an indescribable longing for friendship and a more profound sense of belonging. Thanks to her continued counseling, she understood how the loss of her mother and the intense ache of all she believed she'd missed was the source of her pain, which ultimately caused her to self-medicate. But perspective doesn't always diminish losses into paler specters.

From the crowd, Judy looked across the room in Leo's direction and gave an encouraging smile. Leo wasn't sure if she was looking at her or someone seated directly behind her and was too embarrassed to look around to verify. How do you navigate complicated cues? Leo gave a weak smile back and then, embarrassed that she had misread a signal, bent to retrieve something from her book bag. There were too many pushy bodies around the homework assignment. She would wait until the congregation thinned.

The radiator next to Leo clanked and hissed,

sending off a blast of heat. Leo removed her sweatshirt, then, realizing she still had her sleep shirt on underneath, quickly pulled it back on, hoping no one had noticed. No one had.

Outside, the snowfall continued. Full, lacey crystals spiraled in casual descent. Leo loved how her dull world was washed white, making everything look like the insides of an unfinished, factory-reject snow globe, no content, all snow. She found solace in this space and was grateful the flurry had continued throughout the day. She hadn't been able to build a snowman in a long time. Maybe she could talk her dad into hot chocolate on their walk home. Uncle Paul was away on a business trip, and the house was their own for a few days.

It always felt different when he was gone, quieter, somehow more controlled. Though older, Uncle Paul never acted like it. His high energy and laughter punctuated their lives. He kept things light, bright balloons floating skyward, while her father kept them all safely tethered to the ground.

How different her experience was when Uncle Paul let her drive. The first time Leo climbed into the driver's seat of her uncle's 1996 Ford pick-up, he looked at her with relaxed eyes and yawned. "My last trip was tiring. I'm going to sleep, and you, my niece, will drive. She's easy to handle, with an inline six-cylinder engine, automatic drive, and a belly full of gas. Wake me up if you need me." He bunched up his jacket, placed the makeshift pillow behind his head, and promptly fell asleep.

When he woke two hours and forty minutes later, the truck was parked at the Oklahoma City airport.

"You told me to drive," Leo stated matter-of-factly.

"That I did." Uncle Paul stretched and looked at the trip mileage he had zeroed at the start. "One hundred and seventy miles, great job! Now let's grab some grub. It's tough business being the passenger of a student driver."

They were seated in the bed of the two-toned, mint condition, blue and silver F-150, their legs dangling over the side as they munched on burgers and fried okra and drank thick milkshakes. Leo watched the planes lift, soaring heavenward, carrying their occupants to destinations nearby and places so far-flung and exotic that she hadn't heard of them. The earth, was vast. How little she had seen and experienced. But in that moment, she was content. Leo couldn't imagine the sensation of not having her feet connected to the ground.

"Miss? Miss?" A tap on Leo's shoulder brought her to the present.

"Yes, Mister…?" She looked at the chalkboard to see the substitute teacher's name. "Mr. Frederic?"

"Class is almost over. The assignment is due tomorrow, and everyone else has chosen. Please, pick a soldier and draw a line through their name when you decide."

Leo tugged at her sweatshirt. The classroom was warm, and this busy work seemed pointless. But she remained quiet and respectful. She had a research paper due next week and had to study for an AP American History exam.

The slim teacher did not smile. As if he could read her mind, he pointed to the paper. "I will be here tomorrow. This counts as homework. Therefore, the assignment impacts your final grade, so I suggest you get going."

Leo scanned the names, one blurring into the other. Where was Uncle Paul with his ridiculous English accent when she needed him to make the mundane interesting? She was about to close her eyes and arbitrarily choose when something familiar caught her eye. Near the bottom of the long list was a name Leo recognized. She grabbed the index card and hastily wrote down the Army Post Office address. Tonight, she would sit down and write a letter to Sergeant Ray Shipworth.

****

Leo slid her feet along the icy sidewalk, a fledgling skater, and tipped her head back to catch the fat snowflakes on her tongue. The streets of Tahlequah were tranquil, muted by the expanding blanket. Thwack! Something cold and hard struck her in the back. With lynx-like reflexes, Leo swiftly turned around. There she saw her father, his face flushed from the cold, his eyes sparkling, daring, his arm cocked back, poised with another snowball.

"You did not just do that!" With surprised delight, Leo swiftly bent to gather handfuls of heavy, packing snow. "Bring it on!" She let one fly, and her father, despite his inherent agility, was not quite prepared for her speed. The snowball caught him on his forehead, the explosion of ice spilling into his open jacket and down his flannel shirt. He burst out laughing, and Leo followed, their revelry momentarily piercing the deepening hush.

Much later, after mugs of half marshmallow, half double hot cocoa, and bowls of popcorn were consumed, after the familiar routines of life were completed, Leo sat crossed-legged on her family's worn dark brown corduroy couch. She nestled into a sagging pocket that springs had long ceased supporting, a blanket draped around her shoulders. Gazing into a capering fire her father had built in the wood burner, with genuine intent, Leo composed a candid letter to her assigned soldier, Ray. She licked the envelope and sealed it. *Will he ever get this? And if he does, will he remember me?*

Flight

Iraq

A Chinook whirled through the heavy cloak of night; its lights were off, rendering the helicopter less visible, a camouflaged moving target. When Ray's boots touched the ground on the U.S. Forward Operating Base Rustamiyah, he walked into a world saturated with smell. Situated six miles southeast of Sadr City, on the eastern side of Baghdad, between a waste incineration field and sewage treatment plant, the olfactory assault, a pungent concoction of burning trash laced with feces, was overwhelming.

"Ah, there's nothing like the smell of Camp Rusty in the evening." The flight pilot inhaled deeply, stretched, and grinned at the soldiers as they disembarked and started to choke. "Welcome to your new home, boys."

Transferred directly from intense, specialized training, the company of men entered a new arena, the proving ground. They were dropped into an active war zone, from which there was no retreat. They silently moved through the base, a maze of engineered, rebar-reinforced T-walls, absorbing and cataloging each detail as their new reality sank in. No turning off the television console here, no changing the video game halfway through because you were tired or had run out of ammo. Each soldier became aware of a brutal new truth: unless severely wounded or in a body bag, there was no way out, not before their orders were completed, and before their major announced *game over, you are free to return home.*

As they walked toward their sand-bagged encased barracks, their movements kicked up a fine, powdery, beige sand. The particulate matter settled onto their combat boots, uniforms, and rucksacks and covered everything; even the susurrus full-leafed palm, painted with the moon dust, glistened. Even outside food consumption, sprinkled with Rusty Dust, they would find out later, was a gritty affair.

They neared their quarters, ready to settle for the night when a soft hiss drew their attention. Ray looked skyward as the whistle increased in pitch, slicing through the dark.

"Incoming!" someone yelled.

Around them, seasoned soldiers ran for the nearest concrete bunker, engulfed by sandbags. Those who didn't feel they had time hit the earth, forming compact balls, their hands clasped together, arms protecting their necks. A rocket slammed into the roofed aluminum housing unit, flinging shrapnel debris high into the air, and the earth rattled beneath them.

Ray quickly learned that unlike in the movies, one rarely heard the incoming rockets and mortars. If you were lucky, you did. Then you had a few seconds of warning. The night they arrived in Iraq was the first and last time Ray and his unit stood looking into the night, oblivious, unaware of what the sound heralded. Never again would their bodies not respond, every muscle tensing until an explosion and awareness hit simultaneously. They had survived, escaped destruction and severe bodily injury, at least this time.

After the communication blackout was lifted, they learned a soldier had lost his life, and several more were wounded. And so began the vigilance, a constant state of alertness that would not diminish, even in sleep, even when Ray was no longer in a war zone, long after he returned stateside and there was no need for hardwired watchfulness anymore.

****

In the space between sleep and wakefulness, Ray would have his most vivid dreams or clearest memories. Sometimes tangling them apart was challenging. What was an actual memory? What was a sleep-induced reverie? On this pre-dawn morning, he saw Leo, aged nine. Practice was over. A languid fall evening with deepening purple hues was descending. Coach Lightfoot had them gathered on a corner of the football field. He was giving a pep talk for an upcoming meet. Ray saw Leo scrambling up the empty stadium stairs, barefoot, skinny legs sporting the numerous scratches and bruises one has at that age from living fully, a mane of dark hair flying behind her. A little bundle of Sandy fur, close to her heels. She was racing now, and at the top, she flung her arms wide just as a migratory flock of American white pelicans soared over. They were calling, moving swiftly, and for a fleeting instant, pulled into dusk on the wingspan of a child was Leo. She had become part of this flight. When Ray woke with the army-issued sheet jumbled around his hard hips and beads of perspiration on his torso, he knew this was both: a vision and a flawless memory.

****

Like the rapid-fire of his personal military issued, M249 Squad Automatic Weapon machine gun, flashes of memory would strike in succession. Ray had little control over how his brain presented them, but he did perfect the art of detached observation.

On the battlefield, Ray found his voice. Here, political views and opinions fell away, like a fire destroying all organic material, leaving only the stainless-steel bones of a structure. On the front line, Ray was force-fed an all-out raw experience, pulsing with its own life, terrifying and intoxicating at the same time.

Ray stood atop the third vehicle of the convoy, positioned behind the turret and an M240 Bravo machine gun. They were on Route Gator, following a chewed-up road that skirted the slumbering Tigris River, escorting the Explosive Ordnance Disposal unit to an undetonated roadside bomb. Despite being late afternoon, the temperature hovered close to 110 degrees. Sweat soaked every part of his uniform, including his bulletproof flak jacket and field combat boots, as if he had just emerged from a hot, humid, saltwater shower fully clothed. As a gunner, his job was to look for possible threats.

Ray scanned the surrounding landscape. No human or animal activity was detected. There were no ripples in the river. Even the palms hung limply, debilitated by the heat. The safety and success of a convoy's mission pivoted on the eyes, ears, and muscles of its gunners. Usually, on high alert when out of the wire, Ray felt removed. This last operation lasted thirty-six hours, and he had not eaten or slept. But he wasn't alone. All the men in his unit were beyond exhaustion. Once the EOD detonated the improvised explosive device, everyone could return to base.

In the lull of the moment, all was quiet. Ahead was the carcass of a dead donkey, half on the road, half off. Fighting overwhelming fatigue, Ray slowly closed his eyes, then opened them. Before him rose a mushroom tide of flame and earth. The immense discharge sent the convoy's lead vehicle arching into the air like a toy. The metal door flew off its hinges and splashed into the river. At the same time, the up-armored Humvee landed upside down in the weeds, and his first thought was, this is just a dream.

The explosive concussion and giant chunks of concrete falling from the sky brought him rapidly to a familiar reality. Within seconds, while the gunners pulled security, dismounts extricated the living from the lead vehicle, quickly turning them over to their waiting medic, Specialist Fisher. Following closely on the heels of the medic was a white puppy. Ray was sure he was hallucinating. There was a cognitive disconnect. Then he remembered, during their drawn-out operation, he and Fisher found the pup alone, shivering with malnutrition, in an empty shelled-out house, and they were bringing her back to base. The pocket-sized creature scampered over to the six-foot deep, ten-foot-wide crater created by the explosion and curiously peered down.

Ray was hauled back into full alert by sniper fire aimed directly at their immobilized unit. Sharp snaps from across the river recoiled in the air all around them. This was how attacks often went: a roadside bomb, rendering passage impossible, would stop the convoy dead in its tracks, and then, while attending to their wounded or assessing the damage, the convoy would be ambushed. Using machine guns, the insurgents opened fire on the trapped assemblage of soldiers and their vehicles. As Ray rapidly turned his mounted 240B aiming for the far western bank, he saw Doc Fisher scoop up the pup and gently place her on the floor of a nearby Humvee.

"On, like Donkey Kong!" they cried from the turrets. The gunners and soldiers on the ground were returning fire with every arsenal they had at their disposal. Ray, on his feet, sighted the dust kick-up of a PKM machine gun. Without hesitation, he aimed, using the iron sites, and fired a 5-7 round burst, then another. Two of Ray's brothers were dead.

Also deceased was an eighteen-year-old Iraqi interpreter who called himself Jay. They'd seen pictures of his siblings, and learned of his dream to move to America, go to college, and study green technology for sustainable farming. In moments like these, war became personal. Rage became uncontainable. Ray's sympathetic nervous system, the part of the brain that triggers fight or flight, started a chain reaction, flooding his body with adrenaline, accelerating his cardiac rate and raising his blood pressure. The catecholamine dump pushed his heart, mind, and muscles to perform beyond capacity. Chaos reigned. Survive or die.

Out of the madness, rose a disciplined warrior, who charged into combat, where every decision had ramifications. And history was written with every irrevocable action.

From the Humvee behind him, automatic grenade launchers were spitting hot and fiery. Explosions riddled the west bank. Trees flew in the air, elephant grass caught on fire, and the Tigris churned as if on a high boil. Ray was down to the last of his ammunition and was now firing tracer rounds from his hell belt. He could see them zip across the waterway, joining the immense firepower that shone brighter than the sinking sun.

Like birds of prey, Apache helicopters flew out of the dusk, diving in coordinated flight. They spotted the insurgent bunker from which the attacks originated and let loose 30 mm cannons until nothing was left. As suddenly as the attack started, all was bathed in silence.

Ray collapsed back into his turret, breathing rapidly through his nose and out of his open mouth, trying to regain equilibrium. Once his respirations dropped, he reached into his pocket, extricated a single cigarette (when in a combat zone, he allowed himself two a day), and watched the silhouette of his smoking 240B barrel against the diminishing dusty pink twilight while ash from the burning elephant grass rained peacefully around them. Across the river, he could hear the rounds still on the enemy dead, popping in the fire.

Forty hours after leaving for their mission, they pulled back onto the base. Ray and his men returned their Humvee to the motor pool repair shop to fix the windshield riddled with damage from sniper fire. With exhaustion approximating annihilation, their bodies craving nothing but sleep, they wordlessly dismounted and stepped down into a raucous party.

Salsa and rap music blared simultaneously, emanating from competing speakers, while tee-shirt clad, and shirtless soldiers danced as if no one was watching, sang at the top of their lungs, and drank Saint

Pauli's Girl, non-alcoholic beer as if there was no tomorrow. Ray felt he was moving slowly through an alternate reality, a surrealistic split dimension. Starkly layered, the palpable dichotomy of war included the tediousness of procedural regulation when on base–the predictable patterns he and his fellow soldiers carefully knit, almost superstitiously, around them–as well as the terrifying moments in battle and when running for bunkers to avoid incoming rockets–the times when all there was, was the raw, frantic struggle for life.

The Back Door

"Coach Lightfoot?"

Joseph looked up from his desk. He was between classes when one of the office assistants handed him a message. "This call just came in from Dr. Baker. She said there's no rush. Contact her at your earliest convenience."

As the students filed in, he glanced at his watch. He'd have time after this period ended, during his thirty-minute lunch break, to touch base with his daughter's therapist. He took a deep breath; the pain in his ribs was almost gone, the car accident already weeks behind them.

But what was this about? Leo had been seeing Dr. Baker for years. The changes in Leo and at home were noticeable. Joseph, Leo, and Paul had settled into a comfortable cadence. Leo ranked near the top of her class and had an academic scholarship to Northeastern State University. A call from Dr. Baker now, so close to graduation, was surprising and a little unnerving. He thought he'd been doing a good job, that he had been present and watchful.

Was Leo engaging in risky behavior again? Had he failed to notice the changes? Joseph had never met his daughter's psychologist. The intake family meeting scheduled after Leo started seeing Dr. Baker was canceled because of an emergency. Dr. Baker ended up conducting the session with Joseph and Leo via speakerphone. All of them concluded that was sufficient, but if any of them, at any point, wanted an in-person family session, then they would do so. Joseph's usually steady hands were shaking when he dialed her number.

Dr. Baker pleasantly explained that Leo was doing well, but she had questions, could they arrange a get-together? She used the phrase, "Paramount to Leo's progress is a healthy perspective." What did that even mean? He marked his day calendar with the date, tomorrow, and the time, an hour after school let out. Dr. Baker ended the call as she had started by emphasizing how vital his participation was in this process and by assuring him that Leo had given her permission for them to meet.

****

Why did he feel like he was betraying her? After school, when they usually met to walk home, Joseph told his daughter, "Go on without me. I have a mandatory parent conference."

Her eyebrows furrowed. Usually, these sessions happened around the marking period. That had ended weeks ago. But she took him at his word and nodded. "Okay, Dad." She pushed a straying strand of hair behind her ear and smiled, unabashed and trusting. "See you when you get home."

Joseph watched her tall, thin frame wander down the hall until she opened the door and disappeared into the pale afternoon light. He had been truthful, he rationalized, only he was the parent, and the conference was with Leo's therapist. He couldn't explain why he hadn't been entirely forthright or felt troubled with the cold reality: We're meeting to discuss you, my one and only child.

Joseph arrived on time and settled into a cozy waiting room with an herbal tea station and a wicker basket full of art books and poetry. When the hunter-green door to Dr. Baker's office opened, he didn't pay much attention to the slight figure in the frame, assuming her prior client was leaving. This was before he learned that patients always left out a back stairway to protect their privacy.

"Mr. Lightfoot?" Her voice was airy, barely reaching his auditory canal. Over the years, he had imagined an elderly, curvy woman with silver hair spun into a tight bun. After all, she was a pastry maker, a chef, a baker. He looked at her askance.

She looked so young. Shoulder-length, straight blond hair was pulled off her small, delicate face by two metal clips in the shape of dragonflies. Her slim body was engulfed in a billowing floral print dress that stopped two inches above polished, bright red cowboy boots. And on her left ear, a series of thin silver hoops arched along the pinna's pink curve toward a slightly pointed tip. Had he been transported to middle earth? Joseph felt like he was looking at a Pixie.

Her warm smile let him know she knew exactly what he was thinking. "I get that all the time. I'm not what people expect a psychologist to look like."

"Are you even old enough to be one?" Joseph's question startled even himself. Where had that come from? Ordinarily, he reserved inner observations to himself.

Her laugh was like unassuming wind chimes. "Are you even old enough to be the father of a seventeen-year-old?" Her amity drew him in.

****

"Leo has reached an understanding of why she made precarious choices. A lot of confusion stems from the fact she doesn't know anything about her mother. She tells me that other than a few pictures she keeps in her room, there is no trace of her. You never talk about her, and because of this, Leo has unprocessed grief. She feels like her mother never existed. And that void in her life was one she was trying to fill with the pain medications."

"I didn't talk about the loss because I was gutted. I was trying to protect Leo. That's all I ever wanted. What is the point of bringing up something painful that happened in the past?"

"I understand. But for Leo to heal and move on with her life, she needs the truth, as uncomfortable as that might be."

The thirty minutes they spent together flew. Joseph listened intently to Dr. Baker's probing questions and answered honestly. After all, they were working together for Leo. He straightforwardly told her their story. When he finished, there was moisture in Dr. Jennifer Baker's pale blond lashes.

Once they determined the date and time for their joint session with Leo, Dr. Baker hesitated, as if there was something else she wanted to tell him. Joseph stopped putting on his jacket and paused. There was no questioning his patience, his love, and his desire to help his daughter mend. He waited until Dr. Baker spoke. "You know Leo blames herself for you?"

Joseph was confused.

"She thinks if it weren't for her, for *you being stuck*

to raise her, those are her words, not mine, that you would have moved on by now, found a new wife, a new family, a new life."

"That's ridiculous." Joseph rubbed a shaky hand through his hair. "She's my everything."

Dr. Baker's eyes were calm and assured. "Then we must help Leo see this. You have to tell her everything. You can't hold back. This is between you and your daughter, but I will facilitate."

Joseph nodded and took both of her small hands in his. "Thank you, Dr. Baker. Thank you for helping her and for helping me." He turned and let himself out the back door.

No Turning Back

Joseph gave himself thirty minutes to walk the half-mile to his scheduled meeting with Leo and Dr. Baker. He determined shortly into his foray that he was ill-equipped for the conditions. Winter in Oklahoma, subject to the pressures and systems around her, was mercurial. Yesterday was seventy degrees. Today, overpowering the winter sun, a frigid wind pushed the temperature below freezing. Though long-sleeved, his thin cotton shirt was underperforming. But, as quickly as he felt the bitter conditions turning all exposed flesh raw, he let these sensations go. There was no turning back for additional protection. He needed to be on time. Too much was at stake.

Here he was, weeks after the initial consultation with Dr. Baker, just minutes away from the critical meeting with Leo. He moved quickly, taking a shortcut to the downtown office by following the Tahlequah Creek through the university campus. The thin trickle, which would swell in the rainy season, was fighting to find purchase but persisted, struggling over rock, debris, and shards of ice crystals forming along its edges.

Contained within a sharp gust of air, within its burgeoning swell, he heard someone yell, "Coach Lightfoot." More often than not, he would see one of his former students when he passed through the university grounds. When Joseph lifted his head to see who called, the expanse of frozen terrain was empty, barren of all traces of life.

With five minutes to spare, he grabbed a cup of hot chamomile tea and collected the thoughts he hoped would help his daughter heal.

****

Dying light sliced shadowy ribbons across the sidewalk as Leo cycled through the small downtown to her weekly therapy session with Dr. Baker. For the first time, her dad would be there. She was anxious to bring up the subject of her mother's death. Leo hated causing her father pain, but she needed to know. She would turn eighteen soon. Now was the time. She deserved to have answers.

A sharp series of familiar whistles pierced her contemplation; she slammed on the bike's brakes. Across the street, standing outside of Ned's Bar, smoking a cigarette, was Jake.

He sauntered toward her. "Well, howdy sunshine." Jake drew out the words as his eyes traveled the length of her. He wickedly grinned when he reached her face and blew out a plume of smoke. "Man, have you ever grown up. You're a sight for hungry eyes."

Leo glanced at her watch. She had five minutes. "Thought you moved to Tulsa." His flaxen hair was longer, hanging floppily around his face, which seemed a little harder but still looked handsome to her. He hadn't changed much since she last saw him three years ago. Except now, she thought, I'm taller.

"I did move right after, you know, at the end of that summer." He wasn't apologetic. "I'm visiting friends."

Leo nodded and pushed her bike forward. "Good to

see you, Jake, but I have to get going."

"Wait. Leo, wait!" She turned. "Why don't you come to Tulsa with me?" He threw the words toward her like a dart. He continued, giving her a signature smile that worked so well in the past. "I'm working at Bama now. They love me. I bet I'll be a supervisor soon. For sure I could get you a job. You could move into my apartment, ditch this nowheresville town, move to the big city."

Leo laughed nervously. He was joking. He had to be. Jake seemed excited by her doubt. She remembered this heightened look of his, feeding off her as if he had all the answers.

"Come on, Leo. Remember how I noticed you that first year when no one else did? Remember how good we were?" He moved closer. The sense he needed her stirred past emotions. They did have some good times together. And, when he was around, he knew what to say to make her feel better.

She remembered the first time they were alone in his father's house. The late afternoon sun slanted through angled blinds. Jake was lying by her side, touching her, his blond hair scrubbed clean by the light. "I live with my dad because my old lady kicked me out." He kissed her neck. "So, in a way, I am motherless too." He looked into her eyes as if sizing up the effect of his words. His vulnerability was a testament to his devotion. The last threads of hesitation fell away as she wrapped her arms around him. He was like her, navigating life without a mother.

A year into therapy, Leo admitted the relationship probably wasn't healthy. She explained to Dr. Baker things hadn't started that way, recalling the day everything changed. Leo had stayed home under the pretense of studying for an exam. Uncle Paul was on a business trip, and her dad was at a cross-country meet. Jake took the opportunity to rummage through their bathroom cabinet when his eyes lit up. "Hot damn, your old man has some good stuff here."

He expertly opened the childproof lid, popped two tablets in his mouth, and pushed one into Leo's before she could protest. "They'll help you git through a lot of shit."

Jake was right. Judicious use of the pills helped her navigate the tumultuous landscape of adolescence until that fateful night. Still, Leo wouldn't have taken her dad's prescription medication to the party if not for Jake's urging. Initially, being his mysterious secret made Leo feel cherished and flattered, but as the months progressed, the veneer wore thin. She wanted to be acknowledged and be part of her boyfriend's visible life.

Finally, eleven months in, he said she could tag along with him to a party. She was overjoyed. "But you cain't come if you don't bring something good, and you're too young to buy alcohol. Bring your dad's stuff. You better not embarrass me in front of my friends. Don't make me regret inviting you." Working with Dr. Baker enabled Leo to see why she self-medicated. Together, they developed wiser coping mechanisms for when she felt overwhelmed.

Yes, the relationship wasn't healthy then, but they were three years older. She'd done a lot of growing and changing, and she was confident he had too. Taking the alcohol and pills out of the equation, who could predict how good things might be? How could a freshman-senior relationship of the past be compared to a possibility?

Leo shook her head as if to knock some sense into herself. "That's a sweet offer, but I have months until graduation. You probably won't feel the same way then."

"I probably will." He paused and stroked her from her wrist to the soft indentation underneath her chin, the pressure not particularly gentle. "You're a knock-out, Leo. I remember now why we dated. Hey, you don't have to wait until you graduate. You don't need a worthless piece of paper for this job. I'm pretty high up. I can get you in."

The touch was familiar. He was all Leo had known.

"I don't know, Jake, my..." Her words were cut short by one arm that snaked around her back, his fingers resting between her rib cage and the swell of her breast. He pulled her into a kiss, alcohol mixed with smoke that tasted like the last time they made out on a dirty, sheetless mattress on the factory floor.

"Think about it," he whispered into her neck. His breath was hot. "You don't have to give me an answer right away." He stood back, as if aware of the effect he had. "Give me your cell. Come on, Leo," he coaxed. "Hand it over."

Leo reached into her back pocket.

After a few moments of concentration, he pushed the cell into her palm. "You have my new number. Give me a holler whenever you want, and I'll come git you."

A Cosmos Distilled

Iraq

"Heading to the mailroom. Want to join me?" Doc Fisher pushed back his folding chair. The game of Spades was over. Ray jumped to his feet. They exited Joe's into the rainy afternoon; the dirt beneath their boots, which at times was a fine dust, and at others, was solid and unyielding, was now a sucking mud.

"Which way, Ship?" Fisher's inquiry, though seemingly insignificant, was serious; there were multiple routes to their unit's post office. Off base, back in the United States, in a world not consumed with war, this would never be a consideration. The obvious answer was the most direct, least time-consuming route. But here, on the front line, even the simplest of acts, say walking to your barracks on the first night you arrive or sauntering to the mess hall for chow, could be met by death. Soldiers learned to think everything through, to live in the transcendent quality of each moment.

"Let's swing by our room. I have a letter I want to mail." Ray set their course. Even the smallest of decisions, the slightest of motions, like stepping under a palm to light a cigarette, the same instant a rocket impacts the ground under its roots, can be connected to critically immutable events. Here, in reverse gestalt, the cosmos was distilled to its most elemental parts, a single cup of coffee, a letter from home.

As they left their shared room, an incoming projectile slammed into the ground causing the earth to shudder. They would have been in its path if they had gone directly to get their mail and hadn't taken an alternate route. They would have been, at best, victims of penetrating shrapnel and, at worst, a deadly fatality. With unwavering certainty, they knew this. Shipworth and Fisher looked at each other; there was an unspoken acknowledgment. They held onto this cardinal truth, then moved on.

Letters. Ray couldn't have predicted how much they would mean. During boot camp, stationed stateside, or when in war, they could elevate lagging spirits and give strength. Like a rapid bolus of glucose to a starving body, they infused, enabling the soldier to push on. A nonchalant postal orderly handed Ray two envelopes. One was from his sister, and another with a return address in Tahlequah, which he did not recognize, postmarked over eight weeks ago. Penned in blue ink with small, looped writing, the letter looked battered, as if having gone through a great deal to get to him. Such was the fate of communications sent through the Army Post Office. Sometimes missives would arrive quickly, within ten days to two weeks. But, often, correspondence would be buffeted around from post to post until finally arriving at the intended destination. Ray immediately read the one from Hope and shoved the other in his pocket. He planned on reading the letter later in the night while on tower guard duty to help him pass the time.

****

You hear explosions and gunfire every night here.

You quickly become accustomed to it, though. So, life goes on for the Iraqis and us alike.

Ray had written this in a joint letter to his mom and Hope. He reflected on what happened earlier that day and what he had shared. They were driving through a Baghdad neighborhood with a reputation as an insurgent stronghold. Through very narrow dirt streets filled with mud and garbage, the Humvee driver navigated the piles of refuse and potholes. The Humvee suddenly began to descend into the earth after hitting a giant sinkhole camouflaged with mud and debris. The driver's side tire sunk into four feet of muck, placing the bottom of the vehicle on the ground, leaving them at a 45-degree angle. As they struggled to extricate the car (four-wheel drive didn't work), the spinning tires just flung mud everywhere, making the hole deeper, embedding the Humvee. By the time they hooked up tow straps connecting the stuck vehicle to two Humvees, over two hundred spectators had gathered.

People crowded rooftops, hung out of windows, and pressed in on the ground all around them, good-naturedly laughing and offering advice. Ray and his men would already be dead if the mass had harbored malevolent will. As the two rescue vehicles began to pull, their Humvee driver hit the gas, and the throng chanted loudly. Nothing. Then, as the trapped Humvee driver wildly swung the steering wheel back and forth while accelerating, the vehicle started to move. Inch by inch, out of the abyss, finally, breaking free. The crowd erupted. They waved and clapped and high-fived the soldiers on foot. Ray continued writing.

Although we were in a dangerous area, they were rooting for us to succeed. The way they cheered when we broke free was uplifting, as though our car had just finished first place at an off-road race. As much as you don't want to admit, they are just like us, people trying their best to navigate their daily lives despite being in a combat zone. This is a curious corner of the world and certainly one of the strangest occupations of an army throughout human history.

****

W-7, a forty-foot metal watchtower, looked out over the so-called "waste incineration facility." In reality, the area was little more than an enormous trash field, where periodically spontaneous pockets of fire would break out due to incompatible elements coming together—perhaps a weary land's attempt to diminish an accumulation of wreckage. The midnight watch had been without incident. And for this, Ray was grateful. From his vantage point in the far distance, rising from downtown Baghdad, he could see an upsurging cloud of black smoke and hear dwindling gunfire. Whatever had transpired was winding down.

Directly below the tower, he could see a plastic bottle arrangement, a makeshift marquee. The messaging changed depending on who was on duty and who wanted to ruffle another soldier's feathers, a game of sorts. On this dark evening, the note spelled out in plastic bottles: Post=dick brain. Ray shook his head. What soldiers won't do to get someone else going. Private first classman Post was relieving him at 0300, and he would not find the declaration charming.

On the periphery of the rubbish pile, was a malnourished pack of dogs desperately pawing pieces of trash and smelling for scraps. Sometimes, there were people, children, and elderly alike, using the concealment of night, picking through the detritus, searching for discarded items to make their lives a modicum easier. Tonight, the dogs were alone. The white puppy he and Fisher rescued was now six months old. She sat quietly by Ray's side, observing the scavenging dogs with detached interest.

On some of their missions, Ray's unit worked with Iraqi soldiers and policemen. *The Iraqi police are hilarious,* Ray had noted in a previous letter home. *We are like old friends with some of them. We rip on them, and they tease us. It's kind of cool. We show each other our weapons, trade cigarettes, and share stories. And we all have an absolute love of Mountain Dew. Oh, the caffeine! Despite these seemingly ordinary moments, we remember that the enemy is out there. We still get mortared and rocketed, and we encounter IEDs. This is truly a strange sort of war. The enemy is nowhere and everywhere simultaneously.*

Ray grew to respect the Iraqi soldiers and police officers he served with, men who wanted nothing more than a stable country where they could raise their families and grow old.

Ray sighed. The watch had been uneventful and was almost over. With thirty minutes left until he could rack out, he pulled the mystery letter from his shirt pocket. And as he read, an involuntary smile lit his face.

Dear Blink,

Oh wait, will I get you into trouble for not following protocol and calling you by your official title, Sergeant Shipworth? I hope not. Anyway, this is Leo, AKA Squirt. Another hint, in case you need one, I'm the daughter of your cross-country coach, Joseph

Lightfoot.

Full disclosure, Ray, you are a homework assignment, but the BEST one I've had my entire senior year. So don't feel too bad. Besides my dad and Uncle Paul, you are the person I have known the longest. That means you were (well, still are) my best, first true human friend (sorry, no one can top my beloved dog, Sandy, who remains in my heart).

Since I last beat you at horseshoes, ha-ha, at least that's how I remember it, I've been in therapy (long story), been helping with our high school's musical productions (behind the scenes kind of stuff, like set building) and volunteering at the animal shelter.

I hate that it's still a killing "shelter." And they shouldn't even be allowed to call it that, a place of refuge, if they end up murdering an innocent dog just because no one wants them, just because they are out of space. At first, I wanted to adopt them all, but my dad put his foot down on that one. Then I tried to quit. What you don't know won't hurt you. But Jennifer (my therapist) helped me see that I could make a difference, that at least before they die, they have someone who cares for them, reads to them, and pets them. That must count for something, right?

I don't like to admit this, but I didn't think about you being in a war zone until we drove past your dad's church last month. The sign in front says, "Pray for our troops." Here we are in Tahlequah, Oklahoma, living our lives oblivious to what our soldiers are going through. I feel terrible about that. If ever you want to write to me about things, you can. I'm an excellent listener. Do you ever get scared?

You are the bravest person I know. Ray, you joined

the Army and traveled the world. We are 7,000 miles apart—I looked up the distance. Something I haven't told anyone, even Jennifer, is that I am afraid of many things, like leaving Tahlequah and living with strangers in a dorm. I was accepted into Northeastern State but told my dad I wanted to save money by living at home. Pathetic, right? Someday I'll get the courage like you did, but in the meantime, I still have a lot to figure out.

Snow fell today. What do you see when you look out of your window?

She had drawn a heart, and inside, signed her name, *Leo*.

What do I see when I look out my barrack's window? Ray carefully tucked Leo's letter into a large plastic baggie labeled with a Sharpie, "Letters from Home."

I see nothing, Leo. Nothing. I see a sightless casement reinforced with sandbags, a barrier that absorbs bullets and shrapnel. I see a place meant to keep us alive while we sleep but one that also obscures everything, keeping us in darkness. The enclosure is so impenetrable not even a pinpoint of light shines through.

****

"Iceman?" A voice from his past. His boot camp moniker was long gone. No one had called him that since he left Fort Benning.

Ray snapped to attention. He was bent over the computer terminal, where he had just sent an e-mail to his sister. Standing before him, a Cheshire grin, ear to ear, stretched across a familiar face. Ray leapt up and pulled him into a rough hug, "Mud Cat?! I can't believe it." He slapped him on the back. "What in the heck is a good kitty doing in a place like this?"

"My National Guard Unit finally got its orders. We just got here. We start learning the ropes tomorrow."

"Terrific. We'll have six months together here in paradise before our unit ships out. Just like old times, Cat, minus our guardian angel, Drill Sergeant Sledge." Ray looped an easy arm around his friend. "Well, let me start by giving you an insider's tour of your new digs."

"This here is our 'Internet cafe.' Sounds glamorous, right? We have to make up fancy names for these places. But, as you can see, the space is a room with a handful of computers and phones. There are time limits on everything. Otherwise, you'd never get the Fobbits and oxygen thieves off them."

Cat looked at him askance. "Fobbits? Oxygen thieves?"

Ray grinned. "You'll learn quickly. Remember *The Hobbit*? The little guy who never wanted to leave the shire. A deployed service member who never leaves the FOB, or forward operating base, is a Fobbit. And an oxygen thief, well, you can probably guess, someone who just talks too much."

"Anyway." Ray stepped out of the Internet cafe and closed the door behind them. "You can go online, send off an email, and phone your family and friends, provided, of course, there isn't a communication blackout."

He paused, reality quickly returning, his enthusiasm gone. "It can happen at any time, even in the middle of sending a message home or at the start of a phone call, before you even have a chance to say 'Hello.' A blackout means one thing, someone here has died or was severely wounded." His voice was emotionless. "The blackout lasts until family notification is complete." Ray saw Cat swallow hard. Here was the absoluteness of his new microcosm.

They strolled in silence, walking side by side until Ray started again. "This old hospital houses the Troop Medical Clinic and also what we call our mini-mall." Ray smiled, seeing an old friend triggered a long-forgotten sense of self, and he gestured grandly. "In there, you can find all kinds of treasures. The Iraqis have booths selling various trinkets, including phone cards, swords, knives, bootlegged DVDs, video games, and cigarettes with names you've never heard before, like this fine pack of Miami smokes I have here." Cat nodded.

A small white dog appeared, sporting a bright red collar. Ray reached down, stroked the nape of her neck, and then scooped her up for a proper introduction. "This is our base's mascot, Bolt. She comes and goes, where and when she pleases. We try to keep her under the radar. We don't want the higher-ups to fixate on her. So far, if they've noticed, they're looking the other way." He put her back down, and she scampered off, crawling into a hole she had dug at the base of a building.

Ray refocused on his comrade. "And here is a place you will come to know and love well, Joe's Coffee Shop." He opened the door for Mud Cat as they stepped into the rectangular room and found an empty table. On the small television played an MTV-type station. "They have a barber here. You can smoke cigarettes, or hookah, play cards, make calls, use your laptop, or decompress after a mission. They're open twenty-four/seven. Now, let me treat you to a cup of really bad coffee."

Cat took a sip of the lukewarm joe and shook his head. "Man, that has a bite." He put the beverage on the table and leaned forward to touch the matte-black Combat Infantryman Badge, a patch sewn above Ray's left breast pocket. A Springfield Arsenal Musket was superimposed over an elliptical oak leaf wreath.

Ray remembered the day he and his squad mates lined up and, while standing at attention, were awarded this understated but highly prestigious badge of honor. A testimony of sacrifice, strength of character, and steadfast loyalty to their unit, to the Army, to their country. This United States Army Military decoration was only presented to soldiers who were personally present and under fire while assigned as a member of the Infantry or special forces. After the brief ceremony, the combat veterans gave up trying to act as if earning the ribbon was not a big deal and let forth a collective Hooah!

Ray nodded. "Before long, you'll earn one of these bad boys too. Piece of cake, Cat, you got this." They stayed awake deep into the night, joking and catching up on what life had presented them since they last saw each other at boot camp. Cat showed him pictures of his daughter, who had sprouted since Ray met her at the Turning Blue Ceremony, and of his girlfriend, the mother of his child.

"Hey, me and my baby's momma are going to get hitched after this tour. She's been planning this for a while. It's going to be a pretty big shindig at some fancy place on Table Rock Lake near Branson, Missouri." Cat paused, almost embarrassed to continue. "I want you to be my best man, Ray. You think you'd be up for that?"

"It would be my honor," Ray replied, touched by the request. He knew a lot could happen between now and then, but there was no point in bringing that up. At this moment, Cat's request was sincere, and Ray took the offer in the spirit intended.

Ray glanced at his friend in the feeble morning light and gave him an encouraging smile. He remembered arriving at Rusty and the difficulty of acclimating. "Chuck Norris can play the violin with a piano."

Cat returned, "The dark is afraid of Chuck Norris."

Ray volleyed back, "If you want a list of Chuck Norris' enemies, just check the extinct species list."

Before they separated, each reporting to their respective units for duty, Ray looked Cat in the eyes, a steady, level gaze. How many times during their shared experience had they helped and relied on each other? Ray sensed his friend quietly assessing him. Yes, Ray had survived this place so far. He was still standing and looked, at least on the surface, the same.

Cat nodded. He was merely following in a fellow soldier's footsteps. This was what service meant, what was expected. He grinned. "Once death had a near Chuck Norris experience."

****

The transmission came after a twenty-four-hour mission as Ray and his unit headed back to base. "Nighttime foot patrols' rendezvous point under heavy attack. Soldiers down. Requesting immediate back-up."

Immovable cement slabs blocked the access road. Ray looked at the coordinates, rapidly calculating. "Lieutenant, there's not enough time to drive. By foot, enemy fire is two kilometers away. Requesting permission to leave the vehicle and provide additional support."

"Permission granted. I'm coming with you."

Ray and his first lieutenant leapt out of their Humvee and raced toward the conflict. They navigated small passages and alleys as sporadic gunfire erupted, kicking up debris in front of them. Without hesitation, they continued advancing, following the coordinates and the ever-increasing gunfire. Music to their trained ears was the sound of their fellow soldiers firing their .50 caliber machine guns that mixed with zips and snaps of the insurgents' weapons.

As they rounded the corner of the targeted intersection, there was a symphonic shift. No longer did Ray register the reassuring base rounds of his compatriots. Only present in the air were the insurgent's weapons ringing alto and soprano. And for a fraction of a second, Ray hesitated with bottomless foreboding. He saw disabled army Humvees with no activity around them. Were any of them alive?

"Friendlies! Americans! Don't shoot!" Ray and the lieutenant screamed as they rushed the last stretch, dodging concealed fire while returning heat on the muzzle flashes that popped in the dark. Their cries filled simultaneously with latent hope and abiding dread. They charged toward the mute vehicles, compelled by duty and a promise to leave no man behind.

A surge of relief hit Ray, seeing the soldiers taking cover behind their vehicles. They were still alive, their .50 calibers temporarily rendered useless, overheated from excessive use. Abject defeat rapidly replaced reprieve. One private lay dead.

And further down the convoy, a specialist called out, "We need a medic! Hurry! We've got a soldier replacement down." Ray raced to him. The soldier was bleeding with a thin pulsing arc of bright red coming from a bullet-punctured artery. As Ray's paramedic training kicked in, his lieutenant provided cover.

Ignoring the coppery metallic odor of blood mixing with burned flesh and pungent graphite, Ray unhinged the tourniquet he wore on his left arm and expertly tied the rubber tightly above the infantryman's arterial wound. He continued performing a rapid, efficient assessment of the soldier, fervently wishing he had the medical supplies, intravenous fluids, and medications this man desperately needed. Then, in between a heartbeat, a realization slammed into Ray's chest with the weighted force of mortar.

A hell storm surrounded them. The reinforced unit, with shored-up firepower, all weapons fully functioning now, opened a full-on assault, trying to neutralize the attacks. They provided cover for the small band of warriors, who raced back into the night, carrying their fellow soldiers through errant gunfire toward the waiting convoy two kilometers away. His lieutenant toted the body of the dead private. Ray bore the deeply wounded body of his brother-in-arms, Cat, across his shoulders while he fired his M9 Beretta handgun. *Do not die on me, Cat. Not here, not now. Not on my watch.*

In a flash of light, he could see Cat racing by his side at boot camp during the "battle march." They were knee-deep in this "stress shoot," running in full battle rattle across a wide-open Georgian field. Ray and Cat had shouldered an extra fifty-pound ruck each to help their fellow privates who were falling behind, weighed down by their gear. Ray could see the sweat pouring from his friend's face, and unexpectedly, a grin emerged from behind the grimace. This image pushed Ray beyond the limits of human endurance.

Not in the Playbook

Leo was flushed and breathing hard when she pushed open the door to her therapist's office. Her father sat in the oversized burgundy chair by the window, the one Leo usually occupied. Jennifer stood by her file cabinet, closing a drawer.

"Sorry I'm late." Leo dropped her book bag and moved toward the couch.

"Mr. Lightfoot?" Jennifer's voice was satin. "Leo is more comfortable in that chair if you don't mind."

"Oh, of course. Sorry, I didn't know." He awkwardly stood and moved to the couch section closest to his daughter. He folded his hands on his long legs. Despite the coldness of the late afternoon, which seeped through the series of tall narrow windows of aged glass set into freshly painted wood frames, a thin sheen of sweat appeared on Joseph's forehead.

Leo instantly wanted to stop the meeting; her dad looked miserable. Maybe she didn't need to know. Perhaps she could keep everything the same, go back to her life before she started counseling and before she realized her voice had a right to be heard.

"Leo?" Jennifer's eyes were supportive. Nothing was being pushed on her. Leo knew that though difficult, this was something she had to do to move forward.

"Dad…" Her voice was soft as if she could ease his

pain through gentleness. "…we never, ever, talk about it. There are a few pictures, but I want…" She paused and looked at Jennifer, who nodded in encouragement. "What I need is to know. How did she die? What is my mother's story?"

****

Emily's story. The easy part. Joseph turned to look directly into his daughter's expectant eyes.

"I was eighteen, living with my mother and Paul. I was on the high school football team and working at the local grocery store." Leo listened intently, drinking in this new information. "My experience was limited. You would think being a quarterback, I would be confident. But to tell you the truth, I wasn't quite sure where I fit in. I was shy. On the field, though, I was fast with a strong, accurate arm."

Joseph took a long drink from the glass of water Dr. Baker poured him and continued. "It was my second year as the starting quarterback, the fall of my senior year, our opening game against rival Fort Gibson. The first half was ugly. But early in the fourth quarter, I got in a seven-yard rushing touchdown and two-point conversion to bring us to an even fifteen-fifteen. Fort Gibson fought back, taking an eighteen-fifteen advantage on a twenty-nine-yard field goal."

Am I losing her? Joseph looked questioningly. Leo had not moved an inch, her eyes riveted on her father, she gave a barely perceptible nod, and he continued. "Somehow, with slightly over three minutes left in the game, we pulled together and marched sixty yards down the field. The crowd was cheering wildly, a sea of orange and black. I remember looking into the stands and seeing my brother next to my mother. They were

The Circle of Willis

on their feet, an unlikely pair, stomping and waving their arms back and forth with the chanting throng. With twenty-five yards to go, the plan was to pass to my receiver, but he was being double-teamed. In a way that defies the playbooks, I saw an opening. The path was clear in my mind. I knew I had the speed to do it, and so I followed my inner map. Weaving in and out, maneuvering through the defense, I stumbled into the endzone. With ten seconds left, we took the lead and won the game. The next thing I knew, out of the celebratory crush, the most beautiful girl I had ever seen emerged. She threw her arms around me and kissed my cheek! She said I was amazing, and then she was gone as quickly as she had appeared. I found out later that her name was Emily. She was a cheerleader, and her family had moved to town over the summer. My world changed that night."

How do you explain how new love floods, the way feelings course through your veins, the way once your heart and lungs are reached, your previously nutrient-depleted blood becomes saturated with life-giving oxygen so that you feel an inexplicable fullness, a sense that anything in the world is possible? Joseph painted the picture, to the best of his halting ability, of the evolution of their relationship that started with an unexpected kiss to something secretive but intentional. He explained how the moment he found out he was going to be a father, he was so consumed with joy he was ready to run to the county courthouse. He wanted to shout from the water tower that he was in love and starting a family. He dreamed about this since his father left when he was a boy. He wanted Leo to know how much he had wanted her, how sure he felt, how he knew with absolute certainty Emily was his true love and their lives were just beginning.

"Her family knew nothing about me. Emily said if they knew, they would break us up. I guess I was from the wrong side of town, not what they wanted for her." Joseph was introspective. "Emily knew our time was finite. I was in love, oblivious."

He ran a hand through his hair. "The first time I started fully grasping the gravity of the situation was when she told me about the pregnancy. I wanted, no, I begged her to get married. Emily was terrified, and she said her parents couldn't know. If they found out, she'd be forced to have an abortion. So, we kept you a secret. Your mother was always slender, and as the months advanced, she started wearing longer, baggier tops. The night she went into labor, four weeks early, was the night her parents found out she was pregnant."

Here is where the story gets complicated. He glanced at Dr. Baker. Her expression was solemn, but beneath it, he read support in her calm lake-gray eyes. "Your mother's parents believed that the adoption agency had taken care of everything. They were under the assumption that the closed adoption was complete, that this nasty chapter in their daughter's life was over. You were a guarded secret.

"Emily gave me full custody. She tried to visit every two weeks or so when she knew her parents were out of town or otherwise occupied. As you know, my mom died from a heart attack in the winter of my senior year. With her life insurance money, Paul and I moved from the trailer on the outskirts of Tahlequah to our house in town." He took another drink of water, assessed how his daughter was doing, and plunged ahead.

"I graduated high school and was in college working toward my degree in teaching. A kind lady across the street watched you when I was in class. Between the neighbor, me, and Paul, you were never alone. There was no need for daycare. Emily came when she could. Those moments we had together as a family made the periods of separation bearable.

"Then, one evening, when we were expecting her…" Joseph's voice was almost a whisper. Leo leaned forward. "You were looking out the front window, waiting for her to come. I heard you call Momma, Momma? Momma! And you started to cry. I rushed to open the door for Emily, afraid of what happened to cause you such distress. There, where your mother usually stood, was an envelope with her handwriting on the front."

Leo's face, an expression of intent absorption, was slowly replaced by bewilderment. "What are you trying to say?" Leo leaped to her feet, looking stunned and confused. She started to pace. "Oh no?! Her gravestone has her birthdate…." Leo's whole body suddenly became still, taut, as the realization seeped in, water finding minute cracks in the bedrock. He could tell that her intellect was fighting what her core had just acknowledged. Her utterance was barely audible, "But no death date."

He interrupted, "Leo, I never called the stone a grave." Seeing her face infused with stress, as though she might break at any moment, his voice became a cushion. "I always said memorial stone. And I never said she *died or passed*. I would always say she moved on." This was a simple truth.

Leo put her hands over her face and shook her head back and forth in disbelief. Her body and voice quivered on the edge of hysteria; she dropped her hands by her side. "And tell me, how is a three-year-old supposed to know the difference between a grave and a memorial stone? How is an eight-year-old expected to know that her mother is alive because there is no death date? How is a twelve-year-old, a fifteen-year-old, expected to know these things?" And hitting her, in the center of the hot tears and dazed fury, was the knowledge she was supposed to notice. When she was ready, she was supposed to ask, and her father would have told her.

"I didn't know what to do, Leo," his voice implored, "You were distraught and calling out for her. You stood before me in a yellow gingham dress stained and shredded from your search for your mother with your big brown eyes full of tears. I felt angry and utterly helpless. How do you console a little girl whose mother walked away? I wanted to give you something solid to touch and focus on." He couldn't gauge how his words were impacting his daughter. He wanted to reach out, hold her, and help her, as he thought he had been doing so many years ago. "I did what Lightfoot men have always done when challenged, jumped into hasty, sometimes ill-conceived, action." He sighed. "After a few weeks, when I was sure she wasn't returning, I tucked you into your car seat, and we headed out to the quarry, where you picked out a beautiful rose-colored memorial. You chose the stone, and you chose the spot. The site was meant to be a place where you could seek solace, remember and connect on some level with your mother."

"You let me think she was dead."

"It was never meant to be a deception."

Trickery, fraud, had her whole childhood been built on this? A dismantling foundation, a false narrative? Unabated anger came swiftly. Leo turned for support from Jennifer. The session had deteriorated. Leo was supposed to be in control. Dr. Baker looked apologetic; she bit her lower lip. When she broke eye contact with Leo and looked toward Joseph, an extended exchange passed between them, communication without words, a new level of betrayal was revealed.

"Wait, Dr. Baker, you knew?" The treachery seemed unbearable. Leo steeled herself, willed herself not to break down any further, not in front of the people who purposely concealed her truth, people she had implicitly trusted.

Dr. Baker's voice was even. "Remember when I asked you if I could bring your dad in to clarify some things? You gave me permission."

"But not to perpetuate a lie!" Leo looked from her father to her therapist, who was now standing by his side, deceitfully united against her. Her heart was racing like a caged animal, desperate to escape. "I am done!" She glared at Dr. Baker. "You're FIRED. No more therapy sessions, no more falsehoods!" Leo moved closer to the exit, and then she directed her fierce gaze at her father. "You too, Dad. I can't believe you! I'm finished with you all."

She raced down the rear stairs into the back alley, shadowy with dusk's bitter breath. Razor-sharp particles of ice assaulted her exposed skin. Crouched behind the dumpster, the smell of rotting produce choking the air, her bike on its side to avoid detection, she pulled out her cell phone. With trembling fingers, she found Jake's contact information and sent this message: —I need out, NOW—

Ground Level

Laughter exploded from behind the door of Jake's ground-level apartment. The hall, with more overhead bulbs burned out than functioning, was barely lit. Leo struggled to find her key. Jammed in her backpack was a letter she had just retrieved from their overflowing mail slot. The return address read: Dr. J. Baker. Leo was too tired to read and deal with the content. Later, I'll respond tomorrow or sometime next week. For now, she needed all her strength just to get through the door. The lack of light made seeing the opening where the key fit difficult.

She was exhausted, having just finished her twelve-hour janitorial shift cleaning the toilets, sinks, halls, and classrooms of Lewis and Clark Elementary School. Jake couldn't get her the job he promised; she did need a high school diploma to work in general production at the Bama Pie Factory. She sighed heavily. She didn't have the energy to face what she knew waited for her inside, but she had no other option.

All six heads looked up from their remote video controllers as she entered the apartment. "That's your old lady, Jake?" The living room looked like a bomb had been dropped on it. The air was thick with smoke. She could see Jake and his friends had inhaled more than cigarettes over the night. In discarded beer bottles, ash mixed with spit. Burn marks and soot ground into the carpet. A profusion of open pizza boxes, chip bags, and candy wrappers scattered around the sluggish human forms. There was a whiskey bottle lying at the base of the couch.

"You didn't tell us she was hot."

She didn't recognize the fleshy man who spoke, his pudgy fingers mashing a remote. Before returning to the game, he wagged his tongue at her, which protruded from a round, scarlet face dotted with acne.

"Hot, all right," Jake said as his fingers aggressively tapped the buttons of his control device. "Hot for me. You should have seen how she begged me to marry her after moving in. She can't get enough of me." He paused his gaming and ran his hands down his chest; after grabbing his crotch, he continued, "She wants it all." The other five talking heads snickered at his comments, then roared as their soldiers on the *Call of Duty* video game fearlessly opened fire, resulting in a sudden and bloody death.

Leo reached into the sink full of dirty dishes and pulled out a cup that didn't look too rank. Of course, she hadn't begged Jake for marriage, but she had heard his version, this revised narrative so often that she was beginning to doubt herself. Remembering how she felt months ago when she'd agreed to marry Jake, weeks after moving in with him, was difficult.

He had worked his magic, telling her he loved her and would never lie to her as her father, uncle, therapist, and mother had. He told her how lucky she was to have this chance, that many women would want to be his wife, to be chosen. Besides, Leo had felt so utterly alone. There was nowhere else to go. The life she knew was shattered.

Even worse than a dead mother was one who turned her back on her toddler and walked away. Growing up imagining all the different ways her mother could have died was bad enough: a rare form of cancer, knocked off her bike in a horrific hit-and-run, or choking on a fish bone. But finding out she didn't care enough to hang around while her daughter grew up took the term "motherless" to a new level.

Her life with her dad and Uncle Paul was history. Gone was the possibility of graduating, of going to college on a scholarship. Jake was the only one who seemed to want her. At least he was transparent, and he offered a place of shelter, a degree of familiarity. This was all she had, and she clung to it. Leo rinsed and then filled the mug with tepid tap water.

Leo remembered her wedding day, holding a single pale pink gas station rose she bought for herself while standing alone outside the courthouse in a simple white dress she had purchased from the Goodwill store. Jake, her new husband, and Eric, his buddy, their only witness, had left her to grab some beer to celebrate. Leo would not partake. She made that abundantly clear to Jake from the start, from the moment she climbed into his beat-up pickup after hastily packing a few things, including the protective eye necklace he'd given her. She was steadfast. While she didn't care, well at least wouldn't judge, what Jake did, he couldn't expect her to participate in drinking or consuming drugs. He shrugged. "Suit yourself. Makes no difference to me."

On her way to the bedroom, drink of water in hand, she ran into her husband, who was leaving the bathroom. He grabbed her by the shoulders and pressed his lips hard against hers with a little tongue. "You miss me?"

"Thought you had to work today." Leo glanced at her watch. He was too drunk and high and already an hour late for the start of his shift. She knew what his retort would be. The response had become a pattern.

"I deserve a vacation day, don't you think? You wouldn't even have this apartment if I didn't put down the security deposit. It's your turn to pull some weight." He slapped her on the bottom, a gesture that was no longer playful. Leo wordlessly turned and headed into the bedroom, closing the hollow core door behind her.

Sleep was elusive. Despite the fatigue, her mind would not still. On her side, knees drawn up to her chest, Leo curled, cocooning as if the physical reduction of strain on her veins and internal organs could transfer to sensation and reduce the aching pressure in her heart.

How had she gotten here? Where was the friendly, easy-going boy she met in her first year of high school? The one who had slowly, persistently, worked to gain her trust until her guard lowered, until she felt safe to share her innermost feelings. Where was the boy who argued with a series of feather-soft kisses about the absolute need for secrecy?

Those memories represented another lifetime. This was her new normal. Leo closed her eyes. The whir of the bedside fan shuffling hot, stagnant air did little to mitigate the raucous guffaws punctuated by loud moans, groans and yells as fictional warriors killed and were killed. Over and over again, in waves of auditory assault, the charged noise kept her wary and unable to unwind.

Why can't I sleep? She was despondent, frustrated

with herself and the situation. In a few hours, she would have to get up and work her second job, cashiering at the local Quick Trip. And in that unbidden state where fatigue and anxiousness meet, control over thought and emotion diminish and unite in a point of convergence, yet another memory of her wedding day rose and slid into gauzy focus.

She saw herself quietly slipping out of the closed-in apartment, leaving Jake and Eric inside celebrating. She could see herself leaning against the side of the brick building, trying to make herself as small as possible, and with shaky hands, she called her father to tell him the news. She was hyperventilating as she talked, which left her lightheaded and with a tingling sensation in her lips. After she finished speaking, a prolonged pause ensued, then she heard a deep inhalation of air she knew her father always took when trying to get a handle on things. "Are you happy, Leotie?" was all he said.

"I think so," she replied.

But after the phone call, after her father apologized again for withholding the truth about her mother after they both said they loved each other and planned a time when he would come to Tulsa to take them out for a belated celebratory dinner, she became aware of the silent tears which had soaked the satin piping around the collar of her bridal white cotton sheath. These tears had been falling all along.

A Possum Eating a Sweet Potato

"What do you mean you don't have your high school diploma?" Leo's co-worker at the Quick Trip convenience store, Ronnie, stopped her task and leveled a steady gaze at her friend. "That's some bull crap, a smart sister like you?" She completed her transaction and stepped in front of Leo. "Don't tell me you didn't graduate because of him? If you do, I'll have to whip your ass. I really will. Never let a man get between you and your education."

Leo shrugged apologetically and looked away. "It's a long story." She stopped talking and rang up her customer's purchase of a Triple Stack—Jalapeno, cheddar, and smoked sausage. "Do you need anything else today, sir?"

"And what's up with that freaky-looking eye you wear around your neck?" Ronnie grabbed a pack of cigarettes, took money from the customer, and put the cash in the till.

"Jake gave me this when we started dating. He made a promise to protect me."

Ronnie looked at her skeptically.

"It means a lot to him. His mom gave him the pendant."

"Keep the eye hidden, girl. That thing gives me the creeps."

After the lunch rush abated and they were on

break, Ronnie, smoking a cigarette, and Leo eating her favorite from the roller grill, a cheesy pepper jack taquito, the conversations resumed.

"You got to get your GED. I mean it." With dark brown curls framing an oval-shaped face, Ronnie was usually lighthearted and joking, but there was no merriment now.

"I can't. I work two jobs, and in between those, I have to clean the apartment, shop, and cook. I don't see how I could fit everything all in." Leo doesn't say that if Jake ever found out, he would become enraged, thinking she was trying to become better than him, trying to shirk her responsibilities, trying to be all high and mighty.

"No, Leo. This is non-negotiable. What happens if he kicks you to the curb or you get your poop in a group and decide to leave? You gotta be able to stand on your own. You must have at least a high school diploma. And frankly, with your brains, you shouldn't stop there. There are practice exams online if you don't have time to take a prep class. You can check out study guides from the library."

Leo knew Jake would tear apart the study guides and throw them in the trash if he found them, and he would. She didn't try to hide anything anymore; life was easier this way.

"I just can't." Her voice was barely a whisper, and suddenly the taquito caused her stomach to wretch. She threw the roll into the dumpster. Wisps of long, dark hair escaped from her braid. "I don't have a computer, and even if I did, Jake wouldn't get it. He'd complain about me not doing my fair share, making existence difficult. I couldn't keep this secret. He even checks my phone's history." Sometimes multiple times a day but she didn't say that part out loud.

Ronnie took in the whole of her and softened. "Look, I don't understand what you see in that scrawny, self-centered prick. He's worthless, like gum on a bootheel. Look, you can take the online practice exams and crack the books at my place. Next time I take the kid to the library, I'll check out some course material. We'll figure out what areas you need to bone up on—starting next week, instead of cycling straight to work, go to my place. You can do an hour of cramming before our shift starts. Then when it's time to clock in, I'll throw your ride in my trunk and drive us to work."

Leo opened her mouth to protest.

"No," Ronnie interjected before she had a chance to talk. "You're doing this! All you have to do is tell Jake you have a new start time." She stubbed out her cigarette. As they headed back inside to finish their shift, Ronnie gave her friend a quick hug. "If need be, I'll lie for you. It's that simple."

Nothing is ever simple. But looking into the eager, supportive eyes of the first, well maybe the second, true friend in her life, Leo nodded, and with this gesture, she committed to her friend. Then with tenacity and determination, character strands that had been part of her core since early childhood, she threw herself wholeheartedly into the process.

She quickly realized that as long as she kept up the facade of their lives, routinely did what was expected of her while holding down her two jobs, as long as Jake could continue his gaming, having his cohorts over anytime he wanted, day or night, as long as his life wasn't inconvenienced, and as long as nothing out of line appeared on her phone, Jake actually didn't concern himself with what she did. He took for granted her staunch loyalty and accepted at face value that her boss had extended her shift to incorporate her breaks.

****

Ronnie burst into the low-ceilinged rental unit, a whorl of energy. "Sorry I'm late. I've been running all over hell's half-acre."

Leo looked up from the kitchen table where she had been studying quietly for the past hour and smiled at her friend.

Ronnie pulled her two-year-old daughter off her wide hip, dropped a kiss atop her mass of tight black curls, and placed her in the booster chair snuggly tucked next to Leo. She opened the refrigerator and took out a jar of peaches. "Maya's sitter will be here in five minutes. Are you about done?"

Leo closed the study guide, stood, and stretched; she took in the compactness of Ronnie's home. The walls were lined with varying-sized shelves, scavenged from front yards on trash day, from garage sales and thrift stores. And they were all jammed with books, everything from toddler delights, *Goodnight Moon*, *The Velveteen Rabbit*, to the classics and more, *My Antonia*, *Beloved*, *I Know Why the Caged Bird Sings*, to Ronnie's community college textbooks. Over the past few months, her apartment had become more than a study space. Her home became a sanctuary, a sheltered place where Leo could come five times a week, let herself in with the key under the fake stone in a flower garden that hosted nothing but weeds, let down her guard, drink coffee, and immerse herself in the process.

"I think I'm ready." With a self-effacing laugh, she

met Ronnie's steady scrutiny and continued, "The past few practice exams I've taken, I've passed."

"Girl, look at you!" Ronnie wiped her daughter's face gently with a wet washrag. "I can't believe how fast you got this together. You're grinning like a possum eating a sweet potato. Let's get you signed up for that test!"

Tract Five:

2009-2010

The Suck
Afghanistan

"I am an American fighting in the forces which guard my country and our way of life. I am prepared to give my life in their defense."—Article One of the Code of Conduct for the United States armed forces members.

****

Two separate wars with two different objectives: Operation Iraqi Freedom was a campaign against a single man, Saddam Hussain, and his government; Operation Enduring Freedom in Afghanistan was a crusade against terrorist forces, specifically the Taliban. Intellectually Ray knew there was a difference, but the dimensions and dynamics, the heft of service in a combat zone, seemed the same. On a cellular level, one war felt no different to Ray than the other.

They arrived at Bagram Airfield amidst a massive dust storm. The pilot of the C-17 miraculously found purchase, for the world was choked so thickly that one could not differentiate land from the air. That afternoon, as Ray was shuttled to the transient camp, Forward Operating Base, FOB, Warrior, the windstorm abated briefly, just enough so that he could see his new surroundings. The base was ringed with elevated mounds and disfigured, brown, jagged lumps of earth, like supersized gopher burrow debris, unlike the towering snow-capped peaks he had just seen in Kyrgyzstan. A slip of blue sky appeared, a glimpse of hope. Then the hills and all its air were quickly swallowed again, engulfed in a cloud of burnt sienna dust.

In the military you rush, only to wait and wait. Ray and his platoon found themselves suspended in purgatory, stuffed into a canvas tent with a broken air conditioning unit. They marked time in an overcrowded, hotter than Hades, petri dish warehouse of men. And there they remained for days, which bled, one into the other. The unit they were relieving had already started disembarking. In fact, as Ray and his men waited for advancement, on another part of the intake-outtake hub of Bagram, soldiers from their assigned post were leaving, heading home.

This disrupted transfer of authority happens. In an ideal situation, one company moves in, is shown the ropes, and briefed by the existing unit. Dangerous locations are revealed, the roads to avoid are pointed out, and triggers are explained. By the time The Relief in Place Process is complete, the outgoing troops are confident that the incoming formation understands the missions in the assigned zone of operations and can withdraw—a seamless transition. In war, situations are rarely ideal.

With the dissipating dust, cogs on a reluctant wheel, the stymied impasse shifted, and incrementally, small clusters of soldiers were transported to their respective bases. By the time Ray's platoon reached the remote, austere combat outpost, only a handful of soldiers from the prior unit remained, a fragmented transfer of power. What was accomplished over two weeks was consolidated into twelve hours, better than absolutely nothing, but not by much.

Ray looked around him. Their base was situated in a fertile river valley, a Taliban hotbed, surrounded by forbidding mountains, ones which stretched their sharp, treacherous peaks far into the upper atmosphere as if attempting to escape the land upon which they were tethered. With a high OPTEMPO, a minimum of one mission per day, this would be a place Ray and his platoon would struggle to call home, even though they would be there for twelve months.

****

My Dear Long-Lost Brother,

You are never going to guess what our mother has become. One badass secret agent! Well, you know all about just sending the letters to my address, so Dad doesn't know she's writing to you. Turns out she made a secret hiding place, under the 'Bless this Mess' rug, under a loose floorboard, in the laundry room. So now she takes your letters home with her, hides them, and pulls them out to reread when Dad is out doing his ministerial duties. Also, she's gotten her own email address, which Dad has no idea exists. They still have their joint one, but you can't write her there, of course. It is crazy we still can't talk about you, even though you are now on your second deployment.

Really, Dad? Get over it. So now you can send emails directly to Mom. And if all this isn't enough, Mom has gotten knee-deep into the Family and Friends support group for your unit. The care packages you guys get from this group, well, Mom helps organize them. She does all this behind-the-scenes stuff. She acts all innocent, performing her wifely chores, never giving anything away, and never letting anything slip. She's a stealth aircraft. Conventional dad radar can't detect her. It's great. She has this whole other life that Dad knows nothing about. Mister, "and the Truth shall set you free," would go ballistic!

On another note, I decided to buy the rental home Gabrielle and I have been staying in for the past few years. Our landlord is selling the property to me through a land contract. We can make improvements without checking in with him first, and yes, I still have the few boxes you left behind (now stacked in the garage). I am also thinking about having a baby. This will really send the old man into orbit. One kid, an infantryman, serving on the front line and the other living an "alternative" lifestyle and pregnant out of wedlock—a trifecta of paternal disappointment.

But I've noticed something interesting. Remember the marquee outside of the church, the one you and I used to change each week, putting up Dad's new catchy phrases—one of my all-time favorites, Forbidden fruits, creates many jams. Since you left home for boot camp, Dad hasn't changed it. Not once. The 'Pray for our troops' sign has endured your training, stateside service, and two tours of duty. When a letter falls off the sign, from sheer exhaustion, he goes out and replaces it. Who knows the inner workings of Pastor Bertrand Shipworth, our dear father?

Until next time my favorite brother.

Oh, and remember, 'God answers knee-mail.'

The Circle of Willis

Ray shook his head, smiled though he was alone, and closed his eyes to remember. Without fail, every Monday after school let out, before the evening Bible study classes started, Hope and Ray would change the church's marquee. They went clutching a large cardboard box of letters, and a piece of paper bearing their father's wittily crafted missive typed carefully by the church secretary. This chore had been part of their repertoire since memory began. When they were young, before they could even read, their mother went with them. A word game, who can find me a capital J, an E, or an S? The children scrambled to see who could find the letters first, then helped their mother slide them into place. When they finished, they would look forward, admiring their handiwork, meant to lure in new worshippers. Choose the bread of life, or you will be toast.

When they were adept at reading and spelling and had proved reliable, their mother slipped into the backdrop and let them take the reins. Ray can see in his mind, playing like the reel of an old family movie, ten-year-old twins bent over with uncontainable glee. Prevent truth decay, brush up on your Bible; Don't be so open-minded your brains fall out. Then as teenagers, they laughed with such force that tears coursed down their faces, and they could not catch their breath; he cannot know what this means, or does he? You cannot enter heaven unless Jesus enters you. The best gift you can give God is from a kneeling position. How many countless hours over the years had they spent changing that faithful, long-suffering sign?

On the grassy swell, outside the white-washed church of their lives, they always found things to chatter about, nothing and everything. They laughed at the mundane, the ridiculous. They filled each other in on their observations, bouncing ideas off each other, challenging, and pushing. Sometimes they argued. But always, when they finished, they stood back, side by side, twins whose separate placentas had grown so close together they were fused, impossible for the doctor to tell where one had ended, and the other began, brother and sister, and considered what they had done.

"Hey, Ship, heading to the chow hall. Want to join me?" Fisher peered into the dim particle board-defined room.

Ray folded his sister's note, slid the paper back into the envelope, and put her message in a plastic baggy where he kept all his letters from home. He turned off the 50-watt light and rubbed his heavy eyes. As he swung his legs off the cot, he pulled on his Army Combat uniform top, covering his sand-colored tee. "No, go on ahead. I need to check the M-ATV before we head out of the wire. I don't feel like eating anyway."

"Suit yourself, man. See you in thirty."

The motor pool was quiet, void of any human activity. Ray felt a dull disconnect as he inspected the newly minted Mine-Resistant-Ambush-Protected All-Terrain vehicle. The light tactical tank, designed for harsh and rugged topography, where off-roading was often necessary, was, in theory, structured to withstand ambushes and Improvised Explosive Device (IED) attacks. He had become all too familiar with that during his first tour of duty in Iraq. Where were you then? he thought as he checked the pressure in the tires and the fluids in the engine.

The Circle of Willis

Where were you a few years ago when all we had were up-armored Humvees, those ungainly beasts whose added bulk rendered the existing chassis less stable, whose doors weighed hundreds of pounds and were difficult to open? Where were you when our convoy ran over the IED hidden in the decaying carcass of a donkey…but he stopped himself and pushed back those images. Focus on getting through this day, the here, the now, the suck.

****

Whether on foot or in an up-armored Humvee or riding an off-the-assembly-line M-ATV, nothing could withstand well-placed, deeply concealed, highly concentrated, explosive roadside bombs.

In suspended motion, Ray observed, even as he continued to pull security, the MEDI-VAC arrive. Three more body bags were loaded into its empty, waiting belly. Ray saluted as the chopper took flight, rising straight up in the air. Momentarily, as the aircraft passed over him, he was bathed in a rush of hot air and shadow. The MEDI-VAC had been coming and going all day. He would not allow himself to count the number of body bags that remained.

A Room Stained with Shadow

She waited until Jake had a scheduled day off. He spent the morning, followed by an afternoon of drinking, smoking, and gaming with Eric. When she casually dropped the information that her dad was coming to town to take *them* out to dinner, he blew her off and told her to go without him. The plan worked.

Leo did not want Jake with her tonight. She wanted to celebrate earning her graduate equivalent degree, tantamount to a high school diploma, without him. There was a disconnect here, one she felt on a cellular level. Why could she share this accomplishment with her father but not her husband?

In the marriage's infancy, Leo tried to express what she was feeling and what she wanted. She had learned from her sessions with Dr. Baker that she had a right to be heard and validated. And after all, she thought, sharing was what married people were supposed to do. But Jake had neither been willing, nor was he empathetic. He accused her of being ungrateful. He took her words as a personal attack. And he responded to the perceived criticism with impatient vitriol. He whined, "I don't want an overly sensitive, emotionally immature wife. No wonder your mama left you. You ain't nothing but a crybaby." So, Leo stopped. She internalized thought and emotion and soldiered on doing the best she could in her marriage, trying to ignore the rising anxiety caused by Jake's constant interrupting, put-downs, and reprimands when she failed to get things right. That was why Leo told her dad to pick her up in the parking lot and not at the apartment. She would tell him Jake wasn't feeling well and was in bed sleeping.

She waited by the window, looking for her dad's arrival through a broken blind. A new *Call of Duty*, *The World at War*, had just come out. This time, Jake and Eric were American soldiers fighting the Japanese. They were animatedly talking through headsets to the rest of their team, part of a thriving multiplayer community, a fantasy world Leo had known nothing about but had been introduced to the day she moved in with Jake. She could see Jake sight an enemy climbing over a wall; he rapidly sorted through his available flame throwers, rocket launchers, and an assortment of guns before he settled on a hand grenade and hurled the weapon across the flat screen. When Jake and Eric saw the impact, the profusion of blood from a severed limb, they shrieked with delight. And when Leo saw the lights of her father's patched and battered black Honda pull into the complex, she didn't say a word as she slipped away.

****

"I'm sorry Jake had to miss this celebration." He took a bite of his limoncello cream torte and smiled. "It's an accomplishment, Leo. I am proud of you."

At the sound of Jake's name, she no longer felt like finishing her piece of chocolate tower truffle cake. Since the wedding, Leo had become adept at keeping all other aspects of her life separate from the time she spent at the apartment with Jake. Compartmentalizing had become easy until reminders were injected, puncturing nails snagged in tires. She shrugged.

Her father looked at her across the linen tablecloth. "Your determination reminds me of your mother."

Leo couldn't help herself; she let her fork drop, clattering onto the china. "You've got to be joking. Does Emily have determination? I don't think so. The only thing she was determined to do was to walk away from her kid and a man who wanted to marry her."

Joseph took a deliberate pause before pushing back his empty dessert plate and responding in a low, measured, but sympathetic voice, "That's not fair, Leo. You don't know what she went through. There's more to the story."

****

After dinner, as they strolled along the paved Riverwalk, which hugged the swiftly moving Arkansas River, Joseph's voice rose and fell with the night air. "Your mother was determined. At first, Emily was determined to keep her parents from finding out about you and determined to keep you alive. Then after you were born, she was determined to keep the two of us, you and me, together."

As he told Leo the story, he was transported to an exact moment seared into memory, a heart imprint that happened the second night he slipped into his nascent family's room on the postpartum ward. Long after her parents left, he crept in. He could see Emily's tear-streaked, pale face, almost translucent from the blood loss of childbirth. And he could hear absolute despair in her voice.

"They are forcing me to give her up for adoption, a closed adoption so that I can never know where she is, never ask questions or see pictures of her growing up. My parents promised a huge sum of money to the adoption agency to expedite the process."

Joseph could feel the panic rising as he held his daughter closer to him. Tomorrow, Emily was scheduled for discharge. Was this the last night they would be together as a family? The room started to turn. Orientation was difficult.

"Joseph?" Her voice sounded faint, distant, a diminishing form of echolocation. Emily touched his cheek, then placed her hands on the side of his face, bringing the floating, hazy pieces back into focus. She grazed him gently on his lips before bending to kiss their daughter. "I'm not going to let this happen." Her voice was resolute. Her eyes steadied him, and he exhaled. She pulled out the half-filled birth certificate worksheet. "I have a plan." Then she explained.

When the adoption agency representative met with her the following day, Emily sent her parents to the cafeteria, stating this was hard enough for her that she didn't want them hovering around as she signed the papers. They agreed, all too eager to put this horrid chapter behind them and to have their daughter back on her life's projected course.

"It's a closed adoption, which means my parents can never find out where she went, right?"

The agent pleasantly nodded, smoothed down her pencil skirt, reached into her briefcase for her gold-coated rollerball pen, and flatly stated, "That also means you will never know who adopted her or what state or country she is in. Now let's get the paperwork started."

Standing up to authority figures was not something

Emily had ever done. She swallowed, then unwaveringly stood before the bassinet where her daughter was sleeping. "For the adoption to take place, I have to indicate on the birth certificate that the father is unknown." The director nodded impatiently, and Emily continued, "But that would be a lie. As far as my parents are concerned, I never found the name of the boy I slept with. They think our encounter was a lapse of judgment at a party where alcohol was involved. They thought I never saw him again, that maybe he was from another town. What they do not know, and will never know, is twofold. One, is his name. And two, I am in love with this boy."

The smug look on the representative's face disintegrated and was replaced by incredulity. She stammered and was about to speak when Emily interjected, "Do you want your organization to get the donation my parents guaranteed once this adoption happens?" Afraid of losing ground, the representative blinked her eyes. "I thought so. Let me tell you how we'll do this. The signed birth certificate will be completed after I am discharged. Joseph Lightfoot will be listed as the father of my baby, and I am granting him full custody. Your agency will facilitate this and do whatever is necessary to ensure the documentation is legally binding. My parents will never know Joseph's name, our daughter's name, or the details of this transaction. After all, as you have assured us countless times, this is the basis of a closed adoption. We do everything this way, and your agency gets the donation. If my parents find out what I have done, they will be so mad that you can kiss the money goodbye. But know this, no matter what, Joseph is keeping his daughter.

Understood?"

When Emily's parents returned, with coffee mugs in hand, the adoption broker indicated the paperwork was complete, the closed adoption was in progress, and the adoptive family would come to the hospital to retrieve the infant sometime over the next few days. That afternoon, Emily was discharged, and twenty-four hours later, after Joseph and Paul scrambled to ready their house for a newborn, Joseph took his daughter, Leotie Rose Lightfoot, home.

Joseph looked at his daughter as they walked. The path's nighttime light illuminated tears. "But, Dad, why? Why, after she did all that for us in the hospital and kept us carefully guarded, why, after three years, would she just up and leave? Do you think there was another man?"

He looked toward the river as if answers might arise from its fluid depths. "No. At least, I don't think so. I only know for sure what the letter said. Emily was worn down by her parents, who had been pressuring her to go to college out of state for years. They feared she would run into me again and return to me. Little did they know she never left. Emily loved her parents and always wanted to please them, but they made her life difficult with constant pressure and high expectations. She could never assert herself or stand up to them. It's not a character flaw. It's just part of who she was. Leo, please forgive her for this."

What Joseph knew, which he didn't share with his daughter, was that somewhere along the way, Emily's intense passion for him, the luminous light that had brought the two of them together, encompassed them, insulated them, had dimmed. After Leo's birth, they both were so focused on their shared infant and the need to maintain secrecy that, at first, Joseph did not notice.

One late winter afternoon, Leo had fallen asleep early. Emily kissed her forehead and moved toward the back door, though she wouldn't be expected home for another hour. As threadbare sunlight struggled to infiltrate filmy curtains, he reached for her to pull her into an embrace. The room was stained with shadow. She looked at him sadly and gently pulled away. At that moment, he knew. He realized the life force of Emily, the shooting star that had streaked across the night sky of his life with blinding brilliance, was already moving on, the trail of phosphorescence in her wake, vaporizing high in the earth's upper atmosphere.

When Joseph pulled in front of Leo and Jake's apartment, he got out of the car to hug his daughter. "It's a lot to unpack, I know. But there's something else I want to tell you."

Leo looked at him. Exhaustion etched around her eyes, a dark liner of charcoal. "Don't tell me you know where she is? That she was my high school English teacher, that she's living in the apartment above me?" She gave a contrived laugh.

Joseph looked bemused. "No, nothing like that. Emily left, I never heard from her again, and to this date, I don't know where she is."

Leo nodded. "Okay then, does what you want to share with me have anything to do with Emily?" He shook his head. "Then, Dad,"—she sighed—"can it wait?"

"Of course." He gave her a quick kiss. "Tell Jake I hope he's feeling better." Joseph watched her walk through the door. He would not leave until he was sure she was safely inside until she was with her husband.

The Suck Part II

Afghanistan

"Okay, men, time to move out!" Second Lieutenant Cerelli scanned their camp. He appeared satisfied that the temporary patrol base was packed, and they were leaving the mountainous terrain in approximately the same condition as when they had arrived five days ago. He started to move down the steep, craggy mountainside.

Before Ray donned his ruck, he espied a crystal mountain stream. For a moment, he could see his visage wavering, dark stubble on an angled face. With eyes, the same color as the water, the house of mirrors apparition appeared sightless. Ray did not recognize himself.

He took a long drink, stretched his arms into an unblemished azure firmament, then slung the canvas sack onto his back. Involuntarily, he pressed the pocket of his uniform, the one farthest away from his heart. Feeling the crinkle of a letter he received over thirty days ago, one he'd been carrying ever since, and fell into line as the band of soldiers began their 9,000-foot descent.

He had the letter memorized. Though focused on the steep decline, he could hear her voice as though she was near.

The Circle of Willis

Ray, it's May.
No wonder we were so good together. We rhyme.
About a month ago, I was grocery shopping, and a man came up to me and said I was pretty enough to be a model. This guy hires girls to promote a new energy drink, so guess what. I have a job handing out samples on campus, attending events, and setting up booths. The pay isn't as good as my last job, but I get more exposure. A lot of the girls they hire get discovered, big-time stuff. I mean high-level, like supermodels that end up in catalogs, runways, and even in commercials. Exciting, right? My new boss said the company is thinking about doing one of those calendars, and he asked what month I would want to be in. You don't have to guess what I said.
So, I've been thinking about how nice our apartment was, you understood me. You know how important having a put-together place is, and you always let me decorate the way I wanted. That was nice. I think we should get back together.
Ray and May,
What do you say?

He had re-read the letter so many times the edges of the scalloped floral stationery were translucent. The perfume, her scent, which undoubtedly, she had sprayed, saturating the letter and envelope before posting it, that was barely perceptible upon arrival, was now long gone. Weighted by his rucksack, gravity propelled him forward down the sharp mountainside. The footing was tricky. Triceratops spines of sharp Precambrian metamorphic rocks poked up at odd angles, threatening to snap ankles and cause sudden falls off sheer bluffs if you were not paying full attention.

At first, he felt energized by the prospect of reunification and immediately wrote May back. But now, he was second-guessing that decision, wondering if he had made a mistake. Navigating this inner landscape was difficult. He examined their tenure together with removed rationale. Had he thought about her more than fleetingly since starting his military service? Had he remembered the moments when they were together, with longing or deep affection? Without question, he had been a quick study, learning what made her smile, what brought her joy. And he had been ready to propose. But what had that truly been about? There had been times in their relationship before she started messing around with her boss when she talked of nothing else. She had snuggled by his side and had shown him, for hours on end, rings she loved. At the time, a proposal seemed like the natural progression of a relationship. And he knew the engagement would make his mom and dad feel better about their living arrangements. But was this enough to hang a lifetime of commitment on?

Once May walked out on him, he tried to return the engagement ring, but the saleswoman, who had been so helpful during the purchase, pointed out in the fine print that the store could not refund special order items. Before he left for boot camp, he turned the rock in at the local pawn shop, thinking he could always go back if she changed her mind. That had not happened. And, not once, since his departure, had he thought of the black velvet box or the ring inside.

As the patrol emerged from the foothills onto the open flatland, he scanned the fields with laser-focused vision, noting clear mountain-fed irrigation canals and riverbeds that would provide adequate cover should they take fire.

His thoughts wandered back to May. What were the binding elements that drew them together? And if he hadn't loved her, was entering into a relationship, to go through empty motions, just to have someone waiting for him when he returned home, ethical? Doing so wasn't fair to her. She deserved more. Being a soldier in a combat zone, Ray thought, was far more straightforward than matters of the heart.

May hadn't given him a phone number or an email address where he could reach her, to talk more immediately and figure this out. They were going to be in the field for a few more days. Maybe a letter would be waiting for him when he returned to base. All he could do now was wait. Wait for her reply to his simple response, "I'm all in."

They returned to base a couple of days later, in the late afternoon. Ray spent the next few hours taking apart and carefully cleaning his M4 Carbine and M320 Grenade launcher. He allowed his mind to wander as he focused on each section, rubbing off the dust, mud, and rust. What plans had May been making for them? Would reading her words, feeling her excitement of getting back together, bubble from the page and help ease his lingering doubts? Anticipating a response was within the realm of reason, he thought, while putting his weapons back together. Especially if his reply had only taken a week or two to reach her and if she had written back within a few days. The past two days had given him a chance to conclude: he was ready. He would do anything to try and make this relationship work.

Whatever he had felt for her when they first got together, he was sure would come back with effort, and in time, they would be as they were before. He delayed stopping by the postal center. Instead, he continued to perform the assignments required after a prolonged mission. Holding on to a glimpse of possibility was better than acknowledging a purposeful absence.

No letters were waiting for him. My letter took longer to reach May. Her response is taking an equally long time to return. An anxious heaviness lodged deep in his gut. He withdrew to the empty, sagging wooden structure they called the "recreation room" and found a barely hanging-on treadmill where he could run as fast as his war-weary body and the fraying rubber track would allow. He ran until his muscular, respiratory, and cardiac systems were struggling, but here, and only here, pushed to the upper limits of endurance, was his mind finally able to still.

"Come on, little mermaid, get dried off. We're heading to get some chow," Fisher yelled into the shower stall from outside. Ray quickly toweled down and pulled on his clean army combat uniform. Getting a week's worth of grime off him felt good, but the prospect of hot food after a week of Uncle Sam's packaged, ready-to-eat meals—now that was something to look forward to.

They had finished eating and were decompressing, rehashing their mission, and verbally sparring while playing a long game of Spades. "Ship, you were like Rambo standing on the side of a mountain, returning fire with no helmet or body armor on." Fisher laid down a Jack of Hearts. "What the hell, man? What were you thinking?"

"I was thinking," Ray, sitting to the left of him, threw down a king of hearts, tilted back in his folding chair so that the two front legs were off the ground, and placed his clasped hands behind his head. "I was thinking, what a nice evening to sit on a boulder and read."

To Ray's left, O'Connor threw down two of spades. The soldiers collectively groaned while O'Connor grinned. "Good thing I was protecting your pretty, I'm going to sit and look at the beautiful sunset while reading a book, ass."

"You got that backward. I protected your lazy bottom," Ray replied. "I fired and fired until I ran out of ammo. Helmets and flak jackets are for the weak. Rambo, first blood, is my middle name. I can take on enemy fire with a gun in one hand, a book in the other while watching the sun go down."

The band of brothers burst out laughing. His seasoned fellow soldiers took Ray's grooved swagger in stride and didn't view it as empty bragging. The bravado was seen more as a statement of relaxed confidence and sustained courage, something each recognized and valued in each other, essential warrior skills honed to razor-sharp precision. Each one of the men seated at the table playing Spades had proven themselves, both inside and outside of the wire, time and time again. Their banter, a language born out of shared adversity and mutual experiences, encapsulated the harsh, harrowing, and sometimes exhilarating aspects of military service in a war zone. Peel back the layers of this repartee: strident raucousness, burlesque humor, pointed ridicule, edged bravado, cutting sarcasm, and you can see the true core: the suck is certain, but you are not in this alone.

It was after 2 a.m. when Ray's squad mates disbanded. The blackness of the night sky was absolute, rendering the celestial heavens spectacular. The Scorpio and Sagittarius region of the Milky Way shone forth with such rich brilliance that diffused star shadow splashed upon the ground.

"Hey, guys, I think I'll check if there's a free computer. Now that my mom has her own email account, she's relentless. I told her I'd jot a quick note when we returned from our mission." Ray stopped while the rest of his team continued forward. He lingered outside regarding the stars, smoking his second cigarette of the day, and listening until his comrades' laughter and voices were gone, swallowed by night.

Two soldiers, hunched behind the glowing light of computer screens, did not look up as Ray slid behind an empty terminal and logged on. Navigating the site took a long minute before he found what he was looking for. Sitting in his inbox, impatiently waiting, was an electronic message from May.

"Hey, I am glad you sent me your email. It is faster this way. Just got your letter, which took over four weeks to get here! What is up with that?! Anyway, when I wrote about getting back together, I had just gotten into a big fight with my boyfriend at The Crow's Nest. I thought we broke up. After a few more drinks back home, I thought of you and wrote that letter. But we got back together the next night and are still going strong. I guess you took me seriously. My bad.

Just like that, a thread pulling him back to a tentative world of normalcy was severed. A road he knew intuitively wasn't right for him, destroyed by a mini-improvised explosive device. Looking into his foreseeable future, he could see nothing but an empty gaping crater lined with uncertainty and loneliness.

Rationally, he should have seen this coming. Fool me once and all that. Who had he been kidding? Stupid man. Where did I go wrong? I tried to make her happy, to make us work, but that wasn't enough. I wasn't enough.

As bad as the Iraq and Afghanistan Groundhog Day experience had been, he internally reasoned, at least here on the battlefield, I know my role, my purpose, and I know how to be a good soldier.

With the weight of his new rejection, Ray could feel, in the throbbing of his jugular vein, the lub dub of his heart beating, telling him repeatedly: You suck, you suck, lub dub, lub dub, you suck.

Full Disclosure

Pastor Bert Shipworth's tightly controlled world was falling apart. He was experiencing a crisis of faith, which started with a missing sandwich and a missing wife.

"Maria? Where are you?" He hung his jacket on the hook by the door. The kitchen was quiet, with no signs of recent occupation. There was no note on the counter stating *Heading to the nursing home. Lunch is in the fridge.* He couldn't say why, but he was suddenly afraid. He opened the refrigerator and methodically assembled a sandwich. And in the small space of meal preparation, he sees a lucent autumnal afternoon of his junior year.

High school is letting out, and a swarm of buzzing students move around them. He reaches through the vibrations for Maria's hand. She has become as essential as air; he cannot imagine navigating a world without her. They walk together toward the periphery, and there, just on the other side of the school property line, is a spritely, well-dressed lady in a navy suit who introduces herself as Mrs. Robertson. She is handing out fliers promising salvation and eternal love. All one must do is regularly attend Sunday services and give yourselves to the Lord. Simple enough. How could one single action, on one single afternoon, alter an entire life? At that moment, the bridge he needed appeared, which offered him a way out of his current life. He pulled Maria with him, into a world that provided detailed road maps and lasting protection. Bert knew that first Sunday service as he sat on the unyielding wooden bench, listening to the impactful words of Pastor Goodwin, Maria by his side, that he had found his calling.

The kitchen door screeched open.

"Sorry. I'm running late." Her diminutive presence filled the room. Bert watched her closely, observing every detail. Maria dropped a cloth bag full of vegetables from the farmers' co-op on an empty chair, the one Ray used to sit in as a child and took over making lunch for her husband. Her round face was infused with color, and there was a brightness in her dark eyes. He has not seen this look on her face for a long time. A fracture breaks through his core, the first step onto a sheen-covered lake of ice that will not support his weight. What is going on? Have I been so busy obsessing about my parishioners, my son, and my daughter that I lost sight of the person who means the most to me? My wife. He sized her up; something was different; she was glowing. Was she having an affair?

He slumped heavily into his solid chair at the head of the table. "Where were you?"

She didn't look up as she sliced his sandwich in half and added a scoop of potato salad. "Running errands." She placed the plate before him. And there, in the intonation, in the way her eyes did not meet his, he knew. She might not be lying, but she is not fully disclosing the truth. He studied her intently, trying to find answers in her flushed but unreadable face. Though deeply etched lines splintered around her eyes and mouth, he still saw the fourteen-year-old girl he met all those years ago, quietly and complacently, seated next to him in their freshman life science class. After a quick invocation, he brought the food she prepared to his mouth, but the crust caught in his throat and was impossible to swallow.

****

He knows. Why did she think she could hide anything from her husband? They have been traveling by each other's side since their first year in high school. As Maria sat opposite him and tried to drink her peppermint tea, the lightness she had carried into the door minutes ago dissipated, borne away on the steam of her cooling mug. What she felt now was a sense of disquietude. What was she going to do? Should she remain faithful to the will and calling of her husband, but that meant turning her back on her son? She would have to renounce him, and severing the cord of maternal pull was something she was no longer willing to do.

The taut silence was palpable, almost unbearable. So seldom did Bert remain quiet when there was something to say. Maria stood and took his half-eaten lunch plate to the sink. As she scrubbed clean the remnants, she scanned the backyard. The empty swings on a thin metal structure swayed, pushed by an unrelenting Oklahoma wind. She imagined the swings and barren spaces filled with laughing children, the two she was blessed enough to raise, and the sacred others she conceived but had never been allowed to carry to term.

All Maria wanted for most of her young life was to be a mother, to give her children everything that had been missing in her childhood. Having a new husband who shared the same vision felt wonderful. They planned, they dreamed, and with the youthful assurance of couples starting in life that everything would manifest exactly as they wanted, they tried to conceive.

Melancholy filled her. She put the last dish in the drying rack and turned. "Bert, do you remember when…"

He was no longer seated in his chair at the head of the table; the kitchen was still. She left to find him, running her hands over her soft stomach, feeling the sponge of flesh that had willingly accommodated her two children. She padded down the hall, remembering how a series of early-term miscarriages scattered over the first decade of their union left her despondent. Trying to make sense of what was happening through a lens of faith became increasingly difficult. She believed her body was failing because she was being punished for everything she had done wrong in life. But the duties of being a pastor's wife did not let her linger in the shallows of despair for long. And over time, the congregation became her extended family, and their children became her children. She turned her yearnings to a higher power and accepted 'His will.' Yet every day, for fifteen years, she prayed for biological offspring.

The door to Bert's study was open, but he was not seated behind his desk. Children were a plea she made every morning when she rose, and a supplication offered every night before she closed her eyes. When Maria approached forty, the longing had become a distant dream, faint remembrances of a young girl she no longer recognized. She had never been regular, and now the change of life was coming early. She was resigned. With the altering hormone levels, she gained weight. Mrs. Robertson, the choir director, became concerned when she saw Maria nodding off during the service, something she had never done before. Maria smiled inwardly with the memory as she adjusted the pillows on the living room couch and headed upstairs. Maria had argued with her, but Mrs. Robertson insisted. She made an appointment for Maria with her general practitioner, who examined her and announced that she had a low iron count, which explained the fatigue, her blood pressure was elevated, and, oh, by the way, she was approximately six months pregnant, with what he thought might be twins. He could palpate two distinct heads and spines through her uterine wall. An ultrasound confirmed his suspicions. Her children were finally acknowledged, deferred, prayers. Twins, Hope and Ray.

"There you are." Maria found her husband in Ray's childhood bedroom, rummaging through his closet. Frowning, he pulled out a nylon gym bag with a fiercely growling tiger on the side, the one his son had used for his high school track and cross-country meets. He strode to the hall closet and took out a spare tube of toothpaste, a towel, and a facecloth.

"I'm going to ask you again. Where were you, Maria?"

Since Ray left for boot camp, Bert had forbidden any talk of their only son. She stood before him. In her eyes was an appeal. Please don't make me answer that question. Please do not make me choose. Why can't I be both? A good mother and a good wife? The deception weighed heavily on her conscience. But ever since Hope helped Maria set up an electronic mailbox that was entirely hers, not jointly shared with her husband, or affiliated with the church, the freedom to be in touch with her son gave her new life. She had joined the Family and Friends support group for Ray's company. They banded together, faceless, yet now familiar names, keeping each other afloat. They kept her apprised of the general mission, the progress, the promotions, little victories, and consuming sorrows.

Snail mail worked too, and those letters, the ones that arrived at Hope and Gabrielle's home, she brought back and kept hidden. She took them out and reread every word when her husband was away, storing the substance deep in her being, secreting food for when there would be drought. She now assisted in fundraising, assembling, and mailing care packages. She could control this. Helping was the only way to support her son and the men he served with. Maria took a deep breath, exhaled, and looked toward her husband. "I already answered that question once. I was running errands."

Disappointment, not anger, clouded his face and, in some ways, was worse. Maria had seen that look directed at her children and congregation members, but never, in all their years together, had the stare been concentrated solely on her.

"All right then." He inhaled and pulled his slumped shoulders upright. "Well, I need time to work everything out." Bert grabbed a few more items from the bedroom, zipped up the bag, headed down the stairs and out the door.

Maria extricated Ray's rubber-banded stack of letters from under the baseboard, and from the living room window, she watched Bert drive away. Her son and husband, alone and apart, were each involved in battles she did not understand, and she feared for them both.

Estar roto

(To be Broken)

For the first time in its history, since Pastor Bert Shipworth began his ministerial service with his nascent congregation, the doors to the white clapboard church were bolted shut. He locked himself inside. Forsaking all food, only drinking water when parched, praying for guidance, devouring the Bible for clues, and kneeling on a bed of rice until the small grains became deeply embedded in his flesh. He focused on the agony of the rice pellets lodging in his skin and the pain of his widening hunger. Then he forced himself to let go, to rise above human experience, beyond suffering. Decades upon decades of a carefully structured belief system were being challenged, and to his alarm, the beams were falling all around him. He was desperately seeking answers, within and without.

****

Maria moved through the house, turning off the lights in preparation for bed. Earlier, she had dutifully prepared dinner. When Bert did not show, she put his meal in the oven, warming, waiting. As the hours passed, the food wilted. Her husband had yet to return. She knew where he was, of course. He always retreated there when he needed to think. But he never missed a meal without letting her know he would be late, and he had never stayed away this long. Tonight would be the first time since their marriage, shortly after graduating from high school, right before Bert started his Biblical seminary courses, that he would not be on the other side of their marital bed. His expansive body and his intense energy consumed the space around him. Now, with him gone, the displaced atmosphere closed in. Around her, found in the light dust on the knickknacks and coffee table, gathered in the folds of the cumbersome curtains, lying in the thick piled weave of carpet, were remembrances of their life together. There was a slight torsion in her gut, a pervading sense that something was missing–her husband, her son. She searched the empty home for that which could not be found.

As she waited for the tea kettle to scream, she recognized the same feeling she carried throughout her childhood as an invisible, powerless little girl.

Enough, she thought. Fortified by her commitment to the military support group, tired of feeling helpless, Maria turned off the kettle and did something unthinkable. An act she knew would cause her husband consternation, one he would see as interfering and disrespectful, but he wasn't around, was he? She picked up the landline and called Bert's mentor, the minister who changed the course of his life. She got a machine instead.

"Pastor Goodwin, this is Maria Shipworth. You told us that if we ever needed anything, to call. Your congregation is in Texas now, and the drive is long. I know you have so many other obligations, but I'm desperate. Bert needs your help. So do I. If possible, could you come?" She hung up and turned the kettle back on.

The Circle of Willis

During freshman year in their natural science class, the teacher assigned Bert as her year-long lab partner. Maria surveyed all her other classmates, the countless possibilities, and thought, how did I get stuck with this scrawny boy wearing high-water jeans and a T-shirt with stains underneath the arms? He had the dank, musty smell of furniture stored away from sunlight, stuffed into a moldy basement for decades, the smell of disuse. His eyes were nervous, mistrustful, and darting.

After extinguishing the first-floor lights, Maria climbed the carpeted stairs. Her sleepy-time tea warming her hands, her footsteps heavy. In high school, they both were outcasts, loners of sorts. She knew he was probably thinking the same thing when he looked at her for the first time. How did I get stuck with that? Through his eyes, he probably saw a reclusive, plump, nondescript adolescent girl who never had a professional haircut, whose current style looked as though a madman had taken a pair of pruning shears, closed his eyes, and haphazardly carved away. In desperation, wanting a new look for high school, Maria had cut her curly locks, chopping them shorter and shorter, trying to even everything out until she had run out of raw material. He would also see a girl whose eyes reflected a lifetime of learned timidity. Thus, sitting next to him on that first day, she resolved not to write him off the way she had been her entire life. She knew how being dismissed felt. Maria started their partnership with essential human consideration, asking questions, listening, and then thoughtfully responding. Her lab partner had done the same.

Maria stepped out of her everyday clothes, put them in the laundry basket, and slipped on her white flannel nightgown, the worn cotton touching her skin, as familiar as his hands. She curled on the chair by the window and drank her tea; the curtains drawn against the dark. When did that subtle shift in their relationship happen? Maybe when she realized how turbulent his home life was, how the only peace he had was at school, within an institution's solid, uncaring walls. As she smoothed the fabric over her pulled-up knees, she remembered how, over that first year, as they read lessons and did the corresponding lab work together, Maria learned about her partner. He'd grown up with a father who, when he drank, became abusive. His alcohol-fueled temper was explosive, and no one in the household was immune. If you were in his way, watch out. Bert had spent most of his childhood hidden. His older brother Gus had taken the brunt. But he was gone; his number had come up. He was drafted and serving in Vietnam.

Maria could hear Bert's voice, rising from a chest racked with grief. "I never realized how much he held us together." She could see her husband as a teenager, silent tears running down his face, their course altered by puckered pockets scarred from his struggles with acne. He kicked his legs back and forth over the railroad bridge they were sitting on, the sun making a rapid descent. She scooted closer to him, their sides touching, looking at him while he stared into the deep ravine. "My brother took the heat from us, Mom and me. Whenever Dad was drinking and railing, Gus would appear and make some kind of smart-mouthed remark, which redirected Dad's anger. Then, I just thought he was stupid, but I can now see what he was doing."

The Circle of Willis

Maria reached over and wiped a tear away. He no longer flinched when she touched him. He looked at her, his small eyes full of deep sadness. "But I can't do that for my mother. I can't stand up to him as my brother did. When I hear him losing control, I find a way to disappear, to act like I never heard what was going on. What's wrong with me? Why am I such a coward?" He took both her hands in his and promised, "I will not let them take me away from you. I can't let you down too." And so, he began to eat.

Bert ate out of the pain from his childhood, out of fear of an unknown, unpredictable future. Food provided reliable comfort. He also ate, knowing on one level that if he were grossly overweight and developed diabetes due to his girth, he would be disqualified from the draft when he became of age to register, should his number be drawn.

In the bathroom, Maria rinsed out her tea mug, then brushed her teeth. The sink beside hers, where he usually stood and scrubbed his mouth with such ferocity, remained unblemished. The scrubbed porcelain gleamed, though she could sense him there, looking at her and smiling as he did every night of their marriage. The paste lathered around his mouth. His smile said everything; we survived another day together.

Maria pulled back the multi-colored, cross-patterned quilt and slid into their shared berth contemplating the hesitant way they started their journey. There was never an electric type of attraction the way you read about in books or saw in movies. There were no sparks or juiced hormones. They were merely a product of assignment, of necessity, of survival. As their worlds grew increasingly volatile and unreliable, leaving them isolated in a widening sea, clinging to each other became a last resort, a way of staying afloat in the currents that threatened to pull them under. Over the years, even when life got more manageable, they had not let go. Our desperate adherence might have been our only way out then but look at what our union has wrought. Her mind brought into sharp focus the images of her loved ones, Ray, Hope, Gabrielle, and Bert. Maria closed her eyes, and she prayed. Petitions for her children, parishioners in need, and finally, her husband, who was in deep metaphysical pain. Be with him, please, she offered into the closed-in night, *mi marido esta roto*, and pulled the covers over her head.

****

Bert was in the throes of a spiritual crisis. He had sequestered himself in the sanctuary for four days and nights when memory-laced visions began to appear. His older brother Gus' face resembled his son Ray's. So much that, at times looking at him was painful. Now Gus was holding him at arm's length. "You can do this, bud. You got to be the strong one for Mom now. Being drafted sucks, but that's how it goes. My tour will be over before you know it. Hang in there and keep the family together." Bert was fourteen years old. "No, No, you can't go, Gus!" he cried into the darkness, tears stinging the corner of his eyes, and his brother's face faded. Bert knew how this was going to end. He wanted to stop the reel and leave before the movie finished. He would have done anything in his power to alter the course of events, but he couldn't. The past paralyzed him.

The Circle of Willis

The summer before Bert's senior year of school started, Gus returned from the war as a soul rearranged. His shell looked roughly the same, but that was all. The light in his eyes vanquished. Bert watched in slow-motion horror as a spiral of destruction took over. Within six months, Gus was dead.

Bert didn't sleep or eat; days passed, and the fervor consumed him, an aggressive cancer ravaging his belief system. He kneeled, prayed, read, chastised, and flogged himself. He stood before the cross, suspended by wire over the dais. He bellowed into the blackness, his voice filling the rafters. "I'm sorry, Gus, I let you down. I wasn't what I was supposed to be. I was weak when I should have been strong and a coward when I should have been brave. If I knew then what I know now, I would have been able to save you, to steer you into a field where you would have been safe. But now, what am I going to do? Everything is falling apart. I lost you, and I'm losing my family. My son is at war—I couldn't stop him. What if he dies overseas? What if he doesn't, and the experience crushes him the way it did you? And there is my daughter, my wife. I cannot—"

"Stop. Bertrand Shipworth, get a hold of yourself."

He must be experiencing an auditory hallucination. The voice was no longer that of his brother. The cadence was of his mentor, someone he looked up to and deeply respected, whose advice he had repeatedly sought over the years, Pastor Goodwin. The voice was calm and clear; the words flowed over him. Pastor Shipworth stilled his monologue and listened. "Tell me," the voice continued, "what are your truths?"

Bert opened his swollen orbs. The night was everlasting; when was the last time he saw the light? A shadow moved in the corner of the sanctuary. There was his advisor and friend, the flesh and blood version, who was let into the building's side kitchen door with a key from the head of the cooking committee, Maria. On day five of Bert's fasting journey of penance, Pastor Goodwin arrived. He eased a bewildered Bert into a pew. And with his finger-worn, dog-eared Bible on his lap, he probingly asked the question again. This was the nature of their relationship. "Bert, tell me your conflicts. What do you see before your eyes?"

Bert gathered his thoughts and spoke. "I see an insolent son whose defiance led him into a world of violence, one who blatantly disregarded me and the Word. I see a conniving, disobedient wife, ignoring her responsibility to support me, one who is so ashamed of her activities that she conceals her actions. She is incapable of telling me the truth. I see a wandering, wayward daughter, allowing herself to be distracted and pulled off the path of righteousness."

Inner torment rapidly filled the pit of hunger in his stomach and the blood in his veins. Why was this happening to him? Hadn't he been an obedient and long-suffering servant? Pastor Goodwin gave him the space of experience, allowed him to dwell there momentarily but then steadily led him back. Bert knew Pastor Goodwin could not provide the answers he sought. That was not his role; he could only guide someone experiencing internal conflict to a place where self-analysis and extended mindfulness are critical to finding solutions, a deepening drawn from despair. As Pastor Goodwin began to speak, Bert struggled. He forced himself to quiet the fury, then to let go like the agony from the rice needles driven into his knees. You have to be able to receive that for which you are asking. Listen to his words; he has never let you down before.

Pastor Goodwin was patient, and he was kind. "What you have just described, what you see, is based on fixed doctrine and ego. Did you hear that, Bert? Ego. I want you to close your eyes and let go of your self-pride, open your heart, tap deeply into that source, and let the power fill you. After intense reflection and introspection, expose your heart's vision, speak your truths, and tell me what you see. Then you shall have the answers you seek."

Pastor Goodwin spent the next hour going over sections in the Bible that Bert could turn to for thoughtful deliberation. He led him in prayer, then as silently as he arrived, he slipped back into shadow, leaving his protégé alone. Bert fell to his knees in the silent chapel, and underneath the suspended cross, he let the dagger of darkness and doubt break him open.

There is a tenant hard and fast which you have been taught, which you firmly believe to be true, then there is evolving evidence before your eyes, exposed by expanding awareness, a higher consciousness, and backed by a clear, prayerful understanding of Biblical teaching. And on the sixth day of his soul-searching journey, Pastor Shipworth emerged from the locked chapel doors. His body was slick with porous weeping. Dried and fresh blood alike soaked the knees of his khaki pants. His clothes hung a little more loosely on his still sizeable girth. And if you could peel back the disheveled exterior, you would see a flicker of a reenergized light burning within. He flung open wide the doors to his church with an expansive smile, welcoming his wife and waiting parishioners, and standing on a pulpit of burnished wood, he gave a sermon unlike any they had ever heard.

Under the Cyprus Tree

Saint Patrick's Day, 2010

"Sister, you look like a tall drink of sweet tea." Ronnie shrugged off her green jacket and slid onto a barstool across the high-top from Leo. She gave a low whistle. "He let you out in that?"

Leo laughed uncomfortably, tugging at the hem of her tight skirt as if she could stretch the fabric further down her stockinged legs. Her gaze automatically went to Jake, who was about to break in a round of eight balls. On the corner of the pool table were two twenty-dollar bills. Nothing good ever happened when Jake drank and gambled. A shudder ran through her.

"Believe it or not, he insisted I wear this. He said he wanted me to distract his opponents." A waitress placed a cocktail before Leo, saying the drink was compliments of a mystery admirer. "Now, I think that probably wasn't such a good idea." She pushed the umbrellaed glass toward Ronnie, wearily shrugged her shoulders, and took a sip of her Sprite.

From across the room, a run of whistles pierced the saloon's boisterous chatter, serrated staccato barbs, which created an instant, fearful response in Leo. She knew the signal. Her head snapped up, and she looked in Jake's direction. His needle-pointed eyes focused on her. With a slight uptick of his nose, Leo knew what she had to do. Jake was calling her to him.

"Be back in a second." Leo scooted gracefully off her stool, weaving between tables and patrons, toward the cluster of pocketed billiard tables.

Ronnie jumped down and followed. "I'm tagging along."

Jake, his hair slicked back into a ponytail, thrust his cue in front of Leo. There was a sheen of sweat on his forehead.

"Sugar, I need your lucky touch." All eyes were on her, and she waited. "Kiss the tip, baby. Run your hands down the length." Leo did as instructed, and the crowd around the table hooted and whistled. Behind her, a stranger's calloused hand ran over her backside as Jake successfully banked his last four balls, winning the game. She stood still, not turning to confront the violation, knowing this would somehow be her fault if she acknowledged what had just happened. Enduring those consequences would be worse. Saying something might also cause Jake to "become distracted" to start a losing streak; that too would be her failing. At that moment, pretending nothing transpired was better. Once Jake regained his mojo and had taken two successive games, he dismissed her with a wave of his stick.

"How do you stand that?" Ronnie took a sip of another drink, a chilled flute of champagne, the mystery man had sent to Leo's table. Her voice was not accusing, not judgmental, only gently inquisitive. "Leo, you are like a trusting golden retriever, loyal to a fault."

Leo shrugged. She had started the night with guarded hope. They hadn't spent an evening out in a long time. And usually, those times disintegrated. Why did I think tonight would go differently? Maybe because he'd been playful when they were getting ready. "Don't wear those baggy, ratty old jeans out. I want people to see how sexy you are and know what a hot wife I have." He rummaged through her drawers and came up with a short skirt she had bought with Ronnie's encouragement when they were thrift store shopping. "Wear this," he insisted. He dismissed Leo's hesitations. "I want to show you off, and I'll be there to protect you. No one will mess with you." As they entered the bar together, he gave her a long kiss. "See you around. I'm fixin' to win us some party money."

"Earth to Leo," Ronnie touched her friend's wrist. "I asked, has he ever hit you?"

"Oh, goodness, no. Jake's not abusive." Leo looked startled by the question, but she couldn't meet Ronnie's perceptive scrutiny. She looked down instead, intently focused on an empty glass.

"How he's treating you is a form of abuse, Leo. It's not healthy, and it's not right. He may never lay a hand on you, but a life of verbal assault, belittling, and humiliating put-downs is a form of psychological control, a type of abusive behavior. That man could chew up nails and spit out a barbed wire fence, believe me. I've seen this kind of thing before. Anger and rage bottle up inside them until they explode out of control, and the person they've used as their verbal whipping board becomes their literal punching bag."

"It's not that bad," Leo tried to convince Ronnie. "Really. Most of the time, he leaves me alone. Then I go and do something stupid to set him off." The expression on Ronnie's face indicated she wasn't buying it. "Like yesterday, I went and bought the wrong kind of deli meat to pack in his lunch. Don't know what I was thinking. I know what he likes. He threw out the sandwiches, came home from work hungry and all pissed. My fault."

"Stop defending that snake in the grass." Ronnie sounded exasperated. "For someone as bright as you are, I can see that no amount of talking will change things." She waited until Leo met her gaze. "Okay, before we change topics, promise me this." Leo nodded. "If ever, I mean ever, he slaps you, hits you, pushes you down, or even comes close to doing those things, you will leave immediately, and get help. Trust me, that tiger will never change his stripes."

The waitress put a third drink before Leo. "The mystery donor wants to be revealed. All the drinks are courtesy of the guy sitting at the bar, the one with the white cowboy hat, the handsome one."

Leo reflexively looked up. The seated man rose and took his hat off, tipping the fedora into the air, a limp white flag resuscitated by the promise of a breeze. Leo didn't acknowledge his presence; she knew better, even if Jake wasn't watching. She slid the mug of green beer across the table in front of her friend.

Ronnie giggled, her throaty voice amused. "What are you trying to do? Get a girl drunk?"

Leo laughed, joining her for the first time that night, allowing her guard to fall. How could Leo explain how much this friendship meant? Even after she earned her GED, Leo did not stop going to Ronnie's before her shift at the convenience store. Sometimes Ronnie and her daughter would be out running errands, and Leo would curl in a chair to read. Or she would wander around the comforting space doing a few tasks to help Ronnie out, wash the dishes, sweep, and pick up scattered objects. But most often, Ronnie and Leo would sit at the table together or on the floor playing with Maya, with cups of coffee, talking.

One sunny afternoon, they had been on a quilt under the bald cypress tree on the stretch of green behind Ronnie's apartment. Leo gazed upward into the tall, pyramidal-shaped seedling, at feather-like leaves stroking a pale sky. Ronnie was thoughtful, sitting cross-legged and watching her daughter wander around the perimeter. She probed her friend. "Okay, what's next?" Leo looked at her questioningly. "I mean, Leo Rose Lightfoot, what is your deepest desire? If you could be anything, achieve anything, what would you do?"

No one had ever asked her this before. Leo flipped onto her stomach. Through the cotton and batting, she felt the texture of earth and stone underneath her and opened herself to possibility as she watched Maya toddle toward her. Her chubby thighs were remarkably sturdy, and her sweet smile belied an unflappable disposition. She moved toward Leo with steady expectation. This little life form believed that all before her was worthy, solid, and true.

As Maya stood before Leo, her favorite book of the week, "Fletcher and the Falling Leaves", in one hand, and a much loved, often washed, and repaired second-hand stuffed puppy dangling by the ear in her other hand, Leo knew with certainty two things. One, that her childhood, though unconventional, had been good. Her constants had never wavered and had weaved a tightly knit foundation, one she could still count on, that still existed, even though she was an adult, living another life. The second flash of insight came with such suddenness she understood the knowledge had always been there, beneath the surface, waiting for recognition. She just needed help accessing the content.

Leo leaped to her feet, swept Maya into her arms, and turned around and around. The child's laughter spun around her, delicate honeyed cotton candy strands of happiness. And though all was in motion, Leo had never felt more centered.

She explained to Ronnie, almost embarrassed, that her dream future would be to open a no-kill shelter for abandoned dogs and, yes, she supposed, even cats. To nurse them back to health, to help them find safe, sustaining forever homes. And for the animals deemed disposable, unadoptable, she would provide a protected haven, a place where they could live free from cruelty, ensuring their basic needs would be met. Over the following weeks, Ronnie helped Leo devise a long-term plan of how this could happen. She helped Leo with her research, formulating plan A, then contingency plans B and C, because "Just when you are sure of the road in front of you, a bridge will be out." Ronnie provided support at each juncture. "Baby steps, baby girl, that's what you gotta do." And when doubt crept in, when Leo started accepting what Jake told her and wanted to stop believing and stop dreaming, Ronnie refused to allow her to self-sabotage, to conclude her goal wasn't possible.

"You start by taking the prerequisite classes to get into an accredited veterinary technician program. Then once you are done with that, you move on. A step at a time, nothing overwhelming. You have a lifetime ahead of you, and before you know it, you'll be a full-fledged veterinarian, or if you find yourself on option C or even D, you'll be a tech working with a vet with your same vision. You've got this, girl."

An unfamiliar male voice broke her reverie. "What are you? Stuck up higher than a light pole? Too good to taste the drinks I've been buying you?" The white-hatted cowboy, who Ronnie pointed out earlier was not good-looking at all, forcefully put another drink in front of Leo, this time a shot of whiskey. The contents sloshed but didn't spill.

"No, not at all." Leo's voice was hesitant. She looked at him with a forced smile. "It's just that I don't drink."

He looked incredulous. "Then why in the hell are you at a bar, wearing almost nothing, egging guys on?"

"Who licked the red off your candy?" Ronnie calmly interjected as if trying to dial the stranger's aggression down a notch. She smiled at him as she raised the shot to her mouth. "I've enjoyed every drink. Thank you very much, generous sir."

"They weren't meant for you!" He grabbed the glass out of Ronnie's hand, this time the golden liquid spilled, and shoved it toward Leo. "Drink! Now! I bought this for you. I've been watching you, and I like what I see. Me-n-you is gonna mix."

The next thing Leo knew, Jake was jamming a cue stick into the guy's chest, shoving him back."Get the fuck off. She's mine."

"Oh yeah?" White hat grinned. "Where you been all night, then? She's been eyeing me, encouraging me, dressed in a skirt so tight you can see her religion. If she's yours, then you got yourself a whore."

With that, Jake lifted the cue and brought the stick

crashing down on the white hat's head. The pristine Stetson folded, a trickle of blood following the course of gravity, reached the corner of the man's mouth. "You mother fuc—" Before he could finish, a handful of liquored-up bodies, itching for unchained anarchy, joined in the altercation.

Alcohol, the great liberator, peeled back the layers of conscious control, a bandage ripped off a festering wound, exposing a seething core. Mean-spirited, chemically unbalanced protoplasm, relishing in the opportunity to harm, erupted. Leo and Ronnie ducked under their high top, back-to-back, their knees hugged to their chests. They remained motionless when all around them chaos exploded. In the commotion, Leo surmised that the forms were no longer sure who they were beating or why. The free-for-all continued. Drinks were thrown. Glass shattered, and chairs smashed against tabletops. Cue sticks became weapons, and one innovative patron stuffed a pool ball in his sock and started swinging the contraption like a club. Minutes later, when the police showed up wading heavy and hard into the fray with batons, tasers, and pepper spray, and someone yelled "*COPS,*" the patrons acted as if a bomb had detonated. Everyone flew, frantically dispersing in all directions, climbing over each other, tables, and bar tops, running mad with no goal but to get away.

****

"Are you sure you're going to be okay? You can crash at my place for the rest of the night and sort everything out in the morning." Ronnie turned off the engine and shut off the truck's lights.

Leo tried to appear braver than she felt. "It's all

good. He's probably already passed out." She paused, then said, "If I'm lucky, he got arrested." She felt a little guilty wishing that upon Jake, but all she wanted for the rest of this night was a quiet space to curl. After the police appeared, Ronnie and Leo left, unseen, out of the back exit. Leo had driven them back to Ronnie's place, where she exchanged her snug skirt for a pair of Ronnie's roomy sweatpants. Maya spent the night next door on the neighbor's couch, so they didn't have to worry about waking her up. They drank coffee, rehashed the evening, talked, and laughed until Ronnie felt sober enough to drive Leo home.

The door was unlocked. As she gently closed it behind her, Leo let out a low breath. She quietly turned the deadbolt and headed toward the sofa. She would sleep there, and they could work things out in the morning when he woke sober. Her head pounded, a pressuring pulse of tension. She debated going to the bathroom for some aspirin but decided not to. The entrance was too close to Jake.

She bent to grab a fleece blanket off the floor when she heard the words, "You fucking whore." Shoved from behind, she fell, her head hitting the wall. "Where the hell have you been? And where are your clothes? Whose pants are those?" He grabbed them, pulling them off her thin waist. "Who are you screwing?" His fist slammed into the drywall right above her head, and particles of silica dust rained around her. His breath reeked of whiskey. Leo knew she had made a mistake—the drinking had not stopped at the bar, and he had not passed out.

Leo's heart pounded as she desperately tried to make herself as small as possible, just like a frightened opossum that encountered an out-of-control predator and was trying to play dead. She felt Jake's unwashed strands brush her body as he leaned over and furiously punched the floor around her.

"Next time, won't just be the wall that gets it. You're just like my momma. Dad walked out on her because she didn't do anything right. And I left the backbiter because of all her damn rules. Looks like history come back on itself with me marrying you. And that necklace I gave you, news flash—momma didn't give it to me. I stole the thing from the witch on my way out. What a pathetic wife you are! Ain't worth a lick. You just don't understand. Pigs were there, rounding people up like cattle. I managed to escape. Shit, I'm already on probation, you bitch." This was news to Leo, but she stayed motionless. "That would have been bad! Not going back there, ever! Dammit, Leo, this is all your fault, you slut. If you hadn't gone out practically naked, none of this woulda happened." The banging stopped. As if spent, he stood, pulled a fifth from his back pocket, took a long draw, and half-heartedly kicked Leo's still body.

Leo waited twenty interminable minutes after she was sure he passed out, until his breathing was uniform and slowed, and he hadn't moved for a long time. Though he might stay this way for hours, he could also wake at any moment. Moving swiftly, with silent stealth, she grabbed her cell and charger, stuffed her backpack with toiletries and clothing essentials, and grabbed the key to unlock her bike. She pushed the bottom of the sweats up over her knees so the fabric wouldn't get caught in the spokes, making a note to herself that she needed to return them or buy Ronnie a new pair. She hung the evil eye necklace on the doorknob before exiting the apartment where she had lived for the past two years.

Though she did not look back, she could see him still, fetid fumes rising from his form, lying silently in the darkness, lying in wait.

Tract Six:

Spring-Summer 2010
Gone Girl

A slice of increscent coral stretched across the eastern horizon as Leo cycled toward her childhood home. Before her, she saw the unmistakable flight of a scissortail flycatcher, his incredibly long forked tail flaring wide behind him, a ballasting sail, as he performed his ariel acrobatic maneuvers, all in the pursuit of a bug. She witnessed a sudden flash of the salmon pink flank as he dove straight down, snatching an insect out of midair. Then he darted upward toward a teacup nest perched atop a telephone pole. Moments later, his mate appeared, her dark gray wings flapping as she dropped her catch into an open mouth, a joint effort to feed their young.

With each mile, the tension of the night dissipated. Her body, though thoroughly exhausted, felt strong and alive. Leo knew extrication from her marriage and the life she had structured with Jake would not be easy. Not listening to the inner narrative that accompanied her for most of her life, a belief she was not enough, would be difficult. If she gave in to this, Jake might be able to pull her back. But over the past two years, she had gained confidence in her abilities to navigate difficult situations, and, thanks to Ronnie, she had a plan. If she focused on this and remained resolute in her decision, she had to believe that becoming a veterinarian was possible. Tulsa receded, buildings and structures fell away, and the Oklahoma sky widened and stretched until Leo felt like she could see more of the stratosphere than the earth.

The sound of an approaching truck is unmistakable. Leo braced for the rush of displaced air as this one passed. Then she heard the semi decelerating.

"For goodness' sake," Leo mumbled, "please, leave me alone." Her reserves were depleted. The semi drove slowly past her. She kept pedaling, her eyes straight ahead. She breathed a sigh of relief when he passed, then she saw the turn signal. The truck pulled onto the shoulder, barricading her pathway. She braked, her body taut.

A medium-height, stocky form emerged from the cab into the morning light. Was the rising sun playing tricks on her, luring her into thinking she knew this person? "Uncle Paul?" Acknowledgment kicked in, and in one fluid motion, Leo leaped from her bike, launching herself into her uncle's strong arms.

"Kiddo! I thought that was you! Then I thought, what is my niece doing out here riding like a bat outta hell? But no one else on God's green earth has a pink camo helmet and backpack like you." Even as he talked, he was unhinging the back, throwing her bike and pack into the trailer.

Leo jumped into the passenger side of the cab, relieved. "This isn't your usual truck. I didn't recognize it. You kind of scared me."

"Sorry to give you a start." He reached over and

quickly patted her knee. Before he signaled, he looked at his side mirrors and accelerated back onto the causeway. "A fellow trucker's wife had an event." He turned off the radio. "Not sure what that means, but she's in the hospital, and he couldn't leave his kids alone. I don't have a run until the weekend, so I volunteered–an unexpected business trip."

Leo smiled at their family's inside joke. Ever since her Uncle Paul switched from construction work to truck driving, he called his forays business trips. They agreed. A little glamor in the Lightfoot household couldn't hurt; this sounded more intriguing. Leo sighed and eased into the worn vinyl seat. "I'm just glad it's you. Now I don't have to cycle all the way home. It's a win-win."

"Uncle Paul?"

He glanced expectantly at her and nodded as if he knew there was more to the "I'm done" explanation she gave twenty miles ago.

"What's on your mind?"

"Don't you know these things are on the way out?" Leo picked up his 35 mm camera, the one he always kept with him. "Cellphone cameras are going to make this old guy obsolete." She grinned playfully.

He laughed out loud, the full belly laugh she had grown to love over the years. "Old dinosaurs tend to stick together." He paused, his voice still upbeat. "What's the plan, Leo? Things have changed at home since you left."

"You and Dad don't have to worry. I'm not moving back in." She pushed back a strand of hair over one ear. "I have to learn how to be on my own. It's time. I went from you and Dad to Jake. This is something I must figure out." Leo took in the passing landscape, shifting familiar scenes that her body responded to on a cellular level. "There are a few places in town that are always hiring, finding a job won't be hard. I've been taking some community college courses that will transfer and I'm going to enroll at Northeastern." She didn't tell him that she was already implementing 'Plan B.' She murmured, "Finding a place to stay shouldn't be too hard."

They dropped the semi off and started the mile walk home, Leo pushing her bike, Uncle Paul wearing her pink camouflage backpack.

****

The changes registered in succession, a deck of cards being rapidly shuffled. Over two years had passed since she hastily fled and since she'd seen her childhood home. The clapboard no longer peeled. The siding was sanded and painted a robin's egg blue. The white pebble walkway was weed-free and edged. There were perennial flowers in the bed. On the front porch was a large terracotta pot with purple fountain grass, verbena, and white watermelon geraniums. Annuals in the entryway?

"What's going on?" Leo leaned her bike against the knotted black walnut tree and started to walk toward the front door. "What have you and Dad done with the house I grew up in?"

Through the front picture window, there was movement. Leo first saw her father. He was seated at the table reading the newspaper. Some things haven't changed. Leo exhaled. As she opened the screen door, she saw a woman come up behind her dad and wrap her arms around him, he leaned his head back, and they kissed, not a peck, but something longer and more sensually substantial. For a fleeting instant, Leo thought, is this my mother? Has she returned? Leo's pulse quickened, too late to stop; the opening door startled them both, and they pulled apart.

Dr. Jennifer Baker smiled warmly, her gray eyes pleading as she put her hands up apologetically. "You fired me, remember?"

Leo, with self-deprecating humor, responded, "Well, this isn't awkward at all."

"Leotie!" In one swift motion, her father pushed back his chair and pulled her into his arms. She buried her face in the folds of his flannel shirt. He smelled like her childhood, musky cedar wrapped in vanilla cinnamon, with a citrus orange edge. There she dissolved. As if through osmosis, Leo felt him draw in her pain; the parts that enabled her to survive over the past few years, conformity to rigid expectation, constant vigilance, and submissive fear, were laid bare and began to liquefy. There was no need for words. He held on until she drew away.

****

Leo observed and learned during the unfolding day as they worked together, putting in a deck behind the small house that overlooked the Tahlequah River. Her dad started coaching again once Leo assured him she was doing all right and was married. Joseph and Jennifer began dating a few months after that. Jennifer said she struggled at first. Was going out with him ethical? But she rationalized she'd been "let go" by Leo, her client, and her father pointed out that he had also been terminated from his position as a dad. So really, he said with a wink, "There was no conflict of interest."

Leo replied that a heads-up might have been nice, and her dad agreed. "I tried a couple of times when I visited you in Tulsa. But telling you never felt right. Seemed like you already had too much going on, and I didn't want to pile on." She accepted this explanation now. Her father was lighter somehow. This relationship had changed him. Leo wondered if he ever had this kind of connection with her mother. Really, she mused, how could two eighteen-year-old adolescents navigate parenting, let alone a meaningful partnership? She remembered how she felt at nineteen, a year into her marriage with Jake, which seemed a lifetime ago already. The fact her parents even made the arrangement work for three years was a wonder.

Late afternoon was slowly shrugging off her cloak of light, reluctantly yielding to dusk's plum-infused oranges. Leo's father and Uncle Paul put the final touches on the deck. Jennifer went into town to get carryout food when Leo turned her attention to Sandy's and then Emily's memorial stone. She pulled weeds that had sprouted around the base, fetched some soapy water, and used an old toothbrush to reach the dirt that had settled into the etched letters and numbers. *How could I not have noticed there was only a birth date on my mother's stone? How could I have been so dumb?*

During her self-castigation, a shadow appeared, covering the rock. Leo looked up, toothbrush in hand. Uncle Paul, camera around his neck, stood still. "When ready, I'll take you to see her." His eyes were gentle, but there was no smile on his face. The words moved through her, a seismic wave.

She had to fight to keep her voice steady. "You

know where she is? You and Dad have known all along?"

There was a moment of hesitation as if he wasn't sure he should continue. "We fought to protect you, to shield you from harsh truths. But our strategy backfired and propelled you into a future you were ill-equipped for. Everyone is on the same page now. We won't withhold information anymore." He clenched then unclenched his fists. "This is harder than I thought because I kept things hidden from you and kept them from my brother. Yes, I know where your mother is. Your dad doesn't know. I never told him. He never asked."

Leo bowed her head, feeling a fresh wave of despair. Uncle Paul put his hand on her shoulder, a touch she would know anywhere, familiar and comforting. "I'm sorry, Leo. Grown-ups can make bad decisions. We messed this up."

After learning that her mother was still alive, Leo constructed elaborate stories to fill in the missing gaps: Her mom was kidnapped, she moved overseas, lost her passport and couldn't leave, she had amnesia, or was in prison. Never once did Leo entertain the thought that Emily consciously decided, day after day, year after year, to stay away.

How flawed I must be to have a mother give birth to me, be part of my life for three years, then willingly walk away and never look back. I wasn't good enough as a daughter, and obviously, I wasn't good enough as a wife. No matter how hard I tried, I couldn't make my marriage work. Am I capable of any enduring relationship?

Under twilight's cover, sorrow overtook her. She

tucked her body against the ground and rocked. Surrendering to its overwhelming force, Leo let the waves of humiliation and anguish move her through a landscape of loss. How can the end of a marriage that wasn't healthy and the absence of a woman, a mother she never knew, yet one she intensely imagined and loved, carve out part of her being, leaving her incomplete?

****

The new deck's fairy lights were turned off so they could watch the stars. They relaxed into the night, seated in wooden chairs around the oak kitchen table they hauled from inside, adorned with empty cartons of Thai food and cans of soda. Leo gazed into the inky sky and listened to the river finding its way, even in darkness.

"I have an idea," Uncle Paul's voice broke the companionable silence.

"Oh, no," Leo and her father responded in unison. Jennifer's sunlit laughter joined the Lightfoot's mirth. Having her here felt natural, like she had been with them for a long time. Uncle Paul was indignant. "Hey, my ideas are always good." Leo could hear the merriment in his voice though she could not see his eyes.

"Leo, I know you don't want to live with us, and I can't say I blame you, so why don't you take my old place?"

Leo had never seen the house. Yet, it had become part of their family lore. Uncle Paul built the structure for his wife close to thirty-five years ago. He worked construction at the time and bartered with some of his co-workers to help him build the home on three rugged acres a handful of miles outside of Tahlequah. Over the years, Leo heard numerous stories of how her father, ten at the time, had "helped" erect the structure, how he had a crush on the fancy city girl from Dallas that his brother Paul was bringing into the family, and wondered if he could also marry her and move in with them. When Leo occasionally asked, as she grew, if she could see the mystery dwelling, Uncle Paul would shake his head. "We Lightfoot men are all talk. It's nothing to look at. There's no reason to visit the past." And she, of course, never pushed.

Uncle Paul explained that the curved marital house he designed and crafted out of young love had been for his bride, charming and quaint at first. Less than a year later, however, the aunt Leo never knew sneaked away, stating in her wake that the remoteness of the countryside and the emptiness of her marriage were choking her worse than Oklahoma dust. There was no reason for Paul to stay. He moved back in with his mother and helped her raise his little brother. At first, he rented out the abode, but after a decade of renters trashing the property, failing to make monthly payments, and fleeing in the middle of the night, he decided the effort wasn't worth the trouble and closed shop.

Across the table, he slid a key on an amethyst chain. "Here you go. It's an easy bike ride into town and to campus, but far enough away that you can hear yourself think. I'll drive you out there tomorrow."

****

"Let me help." Jennifer took the bottom of the form-fitting sheet and stretched the cotton over the base while Leo pulled her end over the new sleeper sofa mattress. "Sorry about your old bedroom." She lifted her head, her silver mist eyes shining, considerate.

"You don't have to apologize for anything." Leo slipped a pillow into a case, clutched it tightly to her chest, and collapsed into one of the new living room chairs. "I left home and got married. Expecting him to keep my room forever is crazy. Besides, turning the space into an office for you and Dad makes more sense."

Leo looked around her childhood home. Though the structure was the same, everything seemed fresh and put together. Even the family photos, which had been haphazardly flung on the walls, had new life. They were now placed in neat, organized clusters, their frames uniformly stained, giving the appearance that everything was in the space where it belonged. "This place looks terrific, by the way. Your touch is exactly what the Lightfoot household needed."

Jennifer smiled as if grateful for the grace Leo had shown. She sat in an adjacent chair, slipped off a ruby red sandal, and tucked one leg underneath her doll-like figure, her straight blond hair falling quietly forward, framing a pale face. "Did you ever get my letter, my apology for how everything unfolded at our last session?"

Leo nodded.

Jennifer continued, "Clearly, the meeting got away from me. I feel horrible. My advisor warned us about this when we were in training, about losing control of the situation and leaving your patient feeling abandoned and destroying their trust. I'd only been practicing a year. This isn't an excuse. I should have done better."

Leo released her death grip and held the pillow

more lightly, like a hug. "What happened wasn't intentional." Her voice strained. "I can see that now. Coming to that conclusion took me a while. I always meant to write back, but life got kind of complicated. I was focusing on other things." Like trying to get through each day.

Jennifer replied, her words light with gentleness, "Is that part of the reason you stayed away?"

Tears sprang to the corner of Leo's eyes. "At first, I was mad at the world, angry at Dad, Uncle Paul, my mother, you. Then things got really tough, and coming home, even to visit, seemed impossible." What would be the point to tell Jennifer how Jake repeatedly commented on how her mother had left her and her dad had lied to her because she deserved it? Leo's flaws created her reality. Over the past two years, she had come to believe the truth that her husband had offered to her, wrapped in different veneers, presented in a multitude of ways.

****

Jennifer let out a long breath; so much was contained within the rail-thin body of the young woman she had grown to love. That was the first mistake she made. As a psychologist, you were taught to maintain distance and safeguard the therapist-client relationship. But she had been unprepared for how fifteen-year-old Leo burst into her world. With candor and curiosity, Leo struggled to understand, to become better, and her impetus had been singular in focus. She never wanted to let her father down again. She shared that in her first session. She would do anything for her father, who had put his life on hold to raise her. So, Dr. Baker and Leo had begun the deep dive together into the substance of her life, the events and emotions that had all led her to that fateful night, the night she took some of her father's pain medications and drank too much, the night she was found alone, discarded on the filthy floor of an abandoned warehouse.

And Dr. Jennifer Baker certainly hadn't expected to fall for Leo's handsome, brooding (well, not so brooding, as contemplative) father. With a heart of gold that shone forth steady and true as the North Star, like in one of her romance novels, she had been swept into another dimension. This family that had unintentionally hurt each other as they struggled in their attempts to protect, and shield, had pulled through. They endured. Somehow, they found their way back to each other, humbled yet stronger in resolve. She craved this kind of commitment and fell for this family. Her psyche started to enfold Leo, her father, and even Uncle Paul into her being long before her intellect recognized what was happening, and by then, it was too late.

"Leo, I don't know what you endured. But I can see the profound impact the last few years have had on you." She paused and waited until Leo looked up. "I want you to know that I'm here for you. Not as a therapist, of course, but as a friend who cares about your well-being." Jennifer hoped her words would assuage Leo's angst, an encompassing fleece of comfort.

Where Shade and Light Merge

He had fallen asleep under the willow again. Hope peered out the kitchen window. She could see the dark outline of his body as starlight and wind pushed protective fronds around him. Her brother, an Iraq and Afghanistan combat veteran, had once more found temporary alcohol-induced solace. Ray had been back for months and still, he could not sleep in a bed. There was one for him in her spare bedroom, and another set up in a makeshift living quarter in the detached garage. Sometimes in the pre-dawn light, she would find him hanging off a couch, rounded on the bathroom floor, or face down on the skinny, threadbare carpet by the humming refrigerator door. But mostly, he didn't sleep. Hope recurrently heard him rattling around the house at night, closets and cabinets opened and closed, the television channels surfed, then stilled. Often when she rose, her bladder being pressed upon by her burgeoning baby, she would catch glimpses of him outside, moving with the moon in and out of shadow, trees, or sitting motionless in the crow's nest of the wooden play structure she and Gabrielle had found discarded in pieces and then had laboriously reconstructed for their children to be.

****

When Ray returned from active duty, his system was still hard-wired, and in overdrive. The permanent vigilance and the wakefulness that had ensured survival remained at the ready. Letting go was impossible even though his rational mind understood he was no longer on the battlefield. Unless his guard was temporarily stripped bare by alcohol, a most alluring seductress, he remained watchful beyond the possibility of sleep.

****

First, he felt the gentle stroking of weeping willow fingers across his face. Then he reluctantly acknowledged the dull heaviness of his head, and the cotton absorbed dryness in his mouth. And finally, when the thin wisp branches could no longer keep an insistent sun from pushing in, ribbons of light dancing across his upturned face, he opened his eyes. Not too far from him, seated in oversized colorful plastic Adirondack chairs around the cold fire pit, were his mother and sister. Steady and true, they kept vigil when he was too numb. Since his return, they had been there, trying their best to uphold. He saw their struggle in the tension that stretched across their shoulders and in the way they exchanged furtive glances when they thought he wasn't looking. What are we going to do now? How can we help him? Will he ever be the same?

He knew being with him wasn't easy. He had arrived home and announced while smiling, but with a cold, non-negotiable voice, "No Welcome Home party, I mean it. I just can't." In the car, while his mother drove, he saw his sister frantically texting, sending out a network of messages, and canceling a party she had been planning for years. And even when he walked into Hope and Gabrielle's home, stoically seeing decorations crammed into closets, secrets spilling out, the same Dollar General tablecloths and decorations used to send him off years ago, and a refrigerator full of welcome home food, he couldn't tap into that part of him that felt bad for his sister or his mother. He acted as though nothing had been planned, as though he'd been away for a long weekend.

Out of the spare bedroom window, he watched emotionlessly as Hope and Gabrielle sprinted out the front door, the sound of their voices echoing as they shooed away those they hadn't reached and pushing an ancient Mrs. Robertson in a wheelchair back across their lawn toward the waiting nursing home van. At the same time, she looked around, confused and searching for her favorite Sunday school pupil, her skeleton-thin hands shaking in a shrunken lap. This simple task of reintegration, of mingling with people from his past, of connecting with individuals who would pepper him with questions and demands, seemed overwhelming, almost impossible. Assimilation in a world that had moved on without him was daunting enough. Add to that an overarching confusion. When you are in a war, all you want to do is return home. And when you are home, all you can do is think about the soldiers and what they are sacrificing. He could not stop ruminating about what they were going through, feeling guilty being stateside. Allowing himself to do anything normal seemed like a flagrant disregard for their service. Since his arrival, coping had not gotten easier.

From his perspective, observing his sister and mother through almost translucent, moving willow leaflets, where shade and light rippled and merged, the scene looked like an impressionist's brushed rendition of a reality he no longer felt a part of. They talked quietly, drinking water from jelly jars. He could tell when his sister sensed he was awake; she didn't break conversational stride, but something subtly shifted in her tone, and she quickly glanced his way to confirm what she already knew.

As he stood and staggered, trying to get his stiff body moving, he tucked himself as deeply as possible in the foliage and, using the tree's large, knotted trunk as cover, unable to hold it any longer, he urinated, hitting the base of the tree to prevent any sound, ashamed. He'd passed out again.

What's wrong with me? Where is the high school graduate who dedicated himself to paramedic school, became licensed, and served his community? Where is the disciplined soldier that was forged in boot camp?

The morning bluebell sky reeled. He felt disconnected and disgusted. Before boot camp, the taste and how alcohol made him feel was enough to keep him from imbibing more than a drink or two at a time. Since his honorable discharge from active duty, something had shifted.

She called to him, a most demanding, insatiable mistress, luring him with seductive promises. *I have the power to ease your pain. I alone can help you forget.* And try, as he might, a pattern emerged. Ray would sober up and do what they expected of him, study to take his re-licensure exam, and help Hope and Gabrielle with projects around their home. He was even toying with enrolling at Northeastern, maybe studying to become a nurse, a physician's assistant, or even applying to medical school. He would do well for a week, ten days, or so, then something, a random sight, a smell, a sensation would trigger the deep need in him to escape, and he would start to drink. The purchase would come out of the paper bag; he would tip the bottle back and let the peppermint schnapps blossom in his throat, liquid relief. Even though his intellect knew this was a bad idea, once the need for oblivion started, he would drink and slide into the darkness while everything else around him fell apart.

When he stepped out from under the willow, Hope nonchalantly offered him a tall drink of lemon-infused water. He sat feeling defeated and exhausted. They smiled at him, warm and accepting, trying not to let the worry show, and continued their conversation as if Ray had been sitting with them all along. Ray sighed. He was resigned. Today he would be better. Today, he would start again.

They watched Gabrielle, carrying a pitcher of fresh, iced water, walk across a long stretch of the backyard. His mom glanced at Hope, who gave her a barely perceptible nod. She took a deep breath and started talking. The words sounded rehearsed. "Our church marquee has a new message. Finally, after years of 'Pray for our Troops,' this week is about forgiveness. Forgiveness is swallowing when you would rather spit."

Ray raised an eyebrow at Hope and Gabrielle, who bit back smiles.

Maria, not noticing the exchange, continued in all seriousness. "Anyway, your father has been working on a sermon for a while, and he wonders if you would come to church this Sunday. Ray, I know he's been hard on you, but he has softened. He wanted me to personally invite you and let you know that you are welcome to attend anytime. The doors are always open." She leaned back and blew out a small puff of air as if glad to have completed what she was charged to do. Gabrielle gracefully moved around the small circle, refilling their glasses. She set the half-full pitcher down on the fire pit's red brick rim and slid into the dark blue chair next to Hope.

The weight of his mother's words settled over him. Seeping in was the pain of rejection, of feeling like he had never been enough, of having let down a father he had loved and looked up to. And not once, while he was away, had his father reached out to him or let him know that he was thinking of him or even cared.

"I am not the prodigal son! I am not begging my father for absolution. There's no reason for me to repent and ask forgiveness. I was serving my country, and if that's not honorable enough for him, then so be it."

Maria and Hope tried not to look confused by the forcefulness of his voice. Ray knew this was a side of him they hadn't seen before. Was anger a result of what he had been through, or had the emotions been there, beneath the surface, all along? Heck, if he knew. Seeing the impact of his words, like a slap to his mother's face, Ray took a long drink of water and, with measured temperance, explained. "Dad made his thoughts clear that I have been nothing but a disappointment. Just because I was born? Or because I didn't follow his prescribed script? That's one of the great mysteries of my life, something that will never be solved. But what I know for sure is that I don't need one of his famous sermons pointing out, in front of the whole congregation, the error of my ways and what a terrible person I am." He stopped short of telling the women in his life that he already felt horrible. The titanic weight of his decisions and all he had experienced were like piercing pieces of shrapnel sticking out of his internal organs, causing internal hemorrhaging and jagged soul destruction. How do you find your way out of that?

"Hey, Buddy." The voice behind him caused a visceral reaction.

"Miggy." Ray stood and allowed himself to be pulled into a bear hug. Slung across Miguel's face was a broad grin. Running shoes were around his shoulders. Though from looking at his friend, Ray surmised that he hadn't hit the track since their high school days.

"What's up, Miggy?" Ray plopped back into the bright red deck chair and wiped his brow. He could smell the alcohol evaporating from his pores.

"You, my friend, are going to help me get back into shape." He tapped his rounded, beer-built belly, sending ripples underneath his triple X Tee. "The misses and I are trying to get pregnant. She blames my slow swimmers on my slow body, and she keeps telling me that she doesn't want to, but if she must, she will start shopping around for a newer, more finely tuned model, one that can get her pregnant and won't drop dead while raising her children."

Miguel plopped his large body into the yellow chair, which quietly protested, sinking a good two inches into the sand surrounding the fire pit. He pulled a pair of socks out of his gym shorts, slipped off his sandals, and started tying up his tennis shoes.

"Right now?" Ray was incredulous. His body protested. The night of binge drinking was still working through his system. Yet, another part of him responded. Running was something akin to breathing, something he had done religiously since adolescence. Yet, since his return, he had not gone once.

"No time like the present." Miguel stood and

started going through some stretching exercises Coach Lightfoot would have them do before practice. "Look, I am so out of shape. I'm going to need lots of help. Today I don't work. But maybe, on days I do, we can go for a jog before my shift starts. You'll have to go easy on me. It'll take this body some time to adjust."

Ray quietly observed his friend, who could no longer bend over and touch the ground, his midsection stopping him halfway.

Miguel looked up. "Come on, man, stop gawking at the train wreck. I need your support."

With Ray jogging easily by his side, Miguel lumbered down the long, rut-strewn drive. In the infinite sky, an eagle turned a great circle above them. And so, they began a tentatively renewed friendship. For Ray, the commitment was to help Miggy get back in shape. For Miguel, the far-flung attempt went deeper; prompted by a desperate visit from Hope and Maria to remind Ray of what grounded him.

"We need your help, Miguel." Hope had tears in her eyes, and Maria thrust a newspaper into his hands. The article revealed the results of a recent study. On average, twenty veterans commit suicide daily. "We don't want him to be a statistic." Ray's mother had gripped his arm tightly, pleading, "*Por favor*."

And here Miguel was doing something he told himself he would never do again, exercise regularly. Each step Miguel took, each fraction of a mile, was a labor of love for his friend, an effort to keep him from going further down a rabbit hole, one from which there was no return.

****

A new arrangement emerged. Before dawn, Ray

would lace up and run the two miles to Miguel's house. From there, they would jog together. And when they were done, after Miggy went through his front gate, sweating profusely, breathing heavily, and waving goodbye, Ray would run some more. As he moved across the terrain of his life, running over the roads and paths of his youth, Ray felt lighter. When he pushed his body to the edge, self-doubt, memory, fear, and guilt struggled to find purchase.

One morning, as Ray increased his pace, he saw before him two diametrically opposed identities. The first was a hardened warrior who had been forged at boot camp and had taken over when he was flown into Camp Rustamiyah by Chinook. That was the one who had been in the forefront, the one who had returned impenetrable and numb to his hometown. And somewhere buried deeply, there existed, or at least Ray hoped he was still there, an ordinary denizen of the world, an everyday friend, brother, worker, son, a more centered translation of himself.

Ray was sprinting now, taking a route he usually avoided, one that had more foot and vehicle traffic through the streets of Tahlequah. What was he now—a soldier, a civilian? And where did he fit in? Strong and fleet of foot, he raced across the grocery store's parking lot, less than a mile to go.

****

She would recognize that stride anywhere. Their lives had been loosely entangled for four of her formative years, a total of eight combined cross-country and track-and-field seasons. She had grown up around those memories carrying them within her. And at this moment, seeing him run across the parking lot in the morning light, she felt her pulse quicken as if to match his. Everything in her wanted to call out to him, as she would have done when she was a child, or better yet, to race toward him, to catch up, then match him, stride for stride. How wonderful it would be to run by his side again and hear the laughter of Blink and Squirt. But that image was part of her childhood. The little girl was long gone. Life was simple and uncomplicated then. Ray represented the innocent sweetness of a schoolgirl crush.

While watching his figure recede into the unfolding morning, Leo wistfully hugged the memory and the grocery bag close to her chest. A determined Oklahoma wind rushed by, catching her hair. She felt a charge in the air as the current passed through her.

The Skeleton of Remembrance

"Leo Lightfoot!" A musical voice stopped Leo mid-stride as she crossed the grocery store parking lot.

Uncle Paul took the paper bag from her arms. "Go on, say hello. I'll wait for you in the truck."

"It's so good to see you." Judy's smile was broad. There was no artifice. She rested her arms across a large, pregnant swell and continued, "I heard you married Jake and moved to Tulsa."

"Judy, hi." Leo stood awkwardly, trying to fold into herself. The insecurities and shyness associated with high school returned. Of course, Leo remembered Judy Langard, the star of all of Tahlequah high school's musical productions, the girl everyone said would make a name for their small town, who would burst onto the big screen; her voice and acting had been that good. Leo helped behind the scenes with every production except the one in the spring of their senior year when she left with Jake. She remembered watching Judy perform and sing, wishing she could be more like her, self-assured and confident. She was surprised Judy remembered her name. Self-consciously, Leo brushed a lock of hair from her face. "True, I did marry Jake, but that didn't work out. We're getting a divorce." Saying the words for the first time out loud felt good.

"Glad you woke up. That guy was nothing but bad news." A lump from Judy's mid-abdomen popped upward. The tiny curve of a heel or an elbow made a steady track across her belly. Judy laughed. "Whoa, slow down, little one." She gently touched the protrusion until it disappeared.

Leo watched, fascinated. "When are you due?"

"Two weeks to go, but I don't think he'll wait that long. He wants to join his two-year-old sister and get the party started."

Leo did the calculations quickly. She wanted to ask but refrained.

As if reading her mind, Judy offered, "I tried to hide my pregnancy during our last musical production of the Wizard of Oz. Thank goodness for Dorothy's billowing aproned dress. Brody and I graduated, then got married the following weekend. Our daughter was born a month later. The ride hasn't been easy, that's for sure, but we're doing okay." She paused and looked at her watch. "Oh man, I gotta get going. Brody can't be late for work. Hey, why don't you give me your number? We can get together, you know, talk and catch up." She reached into her purse and pulled out a glittering gold-encased phone.

****

Leo jumped into the pickup. Uncle Paul waited until she buckled up. "Ready to move into your new digs and start your new life, kiddo?"

Leo held the grocery bag in her lap and offered him a quick smile along with a thumbs-up sign as he guided the truck onto Mahaney Avenue.

Just past the peaceful hamlet of Sleepy Hollow, population 206, off the main artery, on the road with no name, just an official number, an iron-rich path stained red from oxidation appeared. Uncle Paul navigated the umbilical cord tough, bumpy excuse of a driveway carefully. A canopy of trees sheltered the drive. As they unhurriedly bounced along, light and shade rippled through the truck's window creating an impression that Leo was holding her breath just under the surface of a lake. The image stayed with her until the vehicle finally burst into a clearing. The long abandoned, round river stone house stood in an extensive field of prairie grass. On one side, a stand of scrub pines leaned inward as if offering a promise of protection. Two hundred yards away, a densely treed grove sprung upward. Leo jumped out of her uncle's truck.

As she surveyed her new home, she had an overwhelming sense of familiarity. "I've been here before."

Uncle Paul stood beside her. "You can't possibly remember, can you?" Was there a catch in his voice? "The last time I brought you here, you were about two years old, maybe two and a half, but never...." He stopped.

"Never after my mom left." Leo finished for him, and he nodded.

After helping Leo unload her bike, the groceries, and a bag of necessities her dad and Jennifer put together, he led her through the front door. Inside was temperate, cocooning. The still air held a sense of mystery, of time suspended. Leo walked through the circular interior, touching the furthermost wall as she moved. One living space flowed seamlessly into the other, without clear delineation, the entrance, sitting area, kitchen, bedroom, and bathroom. And at the center of the home, around which all other spaces revolved, sat a sturdy, cast iron wood-burning stove.

The home's contents contained nothing superfluous but everything essential to living.

Open shelving lined the kitchen with two china plates, two hand-blown glass goblets, and a dark red tea kettle. In a small wicker basket were forks, knives, and spoons, and near the window sat a walnut table with two carved chairs. Underneath a set of slanted, ladder-like stairs, which led to a smaller circular loft, was a raised double bed with built-in storage drawers. A toilet, a pedestal sink, and a sunken open shower with a rain-washed slate floor were in the bathroom. Four arched expansive windows, ones with no coverings, hugged the exterior wall, each perfectly spaced and each one with a purpose, allowing the home's occupants to gaze outward in every direction: due north, south, east, and west. The interior was simple but elegantly designed. Each time Leo made the circuit, she noticed something new, a hidden closet, a recessed shelf for books–unpretentious, charming details, unexpected gifts.

Uncle Paul popped up from the storm cellar underneath the kitchen floor. He brushed cobwebs from his hair and smiled. "You're all set. They turned the electricity back on this morning, and I primed the pump. Wait a few hours before you try and take a hot shower."

It was hard for Leo to tell what he was thinking as he looked around. His usually easy-going expression was thoughtful and distant. What was he like back then? She tried to imagine a twenty-year-old Paul, flush with love and enthusiasm for his unfolding life. She can see him with his construction buddies, carefully crafting this home for his young bride. Her father, ten years old at the time, tagging along with a heavy hammer in his hand, seriously trying to help. She can also see her dad, tired of tediousness, racing around and around the circular interior, laughing out loud. A delighted puppy chasing his tail.

As he surveyed his long ago handy-work, Uncle Paul sighed deeply. He stretched and twisted a dormant vintage Edison-like bulb in its socket, which hung suspended over the kitchen sink. The light sprung to action as if having just awoken from a deep sleep.

"You'll need to clean her up, kick out those field mice, check the bathroom cabinet for scorpions, and brush the spiders off the external stone. She's a bit rough right now, but once you settle in, she'll soften. In the summer, the insulating stone will keep you cool. In the winter, all you'll need is the wood burner, and you'll be warm. She's yours for as long as you need her." He paused and sized up his niece as if checking for broken parts. "There will be countless surprises if you are open to them. My goal was to have the natural world be an extension of our home. I wanted every season to bring something new and unexpected." He laughed quickly and stated more to himself than to Leo, "But we all know how that went. When my wife left, she told me she was suffocating, that marriage and life in this house weren't what she imagined." His words contained no bitterness, the process of aquamation over time leaving little more than a washed, clean skeleton of memory.

"We didn't live here long, and I'm not sure if the land still holds its secrets. My hope for you, Leo, is that this self-contained abode and the surrounding land will help you heal." He stood by his truck, the driver's door already open, and hugged her fiercely. He smiled the patented Lightfoot smile. "This is your journey, Leo, but remember, you're not alone. Visit often, come for a cookout, invite us to dinner, or drop in unannounced. Cell phone coverage is bound to be spotty, but if you need anything, call. Or if you can't reach us, send up a road flare, and we'll be here."

Leo watched until his taillights were no longer visible. From deep inside the stone house behind her, she could hear the faintest of footfalls, steps from the past moving toward her.

A View of the Girl

(From the Bridge)

Daybreak's light grew as he rounded the drive after finishing his morning run with Miguel. Fifty yards away stood his sister hanging the wash on a clothesline suspended between two lacebark elms. She had been up early, doing chores, and had sleepily greeted him before he put on his shoes and slipped into pre-dawn's dusky mantel. Ray stopped the timer on his watch; Hope would soon leave for work.

He walked briskly toward her, ready to take over, to tell her to go and eat breakfast, but something in her movements of bending down to the basket and reaching upward to hang fabric on a swaying line abruptly stopped him. He could not move. An overwhelming wave of vivid awareness washed over him, a layering of time. Ray was carried to a different reality that seemed to be occurring simultaneously with the moment in which he stood. The other all-consuming mental terrain took over and possessed his mind.

He was transported back to Iraq, where he was pulling security on a bridge overlooking one of Baghdad's most dangerous and heavily trafficked highways. On assignment with some of his squad mates and the Iraqi police, they were watching for any untoward activity—the casual disposal of trash, the carcass of an animal, or an abandoned car, all of which could contain an improvised explosive device. The prior days of the watch had been uneventful. As the smog-laden afternoon settled over them, heavy and sedate, all seemed contained. From the bridge, Ray had an eagle's eye view of the low-rise apartment situated on the west side of the causeway. Over the past few days, he had been studying the tenants, watching them go about their daily activities, and he had come to know the routines of many.

Three young children would come onto their first-floor balcony early in the morning, dressed in school uniforms, laughing and boisterous. They slapped together their shoes, ridding them of dust and debris, before leaving the complex, book bags dangling across young shoulders. The next floor up, mid-morning, an elderly couple faithfully appeared, and with slow, measured shuffles, they carefully watered every plant that jammed their small balcony. After they finished, they would sit amidst their lush foliage on a small wooden bench and gaze out at their world.

On the third level, he watched a young mother-to-be step onto the balcony, as she did every afternoon, to hang hand-washed clothes on two ropes loosely slung across the open mezzanine's width. She bent, one hand rested on her swell or sometimes supported her back, and picked up threadbare clothing. From his paramedic training, Ray surmised she was due any day. Every afternoon, he watched her and wondered what her life was like. He had never seen anyone else step outside, nor had he ever seen her leave the apartment. What was her story? What did she think every morning when she rose to rinse and repeat, day after day? He also contemplated what life would be like if he and Hope had been born elsewhere.

As he watched her pick up the basket and turn to go inside, he could vividly see every detail, the sway of damp laundry pushed by a gentle breeze, the swish of the blue hijab covering her hair, her entire body, all but her face, and he could discern a faint smile as she looked over her shoulder at the soldiers and policemen, she knows have been watching her, their girl viewed from the bridge. When she smiled, Ray saw a blinding flash, then another. In a heartbeat, the afternoon was split down the middle, shattered with artillery fire and incoming detonations launched at them from inside the complex. Now there was no light. He was inside a tunnel of expanding darkness, loud with the sounds of explosions and gunfire. The cement in the bridge kicked up around them as they ran for cover and were instructed by their superiors to return the force. Even as he responded, his automatic aiming only at where the shots originated from, but he couldn't be sure. A sense of horror filled him.

As Ray's weapon fired, he screamed, "You cowards. You fucking bastards, hiding behind children, pregnant women, the elderly. Leave them alone! Leave them the hell alone! Show yourselves. Let's fight man to man and leave them out of this!" After the abrupt, furious exchange, in the dreadful silence that followed, as sections of the complex smoked and burned, all Ray could do was send out a missive to the universe. "Please, please let the innocents be okay. They didn't ask for any of this. Please be with the children, the elderly, the girl, and her unborn."

"Ray? Ray!" A voice pulled him to the present, a

hand on his shoulder. "Are you all right? What can I do?" Ray saw his sister's face come into focus through the oppressively thick dissociative cloud. Hope's concern took the place of the visage of the girl seen from the bridge. Ray shook his head, trying to orient himself and awaken from a place where time was suspended, and realities fused. He was profusely sweating and shaking. He felt dazed, searching for his comrades, still feeling the agony of uncertainty, looking for the couple watering their plants, the school children laughing, the girl smiling, but they were all gone. Who had died that day? Had any guiltless people been killed or severely injured? He would never know.

Slowly, the softness of the Oklahoma morning folded warmly around him. The reality he had awoken to that morning was restored. The world returned to him, but it was fractured, and try as he might, he knew he couldn't do anything to repair it.

The pounding of his heart moderated, and Hope, who fiercely grabbed his arm, acting like he might topple over, gently let go, leaving the indentation of her nails in his flesh.

She said, "Come inside. Let's get you some water. I'll have to talk to Miguel about running you too hard."

****

Hope looked up from the kitchen table when Ray emerged from the bathroom. He was shirtless, his hair dripping, a labyrinth of fine lines pulled at his translucent blue eyes, which were tired but clear. In front of the empty chair, the one Ray usually occupied, sat an apple cinnamon muffin on a napkin next to a steaming mug of coffee. She pushed the pastry toward him. "Don't worry. I wasn't anywhere near the kitchen when Gabrielle baked these."

Hope had her hands around a cup of peppermint tea. She looked at her brother and noticed how his muscles had been reduced to whipcord leanness. Around his waist, fighting to stay fixed in place, were a pair of jeans, at least two sizes too big. "Ever hear of belts?" She quickly smiled and subtly dipped her head, motioning for Ray to join her.

He looked at her wearily. "What's up? You're late for work."

She noticed his guardedness, how the skin of his face is pulled tautly across hollowed cheeks, how his whole being somehow seemed reduced, a body worn down from the tremendous weight of actions and consequences. What she wants to say, while accurate, does not speak to her true ulterior motive. Is this the first time there has been subterfuge in their relationship? Will her brother be able to tell?

"I can be late once in a while." She took a sip of tea and waited as Ray dragged the kitchen chair toward him, its sharp edge catching in the linoleum, and he slumped down. "I've been thinking." Hope casually stroked her abdomen.

****

Something had to be bothering Hope; their work ethic, a product of their upbringing, was unrelenting. Ray glanced at his sister. Though she still had two months to go, he could tell the pregnancy was taking its toll; she looked run down. He understood her concern about him was part of the problem, but she had also been diagnosed with gestational diabetes. At her last doctor's visit, her blood pressure was elevated, all reason for concern as the pregnancy advanced. Ray took a sip of coffee and raised an eyebrow.

"Every day we're working short, someone calls in sick or people just up and quit without notice. Then I have to fill in, helping to get the product out. I never have time to get my stuff done." Hope was the Flavorful food manufacturing plant manager. The position enabled her to finance their land contract agreement and provided her with health insurance. Ray knew how important keeping this job was and how easily the owner could find an excuse to fire her.

"So, you're saying you need a brother to help?"

"Just until I can hire reliable employees, or at least until the baby is born. I know you keep talking about enrolling in classes, and I don't want to interfere, but…."

"It's okay. I'll do it." Ray knew as well as Hope that he'd been putting off the tasks of getting on with his life and that her request was not impacting any concrete plans. In fact, the only agenda he had for that day was to head to town to pick up another bottle of forgetfulness. He last imbibed over three weeks ago. But the constant struggle of waging an unrelenting internal war was unbearable at times. He looked at his sister. Her needs superseded his. Liquid respite could wait for another day. This simple act was the least he could do.

Hope's eyes bore into his. "The work is brutal."

"I can handle brutal conditions. Brutal is my middle name," he replied, returning the intense stare.

She nodded. "Okay."

"Do I have to fill out an application or something? Go in for an interview."

"You just completed the interview. I'm the

supervisor, remember? You're hired. You can fill out the payroll paperwork later. I can't offer you more than minimum wage, though. The owner determines the entry-level pay scale. But every sixty days you work, you get an incremental raise."

Ray rinsed out his coffee cup and put the muffin under the glass pastry dome. "When do I start?"

"Put on a shirt. Your one-day orientation starts this morning. Tomorrow, you report as a full-time employee."

****

A painter's stroke of hyacinth bled from the horizon into twilight's lengthening sky, but as Ray walked to the car, he was too exhausted to notice. Every muscle in his body was spent. He hadn't eaten for over twenty-four hours. Hope insisted he share her sandwich and thermos of milk at lunch; after all, he hadn't packed lunch because he was helping her out on such short notice. He adamantly refused. In the long run, he argued, she had been manufacturing a human being for months, and he'd only been producing strawberry jam for a day. Orientation was canceled. One of the shop's regular workers had called an hour after their shift was supposed to start, saying, "I quit." So, Ray stepped in. His job was to stir a large vat of fruit. His shoulders and arms sustained the grueling circular motion for nearly forty minutes as the mixture reached, then sustained, a rolling boil. Yet Ray did not complain. He kept on while the jam simmered until reaching an optimal balance—the consistency of thickened syrup. Vat after vat, all day long, the production of 200 jars of Lucy's Luscious Preserves took enormous effort. Tomorrow, Hope informed him with a fatigued smile, the order was for 250 jars of Holly's Smoking Hot Habanero Sauce.

Hope threw Ray the keys on their way to the car. As tough as Ray's day was, he observed how hard Hope worked keeping everything moving smoothly, stepping in for people to take breaks, filling orders, answering calls, mopping spilled products off the floor so no one slipped, checking temperature gauges, constantly on her feet, trying to keep everything together. Ray came to a complete stop before pulling onto 82A, the blinker quietly clicking. His sister was already asleep. No one was behind him, so he paused to take in the evening sky. *Whatever you do, work heartily*, he could hear his father's low voice recite Colossians 3:23, and for the first time in a long time, he could think of his father without animus.

As Ray turned south onto the open stretch of road, a lone biker, her face obscured by the curve of her protective helmet, cycled past his open window, a scent of jasmine on dusk's breath. Ray breathed deeply, taking in the evening's simple richness, and for the briefest of moments, he felt a heaviness lift into the diminishing day.

But Now I See

Dusk was falling on the Oklahoma countryside as Leo pedaled home from her shift working at Persephone's Burger and Pizza Palace. The smell of an unclaimed carry-out order of mushroom caps and Arti toast wafted from her bicycle basket. She would eat the deliciousness outside, sitting atop the western-facing solid wood picnic table, watching a sinking sun as a steady wind whipped across the tall prairie grass.

How quickly these first few weeks in her new home passed. She carried with her a sense of accomplishment. Northeastern State University accepted the community college courses she'd taken at Ronnie's insistence, without Jake's knowledge. She was on her way to a degree. Not only had she signed up for a few classes, but she had also secured a volunteer position at the animal shelter. Now, thanks to Judy, she was gainfully employed. Everything she earned would go into the new account she set up, one without Jake's name attached to it, one he could not touch, or so the attorney she found through a legal aid flier on campus told her. She had an appointment to start the divorce proceedings next week.

She biked steadily, absorbing the waning light. The unincorporated district called Sleepy Hollow, little more than a whistle-stop appeared. Several blocks later, she passed through the drowsy community and was on the other side. One thing Leo appreciated about rural Oklahoma was as quickly as they rose, small towns disappeared. The landscape was all-encompassing, unlike the sprawling suburbs of big cities, where flat stretches of wide asphalt stretched for miles, tying concrete buildings and concrete lives together.

She shifted the bike into first gear and began a steep ascent, breathing in long, deep air draws as her pace slowed. She was not far from home. A house and a patch of land that already felt familiar enfolded and accepted her.

At first, the isolation was more than she could bear. Though just several miles from campus, she initially felt every inch of that distance. She'd never lived alone before. But as she systematically worked her way around the exterior of the roundhouse, brushing the river stone, washing windows, pulling weeds, and then attending to the interior, cleaning each area, a sense of belonging developed. In one of those still pockets, something unexpected happened. She now had a distinct singular image of her mother, one she knew to be true.

It happened the first time Leo climbed the step ladder at the base of her bed, which led to a small circular loft. As soon as she grasped the wooden rungs, she felt something jolt through her, and when she looked upward, she saw a pair of slender, bare, freckled legs moving before her, climbing the stairs and disappearing into the chamber above. Her mother. They had spent time together in this house, of this Leo was certain. The connection with her new home was now a rope to memory. Maybe more flashbacks would surface the longer she stayed in the house. Leo was hopeful.

As she crested the final incline, she stopped cycling, letting gravity take over, and sped quickly down, heading toward the base of the high hill, which led to her driveway. Yes, she had responsibilities, but her time and life were now hers.

****

Ray slipped into the last pew and scooted down, settling in the perfect spot for one who might need to exit quickly, and unobtrusively. "Tell Dad I'll be there Sunday." Ray surprised himself when talking with his mother a few days earlier.

Eventually, this would have to happen. He couldn't avoid him forever, especially since, week after week, his mother faithfully relayed his father's persistent request. "Your dad personally invites you to the service this week." Already the early summer morning was heating up. But inside, an hour before the service started, was cool and dark.

Though the pew's unyielding wood pressed into the backs of Ray's thighs, he found comfort in the familiar. How many years had he sat with Hope and his mother in a congregation that felt like extended family? The chapel walls contained memories, palpable and strong. The past few nights, sleep was elusive, and even when he closed his eyes, images, and thoughts would shock him back into wakefulness. But here in the silent sanctuary, a place deeply associated with his childhood, a place of refuge in which he had found profound comfort during his formative years, he felt some of the tension dissipate. For a moment, as Ray traced the muted light and shadows cast by the stained-glass windows, he was lured into believing the world could return to the way it had been.

Ray fell into an undisturbed sleep so deep he did not notice as the chapel lights were turned up. As the parishioners slowly filled in the pews around him, a murmur like a low-voltage current passed through them. *He is here. Look, be quiet, don't wake him.* They looked at him slumbering, a man now, someone they had watched grow over the years, who had laughed and played with their children among the pews. The preacher's son, who willingly showed up and helped during their acts of service, who reluctantly joined the choir and, when encouraged by Mrs. Robertson, had shyly found a singing voice pure and true (though he refused to sing a solo, stating he didn't want everyone looking at him) had returned. The churchgoers smiled. *Welcome home, Ray. Welcome back,* their silent offerings were falling around him, threads of garnered support. And still, he slept through the quietly issued opening prayer, the church announcements, mission statements, and bible verses. In a low voice, Pastor Shipworth suggested skipping the opening hymn, and the congregation readily nodded consent.

Some of them, including Mr. Ruggles, one of the church's tithe ushers, turned furtively to look behind them to confirm that Ray was still there and was still asleep. He had returned.

"Today's sermon is titled: Redemption and forgiveness. It's never too late to turn your life around."

Ray stirred, his neck stiff, awkwardly wrenched on the wooden pew bench. He glanced at his watch, he'd been asleep for over an hour and a half, and during that uninterrupted time, he didn't startle awake once. He did not have one vivid nightmare, which often his rewired brain could not separate from reality. He looked around at the assemblage who sat erect, their eyes focused on the elevated dais, which held to one side a communal table, and rising, higher still, from its center, a gleaming polished pulpit. And as his eyes followed theirs, his gaze descended on his father, who always commanded the stage.

The time Ray had been away at boot camp, performing stateside service, training, and two tours of duty, had visibly altered his father. The impact was evidenced in the tremendous weight and hair he'd lost, in the loosely hanging skin folds along his neck. The man standing before him on the platform looked like a shadow of his father's former self. His paunchy, ponderous form was greatly diminished, and he now wore a belt cinched so tightly that folds of fabric rippled around him as he moved. The voice was the same. Ray would recognize the tenor and the cadence anywhere, especially when delivering a sermon.

His mother said he'd changed. Is this what she meant? Having taken stock of the physical transformations, Ray began to focus on his father's words. "Ephesians 4:31 tells us, get rid of all bitterness, rage, anger, brawling, and slander, along with every form of malice." Slowly, Pastor Shipworth pulled off his glasses. He laid them on top of the pulpit and rubbed the bridge of his angled nose while intensely staring at his audience. Ray knew this look well. His father's judgmental, intractable, self-righteous countenance was the same as always. "On this, the Bible is firm. The sins of man are denounced."

Suddenly, there was sourness in Ray's stomach, rising, along with his father's now booming voice. "We were taught that for all who do not repent of their sins, a one-way ticket to Hell awaits." He let the words sink in.

****

Then with more tempered moderation, Pastor Shipworth continued, as he moved his gaze steadily along each pew, staring into each church member's eyes, "But if we read the next section, Verse 32 says: Be kind and compassionate to one another, forgiving each other, just as God through Christ forgave you." Finally, he looked to the last pew, the one on the far left of his vestry, the one to which his long-lost son had finally returned.

The wooden bench was empty. Pastor Shipworth stood still, dismayed. He had lost him again. The words he was planning on saying out loud, directly to his son and in front of his followers, stuck in his throat. He swallowed. Even as he commanded his congregation to bow their heads in prayer, he thought of what he had been prepared to say to Ray. Forgive me, son. Please forgive me for my sins. I was blind, but now I see.

Tract Seven:

Summer 2010, continued
The Wheels on the Bus

"Let's see what grounds we can find for the dissolution of your marriage." Fresh out of law school, the young attorney efficiently typed some commands on her laptop. Her round face, muted with a thin layer of powder, was soft and eager. Leo had followed a hand-painted sign outside the Studs and Suds Laundromat and an arrow pointing to the upstairs office. Candice Kane was beginning her practice and offered Leo a bargain basement deal. The other attorney that Leo called, because she learned from her dad and Uncle Paul that one always had to have at least two quotes before deciding, had given her a staggering initial consultation fee. One that would take over a week's worth of wages to pay. And that had just been for the first hour.

Finances aside, Leo knew she made the right choice when her counsel, exuding a confident, no-nonsense aura, stuck out her cushiony arm for a firm handshake and welcomed Leo to her "starter" office. She was unapologetic about the appearance of the newly acquired space and its sparse furnishings. The room guilelessly held a collapsible card table sporting a pink and purple paisley patterned cloth, which served as her consulting desk and work area, two folding chairs, and a single sleek, black metal, vertical, lockable three-drawer file cabinet. Solicitor Kane listened carefully and respectfully. She waited until Leo finished her sentences and thoughts before asking probing questions.

"Since he's going to fight you on the divorce, our best bet is to find grounds for a judge to grant you one. The first reason for a fault-based divorce in Oklahoma is abandonment. That one is out the window. You left him. Did he ever cheat on you, commit adultery?"

Had he? There were nights he didn't come home, but she always assumed he was out drinking with his friends. He was a big flirt; Leo knew this going into the marriage. There were co-workers and women he talked about in lascivious terms, but this was nothing new. She had no proof of anything. She shook her head. The cell phone in Leo's pocket vibrated, but she refused to look. She knew who was there. Jake, again.

"Impotence?" Her attorney peered through pink plastic-rimmed glasses at the computer screen before her and continued to read, "Extreme cruelty? Fraudulent contract? Habitual drunkenness? Gross neglect of duty?"

The questions made Leo's head spin. What had his duty as a husband been? Where was that defined? And if he had requirements, did that mean she had some legal responsibilities as a wife? Ones that she had known nothing about, and if this was true, had she, in fact, failed him? And yes, he drank and smoked pot, usually daily, but he still managed to work. When he was fired, usually because of a misunderstanding between him and the boss, after a week's vacation or so to recharge, he always found a new job. Extreme cruelty: what constituted that? Besides the night she left, she had never physically been harmed by her husband; even then, the half-hearted kick hadn't been so bad. He hadn't left a mark. Yes, there were times she was terrified of doing something to set him off. Everyone in his sphere knew his temper was legendary, but if you accepted him, you accepted his outbursts. His words were often hurtful and demeaning, but did that constitute cruelty? This all seemed too much.

"Leo, take a breath." Her attorney leaned across the folding table to touch Leo's shaking shoulder. "It's okay. This can seem overwhelming, but I am here to help you with the legal legwork. You're going to get through this."

Leo nodded, though her shoulders slacked with apprehension. The vibration in her pocket resumed an insistent reminder. Focus, Leo, she told herself. "Well, maybe there's something." She took a small sip of water. "I didn't know this when we got married, but apparently, he's on probation."

Candice's pink lipstick mouth widened into an almost perfect O. "Now you're talking. I can look him up on the offender information system. What's his full name?" Her fingers flew over the keyboard. She leaned back, breaking into a full-on smile. Her eyes, magnified through the lens, glinted. "Your soon-to-be ex-husband has a conviction, assault, and battery. He was released on probation in December of 07." Two months before, Leo had run into him outside of Ned's. "And you didn't know this when you married him?" Leo shook her head. "And if you had known this, would you have agreed to matrimony?"

Leo paused. Would she have still married him? With the insight she now possessed, she knew she would have turned and walked (well, biked) away. But then, over two years ago, having felt betrayed by her father and desperate for escape, she couldn't be sure. Still, here was a way out.

"Leo, you cannot prevaricate on this. You must be sure. I need you to say this out loud. You have to convince yourself and me."

Another assertive reverberation from her pocket.

Why don't you leave me alone? That's all I want, Jake, for you to let me go, to let me get on with my life. But you never will. Not until I make this permanent. Leo took a deep breath and looked resolutely, no equivocation here, into her attorney's eyes. "No, I wouldn't have married him if I'd known he'd just been released from prison."

"Perfect. I can argue that the marriage contract was fraudulent. There wasn't full disclosure as to what you agreed to. Oklahoma is a no-fault divorce state now, but some judges want more. If Jake makes it difficult, having this cause will only strengthen our case. Right now, I am a cheap date unknown and underestimated. But I was top in my law class. I know my stuff backward and forward, and I will relentlessly advocate for you, Leo Lightfoot. I will fill out and file the 'Petition for dissolution of Marriage' papers. Jake will be served shortly. He won't know what hit him."

Leo walked down the steps and through the humming laundromat, feeling like she had just gone through a heavy-duty cycle herself. Starting the divorce process stirred all kinds of emotions. But the wheels on the bus were in motion now, and she had to brace herself for the firestorm to come. She forced herself to look at the messages. Nothing new; what did she expect?

When she first left their marriage, his texts started the way they always did after they fought—*Miss U. I need U. Cum back 2 me.* Over the ensuing weeks, they became more militant. *U R MY wife! U CAIN-T leave! U will B SORRY!* She learned never to answer her cell phone when he called. He only did that after he'd worked up an alcohol-induced rage. Seething with incensed vitriol, he was incapable of reason. His sole intent was to let Leo know what a pathetic wife and human being she was. She was the sole reason everything in his life was falling apart. As she thought about him, she became taut, stretched with layered tiers of anxiety and foreboding, reducing her, once again, into insignificance.

She biked unsteadily through the buttery soft afternoon toward Verona's Italian Eatery. Jennifer would be there, the fried ravioli appetizer already ordered, waiting to hear how the meeting with her attorney had gone. They'd talk and catch up as they had done every week since Leo returned to Tahlequah, sharing a late lunch. Then Leo would attend back-to-back classes on campus before her shift at the restaurant started. This is my life was a mantra she had been repeating since she left Jake behind. He is in the past. Don't give him power over you.

****

"Don't give me grief, Ray. Take your lunch break now." Despite the industrial-size fans that blew through open doors, the food manufacturing plant temperature was well above 110 degrees, and droplets of moisture

The Circle of Willis

beaded across Hope's forehead.

Ray started to protest. One of the processing machines was down for service maintenance, putting them behind schedule. He could skip lunch, work through and help them get caught up, but arguing with his sister wasn't worth the effort. When there weren't enough workers, Hope would take over for them while they took a respite.

"It's my responsibility," she told her brother when he first objected. "Let me do my job."

He felt guilty, but she was stubborn. She was the older sister she constantly reminded him, if only by ten minutes, and when she looked at him firmly, with her arms crossed over her chest, he knew the cause was lost.

Ray stepped outside, his paper lunch bag in hand, into the soup of Oklahoma summer. A heavy humid heat oppressively sank around him, blanketing the day, rendering all limp. Even a meager hot wind did not have the energy to stir the nearby bur oak tree's leaves into action. When Ray took a bite of his peanut butter and jelly sandwich, a loud concussion rocked the factory behind him. The noise sounded like someone had shot off a grenade. But that wasn't possible. He stood locked in place, conveyed instantly back to another time. He looked around, stunned. Where was he? Oh my God, where was his weapon? Did he leave it behind? Sergeant Sledge would make him pay for this.

Had his gun been blown out of his hands? Where were his comrades? Were they wounded somewhere? Every muscle in his body was taut, ready for fight or flight. From where did the explosion originate? Even as his body physically responded and prepared for action, his brain registered the world around him, which lay still and unaltered. In a split second after the detonation, chaotic turmoil raged inside him. Just as his intellect pulled him back, attempting to ground him, he heard a blood-curdling scream emanating from the facility's interior. A pitched, piercing wail caused him to run toward the source of the blast. The keening came from Hope.

"My baby, my baby," she was on the ground, rocking back and forth, with fleshy blood on her hands and face splattered all around. He could not process the images before him. The scene looked exactly like the direct impact of an improvised explosive device on a human body. Yet his sister sat before him, seemingly whole.

"What happened, Hope?" He dropped before her, trying to focus, to perform a cursory assessment. Her pregnancy still appeared intact, and even as he was taking her radial pulse, he could see a quick flash of movement beneath her mint green knit maternity top.

"A jar of warm chokecherry jelly exploded in her hands, probably a defect in the glass, or maybe some food bits were trapped under the lid during processing," Pearl Whitehorse was talking on the phone with a 911 dispatcher. That accounted for the pulpy grisly appearance of the residue around her. Another employee rushed over with a plastic bucket of water and a clean cloth and placed the container next to Ray. He gently wiped a significant laceration on Hope's forehead and asked Pearl to hold pressure there while he dipped his sister's hands in the pail of water.

He talked to her in murmurs. "You're going to be okay. Your baby is fine." He deftly examined her appendages. Sharp pieces of glass were embedded in the skin, and blood oozed around the insertion sites. The top dermal layer of several of her fingertips had been peeled away. He palpated lightly for dislocations and broken bones, all the while reassuring her, "You're all right. Your baby is safe," until the paramedics arrived.

****

"Your sister wants you to pick up the hand-tossed pizza she ordered at Persephone's." Gabrielle stood at the door to the garage, Ray's improvised living quarters. Inside was musty and dark. Ray sat in the back corner, in the blue plastic chair he had hauled inside. He took another swallow of peppermint schnapps.

"Just leave me alone." He slumped forward, his elbows on his knees. For goodness' sake, couldn't they just let him be? He and Gabrielle had been by Hope's side in the emergency department all afternoon while the medical team debrided the glass from her hand, skillfully stitched up the two-inch gash in her forehead, and gave her intravenous fluids to address the pre-term contractions she was having due to dehydration. Finally, after a reactive non-stress test and a reassuring fetal ultrasound, after the emergency room doctor was confident that both mother and baby were clinically stable, they were discharged to recover at home. Wasn't that enough? He needed a few hours to process what transpired.

How could he explain to Hope, to Gabrielle, or to anyone who might listen how the sight of the gelatinous chokecherry jelly mixed with his sister's blood that clung to everything after the blast looked just like the pieces of human flesh he had to recover after the series of detonations in Afghanistan? The substance stuck to the surrounding landscape, adhering to the trees, and the bushes, so you couldn't tell to whom the flesh belonged or where the body part came from. Rows of body bags waited for the fragmented remains. Even when you pulled security while others resumed the task of specimen collection, part of you was grateful you were standing on the berm, alive and still breathing, while the other part of you fiercely wanted to take the place of someone who had a wife and children at home. What happened was horrific. If someone had to die, you wished it had been you. You yearned for the nightmare to be over, for it all to be done.

While serving in an active war zone, Ray thought being home would change things, but returning hadn't made a difference. When you thought that life might be getting easier, that maybe you were going to scrabble through the quagmire—a visualization, a singular sound, a smell would bring the experience crashing back. Was there another way of escape? The allure of amnesia, total insensibility, and unconsciousness was overpowering.

Gabrielle was still there, waiting for his response. He yelled in her direction, "You go get the pizza." He took another drag from the bottle he opened ten minutes ago. How did his sister know? Did she have Spidey's senses?

"It's not that I don't approve of drinking," Hope told him weeks before she asked him to help at the manufacturing plant. "It's just that I'm terrified of you doing something irreparable. When you drink, you go so far down that rabbit hole nothing can reach you." What she didn't say to him, but what Ray knew she could see, was how in those moments when Ray self-medicated, he was trying to fill the raw, seared-open depths of despair.

Gabrielle took a measured breath, still speaking through the screened door, making eye contact impossible. "I'm not going to leave her alone, doctor's orders. Besides, knowing that you're in here drinking yourself into oblivion is causing Hope way more stress than that whole jar exploding in her hands did. Believe me. If I had my way, you could do your thing, drink until you blackout if that's what you want." She hesitated, as if unable to assess the efficacy of her words, then pushed forward. "It's not that I don't care about you. I do. You're connected to my partner in ways I'll never fully understand, and I get it. The problem is when you do your thing, it impacts your sister. Hope and this baby are my future." She wavered a shadowy silhouette. "Please, Ray. Just go get the damn pizza."

He screwed the cap back on the bottle and sighed heavily. "Give me the keys."

"Not happening. You've been drinking." She was resolved. "It's a mile there. You can handle the distance. You knock that out running every morning on your way to meet Miguel."

"The pizza will be cold by the time I get back." He let the screen door slam behind him.

Gabrielle gave him a weak smile. "That's what microwaves are for." Written on her face, in her weary eyes, was gratitude, for this one small gesture, for giving Hope one less thing to worry about.

Ray took a deep breath, felt in his back pocket for his wallet and cell phone, looked down the long and winding drive that led toward town, and took the first step.

Temporary Shelter

"He just won't leave me alone." The cell in Leo's apron pocket vibrated as she reached for a pizza box, her back to the entrance. Judy skirted around her to grab an order pad before heading to the newly arrived group of college students talking loudly in the corner booth.

"Give him time," she called over her shoulder. "Guys like that eventually run out of steam. He's too lazy to keep going."

Leo didn't tell Judy how, just two days ago, Jake sat in her dad's driveway, in his pickup, honking and demanding that he tell him where Leo was living and working. Jake refused to listen to her father's reasoned responses, and he refused to leave until her dad had no alternative but to call the police to report a trespasser. Of course, he fled the scene by the time an officer arrived. Leo sighed and leaned against the counter for the first time all afternoon. They had been slammed and running nonstop since the start of her shift hours ago. She took a deep breath and pulled out her cell. There was a new string of text messages: *Be afraid, very afraid! I know where U work. I know where U live!!* She shakily shoved the phone back into her apron pocket, and in the process, her elbow knocked one of the ceramic bovines off the counter onto the ground.

It shattered.

Pieces flew across the black and white checkerboard floor. Oh, for goodness' sake. Here you go again, letting him get under your skin. She bent over, sweeping the cow bits into a pile when she heard the restaurant's entrance bell chime. Her stomach lurched. Was Jake already making good on his threats? The door opened. She looked up and stopped mid-sweep.

First, she noticed his eyes. They were guarded, an eerie impenetrable blue from which no light was reflected. Ray. He moved closer to her and stopped. His intense, edgy gaze traveled over her, but not in the way she was used to with Jake or his friends. Ray took in her entirety, a trained soldier's look that missed no detail. She was not objectified but even more unnerving; she felt uncovered, seen.

****

Ray surveyed the woman before him. Leo had always been slim, but there had also been a softness, an innocence, about her. Now there settled an experience-driven tenacity in her bones, evidenced by how her clavicle and hips subtly protruded from her clothing like a provisional form of body armor shielding her interior. Leo's hair, gathered into a tightly woven French braid, was pulled off her face, emphasizing her ethereal skin, which made her dark brown eyes look haunted and too big for the delicate features of her face. She was frightened of something or someone; of that, he was sure. He knew the shell-shocked look soldiers had after being in a war zone for a while. The unease flickered in her, too, a form of trauma. He wondered if her experience had anything to do with the lighter band of skin around her ring finger. In all the years Ray had known Leo, fear was one emotion he had never seen manifested before.

Their eyes were still locked on each other when they simultaneously said, "What the hell happened to you?" They both stood, taken aback. Leo was the first to laugh.

****

The response was hesitant at first, more like a nervous reaction, an effort to convince herself that everything would be okay. But as her giggling became more full-bodied, spreading through her like a balm, a floodgate opened. She felt a baffling mix of reprieve and confusion. What was happening? Most of all, though, she felt an inexplicable kinship with this boy, now a man from her past, who stood before her, looking at her somewhat askance, trying to contain an amused smile.

Leo caught her breath. "Can I help you?" She managed to say, in her best server's voice possible, trying to tamp down another wave of hilarity.

Her eyes blazed as they had when she looked at him when she was young. His grin widened. When was the last time he had smiled like this? "I'm here to pick up a pie under the name of Hope Shipworth."

"Oh." She paused. Taking her turn to size him up. And she did so from top to bottom. "No wonder you look like crap. You're married."

He was stunned—the absurdity of it all. Leo's light laughter was contagious, and his defenses lowered. Her authentic, astonishingly honest observations pulled back carefully layered strands of protective tissue, reaching him on a deeper level. He laughed for the first time in months, maybe even years. Leo might have never known he had a sister. Even when Hope attended the track meets, which she rarely did because of her after-school activities, they never hung out together afterward. The farewell cookout invitation sent to the Lightfoot household never mentioned that his sister was throwing it.

He laughed, now without restraint. The tension, anger, and anxiety he'd been carrying with him momentarily lifted, a curtain rising on the anticipated first act of a beloved play. As the current swept through their cerebral cortexes, releasing endorphins, the electricity created a charged connection between them, a temporary shelter for two battle-weary beings in an unlikely place, a restaurant chock-full with memorabilia paying homage to Oklahoma's most unassuming gentle giant, the cow.

The Fear Cage

"Ray, I hate to ask you to do this, but our driver broke his leg training for a marathon while running with his dog. I couldn't make this stuff up if I tried. Anyway, we have to get this shipment of pasta sauce over to Muskogee by noon. Can you?"

Ray wiped his salsa-stained hands on his jeans. Hope handed him the keys to the company truck, along with a clipboard with the invoice and address. She was already waddling away before he could respond. He'd worked close to sixty hours a week for Hope for over two months. He was grateful for some new hires who looked like they would work out. Hope's baby was due any day. Ray's exhausting routine was predictable and left little fuel to ignite uninvited spirals.

Anyone looking at him, even those closest to him, his mom, Hope, Gabrielle, and Miguel, would say among themselves that he is doing so much better. He must be finally adjusting, thank goodness. They had no idea of the heavy burden he was carrying, the consequence of war that was slowly sapping away his life. Just because he wasn't showing outward manifestations of his internal struggle, just because he wasn't drinking himself into oblivion, didn't mean he was doing better. There was so much he couldn't share with anyone, even his twin sister. For instance, he hadn't driven once by himself since his return. Of course, they didn't notice this or think to question why he always asked someone to go with him to run errands. When he drove, Hope was with him, or he was with Gabrielle, Miguel, or his mother. Driving by yourself, outside of the wire, off the military base, was tantamount to death.

Now here he was, driving alone. No battle buddy, no one with whom he could converse. Having someone by his side, engaged in meaningless banter, as insignificant as this might seem, kept him tethered to his current reality. How could he describe the odd circuitry of his brain, how neurons overlapped one-time frame in his life with another so seamlessly he couldn't differentiate the two? He had trouble comprehending this himself, let alone being able to explain this phenomenon to another. All he had now was a truck bed full of Percy's Perfect Pasta Sauce and a belly full of dread.

I just have to drive to Muskogee, thirty miles there, thirty miles back, easy, simple. All I have to do is tell myself I'm in Oklahoma, safe and sound. Nothing bad happens here. I can do this.

Ray started the trip home. He was driving a different route than the one he had taken to Muskogee because that was something he was also hard-wired for. Never retrace your route, ever. When you went down a road, a combatant often raced out as soon as you passed, implanting improvised explosive devices, putting them in potholes, covering them up with loose ground or trash, embedding them, and waiting for detonation upon your return.

Always vary your course, and do not be predictable. This action can make the difference between life and death. Iraq and Afghanistan survival lesson number two.

Though he rationally understood this did not apply to life in the United States and how ridiculous the concept would sound to his family or friends. He could not bring himself to retrace a route, ever, not when he ran, but especially when he drove. Ray determined this placid summer afternoon that tomorrow, a rare day off after he and Miguel finished their morning run, he was going to campus. He would meet with a counselor, sign up for classes, and check the apartment listings—time to get on with his life.

Exhaustion, brought on by weeks of strenuous labor, continued alertness, and interrupted sleep patterns, prevailed. He was spent. All was quiet in the lull of the moment. The road was deserted. Ahead, Ray could see the carcass of a large buck, half on the pavement, half off. Just a dead animal. He felt his lids pulling downward. He slowly closed then opened them. Before him, he saw a rising mushroom tide of flame and earth. The immense discharge sent the convoy lead vehicle arching into the air like a toy. He could see the metal door flying off its hinges and splashing into the river at the same time, the up-armored Humvee was landing upside down in the weeds, and he thought, this is just a dream. With his foot off the accelerator, the truck rolled to a stop, thudding into the carcass on the edge of the road, but he did not notice. He plunged into darkness, deep inside a fear cage from which there was no escape.

****

"Ray, Ray!" He could hear the pounding on the door, the thudding of his heart in his ears, and a dull ache in his temples. What was happening? Hope cried and frantically tried to open the locked door. Behind her stood Gabrielle, looking stunned and afraid.

"You called me in a panic. I couldn't understand a word you were saying, then nothing. I thought you'd been in an accident, were sinking underwater, and couldn't talk. Thank goodness our company's vehicles have fleet tracking devices. I might have never found you." Hope aimlessly chatted, something she did when she was nervous, as she drove the company pickup, the steering wheel pushing gently into her swollen belly. "What kind of route home were you taking anyway? You're so far off the beaten path none of this makes sense." She kept glancing in her rear and side-view mirrors to confirm that Gabrielle was following.

He responded with silence.

She glanced at her brother. "What happened, Ray?"

"I can't. Not now. Please, Hope." He slumped against the passenger door. What had transpired was beyond communication. He couldn't begin to try.

"Ray?"

"I don't know!" His voice was more forceful than intended. Hope flinched. He softened and sighed. He always seemed to be hurting the people he cared the most about. She was just trying to help. "I'm sorry, Hope. A flashback? Maybe a panic attack? At least my body felt that way. But you don't black out with panic attacks, do you? The truth is, I don't know what happened. I just don't know."

They stopped at a red light just outside of town. Ray unbuckled his seat belt and reached for the door. "I'm getting out here."

"No! Ray, please! Come home with us and go for a

run. I'll make dinner. We can build a fire and eat outside. We don't have many more nights together before our lives are turned upside down by this little one." She offered him slim branches of normalcy, but they were insubstantial. He needed more.

He saw everything on her face, reading her fear that he would turn to alcohol to escape, the terror that something would happen. And that was his plan. "Hope, let me go. I need space to think. Even if I have a few drinks, I'll be okay." His guarantee carried little weight. Once the seductress started, she was difficult to put aside. But this was all he could give his sister right now. "Go home, be with Gabrielle, make dinner, and put a plate in the fridge for me if you want. I'll be home later."

A Nicked and Battered Dogwood

Leo could not get out of there fast enough. Judy and Domino, the cook, made her wait in the kitchen, until they saw Jake and Eric pull away, and they were sure they weren't coming back. She refused to let them call the police and rejected their advice to file a restraining order. "It'll only make things worse. Please don't call," she pleaded.

Her hands trembled, and tears were still falling, but her breathing slowed as she walked her bike down the street. Half an hour before she was due at the animal shelter, she wanted to use the time to regroup. What happened? She remembered taking an order for the vegetarian special called 'Put out to Pasture' from a sweet elderly couple. She remembered smiling as the lady showed her a picture of her new great-grandson. Then, out of nowhere, she had been tackled and shoved into a nearby wall. In an instant, she was on the ground, and Jake was on her. The evil eye necklace around his neck moved like a pendulum over her. She tried to change focus by looking at the high ceiling fans, which slowly turned, unperturbed, while he spat words of furry, as mad as she'd ever seen him.

"You ain't gittin' out so easy, missy. You think you and your chicken shit attorney are gonna git away with this?" He ripped the divorce notice, thrusting the paper fragments into her face. "I told you, I'm onto you. I know where you work and where you live!"

Judy and Domino ran to her aid, pulling him off her, yelling at him to stop, and threatening to call the police. At that, he hightailed out of there but not before turning to say, with a wicked grin, "Good seeing you again, wifey. Keep your eyes open. I'm fixin' to be there when you ain't lookin'. Be afraid."

****

When Ray stepped out of the liquor store, his paper-bagged purchase in hand, he saw her a block ahead, a determined stride, aggressively pushing her ride as if the bike had done something wrong. He broke into a jog and caught up with her. "Leo?"

She turned. Her eyes had that wild, caged, defeated look you see in the dogs from those animal rescue commercials on television. There were tears in her dark lashes. She nodded acknowledgment but kept walking, and he stepped beside her, matching her stride. They moved in silence. Occasionally, one would look over to the other, size them up, and think, however bad my day was, you look like you had a worse one.

"What happened to your hand?"

Leo picked up her right hand, which sported several heavy, tight stitches, and waved it in the air as one would do to deter an annoying fly. "Banshee bit me." He raised an eyebrow. Leo continued. "Totally my fault, I moved too quickly. The dog was afraid." No more was forthcoming, and Ray did not probe.

Leo leaned her bike against a nicked and battered dogwood situated next to the shelter. "There're cages to be cleaned, some animals need baths, and I'm working with a few who have been the victims of cruelty, trying to get them to trust people again so they don't get put down." She looked him in the eyes. "I could use some help."

Ray walked over to the dumpster behind the shelter and tossed the paper bag he'd been carrying into the contraption's open rusty mouth; the sound of glass breaking followed. "You're in luck then. Help is my middle name." He gave a self-deprecating shrug and, with half a smile, said, "Just don't make me go into a kennel alone with Banshee."

They worked side-by-side. She led, he followed, and as they labored, scrubbing down kennels, putting in fresh bedding, washing toys, and stopping to pet the occupants. As the hours wore on, the events of their prospective days seemed to achromatize.

The tension returned to her shoulders when they stepped back outside. Leo looked around, down the road, reassuring herself that no threat was around. Ray knew about this constant need for environmental assessment. As she reached for her bike, her hands began to shake. He could feel the fear rise off her in invisible, vibratory waves.

Ray started to put a hand over hers as she death-gripped the handlebars, the skin underneath the black stitches blanched, but he stopped. Touch is an intimate thing. What right did he have to breach her space when she was in a place of obvious distress? "What are you afraid of, Leo Lightfoot?" He gently probed, "What's going on?"

The late afternoon stretched languidly before them. Leo, pushing her bike, began to walk quickly. Ray fell in step with her. Frequently, Leo would glance over her shoulder. "I just can't shake the feeling that I'm being watched." Every time she saw a pickup, she would intently stare. As they moved, Leo began to talk. As she openly shared, Ray realized that contrivance had never been part of her makeup, though without a doubt, Leo had grown up, from what he could see, the essential core of her remained true.

"This is so stupid." Leo shored herself up and looked behind her back again just as they turned off the road and started down her root and rock-riddled driveway. "There's no way he figured out where I live. The only people who know are my family. They'd sooner die than give Jake that information. Intellectually, I know he is blowing hot air, trying to make me afraid. Unfortunately, it's working. I don't want to give him that power over me, but I can't help how my body feels."

She stopped before the plank door. A fine tremor ran through her body. She turned to face him. "This was my safe place, and I am letting him ruin it. How do I break out of this panic prison?" Her brown eyes were beseeching, honestly looking to him for the answers he did not have.

How could he offer her anything when he struggled himself? What did he have to give? But there she was standing before him, all five feet eight inches of her, waiting for advice, earnestly trusting that his offer would be true. So, he reached into his experience and spoke. "Each soldier in the United States Army is assigned a partner. I got my first battle buddy at boot camp." Ray swallowed, then continued, "Battle buddies hold each other accountable. They look out for each other. But most importantly, they have each other's back." He inhaled deeply. "I can be your battle buddy until the divorce is final, or you don't need one anymore."

He waited, uncertain of what her response might be. Given what she'd been through and how determined she was to establish her independence, he would understand if this battle buddy concept were something she wouldn't be interested in. "It's just a thought, and you don't have to decide anything now. There isn't anywhere else I have to be. I can check the house with you, make sure nothing is hiding in the closets, and stay until you feel comfortable."

"What about Hope, your wife? Will she mind?"

"Hope is my twin sister."

Leo looked at Ray for a long moment. She nodded and opened the door to the round river stone house, letting him in.

Once they walked through, making sure everything was as she had left it, Ray could see her relax. He could also see how connected she was to her home. Her slim body floated in the contained space as if in a dance, her energy bringing the inanimate alive. Early evening spilled in through the kitchen window, catching her movements and shining off a red tea kettle with wildflowers sprouting from its spigot. The light pooled onto the planked pine floor.

Leo brought in a solar tea jar from outside, smiling as she passed. "I'm trying to make my footprint as small as possible. No man-made energy was used, and you'll see, the taste is great." She pulled the tea bags from the large glass container and added raw sugar.

Placing the lidded decanter, two glasses, and a bag of chips in a cloth bag, which she carefully slung over her shoulder, she winced when the cloth caught one of her stitches. "Come on. I want to show you something."

She climbed the ladder by the base of her bed. Ray watched as Leo ascended. The pale pink cotton shirt she wore rose, exposing a thin piece of smooth flesh over her jeans. He followed her up. They were in an observatory of sorts. On a small wooden desk was a pair of binoculars and a Stokes Field Guide to the Birds of North America. Ray saw a notebook where Leo kept track of the birds she saw, with the date written in parenthesis. He recognized the tidy looped writing from the letter he received in Iraq, how long ago that seemed, a lifetime.

He walked around the upper chamber, looking out the windows, noting bird feeders positioned on the eastern and western fronts, "This is pretty sweet."

Leo's eyes glinted. "True, but there's more. I found this hidden opening while brushing off cobwebs." She sprung open a cleverly concealed door that blended seamlessly into the wall. Outside on the sloping rooftop was a platform, just large enough for two bodies to sit, or lie, side by side and look upward at the sky or toward the horizon. They climbed outside and took a seat next to each other. "Cell phone reception in the house is hit or miss. Usually, it's a miss. But it's pretty good up here."

Ray felt the outline of his phone in his jean pocket. I should shoot Hope a text, he thought, and let her know I'm still alive. But as quickly as he considered this, he let twilights current pull him back into the moment. Much later, long after night fully descended, after he said goodbye to Leo, who reassured him she was okay and would see him soon, he would pull out his phone intending to contact his sister and see one unread message waiting for him:

—Contractions started, water broke, meet us at the hospital.—

Leo unpacked the fabric bag. "About that battle buddy offer." She poured some tea and handed the glass to him. Ray looked at her. He raised an eyebrow. "That goes both ways, right? I mean, for the arrangement to work, this can't be one-sided. We must be equal partners. You have to be willing to let me be there for you."

Leo paused, long strands of dark hair playing across her solemn face, pushed by dusk's deepening breath. "I monopolized your time today. But don't think for one second that I didn't see you, Ray Shipworth. You're going through some heavy-duty stuff. You have to trust me. You have to let me in too."

He sat for a while, silently gazing into a shifting horizon. "What if I can't?"

Leo sized him up. He could tell she was trying to read him. But he wasn't being disingenuous. He honestly wasn't sure of his capabilities.

"Will you at least try?"

Ray nodded. Leo leaned over and bumped into him, shoulder to shoulder, the way she used to jostle him when she was just a kid, and he was an adolescent, the way she used to when they were Squirt and Blink. "Okay, here's to being battle buddies." Her eyes glowed. "Thanks for helping me get through today, battle buddy."

What Ray knew then, what he didn't share with Leo, was the mystifying phenomenon concerning battle buddy relationships. Keeping an eye out for the other, the support, the long-term commitment, the encouragement, the guidance, and the sense that you are never alone often led to a deeper substance. The alliance became something you couldn't imagine yourself being without.

Ray and Leo sat together, drinking sweet solar-infused tea and munching on sea-salted kettle chips. Bantering with the facility of childhood friends, they were equally serene in their silences while watching the sun's last strong rays burn intensity into the colors and shapes of the Oklahoma landscape.

Echo

Somewhere between Caney Creek and Dipping Spring Hollow, Echo lost her way, which is an unfortunate event for a dog. What let her down? Her nares flared, taking in a myriad of odors, quickly filing them. No, it wasn't her sense of smell. It was her sense of direction that turned on itself like a shot from a gun. In fact, that very clap had sent her running in the first place. Maybe it was her imagination. Maybe he hadn't intended to level the gun and point right between her eyes. But every instinct in Echo said *run*. So, she had. And in the volley of shots that followed, she found herself flying—flying through a dense grove of shortleaf pines and trees whose branches bowed under the force of a stiff Oklahoma wind, flying over small tributaries of the river thick with the scent of rabbit and red squirrel. Part of her wanted to stop, inhale deeply, roll in the dry pile of deer dung, and revel in the patches of sunlight between trees, but Echo's inner instincts remained clear, run, run as if life depended upon this single act.

****

At night coyote calls carry. They rise and fall on the wind, weaving an intricate song. Leo crawled onto the platform of her home's roof. She listened to the hunger in the voices of the howling creatures and looked upward at the stars overcrowding the black

Oklahoma night. The heat from the roof radiated through her into a temperate atmosphere.

Six hours ago, there was a preliminary hearing for her divorce petition. Jake had not appeared. Despite his aggressive threats, she hadn't seen him since he accosted her in the restaurant. The rumor was he had a new relationship. She wasn't surprised. Leo remembered how Jake relentlessly pursued her when she was an insecure, naive high school freshman. He worked his well-honed charm and made her feel desired. Though the relationship was clandestine, she had fervently believed the promises he made and never questioned the premise of why they couldn't be seen in public together. At that time, she had zero experience with bad men. When someone said they loved you, you trusted them. She thought about her two-year marriage and knew how despite years of commitment, some relationships are composed of, at best, debilitated threads, nothing more substantial than the diaphanous clouds skittering across a nighttime sky. The coyote's melody cascaded.

Leo understood distant pining and internal desire. Ray. What was she going to do with these developing feelings? For now, nothing. She had to tuck them away and fold them into the fabric of her being. How different the evolution of her relationship with Jake had been from Ray's. Leo held in her heart an abundance of memories of Ray from her childhood. She had grown around those events, carrying them inside her body. For years, their lives had entwined. And for as long as she had known him, he remained steady and true. He never made her feel like she was a pest. He was patient and listened to what she said, no matter how ridiculous. He was ever kind.

The last time she saw him before his departure was at the farewell cookout. Leo thought she wouldn't see him again, but there was a return. And now, in an unforeseen yet remarkable arc, he was her battle buddy. A premise she knew little about but was quickly learning. Being with Ray was a connection renewed, a relationship redefined, like a wet colt, striving to stand on her own for the first time, afraid of knees buckling underneath its weight, yet eager and pushing through, growing stronger and more confident with each fledgling step. Outside, with the Oklahoma night rich with stars and a half-moon that flitted in and out of the scudding clouds, she sighed. Isolation, the sounds of nature woven into stillness, were now comforting, cocooning.

****

Echo hadn't meant to moonlight hunt; foraging was easier in the day. But when she made her nighttime nest, rooting around and around in the pine needles, she startled a rabbit. Meals were never guaranteed. The cottontail was flying, and then so was she–every muscle in her body taut, firing full twitch. In and out of the shadow and silver light, tonight relying on scent more than sight, she trusted these instincts; the drive of the pursuit was exact and true.

****

At first, Leo wasn't sure if the form was the shadow of a cloud racing across the moon or a coyote. The apparition was lean and moved with agile urgency. As the cloud moved past the moon, Leo stood up with a start and whispered, "Oh, puppy, what are you doing here? You're so far away from home."

****

And when Echo was done, her belly full, she looked up and noticed a figure standing on top of a house in the remoteness. She stood stock still, observing the shadowed form who intently surveyed the landscape as if searching for something. Then quite suddenly, the body disappeared, swallowed whole, into an opening. A light from inside the house turned on, and Echo knew the occupant could either cause her great harm or provide a degree of comfort. She would have to watch and see.

When Your Back is to the Wall

"Even when the restaurant is empty, why do you always sit in the same booth, in the farthest corner possible, with your back to the wall? And if that spot isn't available, you stand near the employee's autographed aprons, leaning against the surface like you're holding the entire structure up." Leo leveled a considered gaze at Ray, who was once again seated at his favorite table. "And if the people don't vacate your favorite place, you get carryout and leave?" Her order pad dangled from her right hand, though why she needed it, she didn't know. He always chose the same thing, a veggie and cheese submarine, when he wasn't picking up carryout for his sister.

Ray looked away. "About those aprons, what is the point? No one who works here is ever going to get famous?"

At that moment, Judy Langard walked by carrying a platter of sliders. "Just for that comment, mister, I am going to prove you wrong. One day my apron will be the talk of the town." She smiled seductively over her shoulder, always the flirt. Her friendliness helped in the tip department, but she remained faithful to Brody.

"Don't think you are getting off that easy, Ray." Leo pointedly smiled. "Battle buddy rule number two: when asked, answer questions truthfully." She put his Sprite in front of him.

"What are you now, the maker of all rules?" He took a quick sip of his drink and continued. "I'm the expert on battle buddies. Remember, I introduced the concept to you. And you, Leo Lightfoot, are a mere novice." Though he tried to appear at ease, Leo could tell there was a guarded edge to him. She wasn't going to let this deter her, though. She was taking her battle buddy role seriously. He picked the wrong person if he thought he would get off without effort. Since their pact, Ray would check in with her at least once a day. They'd meet between classes or see each other at the shelter or restaurant. If he didn't reach out, she'd check in with him with a text, a joke, or an observation. And amazingly, Leo found this tentative connection worked. The fear Jake would show up unannounced and harm her, was abating. And even if he did, she rationalized, I will survive. But she needed to help Ray the way he was helping her. If only he would let her.

"Domino put jalapenos on your sub, just as you like it." She slid the plate in front of him and glided into the seat across the table facing him. "I haven't had a break yet, but I am taking one now. You have ten minutes to fill me in. Remember fifty-fifty, the terms of our agreement." She took a drink of water and leaned back in the vinyl booth, watching him as he took a bite of his sandwich. "You told me you would try."

****

Ray nodded and silently ate his sub. Between bites, he looked at her, patiently waiting. He tried to size her up, startled by her astute observations. Until she called him out, this was something he hadn't realized he was doing. Shoot, Leo was getting just as bad as his sister and mother. They could sense when something shrouded him and took him to a dark place, but it wasn't observable or tangible. How did they do that?

What had he gotten himself into with this battle buddy stuff? Why did he care about this woman he'd known since she was eight? He knew nothing about her now except she needed someone, and he offered to be that person. But what if he didn't have the bandwidth in him? What damage would he do if she had these expectations and he failed? Why hadn't he kept his mouth shut?

He felt cornered and pressured by her inquiries. How could he explain the way his rearranged war brain worked? Why did he retreat to the furthest corner? He hadn't thought about this before. He only knew he could see everything before him when he sat in this spot. From this location, he could maintain situational awareness. No one in the restaurant, the patrons, the servers, and even the cooks, could appear without him seeing them first. From this vantage point, in a small beef and pizza joint in rural Oklahoma, there would be no sneak attacks. He had an unobstructed view of the lurking danger his mind expected to materialize at any moment. Ray understood this wasn't rational. What he also couldn't fully grasp, though, was how the behavior had been ingrained in him since boot camp and repeatedly reinforced through his experiences during his two tours of duty. Survival was imperative and was based on figuring out the safest position possible in combat. When your back was to a solid wall, the odds of living to see another moment dramatically improve.

But all he could say, looking into her probing, deep brown eyes, was, "It's a safe place."

****

Leo reached across the plastic-clothed table and carefully put her hands over his. Words were not necessary. She could see Ray's inner turmoil and how he had struggled just to be able to utter that simple phrase: It's a safe place. She slid out of the booth, reached into her apron, and put his tab on the table before him. "Battle buddy code upheld. Thank you, Ray." She smiled. He sat and returned her gaze, looking more relaxed than when he walked into the restaurant. She picked up his plate and empty glass, then walked away.

Leo held something close to her heart, something she wanted to say but held back. She did not want to scare him away, to stop him from sharing with her. As she headed to the kitchen toward the wash sink, she thought, I wish I could be that for you, Ray. I want to be your safe place.

****

When she cupped her hands ever so lightly over his clenched fists, a warmth flowed into him. His hands, clamped with tension, loosened as the electromagnetic current ran the length of his body. He was confused by his reaction. How could such a brief touch transport him to another plane where he glimpsed a future where everything might be okay? Even his on-again, off-again companion, peppermint schnapps, had not been able to take him to such a place.

Ray threw the money, including the tip, on the table and left, his head and heart off balance.

The Risk/Benefit Equation

Out of the corner of his eye, Ray saw movement near the edge of the tree line. He stood still in the sweltering noontime sun, waiting, watching, his bologna sandwich dangling from his left hand.

Hope delivered her baby the night Ray and Leo became battle buddies. She was home on maternity leave. But, still, she packed sandwiches. "For goodness's sake," he argued, "I am a grown man and can make my lunch if I want to."

"But that's the point," his sister returned, her ten-pound son in her arms, facing him, all softness and folds and wide nascent eyes. "If I left it up to you, you wouldn't eat. I can't have you falling into a vat of Checker's Raisin Chutney because your blood sugar is too low."

She was right. If not for his sister's sandwiches, he would skip lunch. And the only reason he ate those was because of the guilt. If Hope made them, he would eat them.

A rich copper shadow rippled through the dense foliage. Ray took a few steps forward, and the movement stopped. He ripped his sandwich down the middle and held half aloft. A russet nose poked through the brush. It quivered, discerning the scent of lunch meat from pickled beets. Soft long ears framed golden eyes which fixed, not on the sandwich as expected, but directly on Ray as if trying to solve the risk-benefit equation before advancing. As she took one more step into the light, Ray could see the lightly built dog's shiny skin pulled tautly, revealing the stark outline of ribs through her short hair.

"Oh, baby girl, you need this way more than I do." Not wanting to startle the skittish creature, Ray placed both halves of the sandwich on the ground and slowly backed away.

Dear Family and Friends

"Hey, Mom." Ray leaned down and dropped a kiss on his mother's silver-streaked head.

"So glad you could come!" Maria beamed and thrust a paint roller on an extension in his hands. "You get the job of going for the high spots. No one else can reach those places without a ladder."

Maria watched closely as her son surveyed the dilapidated house. She was trying to gauge him, to ascertain how present he was. Something she had always taken for granted—a maternal ability to read the barometric pressure of your child had dissipated.

When he returned home, a seasoned war veteran who served two prolonged tours of duty, Maria had been under the false assumption she could finally breathe and let go of the anxiety she'd shouldered the entire time he was gone. While Ray had his burdens to bear, her son would never fully comprehend the weight she and Hope carried while he was away. How their minds would take them to dark trapping corridors where they felt they would never see Ray again, never hear his laugh, never be able to wrap their arms around him, enfolding the weight of his being. Ray would never understand how every time, between the waking hours of 6 a.m. and midnight, when a strange car pulled into the driveway, you'd immediately drop to your knees, shaking and crying because you knew this was the time the uniformed service members would ring your doorbell to state your son had been killed. Ray would never know how her heart jumped into overdrive when the online family support system lit up the second a communication blackout occurred. The clock started ticking once this happened. You knew within the next twelve hours, some family somewhere would be getting the news. Their soldier was seriously injured or dead. Will there be a knock on your door this time? When the notification period ended, when the official word went out by electronic mail, a relief you'd never known, washed over you. On this day, at this moment, your child was still alive.

In this space of quiet rejoicing, however, the devastating knowledge existed that for another family, an agonizing nightmare, from which there was no return, was beginning. And how can you take any form of solace when another family suffers? The process was gut-wrenching and inhumane. Today one of her son's comrades died on the battlefield.

Thank God he's alive, thank you. But for what, taking the life of someone else's son or daughter? There were no victors in this sick, sick, absolute game.

Dear Family and Friends, on November eleventh, our company was involved in an incident that resulted in two soldiers being killed in action. The soldiers' primary and secondary next of kin have been notified. On behalf of our Company, I send my condolences to the families. Memorial services for these heroes will be held at a time and place to be determined. Please remember to keep these soldiers and all other deployed servicemen in your thoughts and prayers. You will receive details from your family readiness group on how to support the family and when the memorial will be.

How naive they had been, thinking all would be restored when Ray returned, physically in one piece. Maria had read the "What to expect after deployment" brochures and knew some adjustments would have to be made and would take time. But she hadn't been prepared for the shattering of her son's core. All the truths he held for a lifetime had been tested. In addition to the parts that made him uniquely Ray, there were layers of confusion, anger, and at times an outright attempt to lose the remaining pieces of himself in destructive behavior. She learned over the past years how to get through a day by focusing on getting through each hour. Maria returned to this strategy.

In this sun-drenched moment, Maria felt blessed. Ray, her only son, her second-born child, was alive, sober, pushing through, and for this, she was grateful. Every night, her daughter sent a text:—He's okay.—

—He's mowing the grass.—

—Barbecue is on the grill. Can U join us?—

And on those dark, starless nights when he turned to the bottle, Maria would bend in prayer. Please ease his pain. Let him get through this night unscathed. Please let him live to see another day.

Maria, Hope, Gabrielle, Miguel, and now Leo, were frantically trying to weave supportive strands underneath him, hoping that even if some of them broke, the rest would not fail from the remaining weight. They were all on Team Ray, even if he couldn't see it.

****

He looked furtively over his shoulder. "You sure

Dad isn't going to be here?" Since he left his father's church mid-sermon, Ray managed to avoid him. The last thing he needed was one of his father's lectures, followed by another of their agonizing confrontations. In Ray's mind, he had taken the first step after his return; he had tried. He had attended church as requested, had lasted through the beginning of the sermon. But as far as he could see, besides physical appearances, his father had not changed.

Ray dipped the roller in the summer wheat exterior enamel and began painting. Their church congregation had been helping down-on-their-luck parishioners, and community members refurbish crumbling domiciles for as long as Ray could remember. Volunteering so many times over the years, they had developed a seamless routine, each person playing to their strengths. They arrived in droves, bringing whatever equipment was needed and food and water to sustain themselves. Under an awning, Ray could see Hope and Gabrielle helping set up the nourishment tent. Gabrielle was wearing baby Hiram in a forward-facing infant carrier, his chubby legs sliced through the sultry air, an Olympian swimming the backstroke. Their goal was to complete the act of service in a day. The group flexed as needed throughout the assignment. They assisted others when necessary, fell out for rest, then returned. All help was welcome; some members came and stayed all day, and others came and went as their schedules allowed. Yet no one was made to feel guilty should they not be able to contribute. And somehow, miraculously, his father always said, at the end of the day, their work was done.

"I wish you and your father would mend those

fences and get on with it." There was a catch in his mother's throat. She wiped her face leaving a streak of pale yellow across her cheek. "But to answer your question, no. He's in Oklahoma City, attending an evangelical pastor round-up. I don't expect him to be back until late tonight."

Ray spoke as he continued painting. "I'm not the son he wanted me to be. In his words, I'm a disappointment. How do I fix that, Mom?" Ray knew she could hear the pain in his voice, the ever-present need for his father's approval. "I can't change who I am, and I shouldn't have to apologize for doing what I thought was right."

"Even though your dad is an orator, I don't think he always chooses the right words. It's not dissatisfaction with you. Your father's personally distressed. He was dismayed he couldn't protect you from the repercussions of war. He felt his job was to shield you. And, of course, he feels if you respected him, you'd have honored his wishes and wouldn't have enlisted."

"We've been down this road before, Mom. Enlisting was never personal. Why doesn't he get that? We see the world differently. I never meant to be disrespectful."

"I know that, son."

****

Maria paused and looked at him. He kept painting, avoiding eye contact. She knew the time had come. Even though she respected her husband's need for privacy, she didn't understand why he wanted to hide this part of his past. Having a functioning family took precedence—enough of this lunacy, this inability to navigate beyond the deadlock.

"There's a reason he's this way," she said. She could see both points of view clearly and understood them. Why couldn't the two most important men in her life get their relationship sorted out? She sighed. "Even though you might not be able to forgive him, if you can see things from his perspective, maybe, at least, you'd understand."

The second wave of volunteers was heading toward the food tent when his father's gold Buick Century pulled into the drive. Ray stopped, dead in his tracks, paint roller in hand, and looked accusingly at his mother. "I thought you said he'd be gone all day!"

"That's what he told me this morning." Ray looked distressed and ready to bolt. "Ray, you must believe me. I had no idea he'd be here."

****

With a whispered surge, Ray heard the members of his father's congregation murmur. "He is here. Pastor Shipworth came!" The acknowledgment moved through the crowd in an undulating swell. The words were imbued with admiration and respect. For Ray, there was a disconnect. As a child, he stood where they were, feeling adoration for his father. Now, there's just an unending sense of let-down, of being constantly judged, and of being found severely lacking. He returned to the task at hand. Ray determined not to back down. *I committed to being here and won't let him bully me into leaving.* He saw his mother steel herself, and, with resigned fortitude, she resumed painting.

What We Carry

We all carry reminders of the person we used to be. For Bert Shipworth, the fat was gone, but the covering, the skin which held all in place for decades, remained. Ray saw folds of sagging epidermis beneath his father's starched button-down shirt, squished underneath his pressed twill dress pants. And he remembered a patient he transported to the hospital once with complications from bariatric surgery. The thirty-five-year-old had shared the unexpected effects of extreme weight loss. When he hit his target weight, everyone around him celebrated, thinking his struggle was over because he had finally achieved his goal. But what they didn't understand, the patient explained, was the physical and emotional pain of obesity merely morphed. The enormous undertaking had shifted and had simply become less apparent. Was this what his father was experiencing now, Ray wondered? The hollowed-out patient likened the experience to living inside a deflated balloon, carrying the excess layers of flesh around. The chafing unrelentingly continued as a constant reminder of what you once were, all the space you had occupied. The membrane mantles would rub together, one thick layer against the other. They would split open from the constant friction, tissue weeping again and again.

Out of the corner of his eye, Ray saw him work the crowd. He shook hands, patted people on the shoulder, and inquired about them. He laughed and told everyone what a good job they were doing. He was getting closer.

Ray heard his father musing, "I must be getting old. I thought the Pastoral round-up was today. Turns out it's next week. My mistake."

Always larger than life, Ray's father had been a looming presence in his world for as long as he could remember. But delayed parenthood had a toll. His mother and father were close to seventy years old. Ray could see a bend in his father's back, his shoulders curled forward, and deep lines etched his face like a cracked windshield. Ray surreptitiously continued to observe as his father drew nearer.

"My wife, my son!" His voice was behind them. They simultaneously turned, acting surprised. Pastor Shipworth beamed, bestowing upon them the look of unabashed welcome he gave to visitors and his congregation alike when they walked through the chapel doors every Sunday morning. Ray was knocked off balance.

Maria stepped forward and put her hand on his arm, a show of affection that was unheard of. "Bert? I thought…"

He put his free hand over hers for the briefest moments. "I made an error, that's all. I penned in the wrong date on my calendar." But while he talked to her, he looked upward into his son's eyes. This was the first time they'd been face to face since before Ray left for boot camp. "So good to see you, son. I am sorry you couldn't stay for the entire sermon—"

"Dad, stop…" Ray was already closing in and ready to leave. Recognition of their patterned history slammed into him. As he turned to go, his father's voice broke through.

"No, Ray. Please, don't leave on account of me." His father threw both hands in the air as if in supplication or under arrest.

"I can see everything is under control. I need to return to the church to do some paperwork. I'm not needed here." He said this without accusation, without animosity. Ray was speechless. He watched his father back away, moving toward the parked Buick. Then he stopped, folded his hands together, and spoke directly to his son. "Ray, I just wanted to tell you…"

Here we go, Ray thought. He couldn't leave without a dig, without letting me know how I failed in life. Pastor Shipworth took a deep inhalation. Pinpoint eyes stared unfaltering. "I've been meaning to tell you that I admire the strength of your conviction and respect your call to service."

Ray and Maria stood side by side, paint roller and brush nearly falling from their hands, stunned. Bert smiled and continued. "Our church has a new sign, did your mom tell you that? Maybe you could try us again, swing by, see the new marquee, and join the congregation for a service."

Ray was about to decline, to forage for an excuse. "In addition to my new job at the hospital, helping Hope at the manufacturing plant, I have classes." But he stopped. For the first time in his life, he could see his father's request was simply an appeal, not a non-negotiable demand.

"Our doors are always open."

Ray swallowed, then nodded, watching his father walk away, folds of concealed skin moving with him.

****

The light shining off the gold hood of Bert Shipworth's car almost rendered him sightless. He reached into his glove box and pulled out a pair of sunglasses. John 9:25 played in his head, *I was blind, but now I can see*, and as he buckled up and pulled away, leaving behind his nuclear and church family, he gave thanks. After almost a week spent in a state of constant fasting, extreme emotional turmoil, extended prayer, biblical study, and kneeling for hours upon a bed of rice, with the guidance of his old mentor, everything changed.

He was granted the gift of sight and insight. Pastor Shipworth no longer saw himself as an ordained enforcer, one tasked with addressing and correcting sinful and destructive behavior. His mission was reborn. Now he was meant to support, honor, and lead with grace and love. Judgment belonged to a higher power. What he ultimately revealed to his higher consciousness, a higher being, one who spoke through the voice of his brother Gus, then his spiritual teacher Pastor Goodwin, during the dark night of his reckoning, he will never forget.

"You ask me what is my truth, what do I see? What I see now is a daughter who is kind, faithful, and searching. I see her in her innocence, laughing and playing as a child with the other children of the congregation, including cherished Gabrielle. I see a young woman who is soul searching, trying to understand who she is, a human being who, no matter what path she travels, is equally worthy of God's love. How I want to protect her from the harsh world. But she's strong and brave and has an inner veracity she must follow.

"I see a devoted wife, a loving mother, struggling to do everything in her power to support her daughter and son. I see a woman of enduring spirit whose invisible suffering and the compounding years of loss enabled her to serve with deep compassion and gentleness. I see a woman of infinite patience and discernment, one who accepts her husband's weakness and frailty, who steadfastly stood by his side during the seasons of ministry when God presented faith-testing obstacles.

"I see a son with an abiding sense of duty, responsibility, and hunger for service. I see a son who is struggling, who doesn't know I have changed. Not only do I accept and honor him, but I am proud of the man he has become. But there will come a time when Ray can see, he will know, and I will be there. The oxen are slow, but the earth is infinitely patient."

The Weight of Love

Near two in the afternoon, Ray and Maria joined Hope and Gabrielle for a late lunch under an ancient sycamore. They formed a loosely knit circle surrounding the sleeping baby. Hiram lay on a quilt, flat on his back, meaty palms facing upward. Over their heads, an open crown of crooked branches arched close to a hundred feet, reaching far into the sky. Maria watched her son. When he sat down, he ran his hand along the massive supporting trunk, feeling where a sheet of bark had scaled away, leaving a smooth, milky interior.

They ate in amiable quiescence, listening to the distant chatter of volunteers working and the single-chirped communications among house finches perched high in the towering tree.

"We were fourteen," Maria began in a low and steady voice. She tried to ignore the look Ray and Hope exchanged. She knew what they were thinking; here is our parent's story, at long last. They continued to eat casually as if she was simply sharing an exchange she had last week with a check-out clerk at the gas station. And as sunlight filtered through the stately sycamore's ovate leaves, playing across her children's familiar and loved features, Maria, uncertain how she would unpack this tightly woven history, forged forward, presenting them with an unglamorous truth, the story of their origins. She was resolved; there was no stopping now.

On the tentative strands of the afternoon, she laid bare the meeting and growing together of two struggling adolescents. She sketched along the outlines of their lives, revealing to Hope and Ray they had an uncle they never knew, one their father looked up to and loved. Skimming surfaces, she explained, her voice centered, how their father's brother was drafted and returned from Vietnam a changed soul. He couldn't find solace, no matter where he searched, and six months after his return, he killed himself. With quick brush strokes, Maria offered her children an insight into why their father chose the ministry and chose to eat, in abundance, food for the body and soul.

"His appetite for food and religion became a way of life, constant, reliable nourishment. As your dad became more committed to his calling, he saw how he could help others avoid the pitfalls in life. He wanted the best for his congregation. There was to be no alcohol, no caffeine, or anything that might alter one's level of consciousness, no gaudy distractions, such as popular music or dancing, and absolutely no straying from the word, all they had to do was follow God's law, his commandments, and they would be rewarded."

Hiram woke. His wide eyes followed the alluring cadence of sound. First, he looked upward to the sycamore's branched limbs holding tucked-away trilling birds, then steadily moved to the deeper timbre of Maria, his beloved grandmother. He smiled a sleepy expression of pure contentment, his gaze trailing around the band of human beings who surrounded him.

Maria scooped him up, cradling him in her arms, kissing the dark hair that curled in cords around his temple. At first, she was taken aback when Hope and Gabrielle announced his name. An older man's moniker for a baby, what were they thinking? But Gabrielle explained the name belonged to her revered grandfather and meant exalted. Hiram suited him perfectly. Maria saw that now. Her grandson, whose existence every day was treasured, filled the name with purpose. She thought of the tentative way she and Bert came together, the improbable journey that led them all to this point, and gently stroked her grandson's limbs.

Hiram squirmed. Maria kissed his head before handing him over to Hope, who discreetly began nursing him under a cotton blanket. "You must understand, by keeping a tight rein on his parishioners and his family, your father finally felt he had control over his life. He thought he could keep everyone he loved and cared about safe and protected. God promised this, and he believed. Clear to him was what happened when people strayed. He didn't want this for anyone, especially the two of you, his flesh and blood." She let her words fall around them. Maria stood.

It was done. She shared the parts they needed to know. What they chose to do with this information was up to them. She began gathering the remains of their meal. Gabrielle and Ray joined her, picking up paper plates, cups, and plastic utensils. Hope leaned against the tree's textured trunk, still holding her son to her breast, and closed her eyes with an expression of beatitude.

Maria understood what her daughter was experiencing. A dynamic permanently changed the moment she learned she was pregnant. She did not explain this. There was no reason, for doing so wouldn't have added to her children's understanding. But she remembered well the ferocity of emotion that slammed into her upon hearing the news. First, she began to cry, overwhelmed with sheer joy. And on the doctor's examining table, a paper gown barely concealing her nakedness, she began her bargains with God.

I will do everything you ask of me for the rest of my life if you protect my growing children and allow them to be born alive, healthy, and full of promise. If you need to take my life so they may live, do so. If there's a choice, God, take me, not my innocent children.

And she did not share with them the look of fear that filled Bert's face when she told him about the miracles growing inside of her. A first-time, geriatric pregnancy with high blood pressure, the potential of losing his wife to complications, the increased probability of having babies with congenital disabilities—his eyes, and his demeanor said everything. Maria could tell what bargains he was making with God. As if bargains could be made. But Maria would not be distracted. She remained focused, no longer on her husband's needs or concerns, but unrelentingly on the future of her unborn children. Maria's reality was laid bare; for decades, before she became pregnant, she had a compartmentalized, tidy, narrowly crafted view of commitment, but as her pregnancy advanced, this perspective was reduced to dust. As she gave birth to not one but two perfect beings in rapid succession, she was shattered, cracked open by the weight of love.

Tract Eight:

Fall 2010
Hope is the thing with Feathers

Ray found Leo sitting on a blanket, legs crossed, in a concrete cage, with an orange, black, and brown patchwork canine by her side. She read out loud an Emily Dickinson poem from one of her college textbooks, Norton's Anthology of American Literature.

"Hope is the Thing with Feathers," her voice lulled the giant dog, who seemed to be listening. "That perches in the soul." Ray stood back and observed, not wanting to interrupt.

"And sings the tune without words." The dog lifted his head, and his black nose twitched. "And never stops at all."

The multicolored beast turned to look at him. Busted. Ray gave an apologetic smile. Leo's face lit up with recognition. She said softly, "Come in. Move slowly, though. He's still getting used to being around people."

Ray unlatched the cage. The dog retreated to the furthermost corner. "It's okay, Surtr. This guy's all right. He won't hurt you." She spoke with a cadence that seemed to put the dog at ease. "Remember your name. You are a strong, albeit ragtag, brave fire giant. There is no need to be afraid." Ray looked at her inquiringly.

Recently, he noticed that sometimes a simple look could ask a question.

She answered, "I was talking to Jennifer, Uncle Paul, and Dad the other night about getting more shelter dogs ready for adoption, and my dad's girlfriend, a child psychologist, had a brilliant idea." The canine warily returned to the edge of the blanket, curling by Leo's now outstretched feet. "A lot of children struggle with reading. Soon, the pups I read to will associate the process with safety and companionship. When they're ready, I'll take them to the elementary school, and children can practice reading out loud. My hope is one of the students will fall in love, and they'll beg their mom or dad to adopt them. If the parents can see how much this relationship has helped their child, surely, they will agree. Surtr is my first courageous candidate."

She never stopped surprising him.

Leo looked at Ray quizzically, her turn to ask an unspoken question. He responded, "I got here a little while ago and saw you were deep in discussion with a dog, so I went and helped unload a shipment of food, hosed out some pens, and thought I'd swing by to check in on my way out."

****

Leo nodded thoughtfully–battle buddy protocol. Ray often appeared at the shelter when she was volunteering. He helped any way they asked, never balking at the tasks demanded of him, no matter how smelly.

Something else was on his mind, Leo could tell. She waited patiently and stroked the dog's coarse hair. Ray reached into his pocket and pulled out a twice-folded envelope. "Got this in the mail yesterday. It's not for another six weeks, in mid-October, but I was wondering if you'd like to be my battle buddy." He handed her the contents.

Leo scanned the embossed invitation. An unrestrained smile broke across her face. She leaned over and shoulder-bumped him. "Ray Shipworth, are you asking me to be your plus one?"

Trying not to respond to her eagerness, to act serious, was difficult. With a suppressed grin, he replied, "I'm asking you to be my battle buddy, that's all. Nothing more, nothing less."

Leo jumped up. Surtr startled and bounced to his feet too. "It's okay, boy." She leaned over and put her arm gently around the dog, offering reassurance. She whispered into his scruffy pointed ears loud enough so he could hear, "Did you hear that, Surtr, you Norse God of the Flames? Ray asked me to be his plus one."

He turned so she could not see his smile. "Whatever." Ray let the cage click behind him. "See you around, battle buddy," he called over his shoulder, looking at her one last time.

She stood tall, the fire giant by her side. "See you, plus one."

****

Leo surveyed the clothes laid out on her bed. "I'm going to be gone for a few nights, sweet girl." She bent down to stroke the glossy ears of her loyal companion. Echo cocked her head to one side, intelligent golden eyes trying to discern a message. "I've left plenty of kibble and water inside the doggy door. Help yourself to my bed. What's mine is yours." Leo kissed the young dog's head and ran her hands gently over the lean, well-defined muscles, searching for errant burrs or tics. Getting to a place where Echo implicitly trusted her had taken months. Leo's consistent commitment to the lost creature had paid off. Incrementally, the pup had allowed her to move in, closer and closer. Now, when Leo was at her river stone house, Echo would be no more than a high-pitched whistle away, and often she was right by her heels or velcroed onto her side when Leo was sitting down.

Over the months, Leo witnessed the unfolding of a lively, gentle-mannered beast who thrived on interaction. They explored the woods, did chores, played and ate together. At night, after Echo's evening foraging was done, without fail, she would let herself in through the dog door Leo installed by herself and curl tightly next to Leo on the raised bed. When Leo cycled into town, the dog would run by her side until she peeled off into a section of dense overgrowth. Echo always disappeared in the same spot. *One of these days, I will follow her and see where she goes.*

"I'm not abandoning you, Echo. I promise I'll be back soon," Leo said, as she carefully folded jeans, T-shirts, and sleep shorts, placing them next to some toiletries in a backpack. "Can I tell you a secret, girl to girl?" Echo intently watched. Her amber eyes tracked Leo's movement as she packed. "I really want Ray to see me as more than a battle buddy, more than a friend. But I am afraid he'll never be able to consider me anything other than a kid. Unless he gives me a sign, I can't do anything. I don't want to be overbearing, and I don't want to ruin things. I may have already pushed too far."

She remembered the day several weeks ago when

they were hanging out between classes, sitting companionably on white bar stools at Afternoon Delights, Leo drinking a Peach Mango smoothie. Ray was talking about the logistics of the upcoming wedding. His battle buddy from boot camp was getting married, and Ray was the best man. Leo asked him questions about his military friend, and he shared some of their adventures. Leo could tell there were parts he kept to himself. He quickly steered the conversation away when Leo got too close.

"There are some amazing hiking trails in the Ozarks," he said, taking a sip of his Butterbeer Float. "Too bad we won't have time to do any of that."

Leo's unabashed enthusiasm took over. She hadn't thought the proposal through, had she? "Let's do it, Ray! Let's stay a couple of extra days and do some hiking. Neither of us has Monday classes, and we have enough time to get our Sunday work shifts covered." Her eagerness was infectious. "Hiking in October when it's not too hot or cold would be perfect. Dad, Uncle Paul, and I have done some of the trails on the Kiamichi Mountains, but I've never been to the Ozarks."

****

What could he say? A fleeting thought once articulated around Leo often found a life of its own. Had he wanted this all along? Is that why he musingly said the words aloud? It would be nice hiking on familiar trails with a battle buddy, someone who would remind him by her presence that he was no longer on the mountainous, dangerous passes in Afghanistan. But more than this, on a deeper level, the isolating loneliness of their separate yet intense experiences made him feel they were partners. Was this sense illusory or real? Ray couldn't tell. His experience with May had been based on the superficial; he could see that now, but at the time, he thought their connection was substantive. All he knew now was that when Leo's fear invaded her, causing her to cower inwardly, it also called out to him. He couldn't turn away. And conversely, when his torment reared unexpectedly and overwhelmingly, she refused to back down—a dog on a bone.

Girl with a Pearl Earring

Jennifer leaned over and, with a steady hand, applied makeup on Leo's upturned face. "This is fun." She continued, putting a smoky blue smudge over lightly mascaraed lashes and a hint of rose-infused blush on high cheekbones. After she outlined Leo's lips with a nude pencil, she applied a thin layer of tinted, strawberry-flavored lip gloss. "Almost perfect, if I do say so myself." Jennifer stepped back; a purple-tiered peasant dress billowed around her. "But you need something else. Let me think." She took in the entirety of her. "I know. Wait here a second."

****

A white and brown, fine-boned cat sauntered nonchalantly into the room. Her plumed tail, in an upright position, was perpendicular to the floor. Leo grinned. "Well, hello, Miss Iris Mirabel Walnut Baker-Lightfoot!" A cascade of names for a Persian mouser with a coat falling around her like a waterfall. When Jennifer adopted her with Leo's unrelenting, enthusiastic urging from the shelter, she couldn't decide what name to give the kitty, so she settled for them all. Iris walked over to Leo, her green almond-shaped eyes aloof. But when Iris rubbed her head and then the length of her body against her legs, Leo understood. The message was received. The gesture was a salutation, a badge of honor of sorts. Cats were very particular about who they chose to bestow their pheromones upon. Did the creature remember the first time they met? Did she retain images of the first bath Leo had given her and her two siblings the morning they had been dropped off at the shelter, their fur a tangled, muddy mess? And oh, what mewling there had been. Leo lightly stroked the cat between her large, pointed, wide-set ears. "What a sight you were, Iris. But look at you now. Look at what a good life you have."

Jennifer returned, holding two tear-drop single pearl earrings. "My parents gave these to me when I graduated with my doctoral degree. Let's see how they look on you. Oh, Leo, come." Jennifer took Leo's hand and pulled her to the full-length mirror behind the door of Lightfoot house's only bathroom. "Look at how beautiful you are!"

Leo stood before the mirror in navy pumps and a simple dark navy sheath that stopped mid-thigh, making her tan stockinged legs appear longer. Raven hair fell in silken columns along a subtly made-up face, and when she turned her head, the dangling, pure white pearls peeped through.

"The earrings are gorgeous, Jennifer, but I can't wear them. Your mom and dad gave them to you. What if I lose one?"

Jennifer brushed this aside. "The memory of the gift, of that important day, is what makes them significant. They're just objects. So what if one or even both gets lost? I'd have no regrets. They are yours for the night."

What will he see when he looks at me? Trying to see herself through Ray's eyes was difficult. All she saw was a gawky, gangling girl playing dress-up. Oh well, she ruminated, regardless of what he thinks, regardless of what happens, the whole experience has been nice. No one had ever helped her prepare for a special occasion. Leo didn't go to the prom or school dances. Even when she had a boyfriend, her freshman year, Jake told her his group of friends wouldn't understand, and they'd give him a really hard time and ride him until he dumped her. She didn't want his life to be harder, did she? He told her to stay home. So she had. Jake had been her first and only high school boyfriend. Even on her wedding day, she had been alone. No one was there to help her prepare for what was supposed to be one of life's most important days.

"Thank you, Jennifer," Leo spoke into the mirror, smiling with gratitude at the petite fairy-like woman by her side.

Jennifer reached around Leo's waist and gave her a quick hug. "My pleasure." She beamed with approval and bubbled, "This is all so romantic, isn't it?"

Leo smiled back. "I wish. He keeps reminding me we're just battle buddies."

"Ray is more like your knight in shining armor, coming to your rescue."

Leo felt hurt as she headed out of the bathroom to pour herself a glass of water. Iris and Jennifer followed her into the kitchen. "Thank you very much, but I don't need a man to rescue me. I'm doing fine by myself."

"Oh, Leo." Jennifer sighed. She sat on the kitchen chair opposite where Leo was standing, tucking a leg underneath her. Her face was open, frank. "Of course, you're doing fine. More than that you're thriving. It's incredible how you've gotten your life in order. It's just me, you know, the hopeless romantic thinking about how Ray found you amidst the debris of the factory that night, how he carried you to safety. I imagine in a kind of *An Officer and Gentleman* style. Forget that reference. That was way before your time. Who knows what would have happened if he hadn't been so careful in his search? What would have happened if he had not found you?"

Leo was confused. She put the glass on the table and slid into the wooden chair. Iris jumped into her lap, her front paws kneading the fabric folds of Leo's dress with a repeated and rhythmic motion. "What do you mean? Jake was with me. He told me he stayed by my side watching me, ensuring I was going to be okay." As Leo thoughtfully stroked Iris' long, silky coat, the cat purred. "And when he thought I might need help, he alone carried me out into the night, drove me to the hospital, and waited until the emergency room doctor came out and took charge. He didn't worry about getting in trouble for being with a minor. He didn't care about his reputation."

As she talked, she could see the empathy in Jennifer's eyes. She'd fallen for another one of Jake's false narratives. Of course, he hadn't stayed with her, and he certainly hadn't driven her to the hospital when he was more intoxicated than Leo had ever seen him.

"Why is this the first time I'm hearing about this?"

"I thought you knew. The paramedics went out for a welfare check based on an anonymous call. Apparently, the caller hung up before they got any details, only that there was a party at the old factory, and someone might still be there."

"And that paramedic who came to check on me was Ray?"

The Circle of Willis

Jennifer nodded and pushed back her pale blonde hair. A crystal suncatcher dangled, catching October's afternoon light as the rays filtered through the kitchen window scattering flickering points of color across the room, over their bodies.

Leo slumped over with her head cradled in her hands. "Just when I think I have the pieces to the puzzle of my life figured out, I find out I've mistakenly jammed the wrong bit into the wrong place, and I have to pull out a whole section and start reassembling the mess again."

"I didn't find out until later. After you married, your father told me about Ray's account, which was written in the paramedic report. I knew Jake had been there with you that night, of course. You told me about your relationship with him, which your dad never knew anything about. But you disclosed this information during our counseling sessions, and even though you fired me, I was still obligated to keep my mouth shut due to doctor-patient confidentiality. I couldn't tell your dad Jake was the one who took you there that night, and he was the one who provided you with the alcohol. As much as I messed up, I never revealed anything you told me in confidence."

Leo sat thoughtfully for a moment, and she was about to reply when the doorbell rang. With extreme gentleness, she dislodged the sleeping cat from her lap, cradling her in her arms. She placed Iris on a kitty bed underneath the windowsill. She pushed the chair to its original position and grabbed her backpack, complete with a sleeping bag rolled up and attached at the bottom.

"He's here, Jennifer. Wish me luck. Hopefully, I

don't mess this up too." Jennifer followed Leo to the door and watched as she stepped onto the front porch and greeted Ray, who stood tall, dark, and handsome in his freshly starched and pressed Army green full-dress uniform.

Two is Enough

"What's this ribbon for?" Leo held his jacket in her lap and pointed to different medals, pins, and ribbons, trying to piece together a service history. The 155-mile drive to Big Cedar Lodge was passing quickly as they effortlessly bantered back and forth and, in comfortable silence, took in the ever-evolving landscape.

Ray quickly looked. "That's an army commendation ribbon." Leo pointed to another, and he told her. "That's for meritorious service. That's for national defense service, overseas service. That's a bronze star service ribbon, and that one symbolizes an honorable discharge."

Leo ran her fingers lightly over the grooved, textured left and right half knots on a light blue circle. "That's my Infantryman cord." Her pointer alighted upon a silver pin, ridged wings holding up a parachute. She looked at him with an inquiry. "Those are my jump wings."

Incredulously, she responded. "Wait, you willingly leaped out of a perfectly good airplane. No one pushed you?"

He gave an abrupt but easy laugh. "Yup, after advanced combat training at Fort Benning, I went through jump school."

"Tell me about it, please!" Her eagerness was sincere. One thing Ray learned about Leo was when she asked a question, the inquiry wasn't a meaningless way to keep a conversation going. She truly wanted to know and to understand. She stored this information away, and she remembered.

"The first time I jumped, I fell out to the side. As the plane passed, the prop blast hurled my body like a piece of trash. You're trained to count, one thousand, two thousand, three thousand, and as you're counting to four thousand, waiting for your chute to automatically deploy for the briefest of moments, you are free-falling through space and time. It's an experience unlike any other. But as you soar, your hands and mind are also ready to pull your reserve chute should your primary fail to open." Ray remembered looking up to check the integrity of his canopy and seeing the door of the plane open, a gaping barrel spitting bullet points of servicemen into the sky. They fell to earth a moving ribbon, like the rapid-fire of his M-16.

He gave Leo the Hollywood version of his first jump, free from encumbrances, a surface-level presentation of reality. For every scintillating projection of experiencing boot camp, airborne school, and war, there were ugly and often mundane underpinnings.

****

Leo was used to Ray reliving events, a faraway look in his circumspect cobalt eyes, but today he seemed at peace with the remembrances. She ran her hands over his jacket, each pin, ribbon, and carefully sewn-on patch representing a part of his history. So many stories were embedded here, interconnecting strands of experience that were now part of the fabric, not only of his dress uniform but of the man sitting beside her. He didn't always go into depth when she asked questions, but he didn't completely shut her down. The glimpses he gave her of a world she knew nothing about rendered insight into how his experiences affected him. His offerings were a start.

Had they been in the car for three and a half hours already? They checked into their separate side-by-side rooms at the luxury lodge, which was tucked into the rugged landscape of Missouri's Ozark Mountains. They arrived just in time, with twenty minutes until the service started.

Antique pine doors flung open, and the wedding began. Leo sat on a wooden pew halfway back on the groom's side and could not take her eyes off the procession. There was the groom, who took an infinitesimal pause before each step, revealing a hitch in his right leg. And then, there was Ray. Leo watched intently as he walked slowly down the aisle. A beautiful matron of honor encased in flounced layers of fluffy rose petal pink chiffon floated by his side. Leo felt transported like she was in an enchanted fairy tale, watching a brilliant sunset as the wedding party stood before the floor-to-ceiling windows at the front of the three-story chapel. With the glassy backdrop of sparkling Table Rock Lake reflecting the deepening colors, the wedding party appeared as though they were mythical creatures, held afloat by invisible wings, empowered to hold court while hovering above crystal clear water.

Leo watched the ceremony unfold, her eyes focused on the interactions between the bride and groom, studying the interplay of a promised eternal love but never losing sight of the best man. The intensifying hues of a striated sky bathed him in alternating overlaps of rich lavender, penetrating orange and gold. Leo was transported by memory to a spring afternoon when she made a decision.

She had just finished running sprints, trying to keep up with her father's high school track team, who was told to take five and hydrate. She walked up to Ray, now a senior. He was on the periphery, drinking deeply from the water bottle, when Leo, in all seriousness, approached him and stated, "Two is enough." Leo knew he understood what she was talking about. Like every middle school student in Tahlequah, they had been taught the heartbreaking history of their town, how 16,000 Cherokee were forcibly driven from their ancestral homelands, how, on the tortured Trail of Tears, over 4,000 Cherokee died, perishing inhumanely from prolonged starvation, protracted exposure, ravaging disease. And everyone knew the local legend. At the end of this Trail of Tears, at least three elders were supposed to meet to agree upon the location of the Cherokee Nation's capital. Two elders arrived and waited for a third to fulfill the quorum. They waited all day. Finally, before night fell, as the sun slipped, momentarily cradled by the horizon, the two senior tribesmen decided *two was enough*. The permanent capital was agreed upon. Derived from the Cherokee word meaning 'two is enough' or 'just two,' *ta-liye-li-quu,* which would later become anglicized to Tahlequah, was born.

Leo stood before Ray. She'd been experiencing all kinds of sensations she didn't understand. Here was a boy who listened carefully, challenged her, made her laugh, and joked with her but was, above all, always kind. The week before, when her dad and Uncle Paul were shingling their roof, she'd been surfing through the television channels, looking for something to watch that normally she couldn't with two men at the helm, something other than sports, the news, or history. And there, on ABC, she had seen a stunning woman with soft sundew kissed hair, dressed all in white. Before this woman knelt a man. He took her hand and asked her to marry him. So that, she thought, is how it's done. Her body had begun to develop at twelve years old, but she was still not self-conscious of the changes. She knelt before a surprised Ray that sun-drenched forsythia afternoon of heightened awareness and took his hand. "Ray Shipworth, two is enough. Will you marry me?"

Ray pulled her to her feet. "Leo, this is probably the best offer I'll ever get." His blue eyes sparkled, sincere and true. She waited, standing motionless. "But I have a lot of things to figure out. I certainly have a ton of growing up, and so do you. But let's shake hands and make a promise to be friends, okay?"

There was a slight quiver in her voice. "Friends, then. Forever?"

Leo waited until he nodded before sticking out her hand. They shook. Then, like a shot, she was off running, calling behind her, "First one to the end zone wins."

****

"There you are," Ray handed her a glass of sparkling water and took a swig of his beer. Leo leaned against a ledge overlooking the lake, which reflected the stars and full moon. Music from the reception hall spilled outside. Ray raised his beer bottle and playfully smiled. "Two is enough."

She laughed self-consciously, raising her glass in

return. "You remember my pathetic proposal."

"Pathetic, never. It was audacious. It was bold. A man always remembers his first." When twelve-year-old Leo proposed, her shiny black hair was matted with sweat and her face beet red from running sprints. She meant every word. And Ray could see that her inner being, the light she carried within, was just beginning to flourish. Leo was on the cusp of womanhood yet still had a child's pure heart.

Ray and Leo looked at one other, simultaneously seeing each other as they were then and assimilating those images with the person that stood before them now. Unaccountable was the way three simple words, *Two is Enough,* could reel back a personal piece of shared history and, for a community, an entire story. Those words represented a period around which they both had grown, like a tree's cambium, the ever-expanding living layer of tissue that encompasses the surface of every branch, stem, and twig. They carried this inside their beings a molecular remembrance.

A shooting star streaked behind them, and Leo shivered. He turned to face her and moved closer; his strong, noble profile outlined by moonlight. Ray tentatively reached out to stroke Leo's face, barely grazing her features, as if they were constructed from light-refracting marble, rising mist, or ephemeral memory. Just as he was cupping her chin upward and bending down to meet her lips, a band of uniformed brothers came careening out onto the deck, laughing and raucous in countenance.

"Iceman! I wondered where you got to. Do you remember these guys?"

"Perry? Yoda? Hollywood, you guys made it?!"

Ray beamed. They pulled each other into awkward bear hugs, pounding each other on their backs upon release. "Don't tell me you have Drill Sergeant Sledge stashed somewhere in there too? If you do, I am going to whip your sorry ass."

Mud Cat, the groom, grinned, sidled over to him, and threw an arm around Ray's shoulder. He was inebriated but flying high. "This man here saved my life." Leo's head snapped to attention. Here was a missing piece. She sat on a low step, wedged in the space of shadow, and listened.

"I wouldn't be here today if not for him. On my second mission outside the wire, a gunshot wound to my femoral artery earned me a purple heart and a one-way ticket to Germany. But for Ray Shipworth, this day, this wedding wouldn't have happened. My little girl wouldn't have a daddy." His voice filled with emotion, and there were tears in his eyes as he looked at Ray. The service members gave a resounding, appreciative HOOAH and toasted Ray, who dipped his head, looking humbled and uncomfortable.

As quickly as the spotlight came, the focus shifted. They continued exchanging easy jibes, inside stories, memories of time served together and apart, an exclusive club for which there was no protracted entry. Leo silently observed her battle buddy, gauging his interactions with the men he served with, watching him laugh and joke while slowly sinking into a comfortable ethanol-aided bubble of obliviousness. Alcohol was a way Ray coped with everything he endured.

She was nonjudgmental in her understanding. She knew he would go through long periods when he didn't self-medicate, but raw struggle was constant. Would there ever be a time when he didn't feel the need? Periodically, Ray scanned his surroundings, seeking Leo out; once his eyes alighted on hers, he would nod or smile, a knowing exchange passed between them. When he was reassured Leo was still there and doing okay, he'd return his attention to his band of brothers.

At the far corner of the deck, Leo saw two young boys, maybe twelve years old, setting up a series of celebratory rocket firecrackers. The band was taking a break; piped-in music took over and played while warm, sweaty bodies piled onto the deck, filling in the empty spaces around the soldiers.

A whistled hiss drew Leo's attention. She and the cacophonous throng looked skyward as the sound increased in pitch, ribbons of light slicing through the dark. They arched higher and higher. From deep in the crowd, she heard a panicked voice. It sounded like Ray yelling, "Incoming." Simultaneously, all the seasoned soldiers, dressed in their starched military best, collapsed. Crumbling onto the ground, they formed compact balls, their hands clasped together, arms protecting their necks. Their bodies reacting with an entrenched response. Fireworks exploded over them. The wedding attendees, who were exalting the majesty of firepower, fell silent as they witnessed the collection of servicemen brought to their knees. Initially, there was reasoned relief. The soldiers looked up from their hunkered-down positions, assessing their fellow soldiers. We are alive. We escaped destruction and severe bodily injury. But there was also an embarrassing realization as they scrambled up, still shaken to their core, unable to laugh the event off. We are forever changed. Nothing will ever be the same.

Free Falling

"You stayed with me all night?"

They had been hiking through the Ozark National Forest for two hours. Early morning was lengthening. At times the rugged trail was so narrow that one person had to follow the other, but often the path widened so that they could move side by side as they were now. The higher the altitude, the deeper autumn's colors became.

"Cat helped me get you back."

Ray groaned. "Sorry, I didn't mean to drink that much last night. Just being with the guys, celebrating something good for once…." His voice trailed off.

"It's okay, Ray, really." And Leo meant this. He hadn't caused her any trouble at all. Last night felt nothing like when Jake drank, and a cruel ugliness overtook him. With Ray, alcohol allowed him to speak more freely, which deepened her understanding of his experience. Looking into his dark blue eyes last night, she hadn't seen the dulled, reduced level of consciousness that she saw every time Jake drank. Instead, she witnessed a chasm of despair, a bottomless sorrow. After the reception, Mud Cat found them sitting on the deck's step, Ray's head resting on her shoulder. He was mumbling how he should have died, not the men he served with who already had children and families. He was beyond consolation. Leo was at a loss.

"Come on, buddy," Cat leaned down and pulled him to his feet, and there was a recognition and shift of emotion.

"Mud Cat! We're alive! We made it out of that hell hole." Ray stumbled sideways in his attempt to slap him on the back.

"We sure did, Iceman. We got to the other side. Come on now, old geezer, let's get you tucked in." Cat helped her guide Ray, effusive in his praise for the groom and his bride, his arms happily draped around their shoulders, back to the lodge. He assisted her in undressing him, down to his T-shirt and boxers, and had given Leo his phone number in case Ray needed anything throughout the night. Though their rooms were next to each other, Leo didn't feel right, leaving him alone in a vulnerable state.

The truth was this battle buddy stuff had created a deep sense of responsibility in her. Did he feel that way about her? She couldn't be sure, but Ray hadn't let a day go by since their pact without checking in with her. "To answer your question, I stayed the night because I wasn't sure what battle buddy etiquette dictated. I didn't want you to wake up, not know where you were, or become disoriented." The forest closed in around them.

****

She matched him stride for stride on the craggy, inclining stretch and showed no sign of letting up or fatigue. He looked over and took stock of this woman who had become more to him in the past several months than he wanted to admit to anyone, let alone himself. He didn't tell her, but he had violently awoken last night. Jerked by the tentacles of recurring horror into the dark and unfamiliar surroundings, he had been about to leap up screaming for backup, but then he saw her and remembered. Leo had fallen asleep, sitting in an easy chair, facing the bed, with her feet propped on the mattress near where he had lain. Ray turned on his side to see her shadowy outline. He stretched out an arm, resting his palm against her bare ankle. And as he did this, his heart rate slowed, his breathing eased, and he tumbled into a secure sleep that continued uninterrupted until dawn.

****

"What do you think went wrong in your last relationship?" Leo asked the question casually. They were climbing a footpath densely bordered by sugar and brandy maples, which created a tunnel of sorts. A vibrant display of clementine orange, rich magenta, and strawberry red encased them. Leo wiped the sweat from her brow. The afternoon, temperatures rising into the low 80s, was unseasonably warm. Shortly after lunch, she had shed her light windbreaker, which was now wrapped around her waist. The arms gently slapped her legs as she walked.

Ray was quiet as they followed the winding route. Leo wondered if he'd heard her. As much as she enjoyed talking with and learning about him, she felt comfortable in the silence. She watched him from behind, the sweat spreading out around his backpack, soaking through his shirt. The path widened, and the terrain changed. She increased her speed and fell into step beside him.

"I wish I knew what happened." His voice was low. "I thought we were happy. I thought we were in love." Leo tried to tread more lightly to hear. "But I guess I wasn't enough. While living with me, she fell in love with her boss. She left me right before I shipped out for boot camp."

"Ouch." Leo gave him an empathetic smile. "That sucks." What more could she say? Like a jackrabbit, she sprinted ahead of him–her turn to lead. On one side of the path, there appeared a bluff. Leo stepped onto the outcropping and stopped. "Look at that, Ray!" An expanse of colors stretched to the horizon. Cutting through this landscape was a clear water river, dancing over rocks and fallen trees. Underneath them, at the base of the dolomite and limestone overhang, was a still pocket of deep, inviting water. Leo quickly shed her backpack and peeled off her shirt, throwing the garment behind her as she scrambled down the steep, rocky embankment. "First one in wins!"

****

The pool reflected a clear sky. Visible from the limestone perch were stones in the river's shallow rifts, water blue, pale green, and earth brown. They had just emerged, refreshed, quietly energized. Leo wrung out her hair and pulled on her white cotton *Live, Love, Bark,* rescue T-shirt, and jeans over wet undergarments. She felt deep into her pockets for Jennifer's pearl teardrop earrings. They were both nestled there; she touched them, a talisman. Ray remained shirtless. The water from his thick hair formed rivulets as they moved over the lean muscles of his stomach, which tapered down into jeans. Leo sat contentedly next to him. The afternoon sun had warmed the rock which radiated through them.

"When I was a child, Sunday was sacred," Ray began. His hands clasped around his knees, his gaze fixed on the horizon ablaze with color. "Sunday mornings were the best. I'd wake with expectation, and without fail, there were carefully polished shoes and neatly pressed clothes on my bedside chair. It felt like Christmas. After we dressed, Hope and I would walk down the stairs into a kitchen rich with the smell of homemade cinnamon doughnut muffins. Yes, that's a thing, and they're delicious." He flashed a quick smile, his blue eyes shining. "Mom would greet us wearing her 'May the Forks be with you' apron, a spatula in one hand, and a smile. 'Good morning, my loves. Take your seats. Your father should be here any moment.' And, as if on cue, he would emerge from his office, infused with calm. No matter how difficult the week had been in preparation for the sermon, Dad would always spend the early morning in prayer."

Leo scooted around so she was facing him, her back to the bluff's edge. She reached over and ran a finger from his wrist to his shoulder. He looked up. "Am I talking too much?"

She shook her head, her damp hair clinging to her neck, her breast. "No, keep talking, please." *I needed to look at you,* but she didn't say this part aloud.

"My dad can be an intense man. But he was never more peaceful than on Sunday mornings. He'd look at the three of us as if we were the most amazing people he'd ever seen and say, 'I'm merely the vehicle. The message is in God's hands now. Let us break bread together.' Those breakfasts were full of quiet joy, no worldly pressures, no expectations, save for arriving at church with a clear heart."

****

Ray looked into her dark brown eyes, which

seemed so deep that they reflected light. There was an enduring glow. "When I look at you—" He paused, almost afraid to say what he felt, but this was Leo, his battle buddy, his sometimes plus one, someone who wasn't afraid to question his actions, to call him out when necessary, to make him look his demons in the eye while being steadfastly by his side. There was no reason not to be honest. "When I look at you, Leo, I see Sunday morning."

****

She felt as though all the oxygen was siphoned from her lungs. Ray's words were the most beautiful thing anyone had ever said to her. She leaned forward, cradled his head in her hands, and carefully bent in to touch her lips to his, gently but without hesitation.

****

The kiss lasted less than a moment, but when she pulled away, Ray knew he was perilously close to the edge.

****

"One more night, as planned?" Ray hesitated and looked at Leo for affirmation before he set up the two-person pup tent on a blanket of pine needles, sheltered a good hundred yards off the footpath. They were two miles from their endpoint, but Leo knew what Ray was asking and nodded. They could finish the remaining distance in forty minutes and be back in Tahlequah by dinner. They'd planned on camping for two nights, so why shouldn't they follow through? Leo did not want this journey to end. How they covered the twenty-plus mile route so quickly, stopping along the way for breaks and occasional off-route exploration, she couldn't say. The time elapsed, a cardiac beat, an inspiratory breath, a sigh.

As they advanced on the trail, set up camp, cooked meals together, exchanged stories, laughed, and moved in a companionable calm, an affinity wound around them, pulling them closer. One person couldn't be described independently of the other–they were a unit, a moving team, hurtling effortlessly through time and space.

Leo unzipped her sleeping bag, creating a makeshift picnic blanket for their late lunch in a dappled stretch between two white oak trees. Ray lay on his back looking upward, alabaster clouds scudding quickly like stones skipping on the surface of the rolling sky. In the far distance, a darkened wedge of weather slowly moved toward them.

Leo propped up on her side and looked at him. "Since I didn't bring my textbooks hiking, can I use you to help me study for my anatomy and physiology exam next week?" A slow smile of consent arched across his face. "Okay, Mr. Shipworth, paramedic whiz, knower of all, blink once if I get the answer right, twice if I am wrong." Leo reached over his capsized face. "Underneath these fine specimens of dark, lush caterpillar hair is the supraorbital foramen." Her fingers traced his eyebrows lightly. Ray blinked once, still looking heavenward. "And oh, what nice zygomatic arches you have." Her fingers slowly moved over his cheekbones.

Ray shut his eyes and opened them, his focus shifting. He looked directly at her. It was almost as though she could see the clouds reflected there.

Leo continued. "And here we have the finest mandibular symphysis this side of the Mississippi

River." Ray softly chuckled as she stroked his chin. He blinked again, once. "But, ladies and gentlemen, nowhere is there a more worthy example of the alveolar processes found underneath these desirable lips."

She reclined her upper body against his, her fingers tracing the contours of his lips, her mouth now so close to his he could feel her sweet breath. Her eyes danced with merriment. He could not help but reply. A laugh was caught between them in a kiss. Ray closed his eyes again for a long moment, in internal debate, and wrapped his arms around her, enfolding her.

Being with her was everything he imagined. For a moment, Ray felt himself soaring, like the night of the wedding. They were sitting side by side on the deck overlooking Table Rock Lake, their legs dangling, the full moon laying down a shimmering moon glade just for them.

"This is magical," she said.

Her face glowed and he felt the joy radiate from her, shining as brightly as the moonshine. On the outstretched sleeping bag, under the autumnal sky, as their bodies moved together, Ray felt like he was finally returning home.

Leo's unbridled joy was overflowing and washed through him, a cleansing of sorts. But just as quickly, sudden realization slammed into him. And now he was plummeting, free-falling without a parachute—*one thousand, two thousand*, hurtling through increasing darkness he knew over time would invade her the way it had him. *Three thousand.* A day didn't go by where Ray's ability to navigate life wasn't impacted by what he had experienced. On the wedding night, for instance, he was felled to his knees by a mere sound. Flashbacks, nightmares, sights, and smells would unexpectedly rear and render him completely useless.

Recalibration sometimes occurred quickly, but could also take hours to find his way back. How could he be in a relationship when he was such a mess? Doing so wouldn't be fair to her. Leo had been through so much already; she didn't deserve another partner who weighed her down with unasked-for baggage. Before he went to war he hadn't been able to meet his partner's needs, what made him think he could do so now, as damaged as he was. The hard truth was Ray did not know himself anymore. He could see who he had been before, but this person who returned from the war was someone he didn't recognize. He was forever changed. This person kept hurting those who loved him and those who were just trying to help. His mere existence caused the people around him to suffer. And even if remotely possible, even if he was the best version of himself, what right did he have to experience even the briefest taste of happiness? Experiencing joy was a betrayal to the soldiers who did not return, to the innocent civilians who lost their lives just for living in a warzone. His job was not to let go, to carry this always inside, to remember all.

The autumnal sun moved behind a ridge of clouds, putting them in a cold shadow. "No, Leo, stop!" He rolled out from under her, trying to ignore the sudden look of bewilderment on her face. "We shouldn't be doing this."

****

Leo knelt before him, dazed, imploring. "I want to be doing this," she said stubbornly, fighting tears that welled in the corners of her eyes. "Are you saying I cannot decide what I do and do not want?"

"Leo, I never said that. That's not what I meant."

"If you don't want me, just tell me." Overwhelmed with self-consciousness and sudden embarrassment, Leo pulled the bottom of her shirt down, covering the unblemished stretch of exposed skin, the sensation of his hands moving over her already burned into memory. "No need to sugarcoat things. I'm a big girl." Her voice became hard-edged and protective. "Come on, battle buddy, the truth. There's no need to let me down easily."

****

How can he say what is inside him when he cannot tangle apart the complexities? He only knows because he cares for her so deeply, he cannot let her get any closer. He will destroy her. That's the last thing in the world that he wants to do. So, he says something he knows she will react to. "I'm not one of your rescue dogs. I don't want to be. I'm not one of your charity cases."

Leo flinched. His words were a slap but somehow worse than anything she had experienced. She was stunned. Is that really what he thinks? Could he not see what had grown between them? But maybe she had gotten it all wrong? Leo wrestled with the conflicting thoughts, but in the end, the rejection hit deeper, burrowing into her core. There was a defect inside of her. She wanted to scream, to demand answers. What's so wrong with me that I'm so easy to toss aside and so impossible to love? My own mother didn't want me. How can I expect anyone else to? Ray had spoken his truth. So be it, then. She shoved her belongings into her pack.

What she had left was widening shame. "Do not follow me. I mean it! No more battle buddy pity for me. I can find my way back. I know how to take care of myself." As she slung the pack onto her back, all she could feel was a gorge in the center of her chest pulsing with self-reproach. "You are hereby relieved of all your battle buddy duties." She couldn't control the tremor in her voice. "Ray Shipworth, you're free." Leo turned her back to him so he couldn't see her tears. She tripped, stumbling away from him. Then regaining her footing, she began to run, heading as fast as possible toward the trailhead, leaving behind her sleeping bag, still open on the ground, an unzipped wish.

Speed Free My Soul

Leo climbed into the passenger side of the black Honda. Joseph Lightfoot took in the defeated slump of her shoulders and the swollen tissue around her eyes, the likes of which he had not seen in his daughter since Sandy, her childhood dog, died. He knew what he had to do. "It is not complicated," Jennifer explained, "be present and listen, truly listen. Don't minimize, don't try to analyze or fix anything, be there for her." Joseph took a deep breath, leaned over, and turned off the radio, looking at Leo fully, his eyes questioning.

She turned slightly, reached back, and grabbed the seat belt, clicking it into place. "I don't want to talk about it." Her puffy, reddened eyes rose to meet him.

"Oh, thank goodness," his response was a spontaneous utterance of relief that he tried to pull back. This was not what Jennifer meant by being supportive. He smiled apologetically. Leo couldn't help it, looking at her father awkwardly, trying his best. A soft sound, somewhere between a chortle and a sob, responded. Grateful to see anything that approximated a laugh, he reached over, gave her a quick hug, and turned the radio back on.

Order was restored. This was their old pattern and what the Lightfoot household did best, acting as if nothing happened. Jennifer would be disappointed in him, but he tried. Despite being exceedingly uncomfortable, he knew he'd been ready, and if his daughter were willing, he would have listened. But now, Leo's wounds were fresh, the hemorrhaging hadn't abated, and he granted her space.

He wished he could scoop her up as he had when she was a child, kiss away the tears, take her for ice cream, anything to ease her anguish. Joseph knew about loss. He knew how when grief is fresh and overwhelming, you think you will never be able to see your way out and how it is only after the ebbing of time that you can tap into inner calm. A peace pulled from pain.

When they entered Tahlequah's city limits, the mustard yellow-smeared horizon gave way to a sky saturated with deep horseradish green. Leaves, pushed by gusts, assaulted the windshield.

"Leo, looks like a front is moving in. Twisters in October happen, and the weather conditions are prime. Why don't you spend the night with us, and I'll drop you off tomorrow."

"I need to get home to Echo. I don't want her to think I completely abandoned her. And I need to be alone for a while to decompress and figure things out." She looked at her father's visage. "I have everything there that I need, Dad. And if worse comes to worst, I have the storm cellar. Uncle Paul has stocked up like a doomsday prepper. I'll be okay, I really will."

What could he do? She was an adult, living independently and making her own decisions. He reluctantly drove away, watching through the rearview mirror as Leo raced across the yard toward her river stone house, dragging her backpack behind her.

****

"Echo! Echo!" Leo called and gave a high-pitched whistle. The winds gathered in their ferocity, tiny hail pellets bit into her flesh.

Please be okay. I'll never forgive myself if anything happened to you while I was off gallivanting. Please don't leave me like Sandy. I should have learned my lesson then.

As she was about to cross the threshold, Leo abruptly stopped. Around the house, worn into the ground, was a circular dirt trail that hadn't been there before she left. Her heart sank. She knew what this meant. Echo had worn the grass away, leaving a footpath like a caged tiger at the zoo, pacing back and forth, wearing a groove in the earth along the fence line, looking for freedom that would never come. Around and around the house, she must have frantically run, searching, sniffing, for the direction in which Leo had left, grinding her bestial truth into the ground. Her dog, the one Leo had spent months trying to gain her trust, now thought she had been deserted, forgotten. *What have I done?* Leo reached down, taking a handful of the earth as if she could divine something from the soil. From her throat came a keening wail. Long and full of anguish, the sound carried across the field into the dense grove of trees until inhaled by the turbulent sky.

An eerie calm descended. At first, Leo thought the quiet was within, as if all she had was spent as if she had finally been sucked empty. But the silence pervaded all. The world was suddenly still. She looked up across the field toward the forest. The prairie grass no longer whipped, the treetops no longer snapped, and the flying leaves ceased. The absence of sound and movement was a vacuum. Until, out of the undergrowth flew a sleek, copper creature, and on Echo's heels, an unleashed violent energy followed—the sound of an unstoppable, quickly approaching locomotive.

"Echo!" Leo cried as the shaking dog flew into her arms, "Come on, girl! Let's go!"

She ran through the bowing pine door, barreling toward the storm cellar. She flung the hatch open.

****

The military transmutes your relationship with death. Before each deployment, you write a farewell letter to loved ones and craft your will. You meet death in person, watch the blackness devour your compatriots, run your hands along the bulging underbelly and smell its eviscerated bowels. All the while feeling its hot, fetid breath against your skin. I am so close, death whispers, just around the corner, you might be next. Dying is the possibility that never leaves. Awareness of its closeness becomes part of your psyche.

Ray pressed down on the accelerator. Not caring about the raging wind and driving rain, he sped over the curving country road, following the headlight beams as they sliced through a screen of infinite darkness. With each bend, each turn, the lights illuminated immediate pockets of his fragmented existence. Failure as a brother, check. Failure as a son, check. Each pass could be his last. Failure as a battle buddy, check. Would a deer be around the next corner, a semi-truck hogging both lanes or a fallen tree? He did not care. The only thing he'd ever done right was being a soldier. Then his life had a purpose. A profound sense of duty overrode everything like a higher calling. Now there was a floundering, an endless cord of suffering. When did meaning ever rise from empty despair? There would be relief in the end, absolute and all-encompassing. It was all he wanted. Let it be over. Just end it now.

A growing light appeared in the distance until a bend in the pavement altered his direction. The flashing was gone, reappearing as he turned west again, growing more prominent as he barreled forward, leaving the winding descent behind him. Accelerating over the open expanse of land, the light beckoned. This is it, game over. If only I can get to the railroad crossing before the train in time to stop on the tracks. He pushed the accelerator to the floor.

The lights flashed red, back and forth, even as the warning dings and train whistle grew louder. The crossing arms, which were mere stubs amputated from a prior accident, seemed ready to embrace him. "I'm sorry," Ray yelled into the darkness. "I'm sorry that I was such an utter failure at everything in life—speed free my soul."

****

Curled in the tightest of balls, Echo slept by Leo's side. Occasionally a tiny whimper would rise as her defined muscles and curled paws trembled in sleep. Leo gently stroked the curve of her back. "It's okay, girl." The creature stilled under her touch. Leo was prepared for the inevitable power outage. She found an air-tight container of Uncle Paul's emergency long burning candles and lit enough to illuminate their resting place.

The darkness of the storm shelter was relegated to the furthermost corners. Hours ago, a can of tuna for Echo and a can of corn for Leo had served as dinner. Now Leo was sitting crossed-legged on the blanketed mattress; another covering lay over her knees as she carefully went through photographs. She had found a shoebox full of them tucked underneath the shelving. Uncle Paul's stashed pictorial history of the Lightfoot men started when he was in high school, and her dad had been a mere five years old. She shuffled through them slowly, scrutinizing each one for clues of lives lived before her arrival. Then there was a sharp intake of breath, the smallest of gasps.

Echo's head shot up, golden eyes quickly assessing Leo's body language and reading her face. Are we on the move again? Do we need to be on heightened alert? Is there a rabbit nearby? "Sorry for disturbing you, girl. It's just that I found some pictures of my mom." Echo tilted her head slightly, listening to the cadence of Leo's voice. "I've never seen these before." Echo's tail thumped the mattress as Leo scratched behind her silky ears. She stretched her lean, ropy body out, and with a deep doggy sigh, she put her head down in Leo's lap.

There were only a few of them. In one, her young and handsome father was grinning while he gazed proudly at a blotchy newborn face cradled in his arms. One large hand cupped the soft, downy head protectively. The infant, tiny matchstick legs sticking out, was swimming in her onesie. Next to him, close to his side but not touching, stood her mother. Her head was turned to face away from them, a distant, detached look in her eyes. The photo must have been taken after her dad brought her home from the hospital on one of Emily's first visits. Leo touched the smooth surface of the print with her fingertip, tracing the outlines of a fledgling family that would not stand the test of time.

She brought the photo closer, trying to discern what her mother had been thinking. Leo had missed her mother so often over the years that the concept of her had become a living organism, and Leo had woven this narrative into the texture of her being. But how could you miss something you never knew? How could this still be so defining of how she saw herself? Motherless, unlovable. That's pretty messed up, Leo thought as she picked up another snapshot. This one, like the last, was faded; the colors leached away. Only now, the baby was a squirming toddler, two years old, possibly three. Again, she was in his arms, wearing only a diaper. The dark-haired little girl was laughing and looking sunny side up toward her father, and she had her arms stretched as if trying to wrap them around his neck or touch the sky. While her father held his daughter aloft in his left arm, he had his right arm in an easy loop around Emily's shoulder, and there was no mistaking his look as he stared adoringly at the slender, auburn-haired woman. She, in turn, clad in stark white shorts and a tight tank top, was looking straight ahead. Leo regarded the picture thoughtfully, then reached over to bring a candle nearer for further examination. The light flickered across the images.

In her mother's features, was a focused intensity Leo hadn't seen before. But it wasn't just in her vibrant eyes or the flushed edges of her face. The secret was in her Mona Lisa smile. Emily was in love, not with the man holding her daughter, not the man who stood by her side, but with someone else. Her love shone through the picture, channeled directly into the camera lens, reaching beyond to the person behind the 35mm monocle.

Oh, snap, Leo thought, not wanting to disrupt Echo's sleep again. Emily had been in love with Paul.

Had her uncle returned that love? Had her father known? She thinks back to their conversation in Tulsa, along the Riverwalk, the night they celebrated Leo getting her GED, and she asked him, do you think there was another man? Her father paused, then had said, "No, at least I don't think so."

****

When he regained consciousness, the rain was falling with such velocity that the cracked glass looked like it was bending. What happened? Ray touched his throbbing forehead. Blood stained his fingers crimson. He remembered jamming on the brakes so he would be in the tracks, ready for a life-ending impact. But he braked a fraction of a second early, just as the tires hit the upward lip of the tracks. The vehicle caught air, left the ground, and landed on the other side, his head slamming into the windshield. The pain was debilitating. And he realized he was so far down the rabbit hole he could no longer see any light. I am in trouble, he thought.

The train hurtled by. The railroad track irons shuddered as it passed.

The Smell of Sorrow

"Shit," Ray mumbled as he pulled into the empty spot where his sister's car, the one he drove now, usually parked. Miguel and his mother's car were also in the driveway. Dawn's sky was a still, blue-glass lake. He pulled out his cell, turned the phone on, and saw over 30 contact attempts, texts, missed calls, and voicemail messages. Their night had been an endless one too. To be, or not to be. The catechism he held last night dissolved. As careful as he might be, he could not drop a single stone into the sky's surface without the waves propagating outward, each small circle ringing into a slightly larger one, an infinite reversal of nesting eggs.

Hope called his name in a sob. "Ray!" She flew out of the house, threw her arms around him, and started crying on his shoulder.

Ray returned her hug. *I'm sorry for what I put you through, what I keep putting you through*, then he let go. "About the windshield, I'll get it fixed this afternoon."

****

Hope held him at arm's length taking in the point of impact, the dried blood, searching his face, reading him. He hadn't been drinking; his breath wasn't peppermint schnapps fueled, and when she hugged him, alcohol did not rise from his pores. But something profound had happened. She could see beyond his resigned exhaustion into a hollowed-out core. Reflected there, in desolate arctic eyes, was an unfathomable hopelessness. This wasn't the time for questions. He was here. He was alive. They had another chance, another hour, another day. "Windshields are a dime a dozen. I only have one brother."

****

Ray knew she was feigning lightheartedness. Her bloodshot eyes darted away. "Come on, breakfast is in progress. You know how Mom and Gabrielle are when they start cooking and talking. They cannot stop."

He didn't smile, but he didn't refuse either. He didn't dismiss his sister or turn and head to the garage, as he had so often done.

****

Sometime during the clear morning after the storm, while Leo and Echo explored the property, picking up fallen twigs, sawing up felled branches, and putting the timber into a wheelbarrow to stack in the woodshed, autumn's remaining leaves began to fall. Last night's wedge twister had shaken the trees in its path with such force that the stalks which managed to survive the night clinging to the branches seemed, in the light of day, to give up from sheer exhaustion. Colored sleeves of silk cascaded from heights, burnt oranges, and apple reds, swirling down, bumblebee yellow and rich merlot, drifting in the air, catching in Leo's hair, eventually falling around her feet.

She tried to examine what happened with Ray analytically. Other than the fact he was not attracted to her and had never reciprocated her feelings beyond the level of friendship, she also knew what she'd done wrong. When she first volunteered at the shelter in high school, she would often hold the cat or dog she was working with so tightly, the creature would claw and scramble to get away. Over time, she learned how to gauge what an animal needed and how to earn their trust. There was a balance, so they felt secure but not trapped. And there was the lesson she learned from Banshee.

Leo rubbed the scar on her right hand, remembering. Sometimes, what an animal had gone through was too overwhelming to process. She had seen that look in Ray's eyes the night he walked into the restaurant to pick up a pizza, and she had seen the same in Banshee (who had yet to earn her name) the morning she found her chained to the dogwood tree outside of the shelter. Something inside of them folded up and retreated deep into their interior, where they couldn't be touched or harmed again. That morning, when Leo gently loosened the heavy chains, quietly talking to the suffering dog, she reassured her, being careful not to make any sudden movements, and the canine seemed to respond. But just as Leo led her inside for the veterinarian to examine her, she turned on Leo. With terrified staccato yelps, the flea-ridden pooch lunged forward and tore into Leo's hand.

"Who's wailing like a banshee out there?" Another volunteer ran to help. The dog's dirt-saturated collar, which had probably been new and bright red when it was put on her as a puppy, had never been loosened or replaced to accommodate her growing neck. Over time, the poor canine's skin stretched around the collar, which became embedded and required surgery to remove. Banshee took over six months before she could trust again and seemed interested in engaging with the world. With Ray, Leo witnessed a slow transition, a re-emergence of sorts, too. She'd seen him become more comfortable in his surroundings and around her. She felt him open to her, trusting her, and what did she do? She double-crossed him by turning his trust into something he never wanted.

If melancholy had a scent, it would be of fading honeysuckle, or a riverbed gone dry. She carried within her a sadness, a pain, that Echo could smell. Throughout the morning, Echo would sidle up to her, brush against her legs, and look up, her steady golden eyes reassuring and appraising. Each time Echo came to her, and Leo paused to touch her, the perfume of sorrow grew fainter. With a sudden burst of speed, Echo began running through the blanketed woods, dodging trunks, leaping over fallen branches in tight circles, turning on a dime, kicking up pine needles, colorful leaflets, and oxidized dirt, earthborn confetti. Never far from Leo, she raced, all cylinders firing, defined musculature rippling in the light. Pulling up short, she came to an abrupt stop. She sat before Leo, looking at her with adoration and expectation. She panted with exertion, her muzzle open as if in a smile; her golden eyes alight with sheer joy. Leo could not help but respond.

She laughed. "You're right, girl." She reached down and stroked the graciously spirited beast, whispering one of her favorite lines from Kurt Vonnegut's graduation essays: If This Isn't Nice, What is?

****

Hiram had fallen asleep in his baby bouncer on the kitchen floor. Hope washed the breakfast dishes while

Ray dried and put them away, a division of duties they had been doing since early childhood. They worked seamlessly together and in silence. A metal spatula slipped from Ray's dishcloth and clattered on the floor by Hiram's feet. His slumbering body startled reflexively, then relaxed. As Ray bent to pick up the kitchen utensil, he could see movement below the lightly veined, paper-thin skin of his nephew's eyes. Hiram was dreaming. Ray looked up at his sister, who was staring intently at him. She was studying him as he had regarded his nephew. At that moment, he knew. No matter how overwhelming or unbearable everything was, his loved ones would never understand. They would take suicide as an act of betrayal. Purposely checking out was not an option anymore. He was defeated before he started, buried under the rubble of a fallen life. But he had no choice. He would have to see this life through, no matter what. He slumped on the floor.

Hope sat next to him. "We're at a loss, Ray." She gently rocked the bouncer while Ray touched his nephew's sturdy but unbelievably small feet.

"I am too." Ray had never admitted this out loud.

"You've been back over nine months, and just when I think you're getting better when I let my guard down, something happens. I'm terrified. We all are. As rough as this patch is, nothing could be worse than not having you here."

Just when I think you are getting better. Better? As if what he carried was a predictable disease process that could be scientifically cured or surgically excised. If only. How could he explain how war attaches itself to your viscera like a virus, invading every aspect of your being, all the way down to your DNA? Everything changes, how your mind works and functions, how you perceive the external world, what you believe, and value, and how you simultaneously crave and fear love. In war. to survive, you detach yourself from emotion. Once you return intellectually, you must allow yourself to feel again. But when you begin this process, the losses pile up, loss of the men you served with, the innocent civilians, and loss of self. And this awareness produces such anguish that moving forward is impossible. Time to shut down again. Will I ever get back inside of myself again, and what is the point if I do? Look at how damaged and useless I have become. Even the most basic tenets Ray carried into war, the concept of good and evil, right and wrong, were shredded.

Ray exploded. "You just don't get it, sis!"

Hope leaned back, stunned. Hiram's pudgy flesh rolled, his legs flailed, his eyes popped open wide, and he started to cry. Ray's tone moderated, but he persisted. "Everyone's life would be better if I hadn't come back. I should have died there." Ray hugged his knees while Hope pulled Hiram out of his bounce seat and began to soothe him. He wanted to continue arguing with his sister, to point out how their lives would be easier if he hadn't returned. The days they inhabited would be normal and stress-free if he weren't here. And over time, the memories of him would compress, condensing his existence into an insubstantial footnote. Their suffering, and his, would be erased–the way tight sutures close around a wound. Years later, the only thing left is a faint whisper, a translucent scar.

Hope settled Hiram in her lap and reached for her brother, placing a hand on his arm. "Like it or not, we're tethered since the womb. If you fall into that dark tunnel, I'll hold on with all my strength to keep you from hitting bottom. And if you crash, I won't be far behind. That's the way we work. But it's not just about us anymore, Ray. This little guy here, my son, your nephew, is the future."

Hope waited until he met her eyes. "We can't do this alone, we're here for you and will always be, but we're not enough. We need help. Last night, when I wasn't sure if I'd ever see you again, I promised the universe that if I had another chance, I wouldn't waste it, that I would fight for you the way you'd fight for me. I called the Veteran Hospital in Muskogee, and they can help. We have to try this, Ray, please. If not for yourself, for Hiram. We can't let him down."

****

Leo sat on the rooftop, surveying the late afternoon, an arm loosely draped around Echo, who leaned into her as if she couldn't get close enough, as if they were one. Leo quietly spoke aloud her inner truths while Echo, with her ever-watchful presence, absorbed. "I miss him, girl. I miss my battle buddy so much my heart hurts. The reality is I've been in love with Ray since I was a little girl. I realize that now. But I can't make him love me. Maybe I'm destined not to have a person in this life, and if that's how it's supposed to be, I'm resigned. For now, it's just us girls, a pack of two. But you know the saying—Two is Enough."

She sighed, grateful for her furry companion, free to come and go as she wanted. This was the way partnerships should be. I don't want anyone to be with me out of obligation or because of some verbal agreement. Echo was by Leo's side because she chose to be there. The dog door was always open. There was always food and fresh water in her bowls. Leo knew enough not to deny Echo's inherent nature and understood how important honoring the creature's biological imperative was. She was a descendant of wolves, but Echo also had her evolved notion of loyalty and what was selflessly required of pack members. Over the months, a wordless connection developed between them. Daily the bond strengthened–a commitment distinctly theirs, unwavering and reciprocal.

Leo reached into her pocket and pulled out her cell and the photograph from last night. She had folded the snapshot into quarters. She tried to smooth the creases out, but they formed a cross, the arms of which sliced through the families' faces rendering their expressions unreadable. She had to do something. She knew personal growth and her ability to move forward with her life depended on this single action. She opened the flip phone, her fingers trembling while tapping out a message to her uncle. Before she stopped to think, she hit the send button. —Ready to meet Emily.

Echo's henna-colored nose, which blended seamlessly with the color of her sleek coat, twitched. She smelled a cottontail; farther down, there was a waft of red squirrel and a trace of mule deer. Echo's protective instincts had kept her by Leo's side all day. The immediacy of the hunt was tempered by the presence of a kibble bowl, which was always full. The ping of a text response punctuated the quietude, but Leo did not move to open the message. Instead, she absorbed the calm, regal bearing of the creature by her side. Velcroed together, they surveyed a widening afternoon. And still, the leaves continued to fall.

Tract Nine:

Winter 2010-Spring 2011
Now that She has Found Her

A patchwork of land and a kaleidoscope of emotion–angled in the passenger seat of Uncle Paul's truck, Leo observed the shifting panorama. Fenced plains of cattle grazing pastures were stitched together with an occasional thicket of trees tethered to barren fields, which, in the fertile season, would give rise to waving acres of grain sorghum and lined rows of soybean. An undulating open prairie grassland, the most frequent, unifying applique, tied the countryside together. Leo was trying to remain somewhat calm. She was on her way to meet Emily.

"And why didn't you tell Dad where she was?" They were less than half an hour away. Kansas City was close, merely two-hundred and fifty miles, yet a continent apart.

"Shortly after your mother left, a typed letter addressed to me arrived. Emily told me where she was, and if your father ever asked about her or wondered where she was, I was to tell him. Every time she moved, she'd send an update."

"So, like me and the gravestone, sorry, memorial stone, the burden was on Dad, the way it was on me. I was supposed to notice that there wasn't a death date.

When I asked, I would have the answers. All Dad had to do was inquire?"

Uncle Paul nodded. "Something like that." His eyes were fixed straight ahead on the highway before them.

"But how was he supposed to know you had her contact information if he never knew she wrote to you? That's messed up." Leo could feel the folded-up photo in the pocket of her jeans. The way her mother gazed at Uncle Paul, that look was unmistakable. She took a jagged breath, "Were you in love with her too?"

The blue and silver F-150 pickup swerved, avoiding a car that pulled into their lane without signaling. "My feelings don't matter. These are things you're going to have to ask your mother."

"She's not my mother!" Leo shot back without thinking, with more ferocity than she intended. "A mother is there for her child, someone who cares enough to stick around." Her voice softened. "Not someone who walks away from her three-year-old daughter and never looks back."

What in the heck am I doing? If Emily could let all these years go by without bothering to reach out to me, why should I care enough to be doing this now? Why am I so desperate for answers? Even as she questioned herself, she knew what needed to be done. She tried another approach. "So, you guys kept in touch?"

"We did." The firm set to Uncle Paul's jaw let her know asking more questions was futile. Leo was more determined than ever to get closure, no matter what that looked like or how difficult the information might be. She leaned wearily against the passenger side window and looked at a changing landscape as ordinary as it was unfamiliar.

Leo felt like a child when she stood before the weathered brick house, so engulfed by ornamental bushes that seeing the front door was impossible. And she reached, as she always had, for the hand of one of the Lightfoot men who had raised her. "I'm afraid. I don't think I can do this."

Uncle Paul gave her a gentle squeeze. "You've known about Emily for a while. There's a reason you asked to meet her now. Maybe she can give you the answers you need, and maybe she can't. But, Leo, you'll never know unless you try. I'll walk you to the door, but then I have to go. Emily is expecting you. You got this. Call or text when you're ready, and I'll pick you up."

****

There was a faint resemblance to the photographs. But if Leo had passed her in the street and hadn't been given time to study them closely, she would never associate the woman before her with the one in the pictures. The essential features were still there, the shape of her eyes, nose, and mouth, but they'd become more voluminous and softer over time. Leo followed the plump curve of her legging-clad hips as Emily led her down a narrow hall filled with solemn-colored, surrealistic oil paintings into a glass-enclosed side veranda. A heavy braid of auburn threaded with barely perceptible silver streaks swished down her back.

"Sweet tea?" Emily handed her a glass, beaded with moisture. The wicker chair sighed as she sat. And there she was, an unremarkable woman with an open face who just happened to give birth to her over two decades ago.

No use in superficial pleasantries, Leo garnered some of the anger that had arisen over the years. She'd been abandoned, and she needed to know why. She pulled out the photograph and handed it to Emily. "You were in love with Uncle Paul." She paused, then pushed through a layer of dread that spread through her like cold liquid mercury since she first saw the picture the night of the tornado. "Tell me, please, that Uncle Paul is not my father."

Emily's cheeks flared a flush of crimson. She stared at the photo for a long time. "No. My feelings for Paul developed later. In the beginning, I was head over heels in love with Joseph. We met when we were so young. At first, all was sweet and overwhelming, everything you associate with new love. But our relationship wasn't sustainable."

"For you, you mean. Dad wanted to get married."

"He did." Emily refilled her glass and took an oatmeal chocolate chip cookie from the ceramic plate. She offered one to Leo, who adamantly shook her head.

"There's no excuse for what I did, for walking away." Emily bit into the cookie, ate it, then brushed the crumbs on the glass table into a tiny pile with a paint-splattered finger. "But I fought for you, Leo, the only way I knew how. I was just a kid, seventeen when I got pregnant and eighteen when I gave birth to you, and I did the best I could. I hid my pregnancy so I wouldn't be forced to have an abortion. I blackmailed the adoption agency so that Joseph could have full custody of you. I signed the birth certificate leaving your name blank so that your father could name you. I knew he would love you beyond measure and always put you first. I knew I wouldn't be able to do that for you. Being an only child, I was spoiled and used to having things my way. It took me having a baby to see that. I also have difficulty holding up to pressure. I recognize these character flaws in myself."

"But Dad said you were brave, that keeping us together took enormous strength. Your life would've been easier if you agreed to a closed adoption and let strangers take me."

"There you have it." Emily brushed her thick braid over her shoulder. Her earth-green eyes were earnest as if trying to prove a point. "That's one of the main reasons I wanted him to raise you. Joseph Lightfoot unfailingly believes in the strength of the women he loves. I knew our relationship had changed, but he still believed in me, in us. The thought of letting him down was too much." She dipped a finger into the accumulation of cookie crumbs and put the bits to her lips. "I don't know, Leo. Leaving before you had any concrete memory of me seemed the right thing to do at the time."

"And you were in love with Uncle Paul. You forgot to mention that."

Emily sighed. "There's that too. If your father found out, he would've been destroyed."

"So, you guys were messing around behind his back."

"Oh no." Emily looked genuinely shocked. "We never meant for it to happen. Leo, you must believe that. Our attraction occurred gradually. As your dad and I drifted apart, there was Paul. The complementary Yin and Yang powers of the Lightfoot men, your dad is soft-spoken, serious, a deep thinker, and then there is Paul."

Leo knows full well the gravitational draw of her uncle, how he can pull you into his orbit with his laughter and high energy, and how he can make you feel like you are the center of the universe. The stable strength of the Lightfoot men was constant, genuine, and true. And she had been lucky enough to have them both in her life.

Emily continued, her eyes distant. "There were lines Paul would not cross. Doing something that would cause you or your father pain is one of them. He knew how I felt, but he also made it clear until he knew Joseph was over me, he would never allow himself to explore his feelings for me. So, I left Tahlequah. I left you all behind."

Her mind spiraled. Leo listed off the things she knew for certain about Emily: an artist, a painter of reality-distorted oils, with a Masters of Fine Arts from The University of Kansas, a woman who at different points in her life loved both her father and uncle, an only child and finally, a footnoted mother, a statistic. She came from a state with one of the highest teenage pregnancy rates in the country. Leo needed a minute alone.

"The bathroom is at the end of the hall, on the right," Emily told her, pouring them another glass of sweetened tea.

On the way, there was a door partially opened. Leo peered into a studio, bathed in natural light, full of green potted vegetation, paints, drop cloths, and canvases. She stepped into Emily's hushed world. What more could she learn about her birth mother now that she found her? One painting was of an empty gray table. Its legs were of varying lengths so that it tipped, a round edge became long, and the table stretched undulating like a river across the entire canvas. The chairs were distorted, too. None of the legs were even. Some chairs overpowered the table, others stood apart, turned facing away, and some were incredibly small. Leo thought one thing was for sure; no family would ever come together and sit down for a meal at this table. The painting contained all the blurred colors of a thunderstorm, and Leo felt an immeasurable sadness within the strokes.

Leaning along the back wall was a vast canvas covered with an even larger cloth. A work in progress, just a peek. Leo pulled back the corner expecting another bleak presentation, but instead of a painting, Leo saw rows upon rows of neatly pinned photographs on a corkboard. And the pictures were all of her, a chronological progression of Leo's life, starting from when she was a toddler. The cloth fell to the ground. The pictorial looked like something you saw on television shows when detectives were trying to crack a case, just minus the red threads of connecting lines. "What is this? A murder board?" Leo exclaimed to the house plants.

"No, it's more like a life board." Emily's voice came from the dark hall, just outside the open door.

"Uncle Paul." Leo recognized the pictures and remembered how a new one would appear on their refrigerator door every so often, then disappear, only to be replaced by another. Some of the more exceptional shots would be enlarged, her dad would make a frame, and they would be hung on the walls of her childhood home. She had never thought about where the discarded photos went, but now she knew. "Uncle Paul mailed these to you?"

Emily moved closer to the display, by Leo's side, and took a deep breath. "At first, Paul mailed them to me as I moved from place to place. But once I settled here, he started dropping them off whenever his 'business trips' brought him in the vicinity." Beneath her words resided wistfulness. The languishing was found in her tone, demeanor, and melancholic movements of her surreal paintings.

Leo regarded Emily in the afternoon light. Her mother had walked away, chosen a different life, and grown a new identity. But she also carried a secret, a guarded spot that hadn't healed, one with gnawed edges–a fragmented wound with the Lightfoot family stuck firmly in the center.

Land Navigation

Breathe in, breathe out–one step at a time, just like land navigation in boot camp. All one had to do was focus on getting to the next checkpoint, point A to point B. Point B to point C. Don't overthink things, don't self-sabotage, look ahead, and keep moving.

"When you are at war, all you want to do is return home. And when you're home, all you can do is think about the soldiers who took your place and everything they sacrificed. Just because you're back doesn't mean you've fully left. This creates a lot of confusion." Ray spoke first. He looked around at the men, none of whom had served with him or experienced exactly what he'd gone through, but all were veterans. They were seated in a loose circle of chairs. Several of them grunted in agreement. One muttered under his breath, "Amen."

Augie, a narrow, angular Vietnam veteran with tufted titmouse gray hair pulled back into a ponytail, was leading the session. He responded to Ray's comment with a quick downward motion, straying strands of hair curling on his forehead like a crest. "Welcome to the psychological mindfuck of war."

"And you can't stop thinking about the men who died and feel guilty for being here, for surviving." Elvis, a soft-spoken man in his mid-thirties who looked like he hadn't slept well in years, gazed down as he spoke, an Iraqi Freedom hat in his lap. Ray dipped his head in agreement. He still could not understand why he, who had no dependents, lived while other soldiers with wives, children, and already established lives had to die. This wasn't right. There had been times over the past few months, before the wedding, before the disastrous hike, when he was with Leo and found himself laughing or experiencing any emotion that approximated happiness. He would pull himself back and remember. The fact he got to go on seemed like a betrayal to those soldiers who lost their lives.

Since Ray left the Veterans Medical Center in Muskogee over six weeks ago, he'd been attending a local weekly support group composed of veterans. As he got to know them, talking and sharing became easier. And even on those days when words were elusive, when you felt the weight of the world embedded in your bones, often just sitting there and listening, helped. The density you carried somehow found a way to seep out. The heaviness traveled through the ring of men in one direction, then altering its course, would circle back. By the time the session was over, the burden had become something shared and somehow lighter. When you left, you knew that your brothers were carrying some of your load inside of them, too, that they absorbed it, that you were not alone.

Next to Ray, another veteran named Felix haltingly spoke. "I keep reliving the afternoon we were ambushed after an IED disabled our lead vehicle. Two of our men were picked off. I was a gunner. I should've seen the attack coming. I should've stopped them. I could've done more. Maybe they'd be here today if only…."

Augie waited to ensure Felix was finished. "There are all kinds of names for this—survivor guilt, hindsight bias, soldier's heart. But the label isn't what's important. The fact is these thoughts and associated feelings are common among veterans."

Felix jerked up as if on a puppet string and gripped the back of his chair, his knuckles blanching. Augie continued. "But if we don't put this survivor's guilt into perspective, the feelings can be incredibly destructive and prevent us from moving forward. Unrealistic thoughts have to be replaced with realistic ones. An ambush after an IED detonation isn't unusual. Every soldier who served in Iraq and Afghanistan can tell you this."

Augie stopped talking until Felix looked up, then he stared him dead in the eyes. "Felix, you couldn't have changed the course of events. No one has that power. Were you the only gunner there that day?" Felix shook his head no. "During the indeterminable time you waited for the recovery team, did you know the exact moment the attack was going to happen? Immediately, ten minutes into the wait, an hour later?" Again, he shook his head. "And how could you predict the direction the ambush would come from, North, South, East, West, from the high-rise apartments, bridge, or bluffs? All these variables make knowing when, or even IF, an attack will occur impossible."

Felix pulled out a cigarette, lit it, and slumped back into his chair as Augie continued. "None of us are Rambo. No one can take on an organized assault alone. Instead of looking at what we think we did wrong, we must look at what we did right. Think of the men your actions *did* save." Augie paused to ascertain no one had questions and to assess if the group was still with him.

He took a drink of his now cool coffee and continued. "I want you all to think about the men you served with and how you would have laid down your lives for any of them at any time. This is the reality. You know it, and they did too. If they were here, sitting in this circle, and you were ten feet under, would you want them to waste their lives in rumination, rage, and regret? What would you tell them from your grave?"

Elvis piped up. "I'd tell them to quit crying, raise a glass to me, then I would tell them to get off their ass and get on with things." Several of the men laughed, self-consciously.

"Exactly." Augie looked around the circle, meeting the eyes of the men who looked up. "The last thing they'd want is another casualty from their unit." Now Augie was on his feet, padding around the collection of men, his voice grounding. "So, what do we do? We replace unrealistic thoughts with realistic ones, remembering all the outside factors beyond our control that led to an event." He put his hands on Felix's slumped shoulders. "We allow ourselves to grieve. We lost good, true, honorable men in terrifying situations and horrific ways. Then we allow ourselves to see everything we did right along the way, honor this, respect this. Equally important, though, is to practice self-forgiveness for all our faults, realistic and perceived. Be as forgiving to yourself as you would the man sitting next to you. You all have my contact information, but I want you to buddy up with someone in the group and exchange numbers. This system provides an added layer of support." With this, Ray's stomach flip-flopped. Not another battle buddy. He had one. He lost one. Leo.

Not thinking about her was an exercise in futility. He thought about how he botched up their friendship and unintentionally led her on because he couldn't figure himself out. He simultaneously wanted more from their relationship but was terrified of what this entailed. He was afraid of being so damaged that he would hurt her. In the long run, he felt he couldn't give her what she needed. He could blame only himself, for who can truly know, or begin to love, a man who does not have access to himself.

Since they became battle buddies, Ray was used to seeing her daily. And even now, a month and a half later, he couldn't change how he missed her. Thoughts of Leo pervaded; they rose unbidden in pockets of stillness, as well as during times of exertion. They came when he was engaged in conversation or reading. They even stretched into his dreams. There were a cascading number of specifics: her laugh's lilt, the smell of her hair, the sweetness of her kiss, and the glow in her eyes. But when he considered the whole of Leo, he thought of her energy and movements. He reflected on how her presence filled space with lightness and an abiding sense of comfort. When you were with her, there was nowhere else you wanted to be. Her earnest attention to the world around her, whether a mangy dog or a jar of solar tea, made everything seem new and significant. Then Ray thought of her mind, her unique observations, and the surprising things she would say. When she talked to you and focused on you, you felt you were the only one who mattered. Finally, he thought of her heart, her intuitive capacity to care, and how this was her greatest asset and most profound vulnerability. Even after she was bitten or knocked down, she believed.

Augie's voice broke Ray's reverie, reluctantly bringing him back to the present. "This week, I also want you to think about ways to do something positive toward helping someone else. Something as simple as opening the door for an older adult, putting a buck in the Salvation Army kettle, or serving soup at the homeless shelter. I have a list of places that could use assistance, and there are quite a few vets around town who could use a hand with their chores. Start small, and if need be, say to yourself, 'I'm doing this to honor you, Private Getty. What you gave will not be forgotten. Your memory is alive.' It's a way to pass the spirit of service on. What else do you have?"

****

Breathe in, breathe out—one step at a time. Don't overthink things, don't self-sabotage, just look ahead, and keep moving. As Ray navigated the external world, this became his mantra. He now had an apartment on the edge of town, close enough to help Hope and Gabrielle around the house and with his nephew. Between running, attending classes, studying, his new job working as a medical assistant at the hospital, attending the veteran's support group, and performing small acts of service through his father's church or on his own, he was always on the move. His interior landscape, however, was more challenging to navigate. Yet, tenaciously, he remained committed to the process. All you have to do is focus on getting to the next checkpoint, point A to point B. Point B to point C. Look forward, keep moving, observe the contour lines, and never lose your compass.

Over time, as weeks were sponged into months, as Ray and the collection of service members in his group listened to Augie's experiences and advice, they found the courage to speak their innermost truths. In this protected setting, they descended into the past, dissected memories, and relived the sensations associated with them, mundane and terrifying alike. They bore witness and received affirmation: what happened to you, what you did was neither right nor wrong. It simply was. And still is. You lived through these events; you carry them with you now. Through purgative witness, unspeakable events diminished. Helium balloons sucked into a vast and equitable sky. As pots of coffee were consumed, cigarettes smoked, histories and experiences exhumed, evidence revealed that while no two stories were the same, the collective realities of service, suffering, dissolution, and loss were enough to bind this fragmented collection of military men together. The result was like industrial strength adhesive, a surgical glue initially designed to quickly close battle wounds in the field when sutures were unavailable.

The Rabbit Hole

This is the way the world ends. Oh wait, Thomas Stearns Eliot, a native of St. Louis, Missouri, I'll change your famous poem here, just slightly, this one time: This is how a marriage end*s*. No, one more modification, if you will allow me. This is the way *my* marriage ends, not with a bang but a whimper. Leo stood before the judge. Her counsel Candice Kane, dressed in a sharp, curve-hugging, burgundy suit, was by her side. Jake hadn't bothered to attend the final hearing. Leo wasn't surprised. Being on time for anything was never one of his strengths. She'd been holding her breath since the proceedings started, hoping that the rumor mill was correct this time. The last she heard from Brody, Judy's husband, was that Jake had found someone else, that as far as he was concerned, Leo was yesterday's news, put out with yesterday's trash.

"I've reviewed the documentation. Everything was filed correctly. The non-filing spouse has had adequate time since being served to respond and has failed to do so."

Leo glanced over her shoulder. Part of her feared Jake might burst through the door. On the wooden bench behind her sat her father, Uncle Paul and Jennifer, who had been consistently supportive throughout the process. They looked at her with encouragement.

"By the power vested in me, I hereby declare this case is closed. Leo Rose Lightfoot, your petition for the dissolution of your marriage is granted."

A small collection of cheers rose behind her, and Leo turned with a smile, pumping her fist in the air. Candice beamed, pushing the pink-framed glasses back on her nose. "It's over, Leo! Let's go celebrate with your family."

****

Ray slid into an empty folding chair, joining the group in progress. He was late. Hope was tied up at the plant, and Gabrielle had to leave for her afternoon shift, so he was left watching his teething, fussing nephew Hiram until the backup sitter, his mother, in this case, could get there. He unzipped his navy jacket and folded the canvas onto his lap.

With a quick dip of his head, Augie acknowledged Ray's presence and asked, "What do Buzz Aldrin, Terry Bradshaw, and Beyonce have in common?" Ray looked around the circle. Was this a joke-telling session? If so, he was all in. He could use some levity.

"They were smart enough to recognize when they needed help, and they had the strength to seek professional assistance." Augie paused. "Who's ever heard of Harold Wobber?" No one responded. "In August of 1937, he was the first to jump off the Golden Gate Bridge. He was also a World War I Veteran suffering from what they called shell shock at the time. Veterans of the Armed Forces are thirty to fifty percent more likely to die from suicide than the average citizen. This is what we're discussing today."

Oh, holy hell, Ray thought, I sure could have used

a joke, but here we go, down the rabbit hole.

"In general, men have been socialized since birth to master their feelings, and if they can't, they better damn well hide them. In the military, this is further reinforced. The display of any emotion is seen as a form of vulnerability. Now, thrown back into the civilian world, we rely on what has been drilled into us; I can handle the problems myself, and I don't need any help. We learn to hide things really well from our family, our friends, and even from ourselves. But guess what, this old way of coping is why our suicide rates are so high."

He darted around the room, handing each participant a small, business-sized card. "Put these in your pockets, your wallets, hang them on your refrigerator, I don't care where, but keep them accessible. They may save a life." Augie took a reorienting breath. "All right, men, time for a deep dive into what drives us to that edge, how we can protect and support each other." He slid back into his waiting chair, making the sphere complete. "We'll also focus on coping skills, what to do when things go horribly wrong, and learn to problem-solve before things get out of control. You've taken a step in the right direction, but being here isn't enough."

****

Ray's hands trembled as he zipped up his jacket against the fierce wind. He was shaken to his core. Something unexpected and unnerving happened during the group meeting. His first instinct was to go to the liquor store, but he couldn't. He'd taken an extra shift at the hospital and was headed there now. Besides, since the wedding, he hadn't imbibed. He found he didn't crave or need alcohol like he once had. What he really wanted to do was to share his experience with someone he implicitly trusted, Leo. The meeting was intense. Something poured out of him, a frightening acknowledgment of the night he stood on the edge and had jumped. But now exposed, he didn't know what to do. How could what he shared be retrieved, and packed away?

She read him in honest and unnerving ways. Leo picked up on things he often couldn't see himself. She would notice a subtle behavior and then ask gentle, probing questions. She listened intently, and once she understood, she would work with unfaltering tenacity to help pull him through.

He hadn't spoken to or seen her since the hike. Yet, thoughts of her overwhelmed him. He remembered clearly, a day she refused to back down when she saw his need.

Ray allowed himself to go there.

He sees her wide smile. "I'm taking my break now." Her melodic voice calms him. Leo slides into the booth across the table, so she is facing him. Every day since he told her, he felt safer with his back to the wall; she saved her break time to spend with him. He wasn't prepared when she said, "Time to switch spots, Ray."

"What?" He protested and felt sweat start to bead on his forehead.

Her voice softened. "Just for one minute. I promise you. I have your back, and nothing will happen."

He reluctantly, hesitantly, changed positions. And while he sat there, unable to see the door, sure that danger was lurking behind him, unable to ascertain what or who was sneaking up for an attack, she placed her hands over his, quietly talked, and reassured him. "The door is opening now. It's just Mr. and Mrs. Ruggles coming in for their weekly date. They usually order the veggie special. Do you know they have a new great-grandson?"

Her voice became distant and distorted. Sixty interminable seconds. Why am I lightheaded? Maybe it's low blood sugar.

Leo's words penetrated the narrowing light. "You'll hear and feel Judy delivering a pie to the table behind us. It's only Judy. You're doing great, Ray. There are only twenty seconds to go."

The restaurant started to spin. Ray's thoughts whirled. Maybe the reaction was exhaustion. In the past few days, he hadn't slept more than three consecutive hours without being woken by a nightmare. And just as he felt a darkness tunnel down, Leo was by his side, pulling him out. "Time's up. Time to switch places again. You did it, Ray!"

Gradually, the amount of time he would sit, unable to see the door, trusting Leo to keep him posted as to who was coming and going lengthened until he could remain seated, without looking back once, for ten straight minutes. During one of these interludes, when the Beef and Pizza Palace fell quiet, with Leo sitting across the table, he found the courage to share what happened to him the day they became battle buddies, how the trigger of the dead animal on the road sent him spiraling into an altered level of consciousness. He also revealed his fear of driving alone and his inability to retrace a route, no matter what he was doing, whether walking, running, or riding in a car.

The way Leo studied him, the way she genuinely

cared about him, the way she thoughtfully considered what he said and then organically responded with word or action was uncanny and belied an intimacy Ray had never experienced. He missed her on so many levels.

****

All she wanted to do was tell Ray it was over. She was finally free of Jake. She needed to thank him for all he'd done to help her through the tough patch, for being her unfailing battle buddy. Leo imagined the scene now. If she hadn't messed things up between them, he'd be celebrating with her and her family. She would have laughed lightly with him, giving him an out, absolving him of his duties now that she was free. And in her mind, he would have deferred. He would have held her, his blue eyes shining. And gently kissing her, he would tell her he couldn't imagine a life without her and that he loved her.

****

Jennifer knew what Leo was thinking. She was an open book. Her face belied how grateful she was the divorce was over, but also how much she still missed Ray. Upon her return after the wedding and hike, before Joseph drove her back home when Leo reached in her pocket to hand Jennifer back her pearl drop earrings and found one was missing, lost on the Ozark trail; she burst into inconsolable tears, her body wracked with grief. There was no way Jennifer could ease her sorrow, nor would this have been therapeutic. Leo had to process the events on her own. Over time, Leo hesitantly shared some of what happened, and Jennifer listened and offered perspective.

****

Wearing a bright green coat over a sunshine yellow

dress, Jennifer's red cowboy boots peeking through, her elfin ears sporting tiny crystals of rainbow color, she raised an ice cream cone high. "To Leo, whose strength and grace inspire all."

"To Leo." Her father dropped a gentle kiss on his daughter's head, then turned beaming, his gaze full of love and gratitude for his fiancée. Uncle Paul and Candice clicked their chocolate-dipped cones, an ice cream toast. "To Leo," they said. "To Leo."

Leo looked around the unlikely band of people gathered around her, all sharing the deliciousness of quiet celebration. Then she thought of her mother. Emily's absence in Leo's life was her choice, not because Leo was unlovable. Walking away was, at the time, the only option Emily felt she had. And the intense emotion, the anger, the pain, the abiding sense of loss that Leo carried fell away.

With distilled clarity, Leo realized she was a product of all she'd been given, of the people who committed their days and tirelessly gave their love, always believing in her and holding her up. And she knew she had everything. For the first time in her life, Leo did not question her value or what she had to offer. For those who loved her and truly cared, she was enough. Enough for her family, enough for her close friends, enough for the shelter dogs, enough for Echo, and finally, she could look within and accept she was enough for herself. In this space, she found, for her mother, forgiveness.

****

The Afternoon Delights Ice Cream Parlor windows were sprayed to make them look frosted for the holiday season. As Ray walked by on his way to work, he had the sudden urge to go in and grab a cone or shake, for memory's sake. He and Leo often went there between classes or after helping at the shelter. Behind the iced glass, as he passed, he could see an iridescence. Yellow, blue, green, and red drifted around the palest of lavender, a celebration of colors.

Musical Memory

Ray stepped out of the food manufacturing plant for his break and looked around. As the workforce improved, he only filled in for Hope when there was a call-in or they were short-staffed. This worked for him. Between taking a full load of classes, working at the hospital, studying, running with Miguel, the veteran's group, and volunteering, he had little time to himself. White thin flakes fell from a low steely sky but melted when they hit the ground. There would be no accumulation this time.

He scanned the tree line watchfully. The last time Hope needed him to fill-in was two weeks ago. But, without fail, every time he worked, the dog appeared. Did she come faithfully every day, or did she somehow intuit when he was here? He didn't like to think of her waiting for him to emerge for a sandwich break and finally retreating when he didn't show.

At the edge, he spotted her. The sleek creature was standing stock still, her tail horizontal to the earth, her front left paw off the ground pointing, her muzzle aimed toward a chipmunk at the base of a tree. Ray watched. The canine soundlessly took a step forward, maintaining her rigidity, now pointing with the other paw. Over several minutes, she moved closer, the chipmunk oblivious. Then with a snapping leap, she was there. The chipmunk was a fraction of a second faster and skittered up the tree, chirping loudly, a warning cry to other furry creatures. The dog bounded over to him. Wasn't that fun? her golden eyes seemed to be saying. Ray ripped his sandwich in half. As Ray shared his lunch, he had this incredible urge to talk to Leo about the dog and how she appeared in the summer, flea-ridden and close to starvation, how she must have found a home. Though she was still lean, you could tell she had a consistent food source, and someone was giving her flea medication. Leo would love a happy ending story involving a dog. "She would adore you, pretty lady." Ray reached down and stroked her silky ears.

****

Across the wide parking lot, for the first time in two months, he saw her. He knew Leo's schedule, and she knew his. They'd done their best to avoid each other. But there she was, heading in the same direction he was going, toward the Nursing Home. Since Ray stopped going to the animal shelter, he shifted his focus and went to the Senior Center to play the piano and sing with the residents. Mrs. Robertson, his old choir director, lived there now. Though her condition was rapidly deteriorating, he promised her a Christmas program. Today was the day. Winter's indigo blue clothed the sky, stretching from horizon to horizon.

Leo was walking quickly, with purpose, with long jean-clad legs, a winter jacket, and a white knit hat pulled down over her dark hair. Next to her side, on a bright red leash, oh my goodness, Ray had to admit that he had never seen such a frightful excuse for a dog. Sandy, Banshee, and Surtr had nothing on him. One of his golden ears was missing, the other was ripped in half, and his tail was bandaged. Frankenstein-style stitch marks stretched from his nose, following a jagged course along his muzzle. Chunks of fur were absent. Wait, was that a comb-over? Leo had reverently attended to the mutt's remaining hair, and where the pile existed, the shining locks had been carefully brushed down, a sorry attempt to camouflage the bare spots. Hate to tell you this, Leo, but that makeover is patchy, at best.

Despite frightful appearances, something about this fellow drew you to him. Ray couldn't look away. He watched, mesmerized. The uncomely creature was strutting. Strutting across the asphalt with his head held high, his nose slightly elevated, and his eyes relaxed. Around his neck loosely hung a festive felt holiday wreath, complete with a bright red bow. Ridiculous. Yet he walked with a confident swagger as if he owned the day. Ray realized the dog had absorbed Leo's light. Her attention, her belief in the canine, had given him lift, the spring in his step. She could do that if you let her. If you opened yourself to her, there would be flight. Ray called her name.

"Leo."

****

She stopped mid-stride, that voice familiar anywhere. Her body responded, in the pulse of her blood, behind her eyes, in the turn of her gut, all of her. When the duo simultaneously turned to regard him, and her eyes alighted upon him, everything fell away. Ray. She could not contain her smile, inner joy. He was by her side in two strides. They walked toward the door.

"Ray Shipworth, I would like to formally introduce you to Casanova. The ladies love this not so little, fine sir. The director is considering adopting him as a therapy companion."

Ray shook his head and grinned. "Why am I not surprised?"

Leo knew there was only a little time. There was something she had to say; there was no use in circling nested truths. She took a deep breath and plunged in. "Casanova, Banshee, Sandy, aren't charity cases. I don't do this out of pity. I volunteer because I like them and because I find them way more interesting than designer pooches, who, of course, are very sweet, innocent, and unblemished." She was serious and talked quickly, with pent words tumbling. "Every dog in the shelter carries in them a wordless story. But if you are patient and sit with them and listen, they'll reveal who they are and tell you what they need." Casanova and Ray stood staring at her intently, listening. "So, it's not being heroic or acting out of charity or pity. I'm being selfish."

She paused for a moment and reached down to gently touch the top of Casanova's head, reassuring him, herself. "I know the horrible sense of being trapped. You have no idea how you ended up there and feel helpless, as if there is no way to escape. But I was fortunate enough to find a friend who showed me a way out. She believed in me, even when I didn't. She wouldn't let me quit. I'm just helping the animals learn the skills they need to find a better life. Dogs need exactly what everyone needs, a chance. I'm with them because I want to be. It's who I am."

****

Her cinnamon-rimmed, almond-shaped eyes looked earnestly at him. She wasn't just talking about the shelter animals. This was Leo's veracity laid bare. He swallowed. He wanted to say something in return. He was unsure how to start, but he had to try. "I'm not the same. I'm no longer Blink." He paused, afraid to go on. A sudden gust of wind swirled around them. Long, dark hair blew across her reflective face. He bent to stroke the dog, his fingers grazing the spot where Leo's had just been.

Leo waited a long moment, then offered softly, "Ray, I know you've changed and are no longer Blink. I'm not Squirt, either. I'm not the same eight-year-old who asked you to race the first day she met you or the twelve-year-old who dropped to her knees to propose to you. You're not the same, I get it, but can I tell you a secret?"

****

With a burst, the automatic sliding doors of the nursing home opened, and a collection of spritely residents came furrowing out into the cold surrounding each of them, enthusiastically guiding them inside. Miss Ponyo's tightly curled, freshly dyed black locks were so lacquered they did not move as she fairly danced with delight. "Oh, there he is. Casanova, you sweet boy, looking so handsome in your Christmas wreath." Slim, weathered digits interlaced with Leo's fingers and pulled her down the hall. "Come this way, Leo. We have the library set up and waiting for you, with a brand-new doggie bed for Casanova."

Olive, dressed in a bright holly red pantsuit, looped an arm through Ray's. "We're so excited about the Christmas pageant. Over here, the lounge is decorated, and there's punch and cookies."

The throngs carried off their beloved volunteers to

their designated rooms. As they were dragged in opposite directions, all Ray and Leo could do was look at each other over their shoulders and shrug.

****

Fifteen minutes into Casanova's American Literature sharing session, the residents became restless. A cacophony of eager voices engulfed her.

"Leo, we don't want to cut our get-together short, and we don't mean any disrespect to you or Casanova, but can we carry this over into next week? I mean, American Literature has been around for a while. Dickinson can wait, right?" Miss Ponyo was on her feet, collecting the volumes and starting to stash them on the library wall. "We want to hear the holiday concert, which only happens once a year. They have delicious refreshments."

A sharply dressed man stepped forward and offered Leo his arm. "Olive has been practicing her flute accompaniment of "Silent Night", which has been anything but silent. And Mr. Scully's guitar riff in the middle of Jungle Bells is actually quite amazing. We must go and support them."

"And besides,"—wink, wink, nudge, nudge, Miss Ponyo was looking at the others who were grinning conspiratorially—"we want to introduce you to this delightful young man. His name is Ray Shipworth. He's a former pupil of Mrs. Robertson, with a voice like Frank Sinatra." The distinguished gentleman furthered, "And he's an honorably discharged Iraq and Afghanistan veteran."

Miss Ponyo gently pushed on Leo's back toward the door. "He's been coming several times a week to play the piano. We get to make song requests and sing along. It's a lot of fun. You and Casanova are going to love it. Come on, let's go."

The next thing Leo knew, she and Casanova were hauled into the festively decorated lounge.

In a peaceful subdued place near the bottom branches of a freshly cut ten-foot Douglas fir, after Leo carefully removed his wreath, Casanova found a spot to rest his head. Leo sat quietly by his side, stroking the varying lengths of his golden coat. Strands of colored mini-lights draped loosely along the branches twinkled, illuminating the dimly lit space.

Across the room, near a snowy white vintage artificial tree, stood an upright piano. Ray sat on the bench, surrounded by men and women, all nattily dressed in their holiday best, some standing, some seated, some bearing instruments, others just bearing punch cups and their voices. Directly to the right of Ray, in a parked wheelchair, sat a withered shell of a lady. Mrs. Robertson. She had introduced herself to Leo at Ray's farewell cookout, full of life and vitality then; her eyes were shut now, her head tilted back, her mouth a small, rounded opening. Yet without missing a beat, Ray often looked over at her and smiled as if she could see, encouraging her as if she could sing. In her lap, resting on a fleece Rudolph the red-nosed reindeer blanket, an occasional tremor rippled through her skeletal right hand, a wave of musical memory stirring.

The Sound of Silence

Leo watched with continued fascination as Ray navigated the program, galvanized participation, slowing down or speeding up his accompaniment to accommodate the instruments, the voices, and the laughter. He seemed such a natural. He looked so handsome, she thought, but more importantly, she felt something different emanate from him–a tentative sense of calm, a pulse of belonging. Did he even know she was there? She didn't think so. Having this time to observe him quietly put her mind at ease. Despite how she botched things between them, her forwardness, her overbearing assumptions, and her abandoning him as a battle buddy, he seemed genuinely pleased to see her. She could tell that he'd moved forward. He hadn't needed her after all. He appeared to be in a good place. Ultimately, this was what she had wanted for him. Of course, she yearned for more, but that was on her. Perhaps we could go back to being platonic companions? Leo could live with that. I'd rather have him in my life as a friend as opposed to nothing at all. Maybe after the concert, I could suggest hot chocolate or coffee? There's a chance he'd be up for that. What do you think, Casanova? She hadn't spoken aloud, but the sleepy dog lifted his head, gently placed his muzzle on her knee, and sighed.

****

How could he not have noticed the commotion as they dragged poor Leo and her sidekick into the lounge? His heart accelerated. What was this continued pull she had on him? Even two months later, the effect was the same. Yet he played the piano as though nothing had happened. The program continued. When he saw her face light up in the parking lot when she saw him, he was grateful to know she was doing well and didn't appear to be carrying a grudge for how badly he treated her, how he'd hurt her. He wanted to respond to her earnest expository, to tell her it wasn't because he didn't want a deeper relationship with her; he was afraid he was too damaged, incapable of giving her what she needed. But maybe, if we're just friends, I wouldn't risk hurting her again. After all, she accepted him and his war-ravaged psyche at face value. She'd never once waivered or biked away. For Leo, loyalty was an action verb. He could feel her eyes on him now, watching, intently observing. Maybe, Ray thought, as he sped up dashing through the snow to match Mr. Scully's remarkably nimble fingers flying over his electric guitar, maybe after the program, we can grab an ice cream or a hot chocolate.

The residents sang the closing song at the top of their lungs. Someone flipped on the bright fluorescent overhead lights as the paneled walls absorbed the final notes and the enthusiastic applause. Leo and Casanova stood by the tree. Ray was by the piano with the buzzing clientele around him. He made eye contact with Leo. She smiled and started to move toward him.

****

"Ray Shipworth!" From the arched entryway of the lounge, a high-pitched shriek rose. Out of the corner of her eye, across the room, Leo saw a tiny, perfectly dressed bundle of white energy bound in his direction. Then with the graceful ease of a dancer confident in her partner's response, she catapulted herself into his arms. He held her with outstretched limbs. Ray looked as though he was holding a Christmas Angel. Bleached blond hair carefully curled, a billowing halo of light around a circular face. A pristine white sweater dress hugged a generous bosom, and knee-high, fur-lined boots, clung to shapely legs. The mystery woman tilted her head back and laughed, flawlessly playing into a crafted image. The woman batted her eyelashes, cemented with glittering purple and gold mascara, the opening and closing of a rare flower's petals. Leo could not look away.

"I heard you were back in town, but you're a hard man to track down." May then snuggled her face into Ray's neck, kissing him there. She whispered, "Ray Shipworth, this is your lucky day. I have some exciting news for you. I'm finally ready to make us work."

Ray looked across the room, still holding May, taking in Leo's stunned expression, her expectant smile shattered. He hurt her again. He would never know how May found him in this out-of-the-way place at this exact moment, but he had to explain to Leo that this wasn't what it looked like. He had to tell her what he couldn't say earlier. This was his last chance. He gently disengaged May's arms from his neck and put her down. He started to walk toward Leo, to clarify, even as May snaked her arms around his waist, trying to hold on.

Leo and Casanova were gone. The spot where they stood a few moments ago was empty. And still, the asynchronous blinking of lights draped across the arms of a dead tree unrelentingly continued.

"Come on, Ray." May moved before him, forcing him to look down. "Let's go grab some dinner at my favorite Italian restaurant." Her heart-shaped visage was beaming. She was self-assured. "I can fill you in on what's been going on in my life. And tell you all the exciting things I have planned for us."

Weary from the daily navigation, from the sense of always letting people down, slipping back into a shiny, orchestrated existence would be so easy. Before him, May represented a path of minimal resistance, but the partnership served her needs alone. Entering a relationship with May would be tentative. How long until the winds of change blew through her again, a month, a year, a decade, until a better opportunity came along? And it always did.

Ray reflected on the differences between May and Leo. Leo's agreement to be his battle buddy was one of thoughtful consideration. And once made, her commitment to the process was unwavering. She demonstrated a kind of grace under pressure, a quality of endurance.

May slipped her arm through his and started dragging him toward the door. "They said they'd hold our reservation until eight. Let's go." Ray allowed himself to be pulled along, surrendering. Going with the flow would be simple and predictable. But when he reached the spot Leo had occupied, he abruptly halted.

"No, May. Stop."

She looked at him with expectation and pushed her body close to his. "Oh, did you forget something? Your jacket? Sheet music?"

He looked at her feeling immeasurable sadness and said as kindly as possible. "This isn't going to happen. We're done."

May batted her lashes in disbelief; purple and gold smudges circled her eyes. She took a moment to size him up and gauge the strength of his conviction. "Well, mister, you just blew it big time." She thrust her shoulders back, sticking her well-endowed chest outward, and strutted past the residents who had been watching the interaction with keen interest. At the entryway, she paused and bellowed for effect, "Ray Shipworth, if you think I'm EVER going to give you another chance, think again!" The sweater dress and fur-lined boots carried her out of the door.

****

No wonder he looked relaxed and at peace. He had a companion. She should have known. Leo felt bad about the designer dog statement because clearly, he found what he needed, a stunning designer girlfriend who looked like she had just stepped out of a fashion magazine. How could she compete with that? The ache in Leo's heart was familiar. Just as she thought the pressure was easing, seeing him again brought the pain crushing back. *Hello darkness, my old friend*, she sang under her breath, in her less-than-perfect voice, one of her favorite Simon and Garfunkel songs, a tune she carried inside. Once more, she had misread him, hoping he wanted to re-establish a friendship, yearning for something deeper. Thank goodness we were interrupted before I made even more of a fool of myself as if that were possible, she thought. He must still see me as a needy, pathetic little girl with scabs on her knees. *And the vision that was planted in my brain.* Of a future, of a life with Ray. *Still remains*. Winter's cold darkness enveloped her. *Within the sound of silence.*

Tract Ten:

Spring-Summer 2011, and Beyond
A.C.E.

"Felix, open up! Come on, man!" Ray knocked loudly on the door to his veteran friend's apartment. Felix hadn't been at the meeting, and Ray was on edge. For over six months, as long as Ray had attended the weekly sessions, Felix was always one of the first people there. He was one of the last to leave, and he never missed a session.

Augie was leading the group in a discussion about reintegration into the workforce when Ray jumped up from his chair, startling those around him who had started to nod off. "Something's not right. I have to check on him." He moved quickly, with a determined purpose, toward the door.

And as he passed Augie, the mentor nodded, a tuft of silver hair bobbing. "Let me know if you need backup."

Ray looked through the shuttered window of the small studio apartment. There were gaps between the blinds, crenellations separated by the persistent fingers of someone always on alert, of someone peering out. He could see Felix there, hunched in a corner, illuminated by the ever-altering images on high-definition television. In a flash of blue light, tears streaked an anguished face, the hue shifted, and the visage plunged into darkness—an almost empty liter of Jack Daniel's tilted by his side.

Ray pounded. Felix shifted his body, and clutched in his right hand was a 9mm Glock 17. "Dammit, Felix, open the door!" The pistol wavered, but still, Felix did not respond to the banging. Ray knew he was either choosing to ignore him or was somehow assimilating the noise into his inner experience. Either way, he had to act quickly. He recalled where the manager of the complex lived, at least he did when he and May lived here years ago.

He flew down the metal exterior staircase, his mind racing. Please, still live there. Please be home. He battered the caretaker's entryway with one hand while the other hit his group leader's contact information, "Augie, get here now," he yelled into the phone before hanging up. From inside, he heard an interminably slow shuffling toward the door.

Mr. Rexall stood, stooped, and wizened. He remembered Ray and took him seriously when he said it was a matter of life and death.

"I've gotta call the police." The hunched older man mumbled as he backed away after unlocking Felix's door. "I know he's a veteran and your friend, but anytime I unlock a unit without the owner's permission, I have to have a justifiable reason. They'll do a welfare check and write a report."

Ray didn't have time to argue. Nothing was simple. He knew he was already walking along a volcanic ledge that could erupt at any moment, the results of which might be catastrophic. Self-inflicted or suicide by cop, an accidental discharge, collateral damage, there were any number of ways this could go.

"A veteran liaison on the way. Let him talk to the police before they come near the apartment. Please, Mr. Rexall, the cops understand the complexities of working with veterans. Have Augie talk to them first." Ray heard a grunt of ascent as the tired caretaker scuffed away.

"Felix. It's me, Ray. I'm coming in." He took a deep breath and opened the door.

****

A shimmering sheath of rain fell from the eaves outside Leo's childhood home. Frondescence had long passed, and the world was now a blur of abundant and blending green. Beyond the distant rose quartz memorial stones, the river churned and fearlessly rose out of her bed, threatening to flood everything–springtime in Oklahoma. Inside, on Leo's lap, was Jennifer's adopted cat, Iris, her long white and brown fur nesting about her as she slept. Seated at the round kitchen table with her was Jennifer, her father, and in the fourth chair, where Uncle Paul usually sat, who was visiting Emily in Kansas City, perched Echo. A family pulled together, addressing wedding invitations.

Leo grabbed another vibrantly hued card. Before penning in the address, she looked at the collection of beings gathered here. Her family, her pack. Besides the most obvious, to avoid being eaten, she considered the advantages of being part of such a group in nature. Members had honed skill sets, they protected, nurtured, found shelter, or foraged for food. They divided and shared labor, cared for and guarded the young, even those who were not their biological offspring—the willingness of a pack to work together increased their chances for survival. Leo thought about the embroidered wall hanging in Ronnie's kitchen, something Leo had committed to memory and held close to her heart. A simple quote from the feisty television star of "Modern Family", Gloria Delgado-Pritchett: Family is family. Whether it's the ones you start with, the ones you end up with, or the ones you meet along the way.

"What are you doing next weekend?" Jennifer checked a name off the list and looked expectantly toward Leo. Her steady gray eyes were drops of pooled rain.

"Shelter work Saturday morning, but other than that, just studying. Why?"

Jennifer pushed a strand of sandy hair behind her ear, a motion Leo now knew meant she was either nervous, excited, or both.

"My mother is driving up from Rubottom. We'll make a day of it. Lunch and wedding dress shopping, a girls-only event. Would you join us? We could pick you up when your shift ends."

Leo couldn't contain her delight. "Count me in." Iris languidly stretched and leaped down. With an erect tail and head, she slowly sashayed, with flaunting steps, underneath the chair where Echo sat. The dog heaved a sigh and rested her head in resignation on the table. Sometimes extended pack members were just barely tolerable.

****

When Ray entered the apartment, and Felix leveled the Glock, pointing straight between Ray's eyes, he wasn't afraid.

"Get outta here! I mean it," Felix shouted, words

dipped in despair and consternation. "Man, don't mess this up…Get the hell outta here, Ray! If you don't leave, I'll have to shoot you. Then I'll off myself. I don't want to kill you, but you're not giving me a choice."

They were no longer on the front line, but the struggle continued. Stripped bare, there was a harsh reality: war is a lethal and ruthless operation. Combat disfigures and destroys. And if you slice open the chest of the consumptive beast, revealed is a thrashing heart, congested and enlarged. Each erratic beat underscores the core of wartime service, an unfaltering willingness to die for another person. I will lay down my life for you as long as I breathe. Even though they were no longer on the battlefield, Ray refused to let Felix go without fighting for him.

"You're not alone. We're in this together." He remained present, non-threateningly calm, and with a low voice looking Felix in the eyes, he spoke with unwavering honesty and compassion. He remained clear-headed and focused until he saw an opening, a slight pistol dip, and a short closing of Felix's pain-infused lens. Ray moved swiftly. He went to the wall, slid down next to Felix, and pulled the now sobbing man into his arms.

Felix had reached an edge. Everyone had one. Once the Glock was unloaded and secured, once the officer was dispatched back to the station, the report filed, Ray and Augie sat by their comrade's side through a dark and heavy night. Felix relived the painstaking events that unfolded on this anniversary date when he lost his comrades to an ambush attack, the day he thought he had failed them. One moment Felix would tuck inside himself, oblivious that they were there. The next, he would laugh like a maniac or turn on them, taking anything around him, an empty bottle or a couch cushion, and hurl the object, lashing out with overwhelming rage. He cried with dissolution. A person can only take so much. Ray knew this. He, too, had stood on the brink of an abyss and jumped.

Ask–are you thinking about killing yourself? Yes. There is no point in living. **C**are-the situation is serious and deserves attention. Stay with them and then **E**scort–them to a trained professional, a chaplain, or a counselor. A.C.E. It was the business card Augie had handed out in his Veteran's support group, with embossed resources and hotline numbers. Ray kept the information in his wallet at all times.

Into the smear of dawn, the world devoid of color, Ray and Augie helped a sobering Felix into a car. They accompanied him to an agreed-upon place that offered reinforced support, knowing there were some things even the strongest soldiers couldn't carry on their own.

Summer's Heart

As the radiating heart of summer burned foliage brown, Leo slid into a cool pocket of water. Heat haze, diaphanous bent rays of light, rose to shimmer into the sultry air around her. Last fall, she discovered the oasis on the northeastern corner of the property line. Freshwater spilled down natural stone slides, and pockets of water collected then flowed over worn, smooth rocks—a miniature spring-fed geological waterpark of sorts. The oasis was an unassuming variant of the much larger bathtub rock formation she used to go to with her dad and uncle in the summers when she was growing up. Echo jumped into the water with her, swam a slow, measured circle, then climbed out. Shaking herself, a spray of droplets flying in the intense sun, she stretched on an edgeless, rounded stone. Her eyes fixed on Leo, a simultaneous commitment to pack vigilance and fur drying.

Leo sighed, leaned her head back against the rock, and closed her eyes, content. In ten days, her father and Jennifer would be married. Beginnings. Life finds a way. Leo had been living in the river stone house for over a year. The seasons knit around her days, those definable pockets of time where lives are lived. And Leo had borne witness to the evolving gifts her new home and the land had given her. The spring-fed pool, a balcony that kept her grounded while holding her close to the stars, after a spring rain, a sudden wash of wildflowers rose. And perhaps most spectacular of all, ringed around her house, was the slowest of color-infused kaleidoscopes.

The first tight circle of floral phosphorescence emerged during the final throes of winter's fling. A ring of hardy hellebores broke through chilled, dormant earth; their saucer-shaped flowers were confident harbingers. As they faded, daffodil and jonquil poked their noses forward, flirty waiting cups, they formed the next concentric circle. Crepe-paper petaled Iris followed, then yielded to airy, sunny Coreopsis which waved pale yellow flowers. Next, a crest of Coneflowers rose, encouraging the attendance of pollinators. They thrived and faded as wispy wands of blue Russian Sage appeared. And at the end, providing the garden's last full meal for bees and butterflies, a ring of rich purple starred Asters exploded, fall's flashing finale. They stayed with her, fighting through the first frost.

During the winter months, as Leo navigated the colder, dormant world, she often thought of the ring of bulbs, hugging her home, dreaming beneath the frozen earth. Leo considered the hard work, truly an intensive labor of love, her uncle had wrapped in this home and land. And here she was bearing the fruits of his attentive industry. Enwombed in the river stone house, insulated by the rich offerings of the land, with a gentle-spirited creature who offered unconditional acceptance, Leo found inner peace, an acknowledgment of all that had been part of her life. Leo pulled her lean body out of the water and stretched next to her faithful companion. Echo continued her watch as the smooth slabs of stone transmitted the sun's absorbed heat into their water-cooled, receptive forms.

Dog Tags

"Come on, Felix, you got this, man." Ray jogged comfortably beside his friend, whose face was beet red, his breath labored. "Not too much further. Look, you can see the finish line from here." Running on Ray's other side was a streamlined Miguel, who offered vocal support. Behind him trotted Augie, who was flanked by Elvis. And somewhere in the sea of walkers, joggers, and sprinters taking part in the first annual 5K, 10K fundraiser for Veterans Support was his sister, Hope, pushing a stroller, Gabrielle by her side.

The streets were lined with community members who rang cowbells, tooted handheld horns, held signs, and yelled words of encouragement. Ray was surprised by the turnout. The whole town had rallied behind the idea of honoring those lost in service, whether on the front line or after they returned. The race was the kickoff event for the annual Arts, Beats, and Eats weekend festival.

What started as a conversation in his veterans' support group had found wings and taken flight with unexpected ease. Throughout the crowd of participants and onlookers were hand-held signs "I am walking this for Private Getty" and "In remembrance of my son." In Felix's arms were combat boots with the two names of the men in his unit who lost their lives during his tour. In Ray's pocket, he carried a handwritten list of the names of the men he served with who lost their lives, names he would hold in his heart, always. If Ray could hover above the runners, joggers, and walkers, he would see that they carried their loved ones with them. Written on boots, tucked in arms, pockets, and minds was a tide of loss, lives forever impacted by the course of war. And if he could continue to rise above and move down, overlooking the stream of participants, there, toward the end, he would see his father and mother, Bert and Maria Shipworth, walking the 5K course, side by side, their hands close to each other but not quite touching. Circling his father's neck, underneath his cotton button-down shirt, not externally visible, snug against his chest was the oblong identification tags his older brother wore when serving in Vietnam. The same silver military dog tags Bert found around his brother's neck the day Gus took his own life, the ones Bert removed from his soul-fled body before the coffin was permanently shut and lowered into the ground.

Since his brother's funeral, Bert kept the markers tucked away in a shoebox buried deep in a dark corner of the storm cellar. The morning Ray was scheduled to leave for boot camp when Maria left the house to deliver their son's favorite muffins "to the residents in the nursing home," who had she been trying to fool anyway, Bert lumbered down the stairs and desperately dug out the cobwebbed covered box.

Pastor Bert Shipworth hadn't taken the dog tags off once since he put them on the day his only son left to start his military service. The chain sometimes caught in his chest hair, tightly pulling–the pain of remembrance. He held them every morning when he rose and every night before he closed his eyes, ending the day as it had begun, with a touch and a prayer.

A wave of support and encouragement swelled from the crowded sidelines as participants neared the end. Sustaining blood flow. Ray was reminded again of the way a body fights to preserve life. How people likewise can pull together, forming protective bands, circles of reinforcement, and how the magnitude of being part of a community dedicated to a more significant cause can ease a sense of hopeless isolation. If insistent and persistent enough, sometimes even the most despairing can be reached. Ray and Felix crossed the finish line together.

****

Leo filled the water bowls and adjusted the red, white, and blue bandannas around the rescue dogs and cats she and some other volunteers brought to the festival. Months of love and attention renewed these once-discarded creatures. They were ready to find their forever homes. Leo was optimistic. The adoption application table already had a family filling out a form. Their little girl, her auburn hair in braids, was sitting under a tree with a volunteer in front of Surtr's cage, tiny fingers stroking his fur, a look of pure contentment on the canine's face.

The smells of food vendors had the dog's nares quivering. The first band began to play. Her dad was running the 10K along with his high school cross-country team. Jennifer and Uncle Paul were near the finish line, noisemakers in hand. On this cloudless morning, where the sky and possibilities seem infinite, she imagined Ray running, with his family and golden-haired girlfriend cheering him on, supporting him through his ongoing journey. And, for a moment, she allowed herself to be with him too.

Sunday Morning Spinning

"See you in twelve hours." As Ray headed toward the employee time clock, exhausted after his midnight shift, he poked his head into the hospital room of Mr. Fresno, a three-day post-operative patient who had been transferred to the step-down unit the night before.

"Mr. Fresno?" Ray looked at the chair where he had last seen the forty-three-year-old father of four. He still sat in the room's nook, in an oversized reclining chair by the window where Ray had spoken to him earlier while taking his vital signs and assessing his pain level. "I keep thinking about my daughters." Mr. Fresno said while looking out the window into the diminishing darkness as Ray measured his blood pressure. "I think about walking them down the aisle and how lucky I'm to have a second chance." He continued sharing. "They have me on a cardiac exercise program. I'm just getting started. I just wish it hadn't taken a heart attack to get my attention."

He probably fell asleep, Ray thought as he moved toward the motionless form. The night had been a difficult one for the solid man. Despite the sleeping pill the doctor ordered, he couldn't find the relief he sought. A level of anxiety stayed with him, preventing somnolence. And between making scheduled blood draws, taking care of other patients, and answering calls, Ray frequently stopped to check on Mr. Fresno and talk.

"I played high school and college football. For some reason, my wife thought I wanted a son. We already had two daughters when we tried for our third. My wife was convinced we were going to have a boy. She had a blue nursery, a small baseball glove, and a football ready to go. Surprise. We had twin daughters. Four girls. People would ask me, don't you wish one of the twins was a boy? And all I could think was: which daughter would I give back for a son? Who would I return? The concept was unfathomable. No, my family is complete, just the way it is."

Ray gently shook the man's heavy shoulders. "Mr. Fresno?" He was unresponsive. Ray placed his index and middle finger over the man's carotid artery, palpating. There wasn't a pulse. He wasn't breathing. Ray's training kicked in. He yelled for help as he hit the code blue button and eased the unresponsive man onto the firm floor to begin chest compressions. *One-one thousand, two-one thousand, three…*Ray pushed on his chest and felt a rib crack underneath the pressure as the critical care response team pressed in, each performing their assigned roles. Ray stayed through the code, performing chest compressions until he was relieved by another responder. He did everything possible, helping the medical team, supporting Mr. Fresno, who, after the second dose of epinephrine, roused once, looking stunned and so afraid. What daughter would I return? After sixty minutes of vigorous resuscitation, he was pronounced dead. Mr. Fresno had stood at the intersection of life and death and was pulled over.

Ray contemplated the crossroad upon which he now stood. His old identity had departed. He knew and accepted this now. What Ray couldn't see but could sense on a deeper level, whether performing cardiac compressions, sitting by a fellow veteran into the night, playing the piano for residents of the senior home, taking classes, and applying for physician's assistant school, was that there had been an inner transformation. Standing in its stead was an amalgamation, an identity reborn. Out of the conflagration of service, the fire of war rose a new kind of soldier. An individual who had taken the essentials of being a warrior and fused them with the core qualities of being human. Decency, compassion, selfless cooperation, a person who operated with conviction, and courage, one who could surrender ego, who could put others first, a human who would submit his own life if necessary to serve the greater good. For the first time since Ray left for boot camp, he felt a semblance of inner cohesion.

"Shipworth?" Across the parking lot, a nurse practitioner who was involved in the prolonged revitalization effort, called out. "I have a flat, no spare. Can you give me a lift?" He ran a hand over his neatly trimmed beard, his eyes rimmed heavy with exhaustion.

"Sure thing, man." Ray opened the door and let him in.

After dropping off his co-worker, Ray navigated the tranquil, sliver-thin road. He planned to return to his apartment and take a long nap before he was due at his sister's house to help her dig a vegetable garden. He slowed down when he drove past the small steepled church on a hill with a solar-powered sign out front.

The parking lot was nearly full. Ray found a spot on the periphery, climbed out of the car, and looked around. Sunday morning spun around him. The atmosphere smelled of recently cut grass with a soft earthy edge. The old church sign he and Hope religiously changed every week with his father's messages was gone. Replaced. In his mind, playing like the familiar video recording of cherished family memory, he can see the aged marquee and ten-year-old twins bent over with irrepressible mirth as they pull the letters from a cardboard box. Give Satan an inch, and he'll become your ruler. If your life stinks, then we have a pew for you. Then he sees teenagers laughing uncontrollably, to the point where they cannot catch their breath, tears coursing down their faces. What did Adam say to Eve? I'll wear the plants in this family. Easter comes once a year. How often do you? How many countless minutes and hours over the years had he and Hope spent changing that faithful, long-suffering vestige? How many memories were contained in the white-washed church of his youth?

Remembrances of life lessons were found here, within his immediate and church family and the larger community in which he lived. They'd also been forged and learned through service to his country. Ray examined the loosely bound pictures of his life and the accompanying lessons of experience and could see that he'd been granted a gift: while he was slowly, moving from point A to point B and from point B to point C, somewhere along the way, he stitched together a whole new life worth living.

The outdoor digital sign was bright. In the colors of the rainbow, read–ALL WELCOME! And underneath, in smaller print: This Week's Sermon: Soul Growth. Ray shook his head in disbelief. Soul development? Soul evolution? Never had these words been part of his father's lexicon. Will wonders ever cease?

In the distance, carried in on a warm breeze, as gentle and compassionate as the breath of God, he heard the mournful cooing of a dove. Then the bird was there, manifested, perched atop the flashing sign, in his black bill, not an olive branch but a slender frond of willow. Somewhere nearby, his mate was building a nest. The bird's soft gray feathers were moist and askew, and the end of his long-tapered tail was bent sharply at an unnatural angle as if he had recently escaped the jowls of a large feral cat. The dove's eyes were dark tannin orbs encased in a ring of light skin. For the briefest moment, Ray met the stoic look of the feathered creature. There was a pull, a recognition. We are all here, surviving the best we can with what life has given us. As the dove took flight, a soft whistling rose from his battered wings. In this ephemeral sonation, Ray could hear Leo's voice, no more than a whisper, reciting Emily Dickinson's words. *Hope is the thing with Feathers-That perches in the soul-And sings the tune without the words-And never stops at all.*

A Long and Winding Road

(Into the Light)

"Come on, girl. I can't take this anymore. I have to clear my head. Let's go for a bike ride."

Echo, who'd been dreaming, curled next to Leo's bare feet, leaped up, instantly ready. Her tail wagged her body, and her eyes were alert.

With a disheartened sigh, Leo flipped the application for veterinary school face down on the walnut kitchen table. The easy stuff, her test scores, grade point average, transcript, and letters of recommendation were complete, but for some reason, she hit a roadblock regarding the personal statement. Finding the words which described the long and winding trail that had led her to this point in her life was daunting. How could an alphabet of just twenty-six letters be strung together in such a way to truly encapsulate what every single cell in her body knew with absolute certainty–Why she wanted to become a veterinarian? Words can reveal, but they also can conceal. If she could not find those segments that would communicate to a faceless admissions committee why she wanted acceptance into their program, would her dream evaporate before she had a chance to begin?

Leo's pace, furious at first, infused with pent-up angst, began to ease. She was here now, in this moment.

She reminded herself not to look too far ahead, don't think about the application and possible rejection. Just be. Echo moved contentedly by her side, sometimes falling back to sniff something particularly delicious at the side of the burnished rocky road, occasionally sprinting ahead. A field of blooming sunflowers swayed in unison, pushed by a mellow breeze. They tilted their youthful heads back, hungrily drinking in light, tracking with orchestrated precision the slow-moving sun.

Wait, where did Echo go? Leo stopped her bike and gave a quick whistle. Fifty yards ahead, Echo poked her nose out of a dense growth of trees and ran toward Leo. After a short, wet nudge on Leo's bare knee, she turned around and raced back to the trees. "Okay, let's see what's got you so excited."

The emerald-infused wood, refreshed and hushed, closed around them. Echo had forged a narrowly grooved path. The passage looked like the one she made around the house when Leo was away for Mud Cat's wedding and the hike. The Hike.

Leo could look to that time now, the entire experience of having Ray in her life, with gratitude. No longer did she feel embarrassed or ashamed of what transpired. She'd been lucky to have traveled on this earth with him, even for the briefest period, the span of a sunflower's existence. But during that interval, she learned about selfless friendship and commitment. How often had he put aside his needs and anxieties to help her, offering her a reassuring hand, a secure shoulder, and a heartening laugh? Perhaps the most important lesson that came not only from Ray but through Banshee, Echo, and every dog she had ever worked with was: life is never just about you or your needs.

When you encounter another creature of this world, another being, your ability to honor their journey and listen to what they are telling you through words or actions makes all the difference. The possibilities are limitless if you allow yourself to learn about them and respect their inner workings while opening yourself to them.

"Oh, my goodness, girl, no wonder you love this place." Leo stepped from the shaded wood into a stretch of warm light that smelled like heaven. Mango and strawberry saturated the air, and hints of blueberry floated in the sunlight. Leo leaned her bike against a tree and twirled around once, her eyes half-closed as she inhaled. Echo scampered around her.

****

Ray was just about to leave the food manufacturing plant for his break when he saw the dog. But when he saw Leo, he abruptly stopped. He stayed in the darkened doorway and observed with a keen eye. The external world was physically the same, yet somehow more vibrant and clearly defined. Everything was distilled. She moved in a swath of sunlight, lean legs emerging from jean shorts, dark hair, and her favorite, an almost threadbare, *Live, Love, Bark,* cotton T-shirt drifting around her waist, a fearless, devoted creature by her side. The canine stretched upward, lifting its front paws in the air and gently placing them on Leo's chest, near her heart. Laughing, Leo bent, returning a hug. He should have known.

Only someone with infinite patience and devotion could have earned the trust of a creature on the brink of starvation and so terrified of life. But Leo was like that. He experienced her compassion firsthand. She would try to bring out the light in you; if she couldn't, she would give you some of hers.

He could see blades of grass move around her sandaled feet. His breath caught. He had a choice, a decision to make. He could step into her light, tell her everything, lay himself bare, expressing what he had wanted for a long time but had been unable to admit to himself. Did he have that right anymore? He'd hurt her. Should he let her be, protect her from any further pain he might inflict, shield her from an uncertain future? He could turn around into the interior, return to work, return to a blunted life, and be thankful for their time together, appreciative for all she'd given him.

War exposes hard truths. Life is transitory. What is done cannot be undone. What is taken is gone forever. You cannot reboot. Death is death. But out of this veracity arises another lesson: since you cannot rewind the movie of life, don't squander your chances, they may never come again. Maybe the opportunity had passed. She was an independent woman, capable of making fully informed choices. Highly probable was the fact she no longer wanted any type of relationship with him, and who could blame her? Leo might have completely moved on, the hope once there, forever gone, closed over. There was only one way to find out.

Ray took a deep breath, his heart accelerating, his sandwich dangling from his left hand, and he stepped outside.

Epilogue

Echo leaps from the car into a bank of snow. They drove after Ray's last final that morning from their rental house on the edge of Oklahoma State's campus. Leo and Ray unload their packs and bags of groceries, happy to be back at the river stone house for their winter break. Freedom. Echo shakes the snow from her silky body, her eyes lively. They are home. With a sudden acceleration of speed, she races through the fields adrift with snow, her muscles moving like a racehorse, defined and rippling, kicking up tides of white flakes in her wake.

Ray puts down his pack and loops an easy arm around Leo's shoulder. She leans into him as they watch Echo fly, leaping over branches, navigating a landscape, though covered with snow, she knows by heart. At the edge of the tree line, Echo turns with tight precision, and she sees them, her pack, watching, waiting. She sprints toward them with utter abandon, at breakneck speed, as if she cannot reach them fast enough. Echo screeches to a halt before them, and a spray of snow covers their laughing forms. The graceful creature lifts her front paws simultaneously and hurls her whole body forward in a bow, an invitation to play. They reach down and touch her, all hands-on dog. She will go with them anywhere, and she has, to a different rhythmed life, a distant place called Stillwater. But here, on this patch of rough Oklahoma earth, they seem most centered. The unseeable weights they carry inside seem to fall from their beings, snowmelt under a persistent winter sun.

Outside the river stone house, the snow continues to fall. Inside, there is warmth. Ice crystals adhere to the glass, and the fire sparks and cracks in the cast iron wood burner. Leo and Ray finished decorating a single pine branch, felled by the weight of the snow, with strings of popcorn, cranberry, and pinecones dipped in earth-friendly glitter. The semester is, thankfully, over. Leo stashes away her second-year veterinary books on a shelf. She pulls down her American Lit book and sits next to Echo, who is before the blaze, chewing a bone on her fleece doggy bed.

Ray has fallen asleep on the couch. The demands of the term have taken their toll. For the first time in a while, they can relax. Leo starts to read.

From the couch rises a guttural sound of anguish. Leo knows immediately where Ray's dreams have taken him, back in time, back to the front line. Though the flashbacks, the triggers of intense anxiety, and the nightmares have diminished, they are still there. The losses and painful truths are part of Ray's inner world. He will serve them for the rest of his life.

Echo cocks her head to one side, then to the other, listening to his low moans. She gracefully unfolds herself and stands. Leaving her bone behind, she goes to Ray. Quietly climbing next to him, she nuzzles her russet muzzle into the crook of his neck and audibly breathes in and out through her nares.

Leo watches with hushed wonder. Never underestimate the intuitive capacity and power of a dog.

Ray's stifled sobs subside as Echo gingerly stretches along the length of his frame, the slight heft of her body grounding him, calm culled from chaos. She keeps her nose nestled in the bend of his nape, and as her breathing slows to match his, she guides him to a deeper, more restive, light-infused place.

A word about the author...

H.G. Hedger, an avid reader and a lover of nature and animals, is a nurse, who grew up in Oklahoma. She currently resides in Michigan, with her husband and rescue dog where they raised three sons. She attended the University of Michigan where she was a Hopwood Undergraduate Award Winner.

Thank you for purchasing
this publication of The Wild Rose Press, Inc.

For questions or more information
contact us at
info@thewildrosepress.com.

The Wild Rose Press, Inc.
www.thewildrosepress.com